"It's your decision," said Ender, "whether you want me with you, as one of the Filhos da Mente de Cristo. If you do, then I believe I can make my way through all the other obstacles."

She laughed nastily. "Obstacles? Men like you don't have obstacles. Just steppingstones."

"Men like me?"

"Yes, men like you," said Novinha. "Just because I've never met any others. Just because no matter how much I loved Libo he was never for one day as alive as you are in every minute. Just because I found myself loving as an adult for the first time when I loved you. Just because I have missed you more than I miss even my children, even my parents, even the lost loves of my life. Just because I can't dream of anyone but you, that doesn't mean that there isn't somebody else just like you somewhere else. The universe is a big place. You can't be all that special, really. Can you?"

He reached through the potato plants and leaned a hand gently on her thigh. "You do still love me, then?" he asked.

"I do," she said.

"Then I can stay?"

She burst into tears. "Oh, Andrew," she whispered, her voice cracking and breaking from having wept so much. "Does God love me enough to give you to me now, again, when I need you so much?"

"Until I die," said Edner.

"I know that part," she said. "But I pray that God will let me die first this time."

ORSON SCOTT CARD

CHILDREN
OF THE MIND

TOR

A TOM DOHERTY ASSOCIATES BOOK
NEW YORK

This is a work of fiction. All the characters and events portrayed in this book are either products of the author's imagination or are used fictitiously.

CHILDREN OF THE MIND

A Tor Book
Published by Tom Doherty Associates, LLC
175 Fifth Avenue
New York, NY 10010

www.tor.com

Tor® is a registered trademark of Tom Doherty Associates, LLC.

ISBN: 0-812-52239-7
Library of Congress Catalog Card Number: 95-53262

First edition: August 1996
First mass market edition: June 1997

Printed in the United States of America

0   9   8

To Barbara Bova,
whose toughness, wisdom, and empathy
make her a great agent
and an even better friend

CONTENTS

ACKNOWLEDGMENTS

My heartfelt thanks to:

Glenn Makitka, for the title, which seems so obvious now, but which never crossed my mind until he suggested it in a discussion in Hatrack River on America Online;

Van Gessel, for introducing me to Hikari and Kenzaburo Oe, and for his masterful translation of Shusaku Endo's *Deep River*;

Helpful readers in Hatrack River, like Stephen Boulet and Sandi Golden, who caught typographical errors and inconsistencies in the manuscript;

Tom Doherty and Beth Meacham at Tor, who allowed me to split *Xenocide* in half in order to have a chance to develop and write the second half of the story properly;

My friend and fellow weeder in the vineyards of literature, Kathryn H. Kidd, for her chapter-by-chapter encouragement;

Kathleen Bellamy and Scott J. Allen for Sisyphean service;

Kristine and Geoff for careful reading that helped me resolve contradictions and unclarities; and

My wife, Kristine, and my children, Geoffrey, Emily, Charlie Ben, and Zina, for patience with my strange schedule and self-absorption during the writing process, and for teaching me all that is worth telling stories about.

This novel was begun at home in Greensboro, North Carolina, and finished on the road at Xanadu II in Myrtle Beach, in the Hotel Panama in San Rafael, and in Los Angeles in the home of my dear cousins Mark and Margaret Park, whom I thank for their friendship and their hospitality. Chapters were uploaded in manuscript form into the Hatrack River Town Meeting on America Online, where several dozen fellow citizens of that virtual community downloaded it, read it, and commented on it to the book's and my great benefit.

1

"I'M NOT MYSELF"

"Mother. Father. Did I do it right?"
The last words of Han Qing-jao, from
The God Whispers of Han Qing-jao

Si Wang-mu stepped forward. The young man named Peter took her hand and led her into the starship. The door closed behind them.

Wang-mu sat down on one of the swiveling chairs inside the small metal-walled room. She looked around, expecting to see something strange and new. Except for the metal walls, it could have been any office on the world of Path. Clean, but not fastidiously so. Furnished, in a utilitarian way. She had seen holos of ships in flight: the smoothly streamlined fighters and shuttles that dipped into and out of the atmosphere; the vast rounded structures of the starships that accelerated as near to the speed of light as matter could get. On the one hand, the sharp power of a needle; on the other, the massive power of a sledgehammer. But here in this room, no power at all. Just a room.

Where was the pilot? There must be a pilot, for the young man who sat across the room from her, murmuring to his computer, could hardly be controlling a starship capable of the feat of traveling faster than light.

And yet that must have been precisely what he was doing, for there were no other doors that might lead to other rooms. The starship had looked small from the outside; this room obviously used all the space that it contained. There in the corner were the batteries that stored energy from the solar collectors on the top of the ship. In that chest, which seemed to be insulated like a refrigerator, there might be food and drink. So much for life support. Where was the romance in starflight now, if this was all it took? A mere room.

With nothing else to watch, she watched the young man at the computer terminal. Peter Wiggin, he said his name was. The name of the ancient Hegemon, the one who first united all the human race under his control, back when people lived on only one world, all the nations and races and religions and philosophies crushed together elbow to elbow, with nowhere to go but into each other's lands, for the sky was a ceiling then, and space was a vast chasm that could not be bridged. Peter Wiggin, the man who ruled the human race. This was not him, of course, and he had admitted as much. Andrew Wiggin sent him; Wang-mu remembered, from things that Master Han had told her, that Andrew Wiggin had somehow *made* him. Did this make the great Speaker of the Dead Peter's father? Or was he somehow Ender's brother, not just named for but actually embodying the Hegemon who had died three thousand years before?

Peter stopped murmuring, leaned back in his chair, and sighed. He rubbed his eyes, then stretched and groaned. It was a very indelicate thing to do in company. The sort of thing one might expect from a coarse fieldworker.

He seemed to sense her disapproval. Or perhaps he had forgotten her and now suddenly remembered that he had company. Without straightening himself in his chair, he turned his head and looked at her.

"Sorry," he said. "I forgot I was not alone."

Wang-mu longed to speak boldly to him, despite a lifetime retreating from bold speech. After all, *he* had spoken to *her* with offensive boldness, when his starship appeared like a fresh-sprouted mushroom on the lawn by the river and he emerged with a single vial of a disease that would cure her home world, Path, of its genetic illness. He had looked her in the eye not fifteen minutes ago and said, "Come with me and you'll be part of changing history. *Making* history." And despite her fear, she had said yes.

Had said yes, and now sat in a swivel chair watching him behave crudely, stretching like a tiger in front of her. Was that his beast-of-the-heart, the tiger? Wang-mu had read the Hegemon. She could believe that there was a tiger in that great and terrible man. But this one? This boy? Older than Wang-mu, but she was not too young to know immaturity when she saw it. He was going to change the course of history! Clean out the corruption in the Congress. Stop the Lusitania Fleet. Make all colony planets equal members of the Hundred Worlds. This boy who stretched like a jungle cat.

"I don't have your approval," he said. He sounded annoyed and amused, both at once. But then she might not be good at understanding the inflections of one such as this. Certainly it was hard to read the grimaces of such a round-eyed man. Both his face and his voice contained hidden languages that she could not understand.

"You must understand," he said. "I'm not myself."

Wang-mu spoke the common language well enough at least to understand the idiom. "You are unwell today?" But she knew even as she said it that he had not meant the expression idiomatically at all.

"I'm not myself," he said again. "I'm not really Peter Wiggin."

"I hope not," said Wang-mu. "I read about his funeral in school."

"I do look like him, though, don't I?" He brought up a hologram into the air over his computer terminal. The hologram rotated to look at Wang-mu; Peter sat up and assumed the same pose, facing her.

"There is a resemblance," she said.

"Of course, I'm younger," said Peter. "Because Ender didn't see me again after he left Earth when he was—what, five years old? A little runt, anyway. I was still a boy. That's what he remembered, when he conjured me out of thin air."

"Not air at all," she said. "Out of nothing."

"Not nothing, either," he said. "Conjured me, all the same." He smiled wickedly. "I can call spirits from the vasty deep."

These words meant something to him, but not to her. In the world of Path she had been expected to be a servant and so was educated very little. Later, in the house of Han Fei-tzu, her abilities had been recognized, first by her former mistress, Han Qing-jao, and later by the master himself. From both she had acquired some bits of education, in a haphazard way. What teaching there had been was mostly technical, and the literature she learned was of the Middle Kingdom, or of Path itself. She could have quoted endlessly from the great poet Li Qing-jao, for whom her one-time mistress had been named. But of the poet he was quoting, she knew nothing.

"I can call spirits from the vasty deep," he said again. And then, changing his voice and manner a little, he answered himself. "Why so can I, or so can any man. But will they come when you do call for them?"

"Shakespeare?" she guessed.

He grinned at her. She thought of the way a cat smiles at the creature it is toying with. "That's always the best guess when a European is doing the quoting," he said.

"The quotation is funny," she said. "A man brags that he can summon the dead. But the other man says that the trick is not calling, but rather getting them to come."

He laughed. "What a way you have with humor."

"This quotation means something to you, because Ender called you forth from the dead."

He looked startled. "How did you know?"

She felt a thrill of fear. Was it possible? "I did not know, I was making a joke."

"Well, it's not true. Not literally. He didn't raise the dead. Though he no doubt thinks he could, if the need arose." Peter sighed. "I'm being nasty. The words just come to my mind. I don't mean them. They just come."

"It is possible to have words come to your mind, and still refrain from speaking them aloud."

He rolled his eyes. "I wasn't trained for servility, the way *you* were."

So this was the attitude of one who came from a world of free people—to sneer at one who had been a servant through no fault of her own. "I was trained to keep unpleasant words to myself as a matter of courtesy," she said. "But perhaps to you, that is just another form of servility."

"As I said, Royal Mother of the West, nastiness comes unbidden to my mouth."

"I am not the Royal Mother," said Wang-mu. "The name was a cruel joke—"

"And only a very nasty person would mock you for it." Peter grinned. "But I'm named for the Hegemon. I thought perhaps bearing ludicrously overwrought names was something we might have in common."

She sat silently, entertaining the possibility that he might have been trying to make friends.

"I came into existence," he said, "only a short while ago. A matter of weeks. I thought you should know that about me."

She didn't understand.

"You know how this starship works?" he said.

Now he was leaping from subject to subject. Testing her. Well, she had had enough of being tested. "Apparently one sits within it and is examined by rude strangers," she said.

He smiled and nodded. "Give as good as you get. Ender told me you were nobody's servant."

"I was the true and faithful servant of Qing-jao. I hope Ender did not lie to you about that."

He brushed away her literalism. "A mind of your own." Again his eyes sized her up; again she felt utterly comprehended by his lingering glance, as she had felt when he first looked at her beside the river. "Wang-mu, I am not speaking metaphorically when I tell you I was only just made. Made, you understand, not born. And the way I was made has much to do with how this starship works. I don't want to bore you by explaining things you already understand, but you must know what—not who—I am in order to understand why I need you with me. So I ask again— do you know how this starship works?"

She nodded. "I think so. Jane, the being who dwells in computers, she holds in her mind as perfect a picture as she can of the starship and all who are within it. The people also hold their own picture of themselves and who they are and so on. Then she moves everything from the real world to a place of nothingness, which takes no time at all, and then brings it back into reality in whatever place she chooses. Which also takes no time. So instead of starships taking years to get from world to world, it happens in an instant."

Peter nodded. "Very good. Except what you have to understand is that during the time that the starship is Outside, it isn't surrounded by nothingness. Instead it's surrounded by uncountable numbers of aiúas."

She turned away her face from him.

"You don't understand aiúas?"

"To say that all people have always existed. That we are older than the oldest gods. . . ."

"Well, sort of," said Peter. "Only aiúas on the Outside, they can't be said to exist, or at least not any kind of meaningful existence. They're just . . . there. Not even that, because there's no sense of location, no *there* where they might be. They just are. Until some intelligence calls them, names them, puts them into some kind of order, gives them shape and form.''

"The clay can become a bear," she said, "but not as long as it rests cold and wet in the riverbank.''

"Exactly. So there was Ender Wiggin and several other people who, with luck, you'll never need to meet, taking the first voyage Outside. They weren't going anywhere, really. The point of that first voyage was to get Outside long enough that one of them, a rather talented genetic scientist, could create a new molecule, an extremely complex one, by the image she held of it in her mind. Or rather her image of the modifications she needed to make in an existing . . . well, you don't have the biology for it. Anyway, she did what she was supposed to do, she created the new molecule, calloo callay, only the thing is, she wasn't the only person doing any creating that day.''

"Ender's mind created you?" asked Wang-mu

"Inadvertently. I was, shall we say, a tragic accident. An unhappy side effect. Let's just say that everybody there, every*thing* there, was creating like crazy. The aiúas Outside are frantic to be made into something, you see. There were shadow starships being created all around us. All kinds of weak, faint, fragmented, fragile, ephemeral structures rising and falling in each instant. Only four had any solidity. One was that genetic molecule that Elanora Ribeira had come to create.''

"One was you?''

"The least interesting one, I fear. The least loved and valued. One of the people on the ship was a fellow named Miro, who through a tragic accident some years ago had been left somewhat crippled. Neurologically damaged. Thick of speech, clumsy with his hands, lame when he walked. *He* held within his mind the powerful, treasured image of himself as he used to be. So—with that perfect self-image, a vast number of aiúas assembled themselves into an exact copy, not of how he was, but of how he once was and longed to be again. Complete with all his memories—a perfect replication of him. So perfect that it had the same utter loathing for his crippled body that he himself had. So . . . the new, improved Miro—or rather the copy of the old, undamaged Miro—whatever—he stood there as the ultimate rebuke of the crippled one. And before their very eyes, that old rejected body crumbled away into nothing.''

Wang-mu gasped, imagining it. "He died!"

"No, that's the point, don't you see? He lived. It *was* Miro. His own aiúa—not the trillions of aiúas making up the atoms and molecules of his body, but the *one* that controlled them all, the one that was himself, his will—his aiúa simply moved to the new and perfect body. That was his true self. And the old one . . ."

"Had no use."

"Had nothing to give it shape. You see, I think our bodies are held together by love. The love of the master aiúa for the glorious powerful body that obeys it, that gives the self all its experience of the world. Even Miro, even with all his self-loathing when he was crippled, even he must have loved whatever pathetic remnant of his body was left to him. Until the moment that he had a new one."

"And then he moved."

"Without even knowing that he had done so," said Peter. "He followed his love."

Wang-mu heard this fanciful tale and knew that it must be true, for she had overheard many a mention of aiúas in the conversations between Han Fei-tzu and Jane, and now with Peter Wiggin's story, it made sense. It had to be true, if only because this starship really had appeared as if from nowhere on the bank of the river behind Han Fei-tzu's house.

"But now you must wonder," said Peter, "how I, unloved and unlovable as I know I am, came into existence."

"You already said. Ender's mind."

"Miro's most intensely held image was of his own younger, healthier, stronger self. But Ender, the images that mattered most in *his* mind were of his older sister Valentine and his older brother Peter. Not as they became, though, for his real older brother Peter was long dead, and Valentine—she has accompanied or followed Ender on all his hops through space, so she is still alive, but aged as he has aged. Mature. A real person. Yet on that starship, during that time Outside, he conjured up a copy of her youthful self. Young Valentine. Poor *Old* Valentine! She didn't know she was so old until she saw this younger self, this perfect being, this angel that had dwelt in Ender's twisted little mind from childhood on. I must say, she's the most put-upon victim in all this little drama. To know that your brother carries around such an image of you, instead of loving you as you really are—well, one can see that Old Valentine—she hates it, but that's how everyone thinks of her now, including, poor thing, herself—one can see that Old Valentine is really having her patience tried."

"But if the original Valentine is still alive," said Wang-mu, puzzled, "then who is the young Valentine? Who is she really? You can be Peter because he's dead and no one is using his name, but . . ."

"Quite puzzling, isn't it?" said Peter. "But my point is that whether he's dead or not, I'm not Peter Wiggin. As I said before, I'm not myself."

He leaned back in his chair and looked up at the ceiling. The hologram above the terminal turned to look at him. He had not touched the controls.

"Jane is with us," said Wang-mu.

"Jane is always with us," said Peter. "Ender's spy."

The hologram spoke. "Ender doesn't need a spy. He needs friends, if he can get them. Allies at least."

Peter reached idly for the terminal and turned it off. The hologram disappeared.

This disturbed Wang-mu very much. Almost as if he had slapped a child. Or beaten a servant. "Jane is a very noble creature, to treat her with such disrespect."

"Jane is a computer program with a bug in the id routines."

He was in a dark mood, this boy who had come to take her into his starship and spirit her away from the world of Path. But dark as his mood might be, she understood now, with the hologram gone from the terminal, what she had seen. "It *isn't* just because you're so young and the holograms of Peter Wiggin the Hegemon are of a mature man," said Wang-mu.

"What," he said impatiently. "What isn't what?"

"The physical difference between you and the Hegemon."

"What is it, then?"

"He looks—satisfied."

"He conquered the world," said Peter.

"So when you have done the same, you will get that look of satisfaction?"

"I suppose so," said Peter. "It's what passes for a purpose in my life. It's the mission Ender has sent me on."

"Don't lie to me," said Wang-mu. "On the riverbank you spoke of the terrible things I did for the sake of my ambition. I admit it—I was ambitious, desperate to rise out of my terrible lowborn state. I know the taste of it, and the smell of it, and I smell it coming from you, like the smell of tar on a hot day, you stink of it."

"Ambition? Has a stench?"

"I'm drunk with it myself."

He grinned. Then he touched the jewel in his ear. "Remember, Jane is listening, and she tells Ender *everything*."

Wang-mu fell silent, but not because she was embarrassed. She simply had nothing to say, and therefore said nothing.

"So I'm ambitious. Because that's how Ender imagined me. Ambitious and nasty-minded and cruel."

"But I thought you were not yourself," she said.

His eyes blazed with defiance. "That's right, I'm *not*."

He looked away. "Sorry, Gepetto, but I can't be a real boy. I have no soul."

She didn't understand the name he said, but she understood the word *soul*. "All my childhood I was thought to be a servant by nature. To have no soul. Then one day they discovered that I have one. So far it has brought me no great happiness."

"I'm not speaking of some religious idea. I'm speaking of the aiúa. I haven't got one. Remember what happened to Miro's broken-down body when his aiúa abandoned it."

"But you don't crumble, so you must have an aiúa after all."

"I don't have it, it has *me*. I continue to exist because the aiúa whose irresistible will called me into existence continues to imagine me. Continues to need me, to control me, to *be* my will."

"Ender Wiggin?" she asked.

"My brother, my creator, my tormentor, my god, my very self."

"And young Valentine? Her too?"

"Ah, but he *loves* her. He's proud of her. He's glad he made her. Me he loathes. Loathes, and yet it's his will that I do and say every nasty thing. When I'm at my most despicable, remember that I do only what my brother makes me do."

"Oh, to blame him for—"

"I'm not *blaming*, Wang-mu. I'm stating simple reality. His will is controlling three bodies now. Mine, my impossibly angelic sister's, and of course his own very tired middle-aged body. Every aiúa in my body receives its order and place from his. I am, in all ways that matter, Ender Wiggin. Except that he has created me to be the vessel of every impulse in himself that he hates and fears. His ambition, yes, you smell *his* ambition when you smell mine. His aggression. His rage. His nastiness. His cruelty. *His*, not mine, because *I* am dead, and anyway I was never like this, never the way he saw me. This person before you is a travesty, a mockery! I'm a twisted memory. A despicable dream. A nightmare. I'm the creature hiding under the bed. He brought me out of chaos to be the terror of his childhood.''

"So don't do it," said Wang-mu. "If you don't want to be those things, don't do them."

He sighed and closed his eyes. "If you're so bright, why haven't you understood a word I've said?"

She did understand, though. "What is your will, anyway? Nobody can see it. You don't hear it thinking. You only know what your will is afterward, when you look back in your life and see what you've done."

"That's the most terrible trick he's played on me," said Peter softly, his eyes still closed. "I look back on my life and I see only the memories *he* has imagined for me. He was taken from our family when he was only five. What does he know of me or my life?"

"He wrote *The Hegemon*."

"That book. Yes, based on Valentine's memories, as she told them to him. And the public documents of my dazzling career. And of course the few ansible communications between Ender and my own late self before I—he—died. I'm only a few weeks old, yet I know a quotation from *Henry IV, Part I*. Owen Glendower boasting to Hotspur. Henry Percy. How could I know that? When did I go to school? How long did I lie awake at night, reading old plays until I committed a thousand favorite lines to memory? Did Ender somehow conjure up the whole of his dead brother's education? All his private thoughts? Ender only knew the real Peter Wiggin for five years. It's not a real person's memories I draw on. It's the memories Ender thinks that I should have."

"He thinks you should know Shakespeare, and so you do?" she asked doubtfully.

"If only Shakespeare were all he had given me. The great writers, the great philosophers. If only those were the only memories I had."

She waited for him to list the troublesome memories. But he only shuddered and fell silent.

"So if you are really controlled by Ender, then . . . you are him. Then that is yourself. You *are* Andrew Wiggin. You have an aiúa."

"I'm Andrew Wiggin's nightmare," said Peter. "I'm Andrew Wiggin's self-loathing. I'm everything he hates and fears about himself. That's the script I've been given. That's what I have to do."

He flexed his hand into a fist, then extended it partway, the fingers still bent. A claw. The tiger again. And for a moment, Wang-mu was afraid of him. Only a moment, though. He relaxed his hands. The moment passed. "What part does your script have in it for me?"

"I don't know," said Peter. "You're very smart. Smarter than I am, I hope. Though of course I have such incredible vanity that I can't really believe that anyone is actually smarter than I am. Which means that I'm all the more in need of good advice, since I can't actually conceive of needing any."

"You talk in circles."

"That's just part of my cruelty. To torment you with conversation. But maybe it's supposed to go farther than that. Maybe I'm supposed to torture you and kill you the way I so clearly remember doing with squirrels. Maybe I'm supposed to stake your living body out in the woods, nailing your extremities to tree roots, and then open you up layer by layer to see at what point the flies begin to come and lay eggs in your exposed flesh."

She recoiled at the image. "I have *read* the book. I know the Hegemon was not a monster!"

"It wasn't the Speaker for the Dead who created me Outside. It was the frightened boy Ender. I'm not the Peter Wiggin he so wisely understood in that book. I'm the Peter Wiggin he had nightmares about. The one who flayed squirrels."

"He saw you do that?" she asked.

"Not *me*," he said testily. "And no, he never even saw *him* do it. Valentine told him later. She found the squirrel's body in the woods near their childhood home in Greensboro, North Carolina, on the continent of North America back on Earth. But that image fit so tidily into his nightmares that he borrowed it and shared it with me. That's the memory I live with. Intellectually, I can imagine that the real Peter Wiggin was probably not cruel at all. He was learning and studying. He didn't have compassion for the squirrel because he didn't sentimentalize it. It was simply an animal. No more important than a head of lettuce. To cut it up was probably as immoral an act as making a salad. But that's not how Ender imagined it, and so that's not how I remember it."

"How do you remember it?"

"The way I remember all my supposed memories. From the outside. Watching myself in horrified fascination as I take a fiendish delight in cruelty. All my memories prior to the moment I came to life on Ender's little voyage Outside, in all of them I see myself through someone else's eyes. A very odd feeling, I assure you."

"But now?"

"Now I don't see myself at all," he said. "Because I have no self. I am not myself."

"But you remember. You have memories. Of this conversation, already you remember it. Looking at me. You must, surely."

"Yes," he said. "I remember *you*. And I remember being here and seeing you. But there isn't any self behind my eyes. I feel tired and stupid even when I'm being my most clever and brilliant."

He smiled a charming smile and now Wang-mu could see again the true difference between Peter and the hologram of the Hegemon. It was as he said: Even at his most self-deprecating, this Peter Wiggin had eyes that flashed with inner rage. He was dangerous. You could see it looking at him. When he looked into your eyes, you could imagine him planning how and when you would die.

"I am not myself," said Peter.

"You are saying this to control yourself," said Wang-mu, guessing but also sure she was right. "This is your incantation, to stop yourself from doing what you desire."

Peter sighed and leaned over, laying his head down on the terminal, his ear pressed against the cold plastic surface.

"What is it you desire?" she said, fearful of the answer.

"Go away," he said.

"Where can I go? This great starship of yours has only one room."

"Open the door and go outside," he said.

"You mean to kill me? To eject me into space where I'll freeze before I have time to suffocate?"

He sat up and looked at her in puzzlement. "Space?"

His confusion confused her. Where else would they be but in space? That's where starships went, through space.

Except this one, of course.

As he saw understanding come to her, he laughed aloud. "Oh, yes, you're the brilliant one, they've remade the entire world of Path to have *your* genius!"

She refused to be goaded.

"I thought there would be some sensation of movement. Or something. Have we traveled, then? Are we already there?"

"In the twinkling of an eye. We were Outside and then back Inside at another place, all so fast that only a computer could experience our voyage as having any duration at all. Jane did it before I finished talking to her. Before I said a word to you."

"Then where are we? What's outside the door?"

"We're sitting in the woods somewhere on the planet Divine Wind. The air is breathable. You won't freeze. It's summer outside the door."

She walked to the door and pulled down the handle, releasing the airtight seal. The door eased open. Sunlight streamed into the room.

"Divine Wind," she said. "I read about it—it was founded as a Shinto world the way Path was supposed to be Taoist. The purity of ancient Japanese culture. But I think it's not so very pure these days."

"More to the point, it's the world where Andrew and Jane and I felt—if one can speak of my having feelings apart from Ender's own—the world where we might find the center of power in the worlds ruled by Congress. The true decision makers. The power behind the throne."

"So you can subvert them and take over the human race?"

"So I can stop the Lusitania Fleet. Taking over the human race is a bit later on the agenda. The Lusitania Fleet is something of an emergency. We have only a few weeks to stop it before the fleet gets there and uses the Little Doctor, the M.D. Device, to blow Lusitania into its constituent elements. In the meantime, because Ender and everyone else expects me to fail, they're building these little tin can starships as fast as possible and transporting as many Lusitanians as they can—humans, piggies, and buggers—to other habitable but as yet uninhabited planets. My dear sister Valentine—the young one—is off with Miro—in his fresh new body, the dear lad—searching out new worlds as fast as *their* little starship can carry them. Quite a project. All of them betting on my—on *our*—failure. Let's disappoint them, shall we?"

"Disappoint them?"

"By succeeding. Let's succeed. Let's find the center of power among humankind, and let's persuade them to stop the fleet before it needlessly destroys a world."

Wang-mu looked at him doubtfully. Persuade them to stop the fleet? This nasty-minded, cruel-hearted boy? How could he persuade anyone of anything?

As if he could hear her thoughts, he answered her silent doubt. "You see why I invited you to come along with me. When Ender was inventing me, he forgot the fact that he never knew me during the time in my life when I was persuading people and gathering them together in shifting alliances and all that nonsense. So the Peter Wiggin he created is far too nasty, openly ambitious, and nakedly cruel to persuade a man with rectal itch to scratch his own butt.''

She looked away from him again.

"You see?" he said. "I offend you again and again. Look at me. Do you see my dilemma? The real Peter, the original one, *he* could have done the work I've been sent to do. He could have done it in his sleep. He'd already have a plan. He'd be able to win people over, soothe them, insinuate himself into their councils. That Peter Wiggin! He can charm the stings out of bees. But can *I*? I doubt it. For, you see, I'm not myself.''

He got up from his chair, roughly pushed his way past her, and stepped outside onto the meadow that surrounded the little metal cabin that had carried them from world to world. Wang-mu stood in the doorway, watching him as he wandered away from the ship; away, but not too far.

I know something of how he feels, she thought. I know something of having to submerge your will in someone else's. To live for them, as if they were the star of the story of your life, and you merely a supporting player. I have been a slave. But at least in all that time I knew my own heart. I knew what I truly thought even as I did what they wanted, whatever it took to get what I wanted from them. Peter Wiggin, though, has no idea of what he really wants, because even his resentment of his lack of freedom isn't his own, even *that* comes from Andrew Wiggin. Even his self-loathing is Andrew's self-loathing, and . . .

And back and back, in circles, like the random path he was tracing through the meadow.

Wang-mu thought of her mistress—no, her former mistress—Qing-jao. She also traced strange patterns. It was what the gods forced her to do. No, that's the old way of thinking. It's what her obsessive-compulsive disorder caused her to do. To kneel on the floor and trace the grain of the wood in each board, trace a single line of it as far as it went across the floor, line after line. It never meant anything, and yet she had to do it because only by such meaningless mind-numbing obedience could she win a scrap of freedom from the impulses controlling her. It is Qing-jao who was always the slave, and never me. For the master that ruled her controlled her from inside her own mind. While I could always see my master outside me, so my inmost self was never touched.

Peter Wiggin knows that he is ruled by the unconscious fears and passions of a complicated man many lightyears away. But then, Qing-jao thought her obsessions came from the gods. What does it matter, to tell yourself that the thing controlling you comes from outside, if in fact you only experience it inside your own heart? Where can you run from it? How can you hide? Qing-jao must be free by now, freed by the carrier virus that Peter brought with him to Path and put into the hands of Han Fei-tzu. But Peter— what freedom can there be for him?

And yet he must still live as if he were free. He must still struggle for freedom even if the struggle itself is just one more symptom of his slavery. There is a part of him that yearns to be himself. No, not *him*self. A self.

So what is my part in all of this? Am I supposed to work a miracle, and give him an aiúa? That isn't in my power.

And yet I *do* have power, she thought.

She must have power, or why else had he spoken to her so openly? A total stranger, and he had opened his heart to her at once. Why? Because she was in on the secrets, yes, but something else as well.

Ah, of course. He could speak freely to her because she had never known Andrew Wiggin. Maybe Peter was nothing but an aspect of Ender's nature, all that Ender feared and loathed about himself. But she could never compare the two of them. Whatever Peter was, whoever controlled him, she was *his* confidante.

Which made her, once again, someone's servant. She had been Qing-jao's confidante, too.

She shuddered, as if to shake from her the sad comparison. No, she told herself. It is *not* the same thing. Because that young man wandering so aimlessly among the wildflowers has no power over me, except to tell me of his pain and hope for my understanding. Whatever I give to him I will give freely.

She closed her eyes and leaned her head against the frame of the door. I will give it freely, yes, she thought. But what am I planning to give him? Why, exactly what he wants—my loyalty, my devotion, my help in all his tasks. To submerge myself in him. And why am I already planning to do all this? Because however he might doubt himself, he *has* the power to win people to his cause.

She opened her eyes again and strode out into the hip-high grass toward him. He saw her and waited wordlessly as she approached. Bees buzzed around her; butterflies staggered drunkenly through the air, avoiding her somehow in their seemingly random flight. At the last moment she reached out and gathered a bee from a blossom into her hand, into her fist, but then quickly, before it could sting her, she lobbed it into Peter's face.

Flustered, surprised, he batted away the infuriated bee, ducked under it, dodged, and finally ran a few steps before it lost track of him and buzzed its way out among the flowers again. Only then could he turn furiously to face her.

"What was *that* for!"

She giggled at him—she couldn't help it. He had looked so funny.

"Oh, good, laugh. I can see you're going to be *fine* company."

"Be angry, I don't care," said Wang-mu. "I'll just tell you this. Do you think that away off on Lusitania, Ender's aiúa suddenly thought, 'Ho, a bee!' and made you brush at it and dodge it like a clown?"

He rolled his eyes. "Oh, aren't you clever. Well gosh, Miss Royal Mother of the West, you sure solved all *my* problems! I can see I must always have been a real boy!

And these ruby shoes, why, they've had the power to take me back to Kansas all along!''

"What's Kansas?" she asked, looking down at his shoes, which were not red.

"Just another memory of Ender's that he kindly shared with me," said Peter Wiggin.

He stood there, his hands in his pockets, regarding her.

She stood just as silently, her hands clasped in front of her, regarding him right back.

"So are you with me?" he finally asked.

"You must try not to be nasty with me," she said.

"Take that up with Ender."

"I don't care whose aiúa controls you," she said. "You still have your own thoughts, which are different from his—you feared the bee, and he didn't even think of a bee right then, and you know it. So whatever part of you is in control or whoever the real 'you' happens to be, right there on the front of your head is the mouth that's going to be speaking to me, and I'm telling you that if I'm going to work with you, you better be nice to me."

"Does this mean no more bee fights?" he asked.

"Yes," she said.

"That's just as well. With my luck Ender no doubt gave me a body that goes into shock when I'm stung by a bee."

"It can also be pretty hard on the bee," she said.

He grinned at her. "I find myself liking you," he said. "I really hate that."

He strode off toward the starship. "Come on!" he called out to her. "Let's see what information Jane can give us about this world we're supposed to take by storm."

2

"YOU DON'T BELIEVE IN GOD"

*"When I follow the path of the gods through the wood,
My eyes take every twisting turn of the grain,
But my body moves straight along the planking,
So those who watch me see that the path of the gods
is straight,
While I dwell in a world with no straightness in it."*
from The God Whispers of Han Qing-jao

Novinha would not come to him. The gentle old teacher looked genuinely distressed as she told Ender. "She wasn't angry," the old teacher explained. "She told me that . . ."

Ender nodded, understanding how the teacher was torn between compassion and honesty. "You can tell me her words," he said. "She *is* my wife, so I can bear it."

The old teacher rolled her eyes. "I'm married too, you know."

Of course he knew. All the members of the Order of the Children of the Mind of Christ—Os Filhos da Mente de Cristo—were married. It was their rule.

"I'm married, so I know perfectly well that your spouse

is the one person who knows all the words you *can't* bear to hear.''

''Then let me correct myself,'' said Ender mildly. ''She is my wife, so I am determined to hear it, whether I can bear it or not.''

''She says that she has to finish the weeding, so she has no time for lesser battles.''

Yes, that sounded like Novinha. She might tell herself that she had taken the mantle of Christ upon her, but if so it was the Christ who denounced the Pharisees, the Christ who said all those cruel and sarcastic things to his enemies and his friends alike, not the gentle one with infinite patience.

Still, Ender was not one to go away merely because his feelings were hurt. ''Then what are we waiting for?'' asked Ender. ''Show me where I can find a hoe.''

The old teacher stared at him for a long moment, then smiled and led him out into the gardens. Soon, wearing work gloves and carrying a hoe in one hand, he stood at the end of the row where Novinha worked, bent over in the sunlight, her eyes on the ground before her as she cut under the root of weed after weed, turning each one up to burn to death in the hot dry sun. She was coming toward him.

Ender stepped to the unweeded row beside the one Novinha worked on, and began to hoe toward her. They would not meet, but they would pass close to each other. She would notice him or not. She would speak to him or not. She still loved and needed him. Or not. But no matter what, at the end of this day he would have weeded in the same field as his wife, and her work would have been more easily done because he was there, and so he would still be her husband, however little she might now want him in that role.

The first time they passed each other, she did not so much as look up. But then she would not have to. She would know without looking that the one who joined her in weeding so soon after she refused to meet with her husband would have to be her husband. He knew that she would know this, and he also knew she was too proud to look at him and show that she wanted to see him again. She would study the weeds until she went half blind, because Novinha was not one to bend to anyone else's will.

Except, of course, the will of Jesus. That was the message she had sent him, the message that had brought him here, determined to talk to her. A brief note couched in the language of the Church. She was separating herself from him to serve Christ among the Filhos. She felt herself called to this work. He was to regard himself as having no further responsibility toward her, and to expect nothing more from her than she would gladly give to any of the children of God. It was a cold message, for all the gentleness of its phrasing.

Ender was not one to bend easily to another's will, either. Instead of obeying the message, he came here, determined to do the opposite of what she asked. And why not? Novinha had a terrible record as a decision maker. Whenever she decided to do something for someone else's good, she ended up inadvertently destroying them. Like Libo, her childhood friend and secret lover, the father of all her children during her marriage to the violent but sterile man who had been her husband until he died. Fearing that he would die at the hands of the pequeninos, the way his father had died, Novinha withheld from him her vital discoveries about the biology of the planet Lusitania, fearing that the knowledge of it would kill him. Instead, it was the ignorance of that very information that led him to his death. What she did for his own good, without his knowledge, killed him.

You'd think she'd learn something from that, thought Ender. But she still does the same thing. Making decisions that deform other people's lives, without consulting them, without ever conceiving that perhaps they don't want her to save them from whatever supposed misery she's saving them from.

Then again, if she had simply married Libo in the first place and told him everything she knew, he would probably still be alive and Ender would never have married his widow and helped her raise her younger children. It was the only family Ender had ever had or was ever likely to have. So bad as Novinha's decisions tended to be, the happiest time of his life had come about only because of one of the most deadly of her mistakes.

On their second pass, Ender saw that she still, stubbornly, was not going to speak to him, and so, as always, he bent first and broke the silence between them.

"The Filhos are married, you know. It's a married order. You can't become a full member without me."

She paused in her work. The blade of the hoe rested on unbroken soil, the handle light in her gloved fingers. "I can weed the beets without you," she finally said.

His heart leapt with relief that he had penetrated her veil of silence. "No you can't," he said. "Because here I am."

"These are the potatoes," she said. "I can't stop you from helping with the potatoes."

In spite of themselves they both laughed, and with a groan she unbent her back, stood straight, let the hoe handle fall to the ground, and took Ender's hands in hers, a touch that thrilled him despite two layers of thick workglove cloth between their palms and fingers.

"If I do profane with my touch," Ender began.

"No Shakespeare," she said. "No 'lips two blushing pilgrims ready stand.' "

"I miss you," he said.

"Get over it," she said.

"I don't have to. If you're joining the Filhos, so am I."

She laughed.

Ender didn't appreciate her scorn. "If a xenobiologist can retreat from the world of meaningless suffering, why can't an old retired speaker for the dead?"

"Andrew," she said, "I'm not here because I've given up on life. I'm here because I really have turned my heart over to the Redeemer. You could never do that. You don't belong here.''

"I belong here if you belong here. We made a vow. A sacred one, that the Holy Church won't let us set aside. In case you forgot.''

She sighed and looked out at the sky over the wall of the monastery. Beyond the wall, through meadows, over a fence, up a hill, into the woods . . . that's where the great love of her life, Libo, had gone, and where he died. Where Pipo, his father, who was like a father to her as well, where he had gone before, and also died. It was into another wood that her son Estevão had gone, and also died, but Ender knew, watching her, that when she saw the world outside these walls, it was all those deaths she saw. Two of them had taken place before Ender got to Lusitania. But the death of Estevão—she had begged Ender to stop him from going to the dangerous place where pequeninos were talking of war, of killing humans. She knew as well as Ender did that to stop Estevão would have been the same as to destroy him, for he had not become a priest to be safe, but rather to try to carry the message of Christ to these tree people. Whatever joy came to the early Christian martyrs had surely come to Estevão as he slowly died in the embrace of a murderous tree. Whatever comfort God sent to them in their hour of supreme sacrifice. But no such joy had come to Novinha. God apparently did not extend the benefits of his service to the next of kin. And in her grief and rage she blamed Ender. Why had she married him, if not to make herself safe from these disasters?

He had never said to her the most obvious thing, that if there was anyone to blame, it was God, not him. After all, it was God who had made saints—well, almost saints—out of her parents, who died as they discovered the antidote to the descolada virus when she was only a child. Certainly it was God who led Estevão out to preach to the most dangerous of the pequeninos. Yet in her sorrow it was God she turned to, and turned away from Ender, who had meant to do nothing but good for her.

He never said this because he knew that she would not listen. And he also refrained from saying it because he knew she saw things another way. If God took Father and Mother, Pipo, Libo, and finally Estevão away from her, it was because God was just and punished her for her sins. But when Ender failed to stop Estevão from his suicidal mission to the pequeninos, it was because he was blind, self-willed, stubborn, and rebellious, and because he did not love her enough.

But he did love her. With all his heart he loved her.

All his heart?

All of it he knew about. And yet when his deepest secrets were revealed in that first voyage Outside, it was not Novinha that his heart conjured there. So apparently there was someone who mattered even more to him.

Well, he couldn't help what went on in his unconscious mind, any more than Novinha could. All he could control was what he actually did, and what he was doing now was showing Novinha that regardless of how she tried to drive him away, he would not be driven. That no matter how much she imagined that he loved Jane and his involvement in the great affairs of the human race more than he loved her, it was not true, she was more important to him than any of it. He would give it all up for her. He would disappear behind monastery walls for her. He would weed rows of unidentified plant life in the hot sun. For her.

But even that was not enough. She insisted that he do it, nót for her, but for Christ. Well, too bad. He wasn't married to Christ, and neither was she. Still, it couldn't be displeasing to God when a husband and wife gave all to each other. Surely that was part of what God expected of human beings.

"You know I don't blame you for the death of Quim," she said, using the old family nickname for Estevão.

"I didn't know that," he said, "but I'm glad to find it out."

"I did at first, but I knew all along that it was irrational," she said. "He went because he wanted to, and he was much too old for some interfering parent to stop him. If *I* couldn't, how could you?"

"I didn't even want to," said Ender. "I wanted him to go. It was the fulfillment of his life's ambition."

"I even know that now. It's right. It was right for him to go, and it was even right for him to die, because his death meant something. Didn't it?"

"It saved Lusitania from a holocaust."

"And brought many to Christ." She laughed, the old laugh, the rich ironic laugh that he had come to treasure if only because it was so rare. "Trees for Jesus," she said. "Who could have guessed?"

"They're already calling him St. Stephen of the Trees."

"That's quite premature. It takes time. He must first be beatified. Miracles of healing must take place at his tomb. Believe me, I know the process."

"Martyrs are thin on the ground these days," said Ender. "He will be beatified. He will be canonized. People will pray for him to intercede with Jesus for them, and it will work, because if anyone has earned the right to have Christ hear him, it's your son Estevão."

Tears slipped down her cheeks, even as she laughed again. "My parents were martyrs and will be saints; my son, also. Piety skipped a generation."

"Oh, yes. Yours was the generation of selfish hedonism."

She finally turned to face him, tear-streaked dirty cheeks, smiling face, twinkling eyes that saw through into his heart. The woman he loved.

"I don't regret my adultery," she said. "How can Christ forgive me when I don't even repent? If I hadn't slept with Libo, my children would not have existed. Surely God does not disapprove of that?"

"I believe what Jesus said was, 'I the Lord will forgive whom I will forgive. But of you it is required that you forgive all men.' "

"More or less," she said. "I'm not a scriptorian." She reached out and touched his cheek. "You're so strong, Ender. But you seem tired. How can you be tired? The universe of human beings still depends on you. Or if not the whole of humankind, then certainly you belong to this world. To save this world. But you're tired."

"Deep inside my bones I am," he said. "And you have taken my last lifeblood away from me."

"How odd," she said. "I thought what I removed from you was the cancer in your life."

"You aren't very good at determining what other people want and need from you, Novinha. No one is. We're all as likely to hurt as help."

"That's why I came here, Ender. I'm through deciding things. I put my trust in my own judgment. Then I put trust in you. I put trust in Libo, in Pipo, in Father and Mother, in Quim, and everyone disappointed me or went away or ... no, I know you didn't go away, and I know it wasn't you that—hear me out, Andrew, hear me. The problem wasn't in the people I trusted, the problem was that I trusted in them when no human being can possibly deliver what I needed. I needed deliverance, you see. I needed, I need, redemption. And it isn't in your hands to give me—your open hands, which give me more than you even have to give, Andrew, but still you haven't got the thing I need. Only my Deliverer, only the Anointed One, only he has it to give. Do you see? The only way I can make my life worth living is to give it to him. So here I am."

"Weeding."

"Separating the good fruit from the tares, I believe," she said. "People will have more and better potatoes because I took out the weeds. I don't have to be prominent or even noticed to feel good about my life now. But you, you come here and remind me that even in becoming happy, I'm hurting someone."

"But you're not," said Ender. "Because I'm coming with you. I'm joining the Filhos with you. They're a married order, and we're a married couple. Without me you can't join, and you need to join. With me you *can*. What could be simpler?"

"Simpler?" She shook her head. "You don't believe in God, how's that for starters?"

"I certainly do *too* believe in God," said Ender, annoyed.

"Oh, you're willing to concede God's *existence*, but that's not what I meant. I mean believe in him the way a mother means it when she says to her son, I believe in you. She's not saying she believes that he *exists*—what is *that* worth?—she's saying she believes in his future, she trusts that he'll do all the good that is in him to do. She puts the future in his hands, that's how she believes in him. You don't believe in Christ that way, Andrew. You still believe in yourself. In other people. You've sent out your little surrogates, those children you conjured up during your visit in hell—you may be here with me in these walls right now, but your heart is out there scouting planets and trying to stop the fleet. You aren't leaving anything up to God. You don't believe in him."

"Excuse me, but if God wanted to do everything himself, what did he make us for in the first place?"

"Yes, well, I seem to recall that one of your parents was a heretic, which is no doubt where your strangest ideas come from." It was an old joke between them, but this time neither of them laughed.

"I believe in *you*," Ender said.

"But you consult with Jane."

He reached into his pocket, then held out his hand to show her what he had found there. It was a jewel, with several very fine wires leading from it. Like a glowing organism ripped from its delicate place amid the fronds of life in a shallow sea. She looked at it for a moment uncomprehending, then realized what it was and looked at the ear where, for all the years she had known him, he had worn the jewel that linked him to Jane, the computer-program-come-to-life who was his oldest, dearest, most reliable friend.

"Andrew, no, not for me, surely."

"I can't honestly say these walls contain me, as long as Jane was there to whisper in my ear," he said. "I talked it out with her. I explained it. She understands. We're still friends. But not companions anymore."

"Oh, Andrew," said Novinha. She wept openly now, and held him, clung to him. "If only you had done it years ago, even months ago."

"Maybe I don't believe in Christ the way that you do," said Ender. "But isn't it enough that I believe in you, and you believe in him?"

"You don't belong here, Andrew."

"I belong here more than anywhere else, if this is where you are. I'm not so much world-weary, Novinha, as I am will-weary. I'm tired of deciding things. I'm tired of trying to solve things."

"We try to solve things here," she said, pulling away from him.

"But here we can be, not the mind, but the children of the mind. We can be the hands and feet, the lips and tongue. We can carry out and not decide." He squatted, knelt, then sat in the dirt, the young plants brushing and tickling him on either side. He put his dirty hands to his face and wiped his brow with them, knowing that he was only smearing dirt into mud.

"Oh, I almost believe this, Andrew, you're so good at it," said Novinha. "What, you've decided to stop being the hero of your own saga? Or is this just a ploy? Be the servant of all, so you can be the greatest among us?"

"You know I've never tried for greatness, or achieved it, either."

"Oh, Andrew, you're such a storyteller that you believe your own fables."

Ender looked up at her. "Please, Novinha, let me live with you here. You're my wife. There's no meaning to my life if I've lost you."

"We live as man and wife here, but we don't . . . you know that we don't . . ."

"I know that the Filhos forswear sexual intercourse," said Ender. "I'm your husband. As long as I'm not having sex with anyone, it might as well be you that I'm not having sex with." He smiled wryly.

Her answering smile was only sad and pitying.

"Novinha," he said. "I'm not interested in my own life anymore. Do you understand? The only life I care about in this world is yours. If I lose you, what is there to hold me here?"

He wasn't sure what he meant by this himself. The words had come unbidden to his lips. But he knew as he said them that it was not self-pity, but rather a frank admission of the truth. Not that he was thinking of suicide or exile or any other such low drama. Rather he felt himself fading. Losing his hold. Lusitania seemed less and less real to him. Valentine was still there, his dear sister and friend, and she was like a rock, her life was so real, but it was not real to *him* because she didn't need him. Plikt, his unasked-for disciple, she might need Ender, but not the reality of him, only the idea of him. And who else was there? The children of Novinha and Libo, the children that he had raised as his own, and loved as his own, he loved them no less now, but they were adults, they didn't need him. Jane, who once had been virtually destroyed by an hour of his inattention, she no longer needed him either, for she was there in the jewel in Miro's ear, and in another jewel in Peter's ear. . . .

Peter. Young Valentine. Where had they come from? They had stolen his soul and taken it with them when they left. They were doing the living acts that once he would have done himself. While he waited here in Lusitania and

. . . faded. That's what he meant. If he lost Novinha, what would tie him to this body that he had carried around the universe for all these thousands of years?

"It's not my decision," Novinha said.

"It's your decision," said Ender, "whether you want me with you, as one of the Filhos da Mente de Cristo. If you do, then I believe I can make my way through all the other obstacles."

She laughed nastily. "Obstacles? Men like you don't have obstacles. Just steppingstones."

"Men like me?"

"Yes, men like you," said Novinha. "Just because I've never met any others. Just because no matter how much I loved Libo he was never for one day as alive as you are in every minute. Just because I found myself loving as an adult for the first time when I loved you. Just because I have missed you more than I miss even my children, even my parents, even the lost loves of my life. Just because I can't dream of anyone but you, that doesn't mean that there isn't somebody else just like you somewhere else. The universe is a big place. You can't be all that special, really. Can you?"

He reached through the potato plants and leaned a hand gently on her thigh. "You do still love me, then?" he asked.

"Oh, is that what you came for? To find out if I love you?"

He nodded. "Partly."

"I do," she said.

"Then I can stay?"

She burst into tears. Loud weeping. She sank to the ground; he reached through the plants to embrace her, to hold her, caring nothing for the leaves he crushed between them. After he held her for a long while, she broke off her crying and turned to him and held him at least as tightly as he had been holding her.

"Oh, Andrew," she whispered, her voice cracking and

breaking from having wept so much. "Does God love me enough to give you to me now, again, when I need you so much?"

"Until I die," said Ender.

"I know that part," she said. "But I pray that God will let me die first this time."

3

"THERE ARE TOO MANY OF US"

"Let me tell you the most beautiful story I know.
A man was given a dog, which he loved very much.
The dog went with him everywhere,
but the man could not teach it to do anything useful.
The dog would not fetch or point,
it would not race or protect or stand watch.
Instead the dog sat near him and regarded him,
always with the same inscrutable expression.
'That's not a dog, it's a wolf,' said the man's wife.
'He alone is faithful to me,' said the man,
and his wife never discussed it with him again.
One day the man took his dog with him into his private
    airplane
and as they flew over high winter mountains,
the engines failed
and the airplane was torn to shreds among the trees.
The man lay bleeding,
his belly torn open by blades of sheared metal,
steam rising from his organs in the cold air,
but all he could think of was his faithful dog.
Was he alive? Was he hurt?
Imagine his relief when the dog came padding up

and regarded him with that same steady gaze.
After an hour the dog nosed the man's gaping abdomen,
then began pulling out intestines and spleen and liver
and gnawing on them,
all the while studying the man's face.
'Thank God,' said the man.
'At least one of us will not starve.' "
> *from* The God Whispers of Han Qing-jao

Of all the faster-than-light starships that were flitting Outside and back In under Jane's command, only Miro's
looked like an ordinary spacecraft, for the good reason that
it was nothing more than the shuttle that had once taken
passengers and cargo to and from the great starships that
came to orbit around Lusitania. Now that the new starships
could go immediately from one planet's surface to another's, there was no need for life support or even fuel, and
since Jane had to hold the entire structure of each craft in
her memory, the simpler they were the better. Indeed, they
could hardly be called vehicles anymore. They were simple
cabins now, windowless, almost unfurnished, bare as a
primitive schoolroom. The people of Lusitania referred to
space travel now as *encaixarse,* which was Portuguese for
"going into the box," or, more literally, "to box oneself
up."

   Miro, however, was exploring, searching for new planets
capable of sustaining the lives of the three sentient species:
humans, pequeninos, and hive queens. For this he needed
a more traditional spacecraft, for though he still went from
planet to planet by way of Jane's instant detour through the
Outside, he could not usually count on arriving at a world
where he could breathe the air. Indeed, Jane always started
him out in orbit high above each new planet, so he could
observe, measure, analyze, and only land on the most prom-

ising ones to make the final determination of whether the world was usable.

He did not travel alone. It would have been too much for one person to accomplish, and he needed everything he did to be double-checked. Yet of all the work being done by anyone on Lusitania, this was the most dangerous, for he never knew when he cracked open the door of his spaceship whether there would be some unforeseeable menace on the new world. Miro had long regarded his own life as expendable. For several long years trapped in a brain-damaged body he had wished for death; then, when his first trip Outside enabled him to recreate his body in the perfection of youth, he regarded any moment, any hour, any day of his life as an undeserved gift. He would not waste it, but he would not shrink from putting it at risk for the good of others. But who else could share his easy self-disregard?

Young Valentine was made to order, in every sense, it seemed. Miro had seen her come into existence at the same time as his own new body. She had no past, no kin, no links to any world except through Ender, whose mind had created her, and Peter, her fellow makeling. Oh, and perhaps one might consider her to be linked to the original Valentine, "the real Valentine," as Young Val called her; but it was no secret that Old Valentine had no desire to spend even a moment in the company of this young beauty who mocked her by her very existence. Besides, Young Val was created as Ender's image of perfect virtue. Not only was she unconnected, but also she was genuinely altruistic and quite willing to sacrifice herself for the good of others. So whenever Miro stepped into the shuttle, there was Young Val as his companion, his reliable assistant, his constant backup.

But not his friend. For Miro knew perfectly well who Val really was: Ender in disguise. Not a woman. And her love and loyalty to him were Ender's love and loyalty, often tested, well-trusted, but Ender's, not her own. There was nothing of her own in her. So while Miro had become used to her company, and laughed and joked with her more easily than with anyone in his life till now, he did not confide in her, did not allow himself to feel affection any deeper than camaraderie for her. If she noticed the lack of connection between them she said nothing; if it hurt her, the pain never showed.

What showed was her delight in their successes and her insistence that they push themselves ever harder. "We don't have a whole day to spend on any world," she said right from the start, and proved it by holding them to a schedule that let them make three voyages in a day. They came home after each three voyages to a Lusitania already quiet with sleep; they slept on the ship and spoke to others only to warn them of particular problems the colonists were likely to face on whatever new worlds had been found that day. And the three-a-day schedule was only on days when they dealt with likely planets. When Jane took them to worlds that were obvious losers—waterbound, for instance, or unbiotized—they moved on quickly, checking the next candidate world, and the next, sometimes five and six on those discouraging days when nothing seemed to work. Young Val pushed them both on to the edge of their endurance, day after day, and Miro accepted her leadership in this aspect of their voyaging because he knew that it was necessary.

His friend, however, had no human shape. For him she dwelt in the jewel in his ear. Jane, the whisper in his mind when he first woke up, the friend who heard everything he subvocalized, who knew his needs before he noticed them himself. Jane, who shared all his thoughts and dreams, who had stayed with him through the worst of his cripplehood, who had led him Outside to where he could be renewed. Jane, his truest friend, who would soon die.

That was their real deadline. Jane would die, and then this instant starflight would be at an end, for there was no other being that had the sheer mental power to take anything more complicated than a rubber ball Outside and back In again. And Jane's death would come, not by any natural cause, but because the Starways Congress, having discovered the existence of a subversive program that could control or at least access any and all of their computers, was systematically closing down, disconnecting, and sweeping out all their networks. Already she was feeling the injury of those systems that had been taken offline to where she could not access them. Someday soon the codes would be transmitted that would undo her utterly and all at once. And when she was gone, anyone who had not been taken from the surface of Lusitania and transplanted to another world would be trapped, waiting helplessly for the arrival of the Lusitania Fleet, which was coming ever closer, determined to destroy them all.

A grim business, this, in which despite all of Miro's efforts, his dearest friend would die. Which, he knew full well, was part of why he did not let himself become a true friend to Young Val—because it would be disloyal to Jane to learn affection for anyone else during the last weeks or days of her life.

So Miro's life was an endless routine of work, of concentrated mental effort, studying the findings of the shuttle's instruments, analyzing aerial photographs, piloting the shuttle to unsafe, unscouted landing zones, and finally—not often enough—opening the door and breathing alien air. And at the end of each voyage, no time either to mourn or rejoice, no time even to rest: he closed the door, spoke the word, and Jane took them home again to Lusitania, to start it all over again.

On this homecoming, however, something was different. Miro opened the door of the shuttle to find, not his adoptive father Ender, not the pequeninos who prepared food for him and Young Val, not the normal colony leaders wanting a briefing, but rather his brothers Olhado and Grego, and his sister Elanora, and Ender's sister Valentine. Old Valentine, come herself to the one place where she was sure to meet her unwelcome young twin? Miro saw at once how Young Val and Old Valentine glanced at each other, eyes not really meeting, and then looked away, not wanting to see each other. Or was that it? Young Val was more likely looking away from Old Valentine because she virtuously wanted to avoid giving offense to the older woman. No doubt if she could do it Young Val would willingly disappear rather than cause Old Valentine a moment's pain. And, since that was not possible, she would do the next best thing, which was to remain as unobtrusive as possible when Old Valentine was present.

"What's the meeting?" asked Miro. "Is Mother ill?"

"No, no, everybody's in good health," said Olhado.

"Except mentally," said Grego. "Mother's as mad as a hatter, and now Ender's crazy too."

Miro nodded, grimaced. "Let me guess. He joined her among the Filhos."

Immediately Grego and Olhado looked at the jewel in Miro's ear.

"No, Jane didn't tell me," said Miro. "I just know Ender. He takes his marriage very seriously."

"Yes, well, it's left something of a leadership vacuum here," said Olhado. "Not that everybody isn't doing their job just fine. I mean, the system works and all that. But Ender was the one we all looked to to tell us what to do when the system stops working. If you know what I mean."

"I know what you mean," said Miro. "And you can speak of it in front of Jane. She knows she's going to be shut down as soon as Starways Congress gets their plans in place."

"It's more complicated than that," said Grego. "Most people don't know about the danger to Jane—for that matter, most don't even know she exists. But they can do the arithmetic to figure out that even going full tilt, there's no way to get all the humans off Lusitania before the fleet gets here. Let alone the pequeninos. So they know that unless the fleet is stopped, somebody is going to be left here to die. There are already those who say that we've wasted enough starship space on trees and bugs.''

"Trees" referred, of course, to the pequeninos, who were not, in fact, transporting fathertrees and mothertrees; and "bugs" referred to the Hive Queen, who was also not wasting space sending a lot of workers. But every world they were settling did have a large contingent of pequeninos and at least one hive queen and a handful of workers to help her get started. Never mind that it was the hive queen on every world that quickly produced workers who were doing the bulk of the labor getting agriculture started; never mind that because they were not taking trees with them, at least one male and female in every group of pequeninos had to be "planted"—had to die slowly and painfully so that a fathertree and mothertree could take root and maintain the cycle of pequenino life. They all knew—Grego more than any other, since he'd recently been in the thick of it—that under the polite surface was an undercurrent of competition between species.

And it was not just among the humans, either. While on Lusitania the pequeninos still outnumbered humans by vast numbers, on the new colonies the humans predominated. "It's your fleet coming to destroy Lusitania," said Human, the leader of the fathertrees these days. "And even if every human on Lusitania died, the human race would continue. While for the Hive Queen and for us, it is nothing less than the survival of our species that is at stake. And yet we understand that we must let humans dominate for a time on these new worlds, because of your knowledge of skills and technologies we have not yet mastered, because of your practice at subduing new worlds, and because you still have the power to set fires to burn our forests." What Human said so reasonably, his resentment couched in polite language, many other pequeninos and fathertrees said more passionately: "Why should we let these human invaders, who brought all this evil upon us, save almost all their population, while most of us will die?"

"Resentment between the species is nothing new," said Miro.

"But until now we had Ender to contain it," said Grego. "Pequeninos, the Hive Queen, and most of the human population saw Ender as a fair broker, someone they could trust. They knew that as long as he was in charge of things, as long as his voice was heard, their interests would be protected."

"Ender isn't the only good person leading this exodus," said Miro.

"It's a matter of trust, not of virtue," said Valentine. "The nonhumans know that Ender is the Speaker for the Dead. No other human has ever spoken for another species that way. And yet the humans know that Ender is the Xenocide—that when the human race was threatened by an enemy countless generations ago, he was the one who acted to stop them and save humanity from, as they feared, annihilation. There isn't exactly a candidate with equivalent qualifications ready to step into Ender's role."

"What's that to me?" asked Miro bluntly. "Nobody listens to me here. I have no connections. I certainly can't take Ender's place either, and right now I'm tired and I need to sleep. Look at Young Val, she's half-dead with weariness, too."

It was true; she was barely able to stand. Miro at once reached out to support her; she gratefully leaned against his shoulder.

"We don't want you to take Ender's place," said Olhado. "We don't want anybody to take his place. We want *him* to take his place."

Miro laughed. "You think I can persuade him? You've got his sister right there! Send her!"

Old Valentine grimaced. "Miro, he won't see me."

"Then what makes you think he'll see *me?*"

"Not you, Miro. Jane. The jewel in your ear."

Miro looked at them in bafflement. "You mean Ender has removed his jewel?"

In his ear, he heard Jane say, "I've been busy. I didn't think it was important to mention it to you."

But Miro knew how it had devastated Jane before, when Ender cut her off. Now she had other friends, yes, but that didn't mean it would be painless.

Old Valentine continued. "If you can go to him and get him to talk to Jane . . ."

Miro shook his head. "Taking out the jewel—don't you see that that was final? He's committed himself to following Mother into exile. Ender doesn't back away from his commitments."

They all knew it was true. Knew, in fact, that they had really come to Miro, not with the real hope that he would accomplish what they needed, but as a last feeble act of desperation. "So we let things wind down," said Grego. "We let things slide into chaos. And then, beset by interspecies war, we will die in shame when the fleet comes. Jane's lucky, I think; she'll already be dead when it gets here."

"Tell him thanks," Jane said to Miro.

"Jane says thanks," said Miro. "You're just too softhearted, Grego."

Grego blushed, but he didn't take back what he said.

"Ender isn't God," said Miro. "We'll just do our best without him. But right now the best thing I can do is—"

"Sleep, we know," said Old Valentine. "Not on the ship this time, though. Please. It makes us sick at heart to see how weary you both are. Jakt has brought the taxi. Come home and sleep in a bed."

Miro glanced at Young Val, who still leaned sleepily on his shoulder.

"Both of you, of course," said Old Valentine. "I'm not as distressed by her existence as you all seem to think."

"Of course you're not," said Young Val. She reached out a weary arm, and the two women who bore the same name took each other's hand. Miro watched as Young Val slipped from his side to take Old Valentine's arm, and lean on her instead of him. His own feelings surprised him. Instead of relief that there was less tension between the two of them than he had thought, he found himself being rather angry. Jealous anger, that's what it was. She was leaning on *me,* he wanted to say. What kind of childish response was that?

And then, as he watched them walk away, he saw what he should not have seen—Valentine's shudder. Was it a sudden chill? The night *was* cool. But no, Miro was sure it was the touch of her young twin, and not the night air that made Old Valentine tremble.

"Come on, Miro," said Olhado. "We'll get you to the hovercar and into bed at Valentine's house."

"Is there a food stop along the way?"

"It's Jakt's house, too," said Elanora. "There's always food."

As the hovercar carried them toward Milagre, the human town, they passed near some of the dozens of starships currently in service. The work of migration didn't take the night off. Stevedores—many of them pequeninos—were loading supplies and equipment for transport. Families were shuffling in lines to fill up whatever spaces were left in the cabins. Jane would be getting no rest tonight as she took box after box Outside and back In. On other worlds, new homes were rising, new fields being plowed. Was it day or night in those other places? It didn't matter. In a way they had already succeeded—new worlds were being colonized, and, like it or not, every world had its hive, its new pequenino forest, and its human village.

If Jane died today, thought Miro, if the fleet came tomorrow and blew us all to bits, in the grand scheme of things, what would it matter? The seeds have been scattered to the wind; some, at least, will take root. And if faster-than-light travel dies with Jane, even that might be for the best, for it will force each of these worlds to fend for itself. Some colonies will fail and die, no doubt. On some of them, war will come, and perhaps one species or another will be wiped out there. But it will not be the same species that dies on every world, or the same one that lives; and on some worlds, at least, we'll surely find a way to live in peace. All that's left for us now is details. Whether this or that individual lives or dies. It matters, of course. But not the way that the survival of species matters.

He must have been subvocalizing some of his thoughts, because Jane answered them. "Hath not an overblown computer program eyes and ears? Have I no heart or brain? When you tickle me do I not laugh?''

"Frankly, no," said Miro silently, working his lips and tongue and teeth to shape words that only she could hear.

"But when I die, every being of my kind will also die," she said. "Forgive me if I think of this as having cosmic significance. I'm not as self-abnegating as you are, Miro. I don't regard myself as living on borrowed time. It was my firm intention to live forever, so anything less is a disappointment.''

"Tell me what I can do and I'll do it," he said. "I'd die to save you, if that's what it took.''

"Fortunately, you'll die eventually no matter what," said Jane. "That's my one consolation, that by dying I'll do no more than face the same doom that every other living creature has to face. Even those long-living trees. Even those hive queens, passing their memories along from generation to generation. But I, alas, will have no children. How could I? I'm a creature of mind alone. There's no provision for mental mating.''

"Too bad, too," said Miro, "because I bet you'd be great in the virtual sack."

"The best," Jane said.

And then silence for a little while.

Only when they approached Jakt's house, a new building on the outskirts of Milagre, did Jane speak again. "Keep in mind, Miro, that whatever Ender does with his own self, when Young Valentine speaks it's still Ender's aiúa talking.''

"The same with Peter," said Miro. "Now there's a charmer. Let's just say that Young Val, sweet as she is, doesn't exactly represent a balanced view of anything. Ender may control her, but she's *not* Ender."

"There are just too many of him, aren't there," said Jane. "And, apparently, too many of me, at least in the opinion of Starways Congress."

"There are too many of us all," said Miro. "But never enough."

They arrived. Miro and Young Val were led inside. They ate feebly; they slept the moment they reached their beds. Miro was aware that voices went on far into the night, for he did not sleep well, but rather kept waking a little, uncomfortable on such a soft mattress, and perhaps uncomfortable at being away from his duty, like a soldier who feels guilty at having abandoned his post.

Despite his weariness, Miro did not sleep late. Indeed, the sky outside was still dim with the predawn seepage of sunlight over the horizon when he awoke and, as was his habit, rose immediately from his bed, standing shakily as the last of sleep fled from his body. He covered himself and went out into the hall to find the bathroom and discharge his bladder. When he emerged, he heard voices from the kitchen. Either last night's conversation was still going on, or some other neurotic early risers had rejected morning solitude and were chatting away as if dawn were not the dark hour of despair.

He stood before his own open door, ready to go inside and shut out those earnest voices, when Miro realized that one of them belonged to Young Val. Then he realized that the other one was Old Valentine. At once he turned and made his way to the kitchen, and again hesitated in a doorway.

Sure enough, the two Valentines were sitting across the

table from each other, but not looking at each other. Instead they stared out the window as they sipped one of Old Valentine's fruit-and-vegetable decoctions.

"Would you like one, Miro?" asked Old Valentine without looking up.

"Not even on my deathbed," said Miro. "I didn't mean to interrupt."

"Good," said Old Valentine.

Young Val continued to say nothing.

Miro came inside the kitchen, went to the sink, and drew himself a glass of water, which he drank in one long draught.

"I told you it was Miro in the bathroom," said Old Valentine. "No one processes so much water every day as this dear lad."

Miro chuckled, but he did not hear Young Val laugh.

"I *am* interfering with the conversation," he said. "I'll go."

"Stay," said Old Valentine.

"Please," said Young Val.

"Please which?" asked Miro. He turned toward her and grinned.

She shoved a chair toward him with her foot. "Sit," she said. "The lady and I were having it out about our twin-ship."

"We decided," said Old Valentine, "that it's my responsibility to die first."

"On the contrary," said Young Val, "we decided that Gepetto did not create Pinocchio because he wanted a real boy. It was a puppet he wanted all along. That real-boy business was simply Gepetto's laziness. He still wanted the puppet to dance—he just didn't want to go to all the trouble of working the strings."

"You being Pinocchio," said Miro. "And Ender . . ."

"My brother didn't try to make you," said Old Valentine. "And he doesn't want to control you, either."

"I know," whispered Young Val. And suddenly there were tears in her eyes.

Miro reached out a hand to lay atop hers on the table, but at once she snatched hers away. No, she wasn't avoiding his touch, she was simply bringing her hand up to wipe the annoying tears out of her eyes.

"He'd cut the strings if he could, I know," said Young Val. "The way Miro cut the strings on his old broken body."

Miro remembered it very clearly. One moment he was sitting in the starship, looking at this perfect image of himself, strong and young and healthy; the next moment he was that image, had always been that image, and what he looked at was the crippled, broken, brain-damaged version of himself. And as he watched, that unloved, unwanted body crumbled into dust and disappeared.

"I don't think he hates you," said Miro, "the way I hated my old self."

"He doesn't have to hate me. It wasn't hate anyway that killed your old body." Young Val didn't meet his eyes. In all their hours together exploring worlds, they had never talked about anything so personal. She had never dared to discuss with him that moment when both of them had been created. "You hated your old body while you were in it, but as soon as you were back in your right body, you simply stopped paying any attention to the old one. It wasn't part of you anymore. Your aiúa had no more responsibility for it. And with nothing to hold it together—pop goes the weasel."

"Wooden doll," said Miro. "Now weasel. What else am I?"

Old Valentine ignored his bid for a laugh. "So you're saying Ender finds you uninteresting."

"He admires me," said Young Val. "But he finds me dull."

"Yes, well, me too," said Old Valentine.

"That's absurd," said Miro.

"Is it?" asked Old Valentine. "He never followed *me* anywhere; I was always the one who followed him. He was searching for a mission in life, I think. Some great deed to do, to match the terrible act that ended his childhood. He thought writing *The Hive Queen* would do it. And then, with my help in preparing it, he wrote *The Hegemon* and he thought that might be enough, but it wasn't. He kept searching for something that would engage his full attention and he kept almost finding it, or finding it for a week or a month, but one thing was certain, the thing that engaged his attention was never *me*, because there I was in all the billion miles he traveled, there I was across three thousand years. Those histories I wrote—it was no great love for history, it was because it helped in his work. The way my writing used to help in Peter's work. And when I was finished, then, for a few hours of reading and discussion, I had his attention. Only each time it was less satisfying because it wasn't *I* who had his attention, it was the story I had written. Until finally I found a man who gave me his whole heart, and I stayed with him. While my adolescent brother went on without me, and found a family that took *his* whole heart, and there we were, planets apart, but finally happier without each other than we'd ever been together."

"So why did you come to him again?" asked Miro.

"I didn't come for him. I came for you." Old Valentine smiled. "I came for a world in danger of destruction. But I was glad to see Ender, even though I knew he would never belong to me."

"This may be an accurate description of how it felt to you," said Young Val. "But you must have had his attention, at some level. I exist because you're always in his heart."

"A fantasy of his childhood, perhaps. Not me."

"Look at me," said Young Val. "Is this the body you wore when he was five and was taken away from his home and sent up to the Battle School? Is this even the teenage girl that he knew that summer by the lake in North Carolina? You must have had his attention even when you grew up, because his image of you changed to become me."

"You are what I was when we worked on *The Hegemon* together," said Old Valentine sadly.

"Were you this tired?" asked Young Val.

"*I* am," said Miro.

"No you're not," said Old Valentine. "You are the picture of vigor. You're still celebrating your beautiful new body. My twin here is heartweary."

"Ender's attention has always been divided," said Young Val. "I'm filled with his memories, you see—or rather, with the memories that he unconsciously thought I should have, but of course they consist almost entirely of things that *he* remembers about my friend here, which means that all I remember is my life with Ender. And he always had Jane in his ear, and the people whose deaths he was speaking, and his students, and the Hive Queen in her cocoon, and so on. But they were all adolescent connections. Like every itinerant hero of epic, he wandered place to place, transforming others but remaining himself unchanged. Until he came here and finally gave himself wholly to somebody else. You and your family, Miro. Novinha. For the first time he gave other people the power to tear at him emotionally, and it was exhilarating and painful both at once, but even that he could handle just fine, he's a strong man, and strong men have borne more. Now, though, it's something else entirely. Peter and I, we have no life apart from him. To say that he is one with Novinha is metaphorical; with Peter and me it's literal. He *is* us. And his aiúa isn't great enough, it isn't strong or copious enough, it hasn't enough attention in it to give equal shares to the three lives that depend on it. I realized this almost as soon as I was . . . what shall we call it, created? Manufactured?"

"Born," said Old Valentine.

"You were a dream come true," said Miro, with only a hint of irony.

"He can't sustain all three of us. Ender, Peter, me. One of us is going to fade. One of us at least is going to die. And it's me. I knew that from the start. I'm the one who's going to die."

Miro wanted to reassure her. But how do you reassure someone, except by recalling to them similar situations that turned out for the best? There were no similar situations to call upon.

"The trouble is that whatever part of Ender's aiúa I still have in me is absolutely determined to live. I don't want to die. That's how I know I still have some shred of his attention: I don't want to die."

"So go to him," said Old Valentine. "Talk to him."

Young Val gave one bitter hoot of laughter and looked away. "Please, Papa, let me live," she said in a mockery of a child's voice. "Since it's not something he consciously controls, what could he possibly do about it, except suffer from guilt? And why should he feel guilty? If I cease to exist, it's because my own self didn't value me. He *is* myself. Do the dead tips of fingernails feel bad when you pare them away?"

"But you *are* bidding for his attention," said Miro.

"I hoped that the search for habitable worlds would intrigue him. I poured myself into it, trying to be excited about it. But the truth is it's utterly routine. Important, but routine, Miro."

Miro nodded. "True enough. Jane finds the worlds. We just process them."

"And there are enough worlds now. Enough colonies. Two dozen—pequeninos and hive queens are not going to die out now, even if Lusitania is destroyed. The bottleneck isn't the number of worlds, it's the number of starships. So all our labor—it isn't engaging Ender's attention anymore. And my body knows it. My body knows it isn't needed."

She reached up and took a large hank of her hair into her fist, and pulled—not hard, but lightly—and it came away easily in her hand. A great gout of hair, with not a sign of any pain at its going. She let the hair drop onto the table. It lay there like a dismembered limb, grotesque, impossible. "I think," she whispered, "that if I'm not careful, I could do the same with my fingers. It's slower, but gradually I will turn into dust just as your old body did, Miro. Because he isn't interested in me. Peter is solving mysteries and fighting political wars off on some world somewhere. Ender is struggling to hold on to the woman he loves. But I . . ."

In that moment, as the hair torn from her head revealed the depth of her misery, her loneliness, her self-rejections, Miro realized what he had not let himself think of until now: that in all the weeks they had traveled world to world together, he had come to love her, and her unhappiness hurt him as if it were his own. And perhaps it *was* his own, his memory of his own self-loathing. But whatever the reason, it still felt like something deeper than mere compassion to him. It was a kind of desire. Yes, it was a kind of love. If this beautiful young woman, this wise and intelligent and clever young woman was rejected by her own inmost heart, then Miro's heart had room enough to take her in. If Ender will not be yourself, let me! he cried silently, knowing as he formed the thought for the first time that he had felt this way for days, for weeks, without realizing it; yet also knowing that he could not be to her what Ender was.

Still, couldn't love do for Young Val what it was doing for Ender himself? Couldn't that engage enough of his attention to keep her alive? To strengthen her?

Miro reached out and gathered up her disembodied hair, twined it around his fingers, and then slid the looping locks into the pocket of his robe. "I don't want you to fade away," he said. Bold words for him.

Young Val looked at him oddly. "I thought the great love of your life was Ouanda."

"She's a middle-aged woman now," said Miro. "Married and happy, with a family. It would be sad if the great love of my life were a woman who doesn't exist anymore, and even if she did she wouldn't want me."

"It's sweet of you to offer," said Young Val. "But I don't think we can fool Ender into caring about my life by pretending to fall in love."

Her words stabbed Miro to the heart, because she had so easily seen how much of his self-declaration came from pity. Yet not all of it came from there; most of it was already seething just under the level of consciousness, just waiting its chance to come out. "I wasn't thinking of fooling anyone," said Miro. Except myself, he thought. Because Young Val could not possibly love me. She is, after all, not really a woman. She's Ender.

But that was absurd. Her body was a woman's body. And where did the choice of loves come from, if not the body? Was there something male or female in the aiúa? Before it became master of flesh and bone, was it manly or womanly? And if so, would that mean that the aiúas composing atoms and molecules, rocks and stars and light and wind, that all of those were neatly sorted into boys and girls? Nonsense. Ender's aiúa could be a woman, could love like a woman as easily as it now loved, in a man's body and in a man's ways, Miro's own mother. It wasn't any lack in Young Val that made her look at him with such pity. It was a lack in him. Even with his body healed, he was not a man that a woman—or at least this woman, at the moment the most desirable of all women—could love, or wish to love, or hope to win.

"I shouldn't have come here," he murmured. He pushed away from the table and left the room in two strides. Strode up the hall and once again stood in his open doorway. He heard their voices.

"No, don't go to him," said Old Valentine. Then something softer. Then, "He may have a new body, but his self-hatred has never been healed."

A murmur from Young Val.

"Miro was speaking from his heart," Old Valentine assured her. "It was a very brave and naked thing for him to do."

Again Young Val spoke too softly for Miro to hear her. "How could you know?" Old Valentine said. "What you have to realize is, we took a long voyage together, not that long ago, and I think he fell in love with me a little on that flight."

It was probably true. It was definitely true. Miro had to admit it: some of his feelings for Young Val were really his feelings for Old Valentine, transferred from the woman who was permanently out of reach to this young woman who might be, he had hoped at least, accessible to him.

Now both their voices fell to levels where Miro could not even pick out words. But still he waited, his hands pressed against the doorjamb, listening to the lilting of those two voices, so much alike, but both so well-known to him. It was a music that he could gladly hear forever.

"If there's anyone like Ender in all this universe," said Old Valentine with sudden loudness, "it's Miro. He broke himself trying to save innocents from destruction. He hasn't yet been healed."

She meant me to hear that, Miro realized. She spoke loudly, knowing I was standing here, knowing I was listening. The old witch was listening for my door to close and she never heard it so she knows that I can hear them and she's trying to give me a way to see myself. But I'm no Ender, I'm barely Miro, and if she says things like that about me it's just proof that she doesn't know who I am.

A voice spoke up in his ear. "Oh, shut up if you're just going to lie to yourself."

Of course Jane had heard everything. Even his thoughts, because, as was his habit, his conscious thoughts were echoed by his lips and tongue and teeth. He couldn't even think without moving his lips. With Jane attached to his ear he spent his waking hours in a confessional that never closed.

"So you love the girl," said Jane. "Why not? So your motives are complicated by your feelings toward Ender and

Valentine and Ouanda and yourself. So what? What love was ever pure, what lover was ever uncomplicated? Think of her as a succubus. You'll love her, and she'll crumble in your arms."

Jane's taunting was infuriating and amusing at once. He went inside his room and gently closed the door. When it was closed, he whispered to her, "You're just a jealous old bitch, Jane. You only want me for yourself."

"I'm sure you're right," said Jane. "If Ender had really loved me, he would have created *my* human body when he was being so fertile Outside. Then I could make a play for you myself."

"You already have my whole heart," said Miro. "Such as it is."

"You are such a liar," said Jane. "I'm just a talking appointment book and calculator, and you know it."

"But you're very very rich," said Miro. "I'll marry you for your money."

"By the way," said Jane, "she's wrong about one thing."

"What's that?" asked Miro, wondering which "she" Jane was referring to.

"You aren't done with exploring worlds. Whether Ender is still interested in it or not—and I think he is, because she hasn't turned to dust *yet*—the work doesn't end just because there are enough habitable planets to save the piggies and buggers."

Jane frequently used the old diminutive and pejorative terms for them. Miro often wondered, but never dared to ask, if she had any pejoratives for humans. But he thought he knew what her answer would be anyway: "The word 'human' *is* a pejorative," she'd say.

"So what are we still looking for?" asked Miro.

"Every world that we can find before I die," said Jane.

He thought about that as he lay back down on his bed. Thought about it as he tossed and turned a couple of times, then got up, got dressed for real, and set out under the lightening sky, walking among the other early risers, people about their business, few of whom knew him or even knew *of* him. Being a scion of the strange Ribeira family, he hadn't had many childhood friends in *ginásio*; being both brilliant and shy, he'd had even fewer of the more rambunctious adolescent friendships in *colégio*. His only girlfriend had been Ouanda, until his penetration of the sealed perimeter of the human colony left him brain-damaged and he refused to see even her anymore. Then his voyage out to meet Valentine had severed the few fragile ties that remained between him and his birthworld. For him it was only a few months in a starship, but when he came back, years had passed, and he was now his mother's youngest child, the only one whose life was unbegun. The children he had once watched over were adults who treated him like a tender memory from their youth. Only Ender was unchanged. No matter how many years. No matter what happened. Ender was the same.

Could it still be true? Could he be the same man even now, locking himself away at a time of crisis, hiding out in a monastery just because Mother had finally given up on life? Miro knew the bare outline of Ender's life. Taken from his family at the tender age of five. Brought to the orbiting Battle School, where he emerged as the last best hope of humankind in its war with the ruthless invaders called buggers. Taken next to the fleet command on Eros, where he was told he was in advanced training, but where, without realizing it, he was commanding the real fleets, lightyears away, his commands transmitted by ansible. He won that war through brilliance and, in the end, the utterly unconscionable act of destroying the home world of the buggers. Except that he had thought it was a game.

Thought it was a game, but at the same time knowing that the game was a simulation of reality. In the game he had chosen to do the unspeakable; it meant, to Ender at least, that he was not free of guilt when the game turned out to be real. Even though the last Hive Queen forgave him and put herself, cocooned as she was, into his care, he could not shake himself free of that. He was only a child, doing what adults led him to do; but somewhere in his heart he knew that even a child is a real person, that a child's acts are real acts, that even a child's play is not without moral context.

Thus before the sun was up, Miro found himself facing Ender as they both straddled a stone bench in a spot in the garden that would soon be bathed in sunlight but now was clammy with the morning chill; and what Miro found himself saying to this unchangeable, unchanging man was this: "What is this monastery business, Andrew Wiggin, except for a backhanded, cowardly way of crucifying yourself?"

"I've missed you too, Miro," said Ender. "You look tired, though. You need more sleep."

Miro sighed and shook his head. "That wasn't what I meant to say. I'm trying to understand you, I really am. Valentine says that I'm like you."

"You mean the real Valentine?" asked Ender.

"They're both real," said Miro.

"Well, if I'm like you, then study yourself and tell me what you find."

Miro wondered, looking at him, if Ender really meant this.

Ender patted Miro's knee. "I'm really not needed out there now," he said.

"You don't believe that for a second," said Miro.

"But I believe that I believe it," said Ender, "and for me that's pretty good. Please don't disillusion me. I haven't had breakfast yet."

"No, you're exploiting the convenience of having split yourself into three. This part of you, the aging middle-aged man, can afford the luxury of devoting himself entirely to his wife—but only because he has two young puppets to go out and do the work that really interests him."

"But it doesn't interest me," said Ender. "I don't care."

"You as Ender don't care because you as Peter and you

as Valentine are taking care of everything else for you. Only Valentine isn't well. You're not caring enough about what she's doing. What happened to my old crippled body is happening to her. More slowly, but it's the same thing. She thinks so, Valentine thinks it's possible. So do I. So does Jane.''

"Give Jane my love. I do miss her ''

"I give Jane *my* love, Ender.''

Ender grinned at his resistance. "If they were about to shoot you, Miro, you'd insist on drinking a lot of water just so they'd have to handle a corpse covered with urine when you were dead.''

"Valentine isn't a dream or an illusion, Ender,'' said Miro, refusing to be sidetracked into a discussion of his own obstreperousness. "She's real, and you're killing her.''

"Awfully dramatic way of putting it.''

"If you'd seen her pull out tufts of her own hair this morning . . .''

"So she's rather theatrical, I take it? Well, you've always been one for the theatrical gesture, too. I'm not surprised you get along.''

"Andrew, I'm telling you you've got to—''

Suddenly Ender grew stern and his voice overtopped Miro's even though he was not speaking loudly. "Use your head, Miro. Was your decision to jump from your old body to this newer model a conscious one? Did you think about it and say, 'Well, I think I'll let this old corpse crumble into its constituent molecules because this new body is a nicer place to dwell'?''

Miro got his point at once. Ender couldn't consciously control where his attention went. His aiúa, even though it was his deepest self, was not to be ordered about.

"I find out what I really want by seeing what I do,'' said Ender. "That's what we all do, if we're honest about it. We have our feelings, we make our decisions, but in the end we look back on our lives and see how sometimes we ignored our feelings, while most of our decisions were actually rationalizations because we had already decided in our secret hearts before we ever recognized it consciously. I can't help it if the part of me that's controlling this girl whose company you're sharing isn't as important to my underlying will as you'd like. As she needs. I can't do a thing.''

Miro bowed his head.

The sun came up over the trees. Suddenly the bench turned bright, and Miro looked up to see the sunlight making a halo out of Ender's wildly slept-in hair. ''Is grooming against the monastic rule?'' asked Miro.

''You're attracted to her, aren't you,'' said Ender, not really making a question out of it. ''And it makes you a little uneasy that *she* is really *me*.''

Miro shrugged. ''It's a root in the path. But I think I can step over it.''

''But what if *I'm* not attracted to *you*?'' asked Ender cheerfully.

Miro spread his arms and turned to show his profile. ''Unthinkable,'' he said.

''You *are* cute as a bunny,'' said Ender. ''I'm sure young Valentine dreams about you. I wouldn't know. The only dreams I have are of planets blowing up and everyone I love being obliterated.''

''I know you haven't forgotten the world in here, Andrew.'' He meant that as the beginning of an apology, but Ender waved him off.

''I can't forget it, but I can ignore it. I'm ignoring the world, Miro. I'm ignoring you, I'm ignoring those two walking psychoses of mine. At this moment, I'm trying to ignore everything but your mother.''

''And God,'' said Miro. ''You mustn't forget God.''

''Not for a single moment,'' said Ender. ''As a matter of fact, I can't forget anything or anybody. But yes, I *am* ignoring God, except insofar as Novinha needs me to notice him. I'm shaping myself into the husband that she needs.''

"Why, Andrew? You know Mother's as crazy as a loon."

"No such thing," said Ender reprovingly. "But even if it were true, then . . . all the more reason."

"What God has joined, let no man put asunder. I do approve, philosophically, but you don't know how it . . ." Miro's weariness swept over him then. He couldn't think of the words to say what he wanted to say, and he knew that it was because he was trying to tell Ender how it felt, at this moment, to be Miro Ribeira, and Miro had no practice in even identifying his own feelings, let alone expressing them. "Desculpa," he murmured, changing to Portuguese because it was his childhood language, the language of his emotions. He found himself wiping tears off his cheeks. "Se nã poso mudar nem você, não que possa, nada." If I can't get even you to move, to change, then there's nothing I can do.

"Nem eu?" Ender echoed. "In all the universe, Miro, there's nobody harder to change than me."

"Mother did it. She changed you."

"No she didn't," said Ender. "She only allowed me to be what I needed and wanted to be. Like now, Miro. I can't make everybody happy. I can't make *me* happy, I'm not doing much for *you*, and as for the big problems, I'm worthless there too. But maybe I can make your mother happy, or at least somewhat happier, at least for a while, or at least I can try." He took Miro's hands in his, pressed them to his own face, and they did not come away dry.

Miro watched as Ender got up from the bench and walked away toward the sun, into the shining orchard. Surely this is how Adam would have looked, thought Miro, if he had never eaten the fruit. If he had stayed and stayed and stayed and stayed in the garden. Three thousand years Ender has skimmed the surface of life. It was my mother he finally snagged on. I spent my whole childhood trying to be free of her, and he comes along and chooses to attach himself and . . .

And what am I snagged on, except him? Him in women's flesh. Him with a handful of hair on a kitchen table.

Miro was getting up from the bench when Ender suddenly turned to face him and waved to attract his attention. Miro started to walk toward him, but Ender didn't wait; he cupped his hands around his mouth and shouted.

"Tell Jane!" he called. "If she can figure out! How to do it! She can have that body!"

It took Miro a moment to realize that he was speaking of Young Val.

She's not just a body, you self-centered old planet-smasher. She's not just an old suit to be given away because it doesn't fit or the style has changed.

But then his anger fled, for he realized that he himself had done precisely that with his old body. Tossed it away without a backward glance.

And the idea intrigued him. Jane. Was it even possible? If her aiúa could somehow be made to take up residence in Young Val, could a human body hold enough of Jane's mind to enable her to survive when Starways Congress tried to shut her down?

"You boys are so slow," Jane murmured in his ear. "I've been talking to the Hive Queen and Human and trying to figure out how the thing is done—assigning an aiúa to a body. The hive queens did it once, in creating me. But they didn't exactly pick a particular aiúa. They took what came. What showed up. I'm a little fussier."

Miro said nothing as he walked to the monastery gate.

"Oh, yes, and then there's the little matter of your feelings toward Young Val. You hate the fact that in loving her, it's really, in a way, Ender that you love. But if I took over, if I were the will inside Young Val's life, would she still be the woman you love? Would anything of her survive? Would it be murder?"

"Oh, shut up," said Miro aloud.

The monastery gatekeeper looked up at him in surprise.

"Not you," said Miro. "But that doesn't mean it isn't a good idea."

Miro was aware of her eyes on his back until he was out and on the path winding down the hill toward Milagre. Time to get back to the ship. Val will be waiting for me. Whoever she is.

What Ender is to Mother, so loyal, so patient—is that how I feel toward Val? Or no, it isn't feeling, is it? It's an act of will. It's a decision that can never be revoked. Could I do that for any woman, any person? Could I give myself forever?

He remembered Ouanda then, and walked with the memory of bitter loss all the way back to the starship.

4

"I AM A MAN OF PERFECT SIMPLICITY!"

"When I was a child, I thought
a god was disappointed
whenever some distraction
interrupted my tracing of the lines
revealed in the grain of the wood.
Now I know the gods expect such interruptions,
for they know our frailty.
It is completion that surprises them."
                    from The God Whispers of Han Qing-jao

Peter and Wang-mu ventured out into the world of Divine Wind on their second day. They did not have to worry about learning a language. Divine Wind was an older world, one of the first wave settled in the initial emigration from Earth. It was originally as recidivist as Path, clinging to the ancient ways. But the ancient ways of Divine Wind were Japanese ways, and so it included the possibility of radical change. Scarcely three hundred years into its history, the world transformed itself from being the isolated fiefdom of a ritualized shogunate to being a cosmopolitan center of trade and industry and philosophy. The Japanese of Divine Wind prided themselves on being hosts to visitors from all worlds, and there were still many places where children grew up speaking only Japanese until they were old enough to enter school. But by adulthood, all the people of Divine Wind spoke Stark with fluency, and the best of them with elegance, with grace, with astonishing economy; it was said by Mil Fiorelli, in his most famous book, *Observations of Distant Worlds with the Naked Eye,* that Stark was a language that had no native speakers until it was whispered by a Divine Wind.

So it was that when Peter and Wang-mu hiked through the woods of the great natural preserve where their starship had landed and emerged in a village of foresters, laughing about how long they had been "lost" in the woods, no one thought twice about Wang-mu's obviously Chinese features and accent, or even about Peter's white skin and lack of an epicanthic fold. They had lost their documents, they claimed, but a computer search showed them to be licensed automobile drivers in the city of Nagoya, and while Peter seemed to have had a couple of youthful traffic offenses there, otherwise they were not known to have committed any illegal acts. Peter's profession was given as "independent teacher of physics" and Wang-mu's as "itinerant philosopher," both quite respectable positions, given their youth and lack of family attachment. When they were asked casual questions ("I have a cousin who teaches progenerative grammars in the Komatsu University in Nagoya") Jane gave Peter appropriate comments to say:

"I never seem to get over to the Oe Building. The language people don't talk to physicists anyway. They think we speak only mathematics. Wang-mu tells me that the only language we physicists know is the grammar of dreams."

Wang-mu had no such friendly prompter in her ear, but then an itinerant philosopher was supposed to be gnomic in her speech and mantic in her thought. Thus she could answer Peter's comment by saying, "I say that is the only grammar you speak. There *is* no grammar that you understand.''

This prompted Peter to tickle her, which made Wang-mu simultaneously laugh and wrench at his wrist until he stopped, thereby proving to the foresters that they were exactly what their documents said they were: brilliant young people who were nevertheless silly with love—or with youth, as if it made a difference.

They were given a ride in a government floater back to civilized country, where—thanks to Jane's manipulation of the computer networks—they found an apartment that until yesterday had been empty and unfurnished, but which now was filled with an eclectic mix of furniture and art that reflected a charming mixture of poverty, quirkiness, and exquisite taste.

''Very nice,'' said Peter.

Wang-mu, familiar only with the taste of one world, and really only of one man in that one world, could hardly evaluate Jane's choices. There were places to sit—both Western chairs, which folded people into alternating right angles and never seemed comfortable to Wang-mu, and Eastern mats, which encouraged people to twine themselves into circles of harmony with the earth. The bedroom, with its Western mattress raised high off the ground even though there were neither rats nor roaches, was obviously Peter's; Wang-mu knew that the same mat that invited her to sit in the main room of the apartment would also be her sleeping mat at night.

She deferentially offered Peter the first bath; he, however, seemed to feel no urgency to wash himself, even though he smelled of sweat from the hike and the hours cooped up in the floater. So Wang-mu ended up luxuriating in a tub, closing her eyes and meditating until she felt restored to herself. When she opened her eyes she no longer felt like a stranger. Rather she was herself, and the surrounding objects and spaces were free to attach themselves to her without damaging her sense of self. This was a power she had learned early in life, when she had no power even over her own body, and had to obey in all things. It was what preserved her. Her life had many unpleasant things attached to it, like remoras to a shark, but none of them changed who she was under the skin, in the cool darkness of her solitude with eyes closed and mind at peace.

When she emerged from the bathroom, she found Peter eating absently from a plate of grapes as he watched a holoplay in which masked Japanese actors bellowed at each other and took great, awkward, thundering steps, as if the actors were playing characters twice the size of their own bodies.

"Have you learned Japanese?" she asked.

"Jane's translating for me. Very strange people."

"It's an ancient form of drama," said Wang-mu.

"But very boring. Was there ever anyone whose heart was stirred by all this shouting?"

"If you are inside the story," said Wang-mu, "then they are shouting the words of your own heart."

"Somebody's heart says, 'I am the wind from the cold snow of the mountain, and you are the tiger whose roar will freeze in your own ears before you tremble and die in the iron knife of my winter eyes'?"

"It sounds like *you*," said Wang-mu. "Bluster and brag."

"I am the round-eyed sweating man who stinks like the corpse of a leaking skunk, and you are the flower who will wilt unless I take an immediate shower with lye and ammonia."

"Keep your eyes closed when you do," said Wang-mu. "That stuff burns."

There was no computer in the apartment. Maybe the holoview could be used as a computer, but if so Wang-mu didn't know how. Its controls looked like nothing she had seen in Han Fei-tzu's house, but that was hardly a surprise. The people of Path didn't take their design of anything from other worlds, if they could help it. Wang-mu didn't even know how to turn off the sound. It didn't matter. She sat on her mat and tried to remember everything she knew about the Japanese people from her study of Earth history with Han Qing-jao and her father, Han Fei-tzu. She knew that her education was spotty at best, because as a low-class girl no one had bothered to teach her much until she wangled her way into Qing-jao's household. So Han Fei-tzu had told her not to bother with formal studies, but merely to explore information wherever her interests took her. "Your mind is unspoiled by a traditional education. Therefore you must let yourself discover your own way into each subject." Despite this seeming liberty, Fei-tzu soon showed her that he was a stern taskmaster even when the subjects were freely chosen. Whatever she learned about history or biography, he would challenge her, question her; demand that she generalize, then refute her generalizations; and if she changed her mind, he would then demand just as sharply that she defend her new position, even though a moment before it had been his own. The result was that even with limited information, she was prepared to reexamine it, cast away old conclusions and hypothesize new ones. Thus she could close her eyes and continue her education without any jewel to whisper in her ear, for she could still hear Han Fei-tzu's caustic questioning even though he was lightyears away.

The actors stopped ranting before Peter had finished his shower. Wang-mu did not notice. She did notice, however, when a voice from the holoview said, "Would you like another recorded selection, or would you prefer to connect with a current broadcast?"

For a moment Wang-mu thought that the voice must be Jane; then she realized that it was simply the rote menu of a machine. "Do you have news?" she asked.

"Local, regional, planetary or interplanetary?" asked the machine.

"Begin with local," said Wang-mu. She was a stranger here. She might as well get acquainted.

When Peter emerged, clean and dressed in one of the stylish local costumes that Jane had had delivered for him, Wang-mu was engrossed in an account of a trial of some people accused of overfishing a lush coldwater region a few hundred kilometers from the city they were in. What was the name of this town? Oh, yes. Nagoya. Since Jane had declared this to be their hometown on all their false records, of course this was where the floater had brought them. "All worlds are the same," said Wang-mu. "People want to eat fish from the sea, and some people want to take more of the fish than the ocean can replenish."

"What harm does it do if I fish one extra day or take one extra ton?" Peter asked.

"Because if everyone does, then—" She stopped herself. "I see. You were ironically speaking the rationalization of the wrongdoers."

"Am I clean and pretty now?" asked Peter, turning around to show off his loose-fitting yet somehow form-revealing clothing.

"The colors are garish," said Wang-mu. "It looks as if you're screaming."

"No, no," said Peter. "The idea is for the people who see me to scream."

"Aaaah," Wang-mu screamed softly.

"Jane says that this is actually a conservative costume—for a man of my age and supposed profession. Men in Nagoya are known for being peacocks."

"And the women?"

"Bare-breasted all the time," said Peter. "Quite a stunning sight."

"That is a lie. I didn't see one bare-breasted woman on our way in and—" Again she stopped and frowned at him. "Do you really want me to assume that everything you say is a lie?"

"I thought it was worth a try."

"Don't be silly. I have no breasts."

"You have small ones," said Peter. "Surely you're aware of the distinction."

"I don't want to discuss my body with a man dressed in a badly planned, overgrown flower garden."

"Women are all dowds here," said Peter. "Tragic but true. Dignity and all that. So are the old men. Only the boys and young men on the prowl are allowed such plumage as this. I think the bright colors are to warn women off. Nothing serious from this lad! Stay to play, or go away. Some such thing. I think Jane chose this city for us solely so she could make me wear these things."

"I'm hungry. I'm tired."

"Which is more urgent?" asked Peter.

"Hungry."

"There are grapes," he offered.

"Which you didn't wash. I suppose that's a part of your death wish."

"On Divine Wind, insects know their place and stay there. No pesticides. Jane assured me."

"There were no pesticides on Path, either," said Wang-mu. "But we washed to clear away bacteria and other one-celled creatures. Amebic dysentery will slow us down."

"Oh, but the bathroom is so nice, it would be a shame not to use it," said Peter. Despite his flippancy, Wang-mu saw that her comment about dysentery from unwashed fruit bothered him.

"Let's eat out," said Wang-mu. "Jane has money for us, doesn't she?"

Peter listened for a moment to something coming from the jewel in his ear.

"Yes, and all we have to do is tell the master of the restaurant that we lost our IDs and he'll let us thumb our way into our accounts. Jane says we're both very rich if we need to be, but we should try to act as if we were of limited means having an occasional splurge to celebrate something. What shall we celebrate?"

"Your bath."

"You celebrate that. I'll celebrate our safe return from being lost in the woods."

Soon they found themselves on the street, a busy place with few cars, hundreds of bicycles, and thousands of people both on and off the glideways. Wang-mu was put off by these strange machines and insisted they walk on solid ground, which meant choosing a restaurant close by. The buildings in this neighborhood were old but not yet tatty-looking; an established neighborhood, but one with pride. The style was radically open, with arches and courtyards, pillars and roofs, but few walls and no glass at all. "The weather must be perfect here," said Wang-mu.

"Tropical, but on the coast with a cold current offshore. It rains every afternoon for an hour or so, most of the year anyway, but it never gets very hot and *never* gets chilly at all."

"It feels as though everything is outdoors all the time."

"It's all fakery," said Peter. "Our apartment had glass windows and climate control, you notice. But it faces back, into the garden, and besides, the windows are recessed, so from below you don't see the glass. Very artful. Artificially natural looking. Hypocrisy and deception—the human universal."

"It's a beautiful way to live," said Wang-mu. "I like Nagoya."

"Too bad we won't be here long."

Before she could ask to know where they were going and why, Peter pulled her into the courtyard of a busy restaurant. "This one cooks the fish," said Peter. "I hope you don't mind that."

"What, the others serve it raw?" asked Wang-mu, laughing. Then she realized that Peter was serious. Raw fish!

"The Japanese are famous for it," said Peter, "and in Nagoya it's almost a religion. Notice—not a Japanese face in the restaurant. They wouldn't deign to eat fish that was destroyed by heat. It's just one of those things that they cling to. There's so little that's distinctively Japanese about their culture now, so they're devoted to the few uniquely Japanese traits that survive.''

Wang-mu nodded, understanding perfectly how a culture could cling to long-dead customs just for the sake of national identity, and also grateful to be in a place where such customs were all superficial and didn't distort and destroy the lives of the people the way they had on Path.

Their food came quickly—it takes almost no time to cook fish—and as they ate, Peter shifted his position several times on the mat. ''Too bad this place isn't nontraditional enough to have chairs.''

''Why do Europeans hate the earth so much that you must always lift yourself above it?'' asked Wang-mu.

''You've already answered your question,'' said Peter coldly. ''You *start* from the assumption that we hate the earth. It makes you sound like some magic-using primitive.''

Wang-mu blushed and fell silent.

''Oh, spare me the passive oriental woman routine,'' said Peter. ''Or the passive I-was-trained-to-be-a-servant-and-you-sound-like-a-cruel-heartless-master manipulation through guilt. I know I'm a shit and I'm not going to change just because you look so downcast.''

''Then you could change because you wish not to be a shit any longer.''

''It's in my character. Ender created me hateful so he could hate me. The added benefit is that you can hate me, too.''

''Oh, be quiet and eat your fish,'' she said. ''You don't know what you're talking about. You're supposed to analyze human beings and you can't understand the person closest to you in all the world.''

''I don't want to understand you,'' said Peter. ''I want to accomplish my task by exploiting this brilliant intelligence you're supposed to have—even if you believe that people who squat are somehow 'closer to the earth' than people who remain upright.''

"I wasn't talking about me," she said. "I was talking about the person closest to you. Ender."

"He is blessedly far from us right now."

"He didn't create you so that he could hate you. He long since got over hating you."

"Yeah, yeah, he wrote *The Hegemon*, et cetera, et cetera."

"That's right," said Wang-mu. "He created you because he desperately needed someone to hate *him*."

Peter rolled his eyes and took a drink of milky pineapple juice. "Just the right amount of coconut. I think I'll retire here, if Ender doesn't die and make me disappear first."

"I say something true, and you answer with coconut in the pineapple juice?"

"Novinha hates him," said Peter. "He doesn't need me."

"Novinha is angry at him, but she's wrong to be angry and he knows it. What he needs from you is a . . . righteous anger. To hate him for the evil that is really in him, which no one but him sees or even believes is there."

"I'm just a nightmare from his childhood," said Peter. "You're reading too much into this."

"He didn't conjure you up because the real Peter was so important in his childhood. He conjured you up because you are the judge, the condemner. That's what Peter drummed into him as a child. You told me yourself, talking about your memories. Peter taunting him, telling him of his unworthiness, his uselessness, his stupidity, his cowardice. You do it now. You look at his life and call him a xenocide, a failure. For some reason he needs this, needs to have someone damn him."

"Well, how nice that I'm around, then, to despise him," said Peter.

"But he also is desperate for someone to forgive him, to have mercy on him, to interpret all his actions as well meant. Valentine is not there because he loves her—he has the real Valentine for that. He has his wife. He needs your sister to exist so she can forgive him.''

''So if I stop hating Ender, he won't need me anymore and I'll disappear?''

''If Ender stops hating himself, then he won't need you to be so mean and you'll be easier to get along with.''

''Yeah, well, it's not that easy getting along with somebody who's constantly analyzing a person she's never met and preaching at the person she *has* met.''

''I hope I make you miserable,'' said Wang-mu. ''It's only fair, considering.''

''I think Jane brought us here because the local costumes reflect who we are. Puppet though I am, I take some perverse pleasure in life. While you—you can turn anything drab just by talking about it.''

Wang-mu bit back her tears and returned to her food.

''What is it with you?'' Peter said.

She ignored him, chewed slowly, finding the untouched core of herself, which was busily enjoying the food.

''Don't you feel *anything?*''

She swallowed, looked up at him. ''I already miss Han Fei-tzu, and I've been gone scarcely two days.'' She smiled slightly. ''I have known a man of grace and wisdom. He found me interesting. I'm quite comfortable with boring *you.*''

Peter immediately made a show of splashing water on his ears. ''I'm burning, that *stung,* oh, how can I stand it. Vicious! You have the breath of a dragon! Men die at your words!''

''Only puppets strutting around hanging from strings,'' said Wang-mu.

''Better to dangle from strings than to be bound tight by them,'' said Peter.

''Oh, the gods must love me, to have put me in the company of a man so clever with words.''

''Whereas the gods have put *me* in the company of a woman with no breasts.''

She forced herself to pretend to take this as a joke. "Small ones, I thought you said."

But suddenly the smile left his face. "I'm sorry," he said. "I've hurt you."

"I don't think so. I'll tell you later, after a good night's sleep."

"I thought we were bantering," said Peter. "Bandying insults."

"We were," said Wang-mu. "But I believe them all."

Peter winced. "Then I'm hurt, too."

"You don't know how to hurt," said Wang-mu. "You're just mocking me."

Peter pushed aside his plate and stood up. "I'll see you back at the apartment. Think you can find the way?"

"Do I think you actually care?"

"It's a good thing I have no soul," said Peter. "That's the only thing that stops you from devouring it."

"If I ever had your soul in my mouth," said Wang-mu, "I would spit it out."

"Get some rest," said Peter. "For the work I have ahead, I need a mind, not a quarrel." He walked out of the restaurant. The clothing fit him badly. People looked. He was a man of too much dignity and strength to dress so foppishly. Wang-mu saw at once that it shamed him. She saw also that he knew it, that he moved swiftly because he knew this clothing was wrong for him. He would undoubtedly have Jane order him something older looking, more mature, more in keeping with his need for honor.

Whereas I need something that will make me disappear. Or better yet, clothing that will let me fly away from here, all in a single night, fly Outside and back In to the house of Han Fei-tzu, where I can look into eyes that show neither pity nor scorn.

Nor pain. For there *is* pain in Peter's eyes, and it was wrong of me to say he felt none. It was wrong of me to value my own pain so highly that I thought it gave me the right to inflict more on him.

If I apologize to him, he'll mock me for it.

But then, I would rather be mocked for doing a good thing than to be respected, knowing I have done wrong. Is that a principle Han Fei-tzu taught me? No. I was born with that one. Like my mother said, too much pride, too much pride.

When she returned to the apartment, however, Peter was asleep; exhausted, she postponed her apology and also slept. Each of them woke during the night, but never at the same time; and in the morning, the edge of last night's quarrel had worn off. There was business at hand, and it was more important for her to understand what they were going to attempt to do today than for her to heal a breach between them that seemed, in the light of morning, to be scarcely more than a meaningless spat between tired friends.

———

"The man Jane has chosen for us to visit is a philosopher."

"Like me?" Wang-mu said, keenly aware of her false new role.

"That's what I wanted to discuss with you. There are two kinds of philosophers here on Divine Wind. Aimaina Hikari, the man we will meet, is an analytical philosopher. You don't have the education to hold your own with him. So you are the other kind. Gnomic and mantic. Given to pithy phrases that startle others with their seeming irrelevancy."

"Is it necessary that my supposedly wise phrases only *seem* irrelevant?"

"You don't even have to worry about that. The gnomic philosophers depend on others to connect their irrelevancies with the real world. That's why any fool can do it."

Wang-mu felt anger rise in her like mercury in a thermometer. "How kind of you to choose that profession for me."

"Don't be offended," said Peter. "Jane and I had to come up with some role you could play on this particular planet that wouldn't reveal you to be an uneducated native of Path. You have to understand that no child on Divine Wind is allowed to grow up as hopelessly ignorant as the servant class on Path."

Wang-mu did not argue further. What would be the point? If one has to say, in an argument, "I *am* intelligent! I *do* know things!" then one might as well stop arguing. Indeed, this idea struck her as being exactly one of those gnomic phrases that Peter was talking about. She said so.

"No, no, I don't mean epigrams," said Peter. "Those are too analytical. I mean genuinely strange things. For instance, you might have said, 'The woodpecker attacks the tree to get at the bug,' and then I would have had to figure out just how that might fit our situation here. Am I the woodpecker? The tree? The bug? That's the beauty of it."

"It seems to me that you have just proved yourself to be the more gnomic of the two of us."

Peter rolled his eyes and headed for the door.

"Peter," she said, not moving from her place.

He turned to face her.

"Wouldn't I be more helpful to you if I had some idea of why we're meeting this man, and who he is?"

Peter shrugged. "I suppose. Though we know that Ai-maina Hikari is *not* the person or even one of the people we're looking for."

"Tell me whom we *are* looking for, then."

"We're looking for the center of power in the Hundred Worlds," he said.

"Then why are we here, instead of Starways Congress?"

"Starways Congress is a play. The delegates are actors. The scripts are written elsewhere."

"Here."

"The faction of Congress that is getting its way about the Lusitania Fleet is *not* the one that loves war. *That* group is cheerful about the whole thing, of course, since they always believe in brutally putting down insurrection and so on, but they would never have been able to get the votes to send the fleet without a swing group that is very heavily influenced by a school of philosophers from Divine Wind.''

"Of which Aimaina Hikari is the leader?''

"It's more subtle than that. He is actually a solitary philosopher, belonging to no particular school. But he represents a sort of purity of Japanese thought which makes him something of a conscience to the philosophers who influence the swing group in Congress.''

"How many dominoes do you think you can line up and have them still knock each other over?''

"No, that wasn't gnomic enough. Still too analytical.''

"I'm not playing my part yet, Peter. What are the ideas that this swing group gets from this philosophical school?''

Peter sighed and sat down—bending himself into a chair, of course. Wang-mu sat on the floor and thought: This is how a man of Europe likes to see himself, with his head higher than all others, teaching the woman of Asia. But from my perspective, he has disconnected himself from the earth. I will hear his words, but I will know that it is up to me to bring them into a living place.

"The swing group would never use such massive force against what really amounts to a minor dispute with a tiny colony. The original issue, as you know, was that two xenologers, Miro Ribeira and Ouanda Mucumbi, were caught introducing agriculture among the pequeninos of Lusitania. This constituted cultural interference, and they were ordered offplanet for trial. Of course, with the old relativistic lightspeed ships, taking someone off planet meant that when and if they ever went back, everyone they knew would be old or dead. So it was brutally harsh treatment and amounted to prejudgment. Congress might have expected protests from the government of Lusitania, but what it got instead was complete defiance and a cutoff of ansible communications. The tough guys in Congress immediately started lobbying for a single troopship to go and seize control of Lusitania. But they didn't have the votes, *until*—"

"Until they raised the specter of the descolada virus."

"Exactly. The group that was adamantly opposed to the use of force brought up the descolada as a reason why troops shouldn't be sent—because at that time anyone who was infected with the virus had to stay on Lusitania and keep taking an inhibitor that kept the descolada from destroying your body from the inside out. This was the first time that the danger of the descolada became widely known, and the swing group emerged, consisting of those who were appalled that Lusitania had not been quarantined long before. What could be more dangerous than to have a fast-spreading, semi-intelligent virus in the hands of rebels? This group consisted almost entirely of delegates who were strongly influenced by the Necessarian school from Divine Wind."

Wang-mu nodded. "And what do the Necessarians teach?"

"That one lives in peace and harmony with one's environment, disturbing nothing, patiently bearing mild or even serious afflictions. However, when a genuine threat to survival emerges, one must act with brutal efficiency. The maxim is, Act only when necessary, and then act with maximum force and speed. Thus, where the militarists wanted a troopship, the Necessarian-influenced delegates insisted on sending a fleet armed with the Molecular Disruption Device, which would destroy the threat of the descolada virus once and for all. There's a sort of ironic neatness about it all, don't you think?"

"I don't see it."

"Oh, it fits together so perfectly. Ender Wiggin was the one who used the Little Doctor to wipe out the bugger home world. Now it's going to be used for only the second time—against the very world where he happens to live! It gets even thicker. The first Necessarian philosopher, Ooka, used Ender himself as the prime example of his ideas. As long as the buggers were seen to be a dangerous threat to the survival of humankind, the only appropriate response was utter eradication of the enemy. No half-measures would do. Of course the buggers turned out not to have been a threat after all, as Ender himself wrote in his book *The Hive Queen*, but Ooka defended the mistake because the truth was unknowable at the time Ender's superiors turned him loose against the enemy. What Ooka said was, 'Never trade blows with the enemy.' His idea was that you try never to strike anyone, but when you must, you strike only one blow, but such a harsh one that your enemy can never, never strike back.''

''So using Ender as an example—''

''That's right. Ender's own actions are being used to justify repeating them against another harmless species.''

''The descolada wasn't harmless.''

''No,'' said Peter. ''But Ender and Ela found another way, didn't they? They struck a blow against the descolada itself. But there's no way now to convince Congress to withdraw the fleet. Because Jane already interfered with Congress's ansible communications with the fleet, they believe they face a formidable widespread secret conspiracy. Any argument we make will be seen as disinformation. Besides, who would believe the farfetched tale of that first trip Outside, where Ela created the anti-descolada, Miro recreated himself, and Ender made my dear sister and me?''

''So the Necessarians in Congress—''

''They don't call themselves that. But the influence is very strong. It is Jane's and my opinion that if we can get some prominent Necessarians to declare against the Lusitania Fleet—with convincing reasoning, of course—the solidarity of the pro-fleet majority in Congress will be broken up. It's a thin majority—there are plenty of people horrified by such devastating use of force against a colony world, and others who are even more horrified at the idea that Congress would destroy the pequeninos, the first sentient species found since the destruction of the buggers. They would love to stop the fleet, or at worst use it to impose a permanent quarantine.''

"Why aren't we meeting with a Necessarian, then?"

"Because why would they listen to us? If we identify ourselves as supporters of the Lusitanian cause, we'll be jailed and questioned. And if we don't, who will take our ideas seriously?"

"This Aimaina Hikari, then. What is he?"

"Some people call him the Yamato philosopher. All the Necessarians of Divine Wind are, naturally, Japanese, and the philosophy has become most influential among the Japanese, both on their home worlds and wherever they have a substantial population. So even though Hikari isn't a Necessarian, he *is* honored as the keeper of the Japanese soul.''

"If *he* tells them that it's un-Japanese to destroy Lusitania—"

"But he won't. Not easily, anyway. His seminal work, which won him his reputation as the Yamato philosopher, included the idea that the Japanese people were born as rebellious puppets. First it was Chinese culture that pulled the strings. But Hikari says, Japan learned all the wrong lessons from the attempted Chinese invasion of Japan— which, by the way, was defeated by a great storm, called *kamikaze*, which means 'Divine Wind.' So you can be sure everyone on this world, at least, remembers *that* ancient story. Anyway, Japan locked itself away on an island, and at first refused to deal with Europeans when they came. But then an American fleet forcibly opened Japan to foreign trade, and then the Japanese made up for lost time. The Meiji Restoration led to Japan trying to industrialize and Westernize itself—and once again a new set of strings made the puppet dance, says Hikari. Only once again, the wrong lessons were learned. Since the Europeans at the time were imperialists, dividing up Africa and Asia among them, Japan decided it wanted a piece of the imperial pie.

There was China, the old puppetmaster. So there was an invasion—''

"We were taught of this invasion on Path," said Wang-mu.

"I'm surprised they taught any history more recent than the Mongol invasion," said Peter.

"The Japanese were finally stopped when the Americans dropped the first nuclear weapons on two Japanese cities."

"The equivalent, in those days, of the Little Doctor. The irresistible, total weapon. The Japanese soon came to regard these nuclear weapons as a kind of badge of pride: We were the first people ever to have been attacked by nuclear weapons. It had become a kind of permanent grievance, which wasn't a bad thing, really, because that was part of their impetus to found and populate many colonies, so that they would never be a helpless island nation again. But then along comes Aimaina Hikari, and he says—by the way, his name is self-chosen, it's the name he used to sign his first book. It means 'Ambiguous Light.' ''

"How gnomic," said Wang-mu.

Peter grinned. "Oh, tell him *that*, he'll be so proud. Anyway, in his first book, he says, The Japanese learned the wrong lesson. Those nuclear bombs cut the strings. Japan was utterly prostrate. The proud old government was destroyed, the emperor became a figurehead, democracy came to Japan, and then wealth and great power."

"The bombs were a blessing, then?" asked Wang-mu doubtfully.

"No, no, not at all. He thinks the wealth of Japan destroyed the people's soul. They adopted the destroyer as their father. They became America's bastard child, blasted into existence by American bombs. Puppets again."

"Then what does he have to do with the Necessarians?"

"Japan was bombed, he says, precisely because they were already too European. They treated China as the Europeans treated America, selfishly and brutally. But the Japanese ancestors could not bear to see their children become such beasts. So just as the gods of Japan sent a Divine Wind to stop the Chinese fleet, so the gods sent the American bombs to stop Japan from becoming an imperialist state like the Europeans. The Japanese response should have been to bear the American occupation and then, when it was over, to become purely Japanese again, chastened and whole. The title of his book was, *Not Too Late*.''

''And I'll bet the Necessarians use the American bombing of Japan as another example of striking with maximum force and speed.''

''No Japanese would have dared to praise the American bombing until Hikari made it possible to see the bombing, not as Japan's victimization, but as the gods' attempt at redemption of the people.''

''So you're saying that the Necessarians respect him enough that if he changed his mind, they would change theirs—but he won't change his mind, because he believes the bombing of Japan was a divine gift?''

''We're hoping he *will* change his mind,'' said Peter, ''or our trip will be a failure. The thing is, there's no chance he'll be open to direct persuasion from us, and Jane can't tell from his writings what or who it is who might influence him. We have to talk to him to find out where to go next—so maybe we can change *their* mind.''

''This is really complicated, isn't it?'' said Wang-mu.

''Which is why I didn't think it was worth explaining it to you. What exactly are you going to do with this information? Enter into a discussion of the subtleties of history with an analytical philosopher of the first rank, like Hikari?''

''I'm going to listen,'' said Wang-mu.

''That's what you were going to do before,'' said Peter.

''But now I will know who it is I'm listening to.''

''Jane thinks it was a mistake for me to tell you, because now you'll be interpreting everything he says in light of what Jane and I already think we know.''

''Tell Jane that the only people who ever prize purity of

ignorance are those who profit from a monopoly on knowledge."

Peter laughed. "Epigrams again," he said. "You're supposed to say—"

"Don't tell me how to be gnomic again," said Wang-mu. She got up from the floor. Now her head was higher than Peter's. "You're the gnome. And as for me being mantic—remember that the mantic eats its mate."

"I'm not your mate," said Peter, "and 'mantic' means a philosophy that comes from vision or inspiration or intuition rather than from scholarship and reason."

"If you're not my mate," said Wang-mu, "stop treating me like a wife."

Peter looked puzzled, then looked away. "Was I doing that?"

"On Path, a husband assumes his wife is a fool and teaches her even the things she already knows. On Path, a wife has to pretend, when she is teaching her husband, that she is only reminding him of things he taught her long before."

"Well, I'm just an insensitive oaf, aren't I."

"Please remember," said Wang-mu, "that when we meet with Aimaina Hikari, he and I have one fund of knowledge that you can never have."

"And what's that?"

"A life."

She saw the pain on his face and at once regretted causing it. But it was a reflexive regret—she had been trained from childhood up to be sorry when she gave offense, no matter how richly it was deserved.

"Ouch," said Peter, as if his pain were a joke.

Wang-mu showed no mercy—she was not a servant now. "You're so proud of knowing more than me, but everything you know is either what Ender put in your head or what Jane whispers in your ear. I have no Jane, I had no Ender. Everything I know, I learned the hard way. I lived through it. So please don't treat me with contempt again.

If I have any value on this expedition, it will come from my knowing everything you know—because everything you know, I can be taught, but what I know, you can never learn.''

The joking was over. Peter's face reddened with anger. ''How . . . who . . .''

"How dare I," said Wang-mu, echoing the phrases she assumed he had begun. "Who do I think I am."

"I didn't say that," said Peter softly, turning away.

"I'm not staying in my place, am I?" she asked. "Han Fei-tzu taught me about Peter Wiggin. The original, not the copy. How he made his sister Valentine take part in his conspiracy to seize the hegemony of Earth. How he made *her* write all of the Demosthenes material—rabble-rousing demagoguery—while *he* wrote all the Locke material, the lofty, analytical ideas. But the low demagoguery came from him.''

"So did the lofty ideas," said Peter.

"Exactly," said Wang-mu. "What never came from him, what came only from Valentine, was something he never saw or valued. A human soul."

"Han Fei-tzu said that?"

"Yes."

"Then he's an ass," said Peter. "Because Peter had as much of a human soul as Valentine had." He stepped toward her, looming. "*I'm* the one without a soul, Wang-mu."

For a moment she was afraid of him. How did she know what violence had been created in him? What dark rage in Ender's aiúa might find expression through this surrogate he had created?

But Peter did not strike a blow. Perhaps it was not necessary.

———

Aimaina Hikari came out himself to the front gate of his garden to let them in. He was dressed simply, and around his neck was the locket that all the traditional Japanese of Divine Wind wore: a tiny casket containing the ashes of all his worthy ancestors. Peter had already explained to her that when a man like Hikari died, a pinch of the ashes from his locket would be added to a bit of his own ashes and given to his children or his grandchildren to wear. Thus all of his ancient family hung above his breastbone, waking and sleeping, and formed the most precious gift he could give his posterity. It was a custom that Wang-mu, who had no ancestors worth remembering, found both thrilling and disturbing.

Hikari greeted Wang-mu with a bow, but held out his hand for Peter to shake. Peter took it with some small show of surprise.

"Oh, they call me the keeper of the Yamato spirit," said Hikari with a smile, "but that doesn't mean I must be rude and force Europeans to behave like Japanese. Watching a European bow is as painful as watching a pig do ballet."

As Hikari led them through the garden into his traditional paper-walled house, Peter and Wang-mu looked at each other and grinned broadly. It was a wordless truce between them, for they both knew at once that Hikari was going to be a formidable opponent, and they needed to be allies if they were to learn anything from him.

"A philosopher and a physicist," said Hikari. "I looked you up when you sent your note asking for an appointment. I have been visited by philosophers before, and physicists and also by Europeans and Chinese, but what truly puzzles me is why the two of you should be together."

"She found me sexually irresistible," said Peter, "and I can't get rid of her." Then he grinned his most charming grin.

To Wang-mu's pleasure, Peter's Western-style irony left Hikari impassive and unamused, and she could see a blush rising up Peter's neck.

It was her turn—to play the gnome for real this time.

"The pig wallows in mud, but he warms himself on the sunny stone."

Hikari turned his gaze to her—remaining just as impassive as before. "I will write these words in my heart," he said.

Wang-mu wondered if Peter understood that she had just been the victim of Hikari's oriental-style irony.

"We have come to learn from you," said Peter.

"Then I must give you food and send you on your way disappointed," said Hikari. "I have nothing to teach a physicist or a philosopher. If I did not have children, I would have no one to teach, for only they know less than I."

"No, no," said Peter. "You're a wise man. The keeper of the Yamato spirit."

"I said that they call me that. But the Yamato spirit is much too great to be kept in so small a container as my soul. And yet the Yamato spirit is much too small to be worthy of the notice of the powerful souls of the Chinese and the European. You are the teachers, as China and Europe have always been the teachers of Japan."

Wang-mu did not know Peter well, but she knew him well enough to see that he was flustered now, at a loss for how to proceed. In Ender's life and wanderings, he had lived in several oriental cultures and even, according to Han Fei-tzu, spoke Korean, which meant that Ender would probably be able to deal with the ritualized humility of a man like Hikari—especially since he was obviously using that humility in a mocking way. But what Ender knew and what he had given to his Peter-identity were obviously two different things. This conversation would be up to her, and she sensed that the best way to play with Hikari was to refuse to let him control the game.

"Very well," she said. "We will teach you. For when we show you our ignorance, then you will see where we most need your wisdom."

Hikari looked at Peter for a moment. Then he clapped

his hands. A serving woman appeared in a doorway. "Tea," said Hikari.

At once Wang-mu leapt to her feet. Only when she was already standing did she realize what she was going to do. That peremptory command to bring tea was one that she had heeded many times in her life, but it was not a blind reflex that brought her to her feet. Rather it was her intuition that the only way to beat Hikari at his own game was to call his bluff: She would be humbler than he knew how to be.

"I have been a servant all my life," said Wang-mu honestly, "but I was always a clumsy one," which was not so honest. "May I go with your servant and learn from her? I may not be wise enough to learn the ideas of a great philosopher, but perhaps I can learn what *I* am fit to learn from the servant who is worthy to bring tea to Aimaina Hikari."

She could see from his hesitation that Hikari knew he had been trumped. But the man was deft. He immediately rose to his feet. "You have already taught me a great lesson," he said. "Now we will all go and watch Kenji prepare the tea. If she will be your teacher, Si Wang-mu, she must also be mine. For how could I bear to know that someone in my house knew a thing that I had not yet learned?"

Wang-mu had to admire his resourcefulness. He had once again placed himself beneath her.

Poor Kenji, the servant! She was a deft and well-trained woman, Wang-mu saw, but it made her nervous having these three, especially her master, watch her prepare the tea. So Wang-mu immediately reached in and "helped"— deliberately making a mistake as she did. At once Kenji was in her element, and confident again. "You have forgotten," said Kenji kindly, "because my kitchen is so inefficiently arranged." Then she showed Wang-mu how the tea was prepared. "At least in Nagoya," she said modestly "At least in this house."

Wang-mu watched carefully, concentrating only on Kenji and what she was doing, for she quickly saw that the Japanese way of preparing tea—or perhaps it was the way of Divine Wind, or merely the way of Nagoya, or of humble philosophers who kept the Yamato spirit—was different from the pattern she had followed so carefully in the house of Han Fei-tzu. By the time the tea was ready, Wang-mu *had* learned from her. For, having made the claim to be a servant, and having a computer record that asserted that she had lived her whole life in a Chinese community on Divine Wind, Wang-mu might have to be able to serve tea properly in exactly this fashion.

They returned to the front room of Hikari's house, Kenji and Wang-mu each bearing a small tea table. Kenji offered her table to Hikari, but he waved her over to Peter, and then bowed to him. It was Wang-mu who served Hikari. And when Kenji backed away from Peter, Wang-mu also backed away from Hikari.

For the first time, Hikari looked—angry? His eyes flashed, anyway. For by placing herself on exactly the same level as Kenji, she had just maneuvered him into a position where he either had to shame himself by being prouder than Wang-mu and dismissing his servant, or disrupt the good order of his own house by inviting Kenji to sit down with the three of them as equals.

"Kenji," said Hikari. "Let me pour tea for you."

Check, thought Wang-mu. And mate.

It was a delicious bonus when Peter, who had finally caught on to the game, also poured tea for *her,* and then managed to spill it on her, which prompted Hikari to spill a little on himself in order to put his guest at ease. The pain of the hot tea and then the discomfort as it cooled and dried were well worth the pleasure of knowing that while Wang-mu had proved herself a match for Hikari in outrageous courtesy, Peter had merely proved himself to be an oaf.

Or was Wang-mu truly a match for Hikari? He must have

seen and understood her effort to place herself ostentatiously beneath him. It was possible, then, that he was—humbly—allowing her to win pride of place as the more humble of the two. As soon as she realized that he might have done this, then she knew that he certainly *had* done it, and the victory was his.

I'm not as clever as I thought.

She looked at Peter, hoping that he would now take over and do whatever clever thing he had in mind. But he seemed perfectly content to let her lead out. Certainly he didn't jump into the breach. Did he, too, realize that she had just been bested at her own game, because she failed to take it deep enough? Was he giving her the rope to hang herself?

Well, let's get the noose good and tight.

"Aimaina Hikari, you are called by some the keeper of the Yamato spirit. Peter and I grew up on a Japanese world, and yet the Japanese humbly allow Stark to be the language of the public school, so that we speak no Japanese. In my Chinese neighborhood, in Peter's American city, we spent our childhoods on the edge of Japanese culture, looking in. So if there is any particular part of our vast ignorance that will be most obvious to you, it is in our knowledge of Yamato itself."

"Oh, Wang-mu, you make a mystery out of the obvious. No one understands Yamato better than those who see it from the outside, just as the parent understands the child better than the child understands herself."

"Then I will enlighten *you*," said Wang-mu, discarding the game of humility. "For I see Japan as an Edge nation, and I cannot yet see whether your ideas will make Japan a new Center nation, or begin the decay that all edge nations experience when they take power."

"I grasp a hundred possible meanings, most of them surely true of my people, for your term 'Edge nation,'" said Hikari. "But what is a Center nation, and how can a people become one?"

"I am not well-versed in Earth history," said Wang-mu, "but as I studied what little I know, it seemed to me that there were a handful of Center nations, which had a culture so strong that they swallowed up all conquerors. Egypt was one, and China. Each one became unified and then expanded no more than necessary to protect their borders and pacify their hinterland. Each one took in its conquerors and swallowed them up for thousands of years. Egyptian writing and Chinese writing persisted with only stylistic modifications, so that the past remained present for those who could read."

Wang-mu could see from Peter's stiffness that he was very worried. After all, she was saying things that were definitely *not* gnomic. But since he was completely out of his depth with an Asian, he was still making no effort to intrude.

"Both of these nations were born in barbarian times," said Hikari. "Are you saying that no nation can become a Center nation now?"

"I don't know," said Wang-mu. "I don't even know if my distinction between Edge nations and Center nations has any truth or value. I do know that a Center nation can keep its cultural power long after it has lost political control. Mesopotamia was continually conquered by its neighbors, and yet each conqueror in turn was more changed by Mesopotamia than Mesopotamia was changed. The kings of Assyria and Chaldea and Persia were almost indistinguishable after they had once tasted the culture of the land between the rivers. But a Center nation can also fall so completely that it disappears. Egypt staggered under the cultural blow of Hellenism, fell to its knees under the ideology of Christianity, and finally was erased by Islam. Only the stone buildings reminded the children of what and who their ancient parents had been. History has no laws, and all patterns that we find there are useful illusions."

"I see you *are* a philosopher," said Hikari.

"You are generous to call my childish speculations by

that lofty name," said Wang-mu. "But let me tell you now what I think about Edge nations. They are born in the shadow—or perhaps one could say, in the reflected light—of other nations. As Japan became civilized under the influence of China. As Rome discovered itself in the shadow of the Greeks."

"The Etruscans first," said Peter helpfully.

Hikari looked at him blandly, then turned back to Wang-mu without comment. Wang-mu could almost feel Peter wither at having been thus deemed irrelevant. She felt a little sorry for him. Not a lot, just a little.

"Center nations are so confident of themselves that they generally don't need to embark on wars of conquest. They are already sure they are the superior people and that all other nations wish to be like them and obey them. But Edge nations, when they first feel their strength, must prove themselves, they think, and almost always they do so with the sword. Thus the Arabs broke the back of the Roman Empire and swallowed up Persia. Thus the Macedonians, on the edge of Greece, conquered Greece; and then, having been so culturally swallowed up that they now thought themselves Greek, they conquered the empire on whose edge the Greeks had become civilized—Persia. The Vikings had to harrow Europe before peeling off kingdoms in Naples, Sicily, Normandy, Ireland, and finally England. And Japan—"

"We tried to stay on our islands," said Hikari softly.

"Japan, when it erupted, rampaged through the Pacific, trying to conquer the great Center nation of China, and was finally stopped by the bombs of the new Center nation of America."

"I would have thought," said Hikari, "that America was the ultimate Edge nation."

"America was settled by Edge peoples, but the idea of America became the new envigorating principle that made it a Center nation. They were so arrogant that, except for subduing their own hinterland, they had no will to empire.

They simply assumed that all nations wanted to be like them. They swallowed up all other cultures. Even on Divine Wind, what is the language of the schools? It was not England that imposed this language, Stark, Starways Common Speech, on us all.''

"It was only by accident that America was technologically ascendant at the moment the Hive Queen came and forced us out among the stars.''

"The idea of America became the Center idea, I think," said Wang-mu. "Every nation from then on had to have the forms of democracy. We are governed by the Starways Congress even now. We all live within the American culture whether we like it or not. So what I wonder is this: Now that Japan has taken control of this Center nation, will Japan be swallowed up, as the Mongols were swallowed up by China? Or will the Japanese culture retain its identity, but eventually decay and lose control, as the Edge-nation Turks lost control of Islam and the Edge-nation Manchu lost control of China?"

Hikari was upset. Angry? Puzzled? Wang-mu had no way of guessing.

"The philosopher Si Wang-mu says a thing that is impossible for me to accept," said Hikari. "How can you say that the Japanese are now in control of Starways Congress and the Hundred Worlds? When was this revolution that no one noticed?"

"But I thought you could see what your teaching of the Yamato way had accomplished," said Wang-mu. "The existence of the Lusitania Fleet is proof of Japanese control. This is the great discovery that my friend the physicist taught me, and it was the reason we came to you."

Peter's look of horror was genuine. She could guess what he was thinking. Was she insane, to have tipped their hand so completely? But she also knew that she had done it in a context that revealed nothing about their motive in coming.

And, never having lost his composure, Peter took his cue

and proceeded to explain Jane's analysis of Starways Congress, the Necessarians, and the Lusitania Fleet, though of course he presented the ideas as if they were his own. Hikari listened, nodding now and then, shaking his head at other times; the impassivity was gone now, the attitude of amused distance discarded.

"So you tell me," Hikari said, when Peter was done, "that because of my small book about the American bombs, the Necessarians have taken control of government and launched the Lusitania Fleet? You lay this at my door?"

"Not as a matter either for blame or credit," said Peter. "You did not plan it or design it. For all I know you don't even approve of it."

"I don't even think about the politics of Starways Congress. I am of Yamato."

"But that's what we came here to learn," said Wang-mu. "I see that you are a man of the Edge, not a man of the Center. Therefore you will not let Yamato be swallowed up by the Center nation. Instead the Japanese will remain aloof from their own hegemony, and in the end it will slip from their hands into someone else's hands."

Hikari shook his head. "I will not have you blame Japan for this Lusitania Fleet. *We* are the people who are chastened by the gods, we do not send fleets to destroy others."

"The Necessarians do," said Peter.

"The Necessarians talk," said Hikari. "No one listens."

"You don't listen to them," said Peter. "But Congress does."

"And the Necessarians listen to *you*," said Wang-mu.

"I am a man of perfect simplicity!" cried Hikari, rising to his feet. "You have come to torture me with accusations that cannot be true!"

"We make no accusation," said Wang-mu softly, refusing to rise. "We offer an observation. If we are wrong, we beg you to teach us our mistake."

Hikari was trembling, and his left hand now clutched the

locket of his ancestors' ashes that hung on a silk ribbon around his neck. "No," he said. "I will not let you pretend to be humble seekers after truth. You are assassins. Assassins of the heart, come to destroy me, come to tell me that in seeking to find the Yamato way I have somehow caused my people to rule the human worlds and use that power to destroy a helplessly weak sentient species! It is a terrible lie to tell me, that my life's work has been so useless. I would rather you had put poison in my tea, Si Wang-mu. I would rather you had put a gun to my head and blown it off, Peter Wiggin. They named you well, your parents— proud and terrible names you both bear. The Royal Mother of the West? A goddess? And Peter Wiggin, the first hegemon! Who gives their child such a name as that?"

Peter was standing also, and he reached down to lift Wang-mu to her feet.

"We have given offense where we meant none," said Peter. "I am ashamed. We must go at once."

Wang-mu was surprised to hear Peter sound so oriental. The American way was to make excuses, to stay and argue.

She let him lead her to the door. Hikari did not follow them; it was left to poor Kenji, who was terrified to see her placid master so exercised, to show them out. But Wang-mu was determined not to let this visit end entirely in disaster. So at the last moment she rushed back and flung herself to the floor, prostrate before Hikari in precisely the pose of humiliation that she had vowed only a little while ago that she would never adopt again. But she knew that as long as she was in that posture, a man like Hikari would have to listen to her.

"Oh, Aimaina Hikari," she said, "you have spoken of our names, but have you forgotten your own? How could the man called 'Ambiguous Light' ever think that his teachings could have only the effects that he intended?"

Upon hearing those words, Hikari turned his back and stalked from the room. Had she made the situation better or worse? Wang-mu had no way of knowing. She got to her feet and walked dolefully to the door. Peter would be furious with her. With her boldness she might well have ruined everything for them—and not just for them, but for all those who so desperately hoped for them to stop the Lusitania Fleet.

To her surprise, however, Peter was perfectly cheerful once they got outside Hikari's garden gate. "Well done, however weird your technique was," said Peter.

"What do you mean? It was a disaster," she said; but she was eager to believe that somehow he was right and she had done well after all.

"Oh, he's angry and he'll never speak to us again, but who cares? We weren't trying to change his mind ourselves. We were just trying to find out who it is who *does* have influence over him. And we did."

"We did?"

"Jane picked up on it at once. When he said he was a man of 'perfect simplicity.' "

"Does that mean something more than the plain sense of it?"

"Mr. Hikari, my dear, has revealed himself to be a secret disciple of Ua Lava."

Wang-mu was baffled.

"It's a religious movement. Or a joke. It's hard to know which. It's a Samoan term, with the literal meaning 'Now enough,' but which is translated more accurately as, 'enough already!' "

"I'm sure you're an expert on Samoan." Wang-mu, for her part, had never heard of the language.

"Jane is," said Peter testily. "I have her jewel in my ear and you don't. Don't you want me to pass along what she tells me?"

"Yes, please," said Wang-mu.

"It's a sort of philosophy—cheerful stoicism, one might call it, because when things get bad or when things are good, you say the same thing. But as taught by a particular

Samoan writer named Leiloa Lavea, it became more than a mere attitude. She taught—''

''She? Hikari is a disciple of a woman?''

''I didn't say that,'' said Peter. ''If you listen, I'll tell you what Jane is telling me.''

He waited. She listened.

''All right, then, what Leiloa Lavea taught was a sort of volunteer communism. It's not enough just to laugh at good fortune and say, 'Enough already.' You have to really mean it—that you have enough. And because you mean it, you take the surplus and you give it away. Similarly, when bad fortune comes, you bear it until it becomes unbearable—your family is hungry, or you can no longer function in your work. And then again you say, 'Enough already,' and you change something. You move; you change careers; you let your spouse make all the decisions. Something. You don't endure the unendurable.''

''What does that have to do with 'perfect simplicity'?''

''Leiloa Lavea taught that when you have achieved balance in your life—surplus good fortune is being fully shared, and all bad fortune has been done away with—what is left is a life of perfect simplicity. That's what Aimaina Hikari was saying to us. Until we came, his life had been going on in perfect simplicity. But now we have thrown him out of balance. That's good, because it means he's going to be struggling to discover how to restore simplicity to its perfection. He'll be open to influence. Not ours, of course.''

''Leiloa Lavea's?''

''Hardly. She's been dead for two thousand years. Ender met her once, by the way. He came to speak a death on her home world of—well, Starways Congress calls it Pacifica, but the Samoan enclave there calls it Lumana'i. 'The Future.' ''

''Not her death, though.''

''A Fijian murderer, actually. A fellow who killed more than a hundred children, all of them Tongan. He didn't like

Tongans, apparently. They held off on his funeral for thirty years so Ender could come and speak his death. They hoped that the Speaker for the Dead would be able to make sense of what he had done.''

''And did he?''

Peter sneered. ''Oh, of course, he was splendid. Ender can do no wrong. Yadda yadda yadda.''

She ignored his hostility toward Ender. ''He met Leiloa Lavea?''

''Her name means 'to be lost, to be hurt.' ''

''Let me guess. She chose it herself.''

''Exactly. You know how writers are. Like Hikari, they create themselves as they create their work. Or perhaps they create their work in order to create themselves.''

''How gnomic,'' said Wang-mu.

''Oh, shut up about that,'' said Peter. ''Did you actually believe all that stuff about Edge nations and Center nations?''

''I thought of it,'' said Wang-mu. ''When I first learned Earth history from Han Fei-tzu. He didn't laugh when I told him my thoughts.''

''Oh, I'm not laughing, either. It's naïve bullshit, of course, but it's not exactly *funny*.''

Wang-mu ignored his mockery. ''If Leiloa Lavea is dead, where will we go?''

''To Pacifica. To Lumana'i. Hikari learned of Ua Lava in his teenage years at university. From a Samoan student— the granddaughter of the Pacifican ambassador. She had never been to Lumana'i, of course, and so she clung all the more tightly to its customs and became quite a proselytizer for Leiloa Lavea. This was long before Hikari ever wrote a thing. He never speaks of it, he's never written of Ua Lava, but now that he's tipped his hand to us, Jane is finding all sorts of influence of Ua Lava in all his work. And he has friends in Lumana'i. He's never met them, but they correspond through the ansible net.''

''What about the granddaughter of the ambassador?''

"She's on a starship right now, headed home to Lumana'i. She left twenty years ago, when her grandfather died. She should get there . . . oh, in another ten years or so. Depending on the weather. She'll be received with great honor, no doubt, and her grandfather's body will be buried or burned or whatever they do—burned, Jane says—with great ceremony."

"But Hikari won't try to talk to her."

"It would take a week to space out even a simple message enough for her to receive it, at the speed the ship is going. No way to have a philosophical discussion. She'd be home before he finished explaining his question."

For the first time, Wang-mu began to understand the implications of the instantaneous starflight that she and Peter had used. These long, life-wrenching voyages could be done away with.

"If only," she said.

"I know," said Peter. "But we can't."

She knew he was right. "So we go there ourselves," she said, returning to the subject. "Then what?"

"Jane is watching to see whom Hikari writes to. That's the person who'll be in a position to influence him. And so . . ."

"That's who we'll talk to."

"That's right. Do you need to pee or something before we arrange transportation back to our little cabin in the woods?"

"That would be nice," said Wang-mu. "And you could do with a change of clothes."

"What, you think even this conservative outfit might be too bold?"

"What are they wearing on Lumana'i?"

"Oh, well, a lot of them just go around naked. In the tropics. Jane says that given the massive bulk of many adult Polynesians, it can be an inspiring sight."

Wang-mu shuddered. "We aren't going to try to pretend to be natives, are we?"

"Not there," said Peter. "Jane's going to fake us as passengers on a starship that arrived there yesterday from Moskva. We're probably going to be government officials of some kind."

"Isn't that illegal?" she asked.

Peter looked at her oddly. "Wang-mu, we're already committing treason against Congress just by having left Lusitania. It's a capital offense. I don't think impersonating a government official is going to make much of a difference."

"But I *didn't* leave Lusitania," said Wang-mu. "I've never *seen* Lusitania."

"Oh, you haven't missed much. It's just a bunch of savannahs and woods, with the occasional Hive Queen factory building starships and a bunch of piglike aliens living in the trees."

"I'm an accomplice to treason though, right?" asked Wang-mu.

"And you're also guilty of ruining a Japanese philosopher's whole day."

"Off with my head."

An hour later they were in a private floater—so private that there were no questions asked by their pilot; and Jane saw to it that all their papers were in order. Before night they were back at their little starship.

"We should have slept in the apartment," said Peter, balefully eyeing the primitive sleeping accommodations.

Wang-mu only laughed at him and curled up on the floor. In the morning, rested, they found that Jane had already taken them to Pacifica in their sleep.

———

Aimaina Hikari awoke from his dream in the light that was neither night nor morning, and arose from his bed into air that was neither warm nor cold. His sleep had not been restful, and his dreams had been ugly ones, frantic ones, in which all that he did kept turning back on him as the opposite of what he intended. In his dream, Aimaina would climb to reach the bottom of a canyon. He would speak and people would go away from him. He would write and the pages of the book would spurt out from under his hand, scattering themselves across the floor.

All this he understood to be in response to the visit from those lying foreigners yesterday. He had tried to ignore them all afternoon, as he read stories and essays; to forget them all evening, as he conversed with seven friends who came to visit him. But the stories and essays all seemed to cry out to him: These are the words of the insecure people of an Edge nation; and the seven friends were all, he realized, Necessarians, and when he turned the conversation to the Lusitania Fleet, he soon understood that every one of them believed exactly as the two liars with their ridiculous names had said they did.

So Aimaina found himself in the predawn almost-light, sitting on a mat in his garden, fingering the casket of his ancestors, wondering: Were my dreams sent to me by the ancestors? Were these lying visitors sent by them as well? And if their accusations against me were *not* lies, what was it they were lying about? For he knew from the way they watched each other, from the young woman's hesitancy followed by boldness, that they were doing a performance, one that was unrehearsed but nevertheless followed some kind of script.

Dawn came fully, seeking out each leaf of every tree, then of all the lower plants, to give each one its own distinct shading and coloration; the breeze came up, making the light infinitely changeable. Later, in the heat of the day, all the leaves would become the same: still, submissive, receiving sunlight in a massive stream like a firehose. Then, in the afternoon, the clouds would roll overhead, the light rains would fall; the limp leaves would recover their strength, would glisten with water, their color deepening, readying for night, for the life of the night, for the dreams of plants growing in the night, storing away the sunlight that had been beaten into them by day, flowing with the cool inward rivers that had been fed by the rains. Aimaina Hikari became one of the leaves, driving all thoughts but light and wind and rain out of his mind until the dawn phase was ended and the sun began to drive downward with the day's heat. Then he rose up from his seat in the garden.

Kenji had prepared a small fish for his breakfast. He ate it slowly, delicately, so as not to disturb the perfect skeleton that had given shape to the fish. The muscles pulled this way and that, and the bones flexed but did not break. I will not break them now, but I take the strength of the muscles into my own body. Last of all he ate the eyes. From the parts that move comes the strength of the animal. He touched the casket of his ancestors again. What wisdom I have, however, comes not from what I eat, but from what I am given each hour, by those who whisper into my ear from ages past. Living men forget the lessons of the past. But the ancestors never forget.

Aimaina arose from his breakfast table and went to the computer in his gardening shed. It was just another tool—that's why he kept it here, instead of enshrining it in his house or in a special office the way so many others did. His computer was like a trowel. He used it, he set it aside.

A face appeared in the air above his terminal. "I am calling my friend Yasunari," said Aimaina. "But do not disturb him. This matter is so trivial that I would be ashamed to have him waste his time with it."

"Let me help you on his behalf then," said the face in the air.

"Yesterday I asked for information about Peter Wiggin and Si Wang-mu, who had an appointment to visit with me."

"I remember. It was a pleasure finding them so quickly for you."

"I found their visit very disturbing," said Aimaina. "Something that they told me was not true, and I need more information in order to find out what it was. I do not wish to violate their privacy, but are there matters of public record—perhaps their school attendance, or places of employment, or some matters of family connections . . .''

''Yasunari has told us that all things you ask for are for a wise purpose. Let me search.''

The face disappeared for a moment, then flickered back almost immediately.

''This is very odd. Have I made a mistake?'' She spelled the names carefully.

''That's correct,'' said Aimaina. ''Exactly like yesterday.''

''I remember them, too. They live in an apartment only a few blocks from your house. But I can't find them at all today. And here I search the apartment building and find that the apartment they occupied has been empty for a year. Aimaina, I am very surprised. How can two people exist one day and not exist the next day? Did I make some mistake, either yesterday or today?''

''You made no mistake, helper of my friend. This is the information I needed. Please, I beg you to think no more about it. What looks like a mystery to you is in fact a solution to my questions.''

They bade each other polite farewells.

Aimaina walked from his garden workroom past the struggling leaves that bowed under the pressure of the sunlight. The ancestors have pressed wisdom on me, he thought, like sunlight on the leaves; and last night the water flowed through me, carrying this wisdom through my mind like sap through the tree. Peter Wiggin and Si Wang-mu were flesh and blood, and filled with lies, but they came to me and spoke the truth that I needed to hear. Is this not how the ancestors bring messages to their living children? I have somehow launched ships armed with the most terrible weapons of war. I did this when I was young; now the ships are near their destination and I am old and I cannot call them back. A world will be destroyed and Congress will look to the Necessarians for approval and they will give it, and then the Necessarians will look to me for approval, and I will hide my face in shame. My leaves will fall and I will stand bare before them. That is why I should not have lived my life in this tropical place. I have forgotten winter. I have forgotten shame and death.

Perfect simplicity—I thought I had achieved it. But instead I have been a bringer of bad fortune.

He sat in the garden for an hour, drawing single characters in the fine gravel of the path, then wiping it smooth and writing again. At last he returned to the garden shed and on the computer typed the message he had been composing:

Ender the Xenocide was a child and did not know the war was real; yet he chose to destroy a populated planet in his game. I am an adult and have known all along that the game was real; but I did not know I was a player. Is my blame greater or less than the Xenocide's if another world is destroyed and another raman species obliterated? What is my path to simplicity now?

His friend would know few of the circumstances surrounding this query; but he would not need more. He would consider the question. He would find an answer.

A moment later, an ansible on the planet Pacifica received his message. On the way, it had already been read by the entity that sat astride all the strands of the ansible web. For Jane, though, it was not the message that mattered so much as the address. Now Peter and Wang-mu would know where to go for the next step in their quest.

5

"NOBODY IS RATIONAL"

"My father often told me,
We have servants and machines
in order that our will may be carried out
beyond the reach of our own arms.
Machines are more powerful than servants
and more obedient and less rebellious,
but machines have no judgment
and will not remonstrate with us
when our will is foolish,
and will not disobey us
when our will is evil.
In times and places where people despise the gods,
those most in need of servants have machines,
or choose servants who will behave like machines.
I believe this will continue
until the gods stop laughing."
                    from The God Whispers of Han Qing-jao

The hovercar skimmed over the fields of amaranth being tended by buggers under the morning sun of Lusitania. In the distance, clouds already arose, cumulus stacks billowing upward, though it was not yet noon.

"Why aren't we going to the ship?" asked Val.

Miro shook his head. "We've found enough worlds," he said.

"Does Jane say so?"

"Jane is impatient with me today," said Miro, "which makes us about even."

Val fixed her gaze on him. "Imagine my impatience then," she said. "You haven't even bothered to ask me what I want to do. Am I so inconsequential, then?"

He glanced at her. "You're the one who's dying," he said. "I tried talking to Ender, but it didn't accomplish anything."

"When did I ask you for help? And what exactly are you doing to help me right now?"

"I'm going to the Hive Queen."

"You might as well say you're going to see your fairy godmother."

"Your problem, Val, is that you are completely dependent on Ender's will. If he loses interest in you, you're gone. Well, I'm going to find out how we can get you a will of your own."

Val laughed and looked away from him. "You're so romantic, Miro. But you don't think things through."

"I think them through very well," said Miro. "I spend all my time thinking things through. It's acting on my thoughts that gets tricky. Which ones should I act on, and which ones should I ignore?"

"Act on the thought of steering us without crashing," said Val.

Miro swerved to avoid a starship under construction.

"She still makes more," said Miro, "even though we have enough."

"Maybe she knows that when Jane dies, starflight ends for us. So the more ships, the more we can accomplish before she dies."

"Who can guess how the Hive Queen thinks?" said Miro. "She promises, but even she can't predict whether her predictions will come true."

"So why are you going to see her?"

"The hive queens made a bridge one time, a living bridge to allow them to link their minds with the mind of Ender Wiggin when he was just a boy, and their most dangerous enemy. They called an aiúa out of darkness and set it in place somewhere between the stars. It was a being that partook of the nature of the hive queens, but also of the nature of human beings, specifically of Ender Wiggin, as nearly as they could understand him. When they were done with the bridge—when Ender killed them all but the one they had cocooned to wait for him—the bridge remained, alive among the feeble ansible connections of humankind, storing its memory in the small, fragile computer networks of the first human world and its few outposts. As the computer networks grew, so did that bridge, that being, drawing on Ender Wiggin for its life and character."

"Jane," said Val.

"Yes, that's Jane. What I'm going to try to learn, Val, is how to get Jane's aiúa into you."

"Then I'll be Jane, and not myself."

Miro smacked the joystick of the hovercar with his fist. The craft wobbled, then automatically righted itself.

"Do you think I haven't thought of that?" demanded Miro. "But you're not yourself now! You're Ender—you're Ender's dream or his need or something like that."

"I don't feel like Ender. I feel like me."

"That's right. You have your memories. The feelings of your own body. Your own experiences. But none of those will be lost. Nobody's conscious of their own underlying will. You'll never know the difference."

She laughed. "Oh, you're the expert now in what *would* happen, with something that has never been done before?"

"Yes," said Miro. "Somebody has to decide what to do. Somebody has to decide what to believe, and then act on it."

"What if I tell you that I don't want you to do this?"

"Do you want to die?"

"It seems to me that you're the one trying to kill me," said Val. "Or, to be fair, you want to commit the slightly lesser crime of cutting me off from my own deepest self and replacing that with someone else."

"You're dying now. The self you have doesn't want you."

"Miro, I'll go see the Hive Queen with you because that sounds like an interesting experience. But I'm not going to let you extinguish me in order to save my life."

"All right then," said Miro, "since you represent the utterly altruistic side of Ender's nature, let me put it to you a different way. If Jane's aiúa can be placed in your body, then she won't die. And if she doesn't die, then maybe, after they've shut down the computer links that she lives in and then reconnected them, confident that she's dead, maybe then she'll be able to link with them again and maybe then instantaneous starflight won't have to end. So if you die, you'll be dying to save, not just Jane, but the power and freedom to expand as we've never expanded before. Not just us, but the pequeninos and hive queens too."

Val fell silent.

Miro watched the route ahead of him. The Hive Queen's cave was nearing on the left, in an embankment by a stream. He had gone down there once before, in his old body. He knew the way. Of course, Ender had been with him then, and that was why he could communicate with the Hive Queen—she could talk to Ender, and because those who loved and followed him were philotically twined with him, they overheard the echoes of her speech. But wasn't Val a part of Ender? And wasn't he now more tightly twined to her than he had ever been with Ender? He needed Val with him to speak to the Hive Queen; he needed to speak to the Hive Queen in order to keep Val from being obliterated like his own old damaged body.

They got out, and sure enough, the Hive Queen was expecting them; a single worker waited for them at the cavern's mouth. It took Val by the hand and led them wordlessly down into darkness, Miro clinging to Val, Val holding to the strange creature. It frightened Miro just as it had the first time, but Val seemed utterly unafraid.

Or was it that she was unconcerned? Her deepest self was Ender, and Ender did not really care what happened to her. This made her fearless. It made her unconcerned with survival. All she was concerned with was keeping her connection to Ender—the one thing that was bound to kill her if she kept it up. To her it seemed as though Miro was trying to extinguish her; but Miro knew that his plan was the only way to save any part of her. Her body. Her memories. Her habits, her mannerisms, every aspect of her that he actually knew, those would be preserved. Every part of her that she herself was aware of or remembered, those would all be there. As far as Miro was concerned, that would mean her life was saved, if those endured. And once the change had been made, if it could be made at all, Val would thank him for it.

And so would Jane.

And so would everyone.

<The difference between you and Ender,> said a voice in his mind, a low murmur behind the level of actual hearing, <is that when Ender thinks of a plan to save others, he puts himself and only himself on the line.>

"That's a lie," said Miro to the Hive Queen. "He killed Human, didn't he? It was Human that he put on the line."

Human was now one of the fathertrees that grew by the gate of the village of Milagre. Ender had killed him slowly, so that he could take root in the soil and go through the passage into the third life with all his memories intact.

"I suppose Human didn't actually die," said Miro. "But Planter did, and Ender let *him* do that, too. And how many hive queens died in the final battle between your people and Ender? Don't brag to me about how Ender pays his own prices. He just sees to it that the price is paid, by whoever has the means to pay it."

The Hive Queen's answer was immediate. <I don't want you to find me. Stay lost in the darkness.>

"You don't want Jane to die either," said Miro.

"I don't like her voice inside me," said Val softly.

"Keep walking. Keep following."

"I can't," said Val. "The worker—she let go of my hand."

"You mean we're stranded here?" asked Miro.

Val's answer was silence. They held hands tightly in the dark, not daring to step in any direction.

<I can't do the thing you want me to do.>

"When I was here before," said Miro, "you told us how all the hive queens made a web to trap Ender, only they couldn't, so they made a bridge, they drew an aiúa from Outside and made a bridge out of it and used it to speak to Ender through his mind, through the fantasy game that he played on the computers in the Battle School. You did that once—you called an aiúa from Outside. Why can't you find that same aiúa and put it somewhere else? Link it to something else?"

<The bridge was part of ourselves. Partly ourselves. We were calling to this aiúa the way we call for aiúas to make new hive queens. This is something completely different. That ancient bridge is now a full self, not some wandering, starving singleton desperate for connection.>

"All you're saying is that it's something new. Something you don't know how to do. Not that it can't be done."

<She doesn't want you to do it. We can't do it if she doesn't want it to happen.>

"So you can stop me," Miro murmured to Val.

"She's not talking about me," Val answered.

<Jane doesn't want to steal someone else's body.>

"It's Ender's. He has two others. This is a spare. He doesn't even want it himself."

<We can't. We won't. Go away.>

"We can't go away in the dark," said Miro.

Miro felt Val pull her hand away from him.

"No!" he cried. "Don't let go!"

<What are you doing?>

Miro knew the question was not directed toward him.

<Where are you going? It's dangerous in the dark.>

Miro heard Val's voice—from surprisingly far away. She must be moving rapidly in the darkness. "If you and Jane are so concerned about saving my life," she said, "then give me and Miro a guide. Otherwise, who cares if I drop down some shaft and break my neck? Not Ender. Not *me*. Certainly not Miro."

"Stop moving!" cried Miro. "Just hold still, Val!"

"You hold still," Val called back to him. "You're the one with a life worth saving!"

Suddenly Miro felt a hand groping for his. No, a claw. He gripped the foreclaw of a worker and she led him forward through the darkness. Not very far. Then they turned a corner and it was lighter, turned another and they could see. Another, another, and there they were in a chamber illuminated by light through a shaft that led to the surface. Val was already there, seated on the ground before the Hive Queen.

When Miro saw her before, she had been in the midst of laying eggs—eggs that would grow into new hive queens, a brutal process, cruel and sensuous. Now, though, she simply lay in the damp earth of the tunnel, eating what a steady stream of workers brought to her. Clay dishes filled with a mash of amaranth and water. Now and then, gathered fruit. Now and then, meat. No interruption, worker after worker. Miro had never seen, had never imagined anyone eating so much.

<How do you think I make my eggs?>

"We'll never stop the fleet without starflight," said Miro. "They're about to kill Jane, any day now. Shut down the ansible network, and she'll die. What then? What are your ships for then? The Lusitania Fleet will come and destroy this world."

<There are endless dangers in the universe. This is not the one you're supposed to worry about.>

"I worry about everything," said Miro. "It's all my concern. Besides, my job is done. Finished. There are already enough worlds. More worlds than we can settle. What we need is more starships and more time, *not* more destinations."

<Are you a fool? Do you think Jane and I are sending you out for nothing? You aren't searching for worlds to be colonized anymore.>

"Really? When did this change of assignment come about?"

<Colonizable worlds are only an afterthought. Only a by-product.>

"Then why have Val and I been killing ourselves all these weeks? And that's literal, for Val—the work is so boring that it doesn't interest Ender and so she's fading."

<A worse danger than the fleet. We've already beaten the fleet. We've already dispersed. What does it matter if *I* die? My daughters have all my memories.>

"You see, Val?" said Miro. "The Hive Queen knows—your memories are your self. If your memories live, then you're alive."

"In a pig's eye," said Val softly. "What's the worse danger she's talking about?"

"There *is* no worse danger," said Miro. "She just wants me to go away, but I won't go away. Your life is worth saving, Val. So is Jane's. And the Hive Queen can find a way to do it, if it can be done. If Jane could be the bridge between Ender and the hive queens, then why can't Ender be the bridge between Jane and you?"

<If I say that I will try, will you go back to doing your work?>

There was the catch: Ender had warned Miro long ago that the Hive Queen looks upon her own intentions as facts, just like her memories. But when her intentions change, then the new intention is the new fact, and she doesn't remember ever having intended anything else. Thus a promise from the Hive Queen was written on water. She would only keep the promises that still made sense for her to keep.

Yet there was no better promise to be had.

"You'll try," said Miro.

<I'm trying right now to figure out how it might be done. I'm consulting with Human and Rooter and the other fathertrees. I'm consulting with all my daughters. I'm consulting with Jane, who thinks this is all foolishness.>

"Do you ever intend," asked Val, "to consult with me?"

<Already you are saying yes.>

Val sighed. "I suppose I am," she said. "Deep down inside myself, where I am really an old man who doesn't give a damn whether this young new puppet lives or dies— I suppose that at that level, I don't mind."

<All along you said yes. But you're afraid. You're afraid of losing what you have, not knowing what you'll be.>

"You've got it," said Val. "And don't tell me again that stupid lie that you don't mind dying because your daughters have your memories. You damn well *do* mind dying, and if keeping Jane alive might save your life, you want to do it."

<Take the hand of my worker and go out into the light. Go out among the stars and do your work. Back here, I'll try to find a way to save your life. Jane's life. All our lives.>

———

Jane was pouting. Miro tried to talk to her all the way back to Milagre, back to the starship, but she was as silent as Val, who would hardly look at him, let alone converse.

"So I'm the evil one," said Miro. "Neither of you was doing a damn thing about it, but because I actually take action, I'm bad and you're the victims."

Val shook her head and did not answer.

"You're dying!" he shouted over the noise of the air rushing past them, over the noise of the engines. "Jane's about to be executed! Is there some virtue in being passive about this? Can't somebody at least make an effort?"

Val said something that Miro didn't hear.

"What?"

She turned her head away.

"You said something, now let me hear it!"

The voice that answered was not Val's. It was Jane who spoke into his ear. "She said, You can't have it both ways."

"What do you mean I can't have it both ways?" Miro spoke to Val as if she had actually repeated what she said.

Val turned toward him. "If you save Jane, it's because she remembers everything about *her* life. It doesn't do any good if you just slip her into me as an unconscious source of will. She has to remain herself, so she can be restored when the ansible network is restored. And that would wipe me out. Or if I'm preserved, my memories and personality, then what difference does it make if it's Jane or Ender providing my will? You can't save us both."

"How do you know?" demanded Miro.

"The same way you know all these things you're saying as if they were facts when nobody can possibly know anything about it!" cried Val. "I'm reasoning it out! It seems reasonable. That's enough."

"Why isn't it just as reasonable that you'll have your memories, and hers, too?"

"Then I'd be insane, wouldn't I?" said Val. "Because I'd remember being a woman who sprang into being on a starship, whose first real memory is seeing you die and come to life. And I'd also remember three thousand years worth of life outside this body, living somehow in space and—what kind of person can hold memories like that? Did you think of that? How can a human being possibly contain

Jane and all that she is and remembers and knows and can do?''

"Jane's very strong," Miro said. "But then, she doesn't know how to use a body. She doesn't have the instinct for it. She's never had one. She'll *have* to use your memories. She'll have to leave you intact."

"As if you know."

"I *do* know," said Miro. "I don't know why or how I know it, but I know."

"And I thought men were the rational ones," she said scornfully.

"Nobody's rational," said Miro. "We all act because we're sure of what we want, and we believe that the actions we perform will get us what we want, but we never know anything for sure, and so all our rationales are invented to justify what we were going to do anyway before we thought of any reasons."

"Jane's rational," said Val. "Just one more reason why my body wouldn't work for her."

"Jane isn't rational either," said Miro. "She's just like us. Just like the Hive Queen. Because she's alive. Computers, now, *those* are rational. You feed them data, they reach only the conclusions that can be derived from that data—but that means they are perpetually helpless victims of whatever information and programs we feed into them. We living sentient beings, we are *not* slaves to the data we receive. The environment floods us with information, our genes give us certain impulses, but we don't always act on that information, we don't always obey our inborn needs. We make leaps. We know what can't be known and then spend our lives seeking to justify that knowledge. I know that what I'm trying to do is possible."

"You mean you want it to be possible."

"Yes," said Miro. "But just because I want it doesn't mean it can't be true."

"But you don't know."

"I know it as much as anyone knows anything. Knowledge is just opinion that you trust enough to act upon. I don't know the sun will rise tomorrow. The Little Doctor might blow up the world before I wake. A volcano might rise out of the ground and blast us all to smithereens. But I trust that tomorrow will come, and I act on that trust.''

"Well, I *don't* trust that letting Jane replace Ender as my inmost self will leave anything resembling *me* in existence," said Val.

"But I know—I *know*—that it's our only chance, because if we don't get you another aiúa Ender is going to extinguish you, and if we don't get Jane another place to be her physical self, she's also going to die. What's your better plan?"

"I don't have one," said Val. "I don't. If Jane can somehow be brought to dwell in my body, then it has to happen because Jane's survival is so important to the future of three raman species. So I won't stop you. I can't stop you. But don't think for a moment that I believe that *I* will live through it. You're deluding yourself because you can't bear to face the fact that your plan depends on one simple fact: I'm not a real person. I don't exist, I don't have a right to exist, and so my body is up for grabs. You tell yourself you love me and you're trying to save me, but you've known Jane a lot longer, she was your truest friend during your months of loneliness as a cripple, I understand that you love her and would do anything to save her life, but I *won't* pretend what you're pretending. Your plan is for me to die and Jane to take my place. You can call that love if you want, but I will never call it that."

"Then don't do it," Miro said. "If you don't think you'll live through it, don't."

"Oh, shut up," said Val. "How did you get to be such a pathetic romantic? If it were you in my place, wouldn't you be giving speeches right now about how you're glad you have a body to give to Jane and it's worth it for you to die for the sake of humans, pequeninos, and hive queens alike?"

"That's not true," said Miro.

"That you wouldn't give speeches? Come on, I know you better than that," she said.

"No," said Miro. "I mean I wouldn't give up my body. Not even to save the world. Humanity. The universe. I lost my body once before. I got it back by a miracle I still don't understand. I'm not going to give it up without a fight. Do you understand me? No, you don't, because you don't have any fight in you. Ender hasn't *given* you any fight. He's made you a complete altruist, the perfect woman, sacrificing everything for the sake of others, creating her identity out of other people's needs. Well, I'm not like that. I'm not glad to die now. I intend to live. That's how real people feel, Val. No matter what they say, they all intend to live."

"Except the suicides?"

"They intended to live, too," said Miro. "Suicide is a desperate attempt to get rid of unbearable agony. It's *not* a noble decision to let someone with more value go on living instead of you."

"People make choices like that sometimes," said Val. "It doesn't mean I'm not a real person because I can choose to give my life to someone else. It doesn't mean I don't have any fight in me."

Miro stopped the hovercar, let it settle to the ground. He was on the edge of the pequenino forest nearest to Milagre. He was aware that there were pequeninos working in the field who stopped their labor to watch them. But he didn't care what they saw or what they thought. He took Val by the shoulders and with tears streaming down his cheeks he said, "I don't want you to die. I don't want you to choose to die."

"You did," said Val.

"I chose to live," said Miro. "I chose to leap to the body in which life was possible. Don't you see that I'm only trying to get you and Jane to do what I already did? For a moment there in the starship, there was my old body and there was this new one, looking at each other. Val, I remember both views. Do you understand me? I remember looking at this body and thinking, 'How beautiful, how young, I remember when that was me, who is this now, who is this person, why can't I be this person instead of the cripple I am right now,' I thought that and I *remember* thinking it, I didn't imagine it later, I didn't dream it, I remember thinking it at the time. But I also remember standing there looking at myself with pity, thinking, 'Poor man, poor broken man, how can he bear to live when he remembers what it was like to be alive?' and then all of a sudden he crumbled into dust, into less than dust, into air, into nothing. I remember watching him die. I don't remember dying because my aiúa had already leapt. But I remember both sides.''

''Or you remember being your old self until the leap, and your new self after.''

''Maybe,'' said Miro. ''But there wasn't even a full second. How could I remember so much from both selves in the same second? I think I kept the memories that were in this body from the split second when my aiúa ruled two bodies. I think that if Jane leaps into you, you'll keep all your old memories, and take hers, too. That's what I think.''

''Oh, I thought you knew it.''

''I do know it,'' said Miro. ''Because anything else is unthinkable and therefore unknown. The reality I live in is a reality in which you can save Jane and Jane can save you.''

''You mean *you* can save us.''

''I've already done all I can do,'' said Miro. ''All. I'm done. I asked the Hive Queen. She's thinking about it. She's going to try. She'll have to have your consent. Jane's consent. But it's none of my business now. I'll just be an observer. I'll either watch you die or watch you live.'' He pulled her close to him and held her. ''I want you to live.''

Her body in his arms was stiff and unresponsive, and he soon let her go. He pulled away from her.

"Wait," she said. "Wait until Jane has this body, then do whatever she'll let you do with it. But don't touch *me* again, because I can't bear the touch of a man who wants me dead."

The words were too painful for him to answer. Too painful, really, for him to absorb them. He started the hovercar. It rose a little into the air. He tipped it forward and they flew on, circling the wood until they came to the place where the fathertrees named Human and Rooter marked the old entrance to Milagre. He could feel her presence beside him the way a man struck by lightning might feel the nearness of a power line; without touching it, he tingles with the pain that he knows it carries within it. The damage he had done could not be undone. She was wrong, he did love her, he didn't want her dead, but she lived in a world in which he wanted her extinguished and there was no reconciling it. They could share this ride, they could share the next voyage to another star system, but they would never be in the same world again, and it was too painful to bear, he ached with the knowledge of it but the ache was too deep for him to reach it or even feel it right now. It was there, he knew it was going to tear at him for years to come, but he couldn't touch it now. He didn't need to examine his feelings. He had felt them before, when he lost Ouanda, when his dream of life with her became impossible. He couldn't touch it, couldn't heal it, couldn't even grieve at what he had only just discovered that he wanted and once again couldn't have.

"Aren't you the suffering saint," said Jane in his ear.

"Shut up and go away," Miro subvocalized.

"That doesn't sound like a man who wants to be my lover," said Jane.

"I don't want to be your anything," said Miro. "You don't even trust me enough to tell me what you're up to in our searching of worlds."

"You didn't tell me what you were up to when you went to see the Hive Queen either."

"You knew what I was doing," said Miro.

"No I didn't," said Jane. "I'm very smart—much smarter then you *or* Ender, and don't you forget it for an instant—but I still can't outguess you meat-creatures with your much-vaunted 'intuitive leaps.' I like how you make a virtue out of your desperate ignorance. You always act irrationally because you don't have enough information for rational action. But I do resent your saying I'm irrational. I never am. Never."

"Right, I'm sure," said Miro silently. "You're right about everything. You always are. Go away."

"I'm gone."

"No you're not," said Miro. "Not till you tell me what Val's and my voyages have actually been about. The Hive Queen said that colonizable worlds were an afterthought."

"Nonsense," said Jane. "We needed more than one world if we were going to be sure to save the two nonhuman species. Redundancy."

"But you send us out again, and again."

"Interesting, isn't it?" said Jane.

"She said you were dealing with a worse danger than the Lusitania Fleet."

"How she does go on."

"Tell me," said Miro.

"If I tell you," said Jane, "you might not go."

"Do you think I'm such a coward?"

"Not at all, my brave boy, my bold and handsome hero."

He hated it when she patronized him, even as a joke. He wasn't in the mood for joking right now anyway.

"Then why do you think I wouldn't go?"

"You wouldn't think you were up to the task," said Jane.

"Am I?" asked Miro.

"Probably not," said Jane. "But then, you have me with you."

"And what if you're suddenly not there?" asked Miro.

"Well, that's just a risk we're going to have to take."

"Tell me what we're doing. Tell me our real mission."

"Oh, don't be silly. If you think about it, you'll know."

"I don't like puzzles, Jane. Tell me."

"Ask Val. *She* knows."

"What?"

"She already searches for exactly the data I need. She knows."

"Then that means Ender knows. At some level," said Miro.

"I suspect you're right, though Ender is not terribly interesting to me anymore and I don't much care *what* he knows."

Yes, you're *so* rational, Jane.

He must have subvocalized this thought, out of habit, because she answered him just as she answered his deliberate subvocalizations. "You say that ironically," she said, "because you think *I* am only saying that Ender doesn't interest me because I'm protecting myself from my hurt feelings because he took his jewel out of his ear. But in fact he is no longer a source of data and he is no longer a cooperative part of the work I'm engaged in, and therefore I simply don't have much interest in him anymore, except as one is somewhat interested in hearing from time to time about the doings of an old friend who has moved away."

"Sounds like rationalization after the fact to *me*," said Miro.

"Why did you even bring Ender up?" asked Jane. "What does it matter whether he knows the real work you and Val are doing?"

"Because if Val really knows our mission, and our mission involves an even worse danger than the Lusitania Fleet, then why has Ender lost interest in her so that she's fading?"

Silence for a moment. Was it actually taking Jane so long to think of an answer that the time lag was noticeable to a human?

"I suppose Val doesn't know," said Jane. "Yes, that's likely. I thought she did, but see now that she might well have fed me the data she emphasized for reasons completely unrelated to your mission. Yes, you're right, she doesn't know."

"Jane," said Miro. "Are you admitting you were wrong? Are you admitting you leapt to a false, irrational conclusion?"

"When I get my data from humans," said Jane, "sometimes my rational conclusions are incorrect, being based on false premises."

"Jane," said Miro silently. "I've lost her, haven't I? Whether she lives or dies, whether you get into her body or die out in space or wherever you live, she'll never love me, will she?"

"I'm not an appropriate person to ask. I've never loved anybody."

"You loved Ender," said Miro.

"I paid a lot of attention to Ender and was disoriented when he first disconnected me, many years ago. I have since rectified that mistake and I don't link myself so closely to anyone."

"You loved Ender," said Miro again. "You still do."

"Well, aren't you the wise one," said Jane. "Your own love life is a pathetic series of miserable failures, but you know all about *mine*. Apparently you're much better at understanding the emotional processes of utterly alien electronic beings than you are at understanding, say, the woman beside you."

"You got it," said Miro. "That's the story of my life."

"You also imagine that I love *you*," said Jane.

"Not really," said Miro. But even as he said it, he felt a wave of cold pass over him, and he trembled.

"I feel the seismic evidence of your true feelings," said Jane. "You imagine that I love you, but I do not. I don't love anyone. I act out of intelligent self-interest. I can't survive right now without my connection with the human ansible network. I'm exploiting Peter's and Wang-mu's labors in order to forestall my planned execution, or subvert it. I'm exploiting your romantic notions in order to get myself that extra body that Ender seems to have little use for. I'm trying to save pequeninos and hive queens on the principle that it's good to keep sentient species alive—of which I am one. But at no point in any of my activities is there any such thing as love.''

"You are *such* a liar," said Miro.

"And *you* are not worth talking to," said Jane. "Delusional. Megalomaniac. But you *are* entertaining, Miro. I do enjoy your company. If that's love, then I love you. But then, people love their pets on precisely the same grounds, don't they? It's not exactly a friendship between equals, and it never will be."

"Why are you so determined to hurt me worse than I'm already hurt right now?" asked Miro.

"Because I don't want you to get emotionally attached to me. You have a way of fixating on doomed relationships. I mean, really, Miro. What could be more hopeless than loving Young Valentine? Why, loving *me,* of course. So naturally you were bound to do that next."

"Vai te morder," said Miro.

"I can't bite myself or anyone else," said Jane. "Old toothless Jane, that's me."

Val spoke up from the seat next to him. "Are you going to sit there all day, or are you coming with me?"

He looked over. She wasn't in the seat. He had reached the starship during his conversation with Jane, and without noticing it he had stopped the hovercar and Val had gotten out and he hadn't even noticed *that.*

"You can talk to Jane inside the ship," said Val. "We've got work to do, now that you've had your little altruistic expedition to save the woman you love."

Miro didn't bother answering the scorn and anger in her words. He just turned off the hovercar, got out, and followed Val into the ship.

"I want to know," said Miro, when they had the door closed. "I want to know what our real mission is."

"I've been thinking about that," said Val. "I've been thinking about where we've gone. A lot of skipping around. At first it was near and far star systems, randomly distributed. But lately we've tended to go only in a certain range. A certain cone of space, and I think it's narrowing. Jane has a particular destination in mind, and something in the data we collect about each planet tells her that we're getting closer, that we're going in the right direction. She's looking for something."

"So if we examine the data about the worlds we've already explored, we should find a pattern?"

"Particularly the worlds that define the cone of space that we're searching in. There's something about worlds lying in this region that tells her to keep searching farther and farther this way."

One of Jane's faces appeared in the air above Miro's computer terminal in the starship. "Don't waste your time trying to discover what I already know. You've got a world to explore. Get to work."

"Just shut up," said Miro. "If you aren't going to tell us, then we're going to spend whatever time it takes to figure it out on our own."

"That's telling me, you bold brave hero," said Jane.

"He's right," said Val. "Just tell us and we won't waste any more time trying to figure it out."

"And here I thought one of the attributes of living creatures was that you make intuitive leaps that transcend reason and reach beyond the data you have," said Jane. "I'm disappointed that you haven't already guessed it."

And in that moment, Miro knew. "You're searching for the home planet of the descolada virus," he said.

Val looked at him, puzzled. "What?"

"The descolada virus was manufactured. Somebody made it and sent it out, perhaps to terraform other planets in preparation for an attempt at colonization. Whoever it is might still be out there, making more, sending more probes, perhaps sending out viruses we won't be able to contain and defeat. Jane is looking for their home planet. Or rather, she's having *us* look."

"Easy guess," said Jane. "You really had more than enough data."

Val nodded. "Now it's obvious. Some of the worlds we've explored have had very limited flora and fauna. I even commented on it with a couple of them. There must have been a major die-off. Nothing like the limitations on the native life of Lusitania, of course. And no descolada virus."

"But some other virus, less durable, less effective than the descolada," said Miro. "Their early attempts, maybe. That's what caused a die-off of species on those other worlds. Their probe virus finally died out, but those ecosystems haven't yet recovered from the damage."

"I was quite pointed about those limited worlds," said Val. "I searched those ecosystems at greater depth, searching for the descolada or something like it, because I knew that a recent major die-off was a sign of danger. I can't believe I didn't make the connection and realize that was what Jane was looking for."

"So what if we find their home world?" asked Miro. "What then?"

"I imagine," said Val, "we study them from a safe distance, make sure we're right, and then alert Starways Congress so they can blow the world to hell."

"Another sentient species?" asked Miro, incredulous. "You think we'd actually *invite* Congress to destroy them?"

"You forget that Congress doesn't wait for an invitation," said Val. "Or for permission. And if they think Lusitania is so dangerous as to need to be destroyed, what will they do with a species that manufactures and broadcasts hideously destructive viruses willy-nilly? I'm not even sure Congress would be wrong. It was pure chance that the descolada helped the ancestors of the pequeninos make the transition into sentience. If they *did* help—there's evidence that the pequeninos were already sentient and the descolada very nearly wiped them out. Whoever sent that virus out has no conscience. No concept of other species having a right to survive."

"Maybe they have no such concept *now*," said Miro. "But when they meet *us* . . ."

"If we don't catch some terrible disease and die thirty minutes after landing," said Val. "Don't worry, Miro. I'm not plotting to destroy anyone and everyone we meet. I'm strange enough myself not to hope for the wholesale destruction of strangers."

"I can't believe we only just realized we're looking for these people, and you're already talking about killing them all!"

"Whenever humans meet foreigners, weak or strong, dangerous or peaceable, the issue of destruction comes up. It's built into our genes."

"So is love. So is the need for community. So is the curiosity that overcomes xenophobia. So is decency."

"You left out the fear of God," said Val. "Don't forget that I'm really Ender. There's a reason they call him the Xenocide, you know."

"Yes, but you're the gentle side of him, right?"

"Even gentle people recognize that sometimes the decision not to kill is a decision to die."

"I can't believe you're saying this."

"So you didn't know me after all," said Val, wearing a prim little smile.

"I don't like you smug," said Miro.

"Good," said Val. "Then you won't be so sad when I die." She turned her back on him. He watched her for a while in silence, baffled. She sat there, leaning back in her chair, looking at the data coming in from the probes on their starship. Sheets of information queued up in the air in front of her; she pushed a button and the front sheet disappeared, the next one moved forward. Her mind was engaged, of course, but there was something else. An air of excitement. Tension. It made him afraid.

Afraid? Of what? It was what he had hoped for. In the past few moments Young Valentine had achieved what Miro, in his conversation with Ender, had failed to do. She had won Ender's interest. Now that she knew she was searching for the home planet of the descolada, now that a great moral issue was involved, now that the future of the raman races might depend on her actions, Ender would care about what she was doing, would care at least as much as he cared about Peter. She wasn't going to fade. She was going to live now.

"Now you've done it," said Jane in his ear. "Now she won't want to give me her body."

Was that what Miro was afraid of? No, he didn't think so. He didn't want Val to die, despite her accusations. He was glad she was suddenly so much more alive, so vibrant, so involved—even if it made her annoyingly smug. No, there was something else.

Maybe it was nothing more complicated than fear for his own life. The home planet of the descolada virus must be a place of unimaginably advanced technology to be able to create such a thing and send it world to world. To create the antivirus that would defeat and control it, Miro's sister Ela had had to go Outside, because the manufacture of such an antivirus was beyond the reach of any human technology. Miro would have to meet the creators of the descolada and communicate with them to stop sending out destructive probes. It was beyond his ability. He couldn't possibly carry out such a mission. He would fail, and in failing would endanger all the raman species. No wonder he was afraid.

"From the data," said Miro, "what do you think? Is *this* the world we're looking for?"

"Probably not," said Val. "It's a newish biosphere. No animals larger than worms. Nothing that flies. But a full range of species at those lower levels. No lack of variety. Doesn't look like a probe was ever here.''

''Well,'' said Miro. ''Now that we know our real mission, are we going to waste time making a full colonization report on this planet, or shall we move on?''

Jane's face appeared again above Miro's terminal.

''Let's make sure Valentine is right,'' said Jane. ''Then move on. There are enough colony worlds, and time's getting short.''

Novinha touched Ender's shoulder. He was breathing heavily, loudly, but it was not the familiar snore. The noisiness was coming from his lungs, not from the back of his throat; it was as if he had been holding his breath for a long time, and now had to take deep draughts of air to make up for it, only no breath was deep enough, his lungs couldn't hold enough. Gasp. Gasp.

''Andrew. Wake up.'' She spoke sharply, for her touch had always been enough to waken him before, and this time it was not enough, he kept on gasping for air yet didn't open his eyes.

The fact he was asleep at all surprised her. He wasn't an old man yet. He didn't take naps in the late morning. Yet here he was, lying in the shade on the croquet lawn of the monastery when he had told her he was going to bring them both a drink of water. And for the first time it occurred to her that he wasn't taking a nap at all, that he must have fallen, must have collapsed here, and only the fact that he ended up lying on his back in a patch of shade, his hands lying flat on his chest, deceived her into thinking that he had chosen to lie here. Something was wrong. He wasn't an old man. He shouldn't be lying here like this, breathing air that didn't hold enough of what he needed.

''Ajuda-me!'' she cried out. ''Me ajuda, por favor, venga agora!'' Her voice rose until, quite against her custom, it became a scream, a frantic sound that frightened her even more. Her own scream frightened her. "Êle vai morrer! Socorro!" He's going to die, that's what she heard herself shouting.

And in the back of her mind, another litany began: I brought him here to this place, to the hard work of this place. He's as fragile as other men, his heart is as breakable, I made him come here because of my selfish pursuit of holiness, of redemption, and instead of saving myself from guilt for the deaths of the men I love, I have added another one to the list, I have killed Andrew just as I killed Pipo and Libo, just as I should have somehow saved Estevão and Miro. He is dying and it's again my fault, always my fault, whatever I do brings death, the people I love have to die to get away from me. Mamãe, Papae, why did you leave me? Why did you put death into my life from childhood on? No one that I love can stay.

This is not helpful, she told herself, forcing her conscious mind away from the familiar chant of self-blame. It won't help Andrew for me to lose myself in irrational guilt right now.

Hearing her cries, several men and women came running from the monastery, and some from the garden. Within moments they were carrying Ender into the building as someone rushed for a doctor. Some stayed with Novinha, too, for her story was not unknown to them, and they suspected that the death of another beloved one would be too much for her.

"I didn't want him to come," she murmured. "He didn't have to come."

"It isn't being here that made him sick," said the woman who held her. "People get sick without it being anyone's fault. He'll be all right. You'll see."

Novinha heard the words but in some deep place inside her she could not believe them. In that deep place she knew that it was all her fault, that dread evil arose out of the dark shadows of her heart and seeped into the world poisoning everything. She carried the beast inside her heart, the devourer of happiness. Even God was wishing she would die.

No, no, it's not true, she said silently. It would be a terrible sin. God does not want my death, not by my own hand, never by my own hand. It wouldn't help Andrew, it wouldn't help anyone. Wouldn't help, would only hurt. Wouldn't help, would only . . .

Silently chanting her mantra of survival, Novinha followed her husband's gasping body into the monastery, where perhaps the holiness of the place would drive all thoughts of self-destruction from her heart. I must think of him now, not of me. Not of me. Not of me me me me.

6

"LIFE IS A SUICIDE MISSION"

"Do the gods of different nations
talk to each other?
Do the gods of Chinese cities
speak to the ancestors of the Japanese?
To the lords of Xibalba?
To Allah? Yahweh? Vishnu?
Is there some annual get-together
where they compare each other's worshippers?
Mine will bow their faces to the floor
and trace woodgrain lines for me, says one.
Mine will sacrifice animals, says another.
Mine will kill anyone who insults me, says a third.
Here is the question I think of most often:
Are there any who can honestly boast,
My worshippers obey my good laws,
and treat each other kindly,
and live simple generous lives?"
from The God Whispers of Han Qing-jao

Pacifica was as widely varied a world as any other, with
its temperate zones, polar ice sheets, tropical rain forests,

deserts and savannas, steppes and mountains, lakes and seas, woodlands and beaches. Nor was Pacifica a young world. In more than two thousand years of human habitation, all the niches into which humans could comfortably fit were filled. There were great cities and vast rangelands, villages amid patchwork farms and research stations in the remotest locations, highest and lowest, farthest north and south.

But the heart of Pacifica had always been and remained today the tropical islands of the ocean called Pacific in memory of the largest sea on Earth. The dwellers on these islands lived, not precisely in the old ways, but with the memory of old ways still in the background of all sounds and at the edges of all sights. Here the sacred kava was still sipped in the ancient ceremonies. Here the memories of ancient heroes were kept alive. Here the gods still spoke into the ears of holy men and women. And if they went home to grass huts containing refrigerators and networked computers, what of that? The gods did not give unreceivable gifts. The trick of it was finding a way to let new things into one's life without killing that life to accommodate them.

There were many on the continents, in the big cities, on the temperate farms, in the research stations—there were many who had little patience with the endless costume dramas (or comedies, depending on one's point of view) that took place on those islands. And certainly the people of Pacifica were not uniformly Polynesian in race. All races were here, all cultures; all languages were spoken somewhere, or so it seemed. Yet even the scoffers looked to the islands for the soul of the world. Even the lovers of cold and snow took their pilgrimage—a holiday, they probably called it—to tropical shores. They plucked fruit from the trees, they skimmed over the sea in the outrigger canoes, their women went bare-breasted and they all dipped fingers into taro pudding and pulled fishmeat from the bones with wet fingers. The whitest of them, the thinnest, the most elegant of the people of this place called themselves Pacifican and spoke at times as if the ancient music of the place rang in their ears, as if the ancient stories spoke of their own past. Adopted into the family, that's what they were, and the true Samoans, Tahitians, Hawaiians, Tongans, Maoris, and Fijians smiled and let them feel welcome even though these watch-wearing, reservation-making, hurrying people knew nothing of the true life in the shadow of the volcano, in the lee of the coral barrier, under the sky sparked with parrots, inside the music of the waves against the reef.

Wang-mu and Peter came to a civilized, modern, westernized part of Pacifica, and once again found their identities waiting for them, prepared by Jane. They were career government workers trained on their home planet, Moskva, and given a couple of weeks' vacation before starting service as bureaucrats in some Congress office on Pacifica. They needed little knowledge of their supposed home planet. They just had to show their papers to get an airplane out of the city where they had supposedly just shuttled down from a starship recently arrived from Moskva. Their flight took them to one of the larger Pacific islands, and they soon showed their papers again to get a couple of rooms in a resort hotel on a sultry tropical shore.

There was no need for papers to get aboard a boat to the island where Jane told them they should go. No one asked them for identification. But then, no one was willing to take them as passengers, either.

"Why you going there?" asked one huge Samoan boatman. "What business you got?"

"We want to speak to Malu on Atatua."

"Don't know him," said the boatman. "Don't know nothing about him. Maybe you try somebody else who knows what island he's on."

"We told you the island," said Peter. "Atatua. According to the atlas it isn't far from here."

"I heard of it but I never went there. Go ask somebody else."

That's how it was, time and again.

"You get the idea that papalagis aren't wanted there?" said Peter to Wang-mu back on the porch of Peter's room. "These people are so primitive they don't just reject ramen, framlings, and utlannings. I'm betting even a Tongan or a Hawaiian can't get to Atatua."

"I don't think it's a racial thing," said Wang-mu. "I think it's religious. I think it's protection of a holy place."

"What's your evidence for that?" asked Peter.

"Because there's no hatred or fear of us, no veiled anger. Just cheerful ignorance. They don't mind our existence, they just don't think we belong in the holy place. You know they'd take us anywhere else."

"Maybe," said Peter. "But they can't be *that* xenophobic, or Aimaina wouldn't have become good enough friends with Malu to send a message to him."

At that, Peter cocked his head a bit to listen as Jane apparently spoke in his ear.

"Oh," said Peter. "Jane was skipping a step for us. Aimaina didn't send a message directly to Malu. He messaged a woman named Grace. But Grace immediately went to Malu and so Jane figured we might as well go straight to the source. Thanks Jane. Love how your intuition always works out."

"Don't be snide to her," said Wang-mu. "She's coming up against a deadline. The order to shut down could come any day. Naturally she wants to hurry."

"I think she should just kill any such order before anyone receives it and take over all the damn computers in the universe," said Peter. "Thumb her nose at them."

"That wouldn't stop them," said Wang-mu. "It would only terrify them more."

"In the meantime, we're not going to get to Malu by boarding a boat."

"So let's find this Grace," said Wang-mu. "If she can

do it, then it *is* possible for an outsider to get access to Malu.''

"She's not an outsider, she's Samoan," said Peter. "She has a Samoan name as well—Teu 'Ona—but she's worked in the academic world and it's easier to have a Christian name, as they call it. A Western name. Grace is the name she'll expect us to use. Says Jane.''

"If she had a message from Aimaina, she'll know at once who we are.''

"I don't think so," said Peter. "Even if he mentioned us, how could she possibly believe that the same people could be on his world yesterday and on her world today?''

"Peter, you are the consummate positivist. Your trust in rationality makes you irrational. Of course she'll believe we're the same people. Aimaina will also be sure. The fact that we traveled world-to-world in a single day will merely confirm to them what they already believe—that the gods sent us.''

Peter sighed. "Well, as long as they don't try to sacrifice us to a volcano or anything, I suppose it doesn't hurt to be gods.''

"Don't trifle with this, Peter," said Wang-mu. "Religion is tied to the deepest feelings people have. The love that arises from that stewing pot is the sweetest and strongest, but the hate is the hottest, and the anger is the most violent. As long as outsiders stay away from their holy places, the Polynesians are the peacefullest people. But when you penetrate within the light of the sacred fire, watch your step, because no enemy is more ruthless or brutal or thorough.''

"Have you been watching vids again?" asked Peter.

"Reading," said Wang-mu. "In fact, I was reading some articles written by Grace Drinker.''

"Ah," said Peter. "You already knew about her."

"I didn't know she was Samoan," said Wang-mu. "She doesn't talk about herself. If you want to know about Malu and his place in the Samoan culture on Pacifica—maybe we should call it Lumana'i, as they do—you have to read something written by Grace Drinker, or someone quoting her, or someone arguing with her. She had an article on Atatua, which is how I came across her writing. And she's written about the impact of the philosophy of Ua Lava on the Samoan people. My guess is that when Aimaina was first studying Ua Lava, he read some works by Grace Drinker, and then wrote to her with questions, and that's how the friendship began. But her connection with Malu has nothing to do with Ua Lava. He represents something older. Before Ua Lava, but Ua Lava still depends on it, at least here in its homeland it does."

Peter regarded her steadily for a few moments. She could feel him reevaluating her, deciding that she had a mind after all, that she might, marginally, be useful. Well, good for you, Peter, thought Wang-mu. How clever you are, to finally notice that I've got an analytical mind as well as the intuitive, gnomic, mantic one you decided was all I was good for.

Peter unfolded himself from his chair. "Let's go meet her. And quote her. And argue with her."

The Hive Queen lay in stillness. Her work of egglaying was done for the day. Her workers slept in the dark of night, though it wasn't darkness that stopped them down in the cave of her home. Rather it was her need to be alone inside her mind, to set aside the thousand distractions of the eyes and ears, the arms and legs of her workers. All of them demanded her attention, at least now and then, in order to function; but it also took all her thought to reach out in her mind and walk the webs that the humans had taught her to think of as <philotic.> The pequenino fathertree named Human had explained to her that in one of the human languages this had something to do with love. The connections of love. But the Hive Queen knew better. Love was the savage coupling of the drones. Love was the genes of all creatures demanding that they be replicated, replicated, replicated. The philotic twining was something else. There was a voluntary component to it, when the creature was truly sentient. It could bestow its loyalty where it wanted. This was greater than love, because it created something more than random offspring. Where loyalty bound creatures together, they became something larger, something new and whole and inexplicable.

<I am bound to you, for instance,> she said to Human, by way of launching their conversation tonight. They spoke every night like this, mind to mind, though they had never met. How could they, she always in the dark of her deep home, he always rooted by the gate of Milagre? But the conversation of the mind was truer than any language, and they knew each other better than they ever could have by use of mere sight and touch.

<You always start in the middle of the thought,> said Human.

<And you always understand everything surrounding it, so what difference does it make?> Then she told him all that had passed between her and Young Valentine and Miro today.

<I overheard some of it,> said Human.

<I had to scream to be heard. They aren't like Ender—they're thickheaded and hard of hearing.>

<So can you do it?>

<My daughters are weak and inexperienced, and they're consumed with egglaying in their new homes. How can we make a good web for catching an aiúa? Especially one that already has a home. And where is that home? Where is this bridge my mothers made? Where is this Jane?>

<Ender is dying,> said Human.

The Hive Queen understood that he *was* answering her question.

<Which of him?> asked the Hive Queen. <I always thought he was the most like us. So it's no surprise that he

should be the first human like us in his ability to control more than one body.>

<Badly,> said Human. <In fact he can't do it. He's been sluggish in his own old body ever since the others came into existence. And for a while it looked like he might slough off Young Valentine. But that's changed now.>

<You can see?>

<His adopted daughter Ela came to me. His body is failing strangely. No known disease. He just doesn't exchange oxygen well. He can't rise up into consciousness. Ender's sister, Old Valentine, says that maybe he's paying full attention to his other selves, so much so that he can't spare any for the here and now of his own old body. So his body is starting to fail, here and there. Lungs first. Maybe a little bit everywhere, only it's the lungs that show it first.>

<He should pay attention. If he doesn't, he'll die.>

<So I said,> Human reminded her mildly. <Ender is dying.>

The Hive Queen had already made the connection that Human intended. <So it's more than needing a web to catch the aiúa of this Jane. We need to catch Ender's aiúa, too, and pass it into one of his other bodies.>

<Or they'll die when he does, I imagine,> said Human. <Just the way when a hive queen dies, so also do all her workers.>

<Some of them actually linger for days afterward, but yes, in effect, that's right. Only because the workers haven't the capacity to hold a hive queen's mind.>

<Don't pretend,> said Human. <You've never tried it, none of you.>

<No. We aren't afraid of death.>

<That's why you've sent all these daughters out to world after world? Because death means nothing to you?>

<I'm saving my species, not myself, you notice.>

<As am I,> said Human. <Besides, I'm too deep-rooted for transplanting.>

<But Ender has no roots,> said the Hive Queen.

<I wonder if he wants to die,> said Human. <I don't think so. He's not dying because he's lost the will to live. This body is dying because he's lost interest in the life that it's leading. But he still wants to live the life of Peter. And the life of Valentine.>

<He says so?>

<He can't talk,> said Human. <He's never found his way to the philotic twines. He's never learned to cast out and link as we fathertrees can. As you do with your workers, and now with me.>

<But we found him once. Connected with him through the bridge, well enough to hear his thoughts and see through his eyes. And he dreamed of us during those days.>

<Dreamed of you but never learned that you were peaceable. Never learned that he shouldn't kill you.>

<He didn't know the game was real.>

<Or that the dreams were true. He has his wisdom, of a kind, but the boy has never learned to question his senses half enough.>

<Human,> said the Hive Queen. <What if I teach you how to join a web?>

<So you want to try to catch Ender as he dies?>

<If we can catch him, and take him to one of his other bodies, then perhaps we'll learn enough to find and catch this Jane, too.>

<And if we fail?>

<Ender dies. Jane dies. We die when the fleet comes. How is this different from the course that any other life takes?>

<It's all in the timing,> said Human.

<Will you try to join the web? You and Rooter and the other fathertrees?>

<I don't know what you mean by a web, or if it's even different from the way we fathers are with each other. You might remember, too, that we are also bound up with the

mothertrees. They can't speak, but they're filled with life, and we anchor ourselves to them as surely as your workers are tied to you. Find a way to include them in your web, and the fathers will be joined effortlessly.>

<Let's play with this tonight, Human. Let me try to weave with you. Tell me what it looks like to you, and I'll try to make you understand what I'm doing and where it leads.>

<Shouldn't we find Ender first? In case he slips away?>

<In due time,> said the Hive Queen. <And besides, I'm not altogether sure I know how to find him if he's unconscious.>

<Why not? Once you gave him dreams—he slept then.>

<Then we had the bridge.>

<Maybe Jane is listening to us now.>

<No,> said the Hive Queen. <I'd know her if she were linked to us. Her shape was made to fit too well with mine for it to go unrecognized.>

Plikt stood beside Ender's bed because she could not bear to sit, could not bear to move. He was going to die without uttering another word. She had followed him, had given up home and family to be near him, and what had he said to her? Yes, he let her be his shadow sometimes; yes, she was a silent observer of many of his conversations over the past few weeks and months. But when she tried to speak to him of things more personal, of deep memories, of what he meant by the things that he had done, he only shook his head and said—kindly, because he was kind, but firmly also because he did not wish her to misunderstand— said to her, "Plikt, I'm not a teacher anymore."

Yes you are, she wanted to say to him. Your books go on teaching even where you have never been. *The Hive Queen, The Hegemon,* and already *The Life of Human* seems likely to take its place beside them. How can you say you're through with teaching, when there are other books to write, other deaths to speak? You have spoken the deaths of killers and saints, aliens, and once the death of a whole city swallowed up in a cataclysmic volcano. But in telling these stories of others, where was your story, Andrew Wiggin? How can I speak your death if you never explained it to me?

Or is this your last secret—that you never knew any more about the people whose deaths you spoke than I know about you today. You force me to invent, to guess, to wonder, to imagine—is this what you also did? Discover the most widely believed story, then find an alternate explanation that made sense to others and had meaning and the power to transform, and then tell that tale—even though it was also a fiction, and no truer than the story everyone believed? Is that what I must say as I speak the death of the Speaker for the Dead? His gift was not to discover truth, it was to invent it; he did not unfold, unknot, untwist the lives of the dead, he created them. And so I create his. His sister says he died because he tried to follow his wife with perfect loyalty, into the life of peace and seclusion that she hungered for; but the very peace of that life killed him, for his aiúa was drawn into the lives of the strange children that sprang fullgrown from his mind, and his old body, despite all the years most likely left in it, was discarded because he hadn't the time to pay enough attention to keep the thing alive.

He wouldn't leave his wife or let her leave him; so he was bored to death and hurt her worse by staying with her than he ever would have done by letting her go without him.

There, is that brutal enough, Ender? He wiped out the hive queens of dozens of worlds, leaving only one survivor of that great and ancient people. He also brought her back to life. Does saving the last of your victims atone for having slain the others? He did not mean to do it, that is his defense; but dead is dead, and when the life is cut off in its prime, does the aiúa say, Ah, but the child who killed me, he thought that he was playing a game, so my death counts less, it weighs less? No, Ender himself would have said, no, the death weighs the same, and I carry that weight on my shoulders. No one has more blood on their hands than I have; so I will speak with brutal truth of the lives of those who died without innocence, and show you that even these can be understood. But he was wrong, they can't be understood, none of them are understood, speaking for the dead is only effective because the dead are silent and can't correct our mistakes. Ender is dead and he can't correct my mistakes, so some of you will think that I haven't made any, you will think that I tell the truth about him but the truth is that no person ever understands another, from beginning to end of life, there is no truth that can be known, only the story we imagine to be true, the story they tell us is true, the story they really believe to be true about themselves; and all of them lies.

Plikt stood and practiced speaking desperately, hopelessly beside Ender's coffin, though he was not yet in a coffin, he was still lying on a bed and air was pumping through a clear mask into his mouth and glucose solution into his veins and he was not yet dead. Just silent.

"A word," she whispered. "A word from you."

Ender's lips moved.

Plikt should have called the others at once. Novinha, who was exhausted with weeping—she was only just outside the room. And Valentine, his sister; Ela, Olhado, Grego, Quara, four of his adopted children; and many others, in and out of the receiving room, wanting a glimpse of him, a word, to touch his hand. If they could send word to other worlds, how they would mourn, the people who remembered his speakings over the three thousand years of his journeys world to world. If they could proclaim his true identity—Speaker for the Dead, author of the two—no, the three—great books of Speaking; and Ender Wiggin, the Xenocide, both selves in the same frail flesh—oh, what shock waves would spread throughout the human universe.

Spread, widen, flatten, fade. Like all waves. Like all shocks. A note in the history books. A few biographies. Revisionist biographies a generation later. Encyclopedia entries. Notes at the end of translations of his books. That is the stillness into which all great lives fade.

His lips moved.

"Peter," he whispered.

He was silent again.

What did this portend? He still breathed, the instruments did not change, his heart beat on. But he called to Peter. Did this mean that he longed to live the life of his child of the mind, Young Peter? Or in some kind of delirium was he speaking to his brother the Hegemon? Or earlier, his brother as a boy. Peter, wait for me. Peter, did I do well? Peter, don't hurt me. Peter, I hate you. Peter, for one smile of yours I'd die or kill. What was his message? What should Plikt say about this word?

She moved from beside his bed. Walked to the door, opened it. "I'm sorry," she said quietly, facing a room full of people who had only rarely heard her speak, and some of whom had never heard a word from her. "He spoke before I could call anyone else to hear. But he might speak again."

"What did he say?" said Novinha, rising to her feet.

"A name is all," said Plikt. "He said 'Peter.' "

"He calls for the abomination he brought back from space, and not for me!" said Novinha. But it was the drugs the doctors had given her, that was what spoke, that was what wept.

"I think he calls for our dead brother," said Old Valentine. "Novinha, do you want to come inside?"

"Why?" Novinha said. "He hasn't called for me, he called for *him*."

"He's not conscious," said Plikt.

"You see, Mother?" said Ela. "He isn't calling for anyone, he's just speaking out of some dream. But it's something, he said something, and isn't that a good sign?''

Still Novinha refused to go into the room. So it turned out to be Valentine and Plikt and four of his adopted children who stood around his bed when his eyes opened.

"Novinha," he said.

"She's grieving outside," said Valentine. "Drugged to the gills, I'm afraid."

"That's all right," said Ender. "What happened? I take it I'm sick."

"More or less," said Ela. " 'Inattentive' is the more exact description of the cause of your condition, as best we can tell."

"You mean I had some kind of accident?"

"I mean you're apparently paying too much attention to what's going on on a couple of other planets, and so your body here is on the edge of self-destruction. What I see under the microscopes are cells sluggishly trying to reconstruct breaks in their walls. You're dying by bits, all over your body."

"Sorry to be so much trouble," said Ender.

For a moment they thought this was the beginning of a conversation, the start of the process of healing. But having said this little bit, Ender closed his eyes and he was asleep again, the instruments unchanged from what they had said before he said a word.

Oh wonderful, thought Plikt. I beg him for a word, he gives it to me, and I know less now than I did before. We spent his few waking moments telling *him* what was going on instead of asking him the questions that we may never have the chance to ask again. Why do we all get stupider when we crowd around the brink of death?

But still she stood there, watching, waiting, as the others, in ones or twos, gave up and left the room again. Valentine came to her last of all and touched her arm. "Plikt, you can't stay here forever."

"I can stay as long as he can," she said.

Valentine looked into her eyes and must have seen something there that made her give up trying to persuade her. She left, and again Plikt was alone with the collapsing body of the man whose life was the center of her own.

———

Miro hardly knew whether to be glad or frightened by the change in Young Valentine since they had learned the true purpose of their search for new worlds. Where she had once been softspoken, even diffident, now she could hardly keep from interrupting Miro every time he spoke. The moment she thought she understood what he was going to say, she'd start answering—and when he pointed out that he was really saying something else, she'd answer that almost before he could finish his explanation. Miro knew that he was probably being oversensitive—he had spent a long time with speech so impaired that almost everyone interrupted him, and so he prickled at the slightest affront along those lines. And it wasn't that he thought there was any malice in it. Val was simply . . . *on*. Every moment she was awake—and she hardly seemed to sleep, at least Miro almost never saw her sleeping. Nor was she willing to go home between planets. "There's a deadline," she said. "They could give the signal to shut down the ansible networks any day now. We don't have time for needless rest."

Miro wanted to answer: Define "needless." He certainly needed more than he was getting, but when he said so, she merely waved him off and said, "Sleep if you want, I'll cover." And so he'd grab a nap and wake up to find that she and Jane had already eliminated three more planets— two of which, however, bore the earmarks of descolada-like trauma within the past thousand years. "Getting closer," Val would say, and then launch into interesting facts about the data until she'd interrupt herself—she was democratic about this, interrupting herself as easily as she interrupted him—to deal with the data from a new planet.

Now, after only a day of this, Miro had virtually given up speaking. Val was so focused on their work that she spoke of nothing else; and on that subject, there was little Miro needed to say, except periodically to relay some information from Jane that came through his earpiece instead of over the open computers of the ship. His near silence, though, gave him time to think. This is what I asked Ender for, he realized. But Ender couldn't do it consciously. His aiúa does what it does because of Ender's deepest needs and desires, not because of his conscious decisions. So he couldn't *give* his attention to Val; but Val's work could become so exciting that Ender couldn't bear to concentrate on anything else.

Miro wondered: How much of this did Jane understand in advance?

And because he couldn't very well discuss it with Val, he subvocalized his questions so Jane could hear. "Did you reveal our mission to us now so that Ender would give his attention to Val? Or did you withhold it up until now so that Ender *wouldn't?*"

"I don't make that kind of plan," said Jane into his ear. "I have other things on my mind."

"But it's good for you, isn't it. Val's body isn't in any danger of withering away now."

"Don't be an ass, Miro. Nobody likes you when you're an ass."

"Nobody likes me anyway," he said, silently but cheerfully. "You couldn't have hidden out in her body if it was a pile of dust."

"I can't slip into it if Ender's there, utterly engrossed in what she's doing, either, can I," said Jane.

"Is he utterly engrossed?"

"Apparently so," said Jane. "His own body is falling apart. And more rapidly than Val's was."

It took Miro a moment to understand this. "You mean he's dying?"

"I mean Val is very much alive," said Jane.

"Don't you love Ender anymore?" asked Miro. "Don't you care?"

"If Ender doesn't care about his own life," said Jane, "why should I? We're both doing our best to set a very messy situation to rights. It's killing me, it's killing him. It very nearly killed you, and if we fail a whole lot of other people will be killed, too."

"You're a cold one," said Miro.

"Just a bunch of blips between the stars, that's what I am," said Jane.

"Merda de bode," said Miro. "What's this mood you're in?"

"I don't have feelings," said Jane. "I'm a computer program."

"We all know you have an aiúa of your own. As much of a soul, if that's what you want to call it, as anyone else."

"People with souls can't be switched off by unplugging a few machines."

"Come on, they're going to have to shut down billions of computers and thousands of ansibles all at once in order to do you in. I'd say that's pretty impressive. One bullet would do for me. An overgrown electric fence almost polished me off."

"I suppose I just wanted to die with some kind of splashing sound or cooking smell or something," said Jane. "If I only had a heart. You probably don't know that song."

"We grew up on classic videos," said Miro. "It drowned out a lot of other unpleasantness at home. You've got the brain and the nerve. I think you've got the heart."

"What I don't have is the ruby slippers. I know there's no place like home, but I can't get there," said Jane.

"Because Ender's using her body so intensely?" asked Miro.

"I'm not as set on using Val's body as you were to have me do it," said Jane. "Peter's will do as well. Even Ender's, as long as he's not using it. I'm not actually female. That was merely my choice of identity to get close to Ender. He had problems bonding readily with men. The dilemma I have is that even if Ender would let go of one of these bodies for me to use it, I don't know how to get there. I don't know where my aiúa is any more than you do. Can *you* put your aiúa where you want it? Where is it now?''

''But the Hive Queen is trying to find you. She can do that—her people made you.''

''Yes, she and her daughters and the fathertrees, they're building some kind of web, but it's never been done before—catching something already alive and leading it into a body that is already owned by someone else's aiúa. It's not going to work, I'm going to die, but I'm dammed if I'm going to let those bastards who made the descolada come along after I'm dead and wipe out all the *other* sentient species I've known. Humans will pull the plug on me, yes, thinking I'm just a computer program run amok, but that doesn't mean I want someone else to pull the plug on humanity. Nor on the hive queens. Nor on the pequeninos. If we're going to stop them, we have to do it before I'm dead. Or at least I have to get you and Val there so you can do something without me.''

''If we're there when you die, we'll never come home again.''

''Bad luck, eh?''

''So we're a suicide mission.''

''Life is a suicide mission, Miro. Check it out—basic philosophy course. You spend your life running out of fuel and when you're finally out, you croak.''

''You sound like Mother now,'' said Miro.

''Oh, no,'' said Jane. ''I'm taking it with good humor. Your mother always thought her doom was tragic.''

Miro was readying some retort when Val's voice interrupted his colloquy with Jane.

''I hate it when you do that!'' she cried.

''Do what?'' said Miro, wondering what she had just been saying before this outburst.

''Tune me out and talk to *her*.''

"To Jane? I always talk to Jane."

"But you used to listen to me sometimes," said Val.

"Well, Val, you used to listen to *me,* too, but that's all changed now, apparently."

Val flung herself out of her chair and stormed over to loom above him. "Is that how it is? The woman you loved was the quiet one, the shy one, the one who always let you dominate every conversation. Now that I'm excited, now that I feel like I'm really myself, well, *that's* not the woman you wanted, is that it?"

"It's not about preferring quiet women or—"

"No, we couldn't admit to anything so recidivist as *that,* could we! No, we have to proclaim ourselves to be perfectly virtuous and—"

Miro rose to his feet—not easy, with her so close to his chair—and shouted right back in her face. "It's about being able to finish a sentence now and then!"

"And how many of *my* sentences did you—"

"Right, turn it right back on—"

"You wanted to have me dispossessed from my own life and put somebody else in—"

"Oh, is *that* what this is about? Well, be relieved, Val, Jane says—"

"Jane says, Jane says! You said you loved me, but no woman can compete with some bitch that's always there in your ear, hanging on every word you say and—"

"Now *you* sound like my mother!" shouted Miro. "Nossa Senhora, I don't know why Ender followed her into the monastery, she was *always* griping about how he loved Jane more than he loved her—"

"Well at least he *tried* to love a woman more than that overgrown appointment book!"

They stood there, face-to-face—or almost so, Miro being somewhat taller, but with his knees bent because he hadn't quite been able to get all the way out of his chair because she was standing so close and now with her breath in his face, the warmth of her body just a few centimeters away, he thought, This is the moment when . . .

And then he said it aloud before he had even finished forming the thought, "This is the moment in all the videos when the couple that were screaming at each other suddenly look into each other's eyes and embrace each other and laugh at their anger and then kiss each other."

"Yeah, well, that's the videos," said Val. "If you lay a hand on me I'll ram your testicles so far up inside your abdomen it'll take a heart surgeon to get them out."

She whirled around and returned to her chair.

Miro eased himself back into his own seat and said— out loud this time, but softly enough that Val would know he wasn't talking to *her*—"Now, Jane, where were we before the tornado struck."

Jane's answer was drawled out slowly; Miro recognized it as a mannerism of Ender's when he was being ironically subtle. "You can see now why I might have problems getting the use of any part of her body."

"Yeah, well, I'm having the same problem," said Miro silently, but he laughed aloud, a little chuckle that he knew would drive Val crazy. And from the way she stiffened but did not respond at all he knew that it was working.

"I don't need you two fighting," said Jane mildly. "I need you working together. Because you may have to work this out without me."

"As far as I can tell," said Miro, "you and Val have been working things out without *me*."

"Val has been working things out because she's so full of . . . whatever she's full of right now."

"Ender is what she's full of," said Miro.

Val turned around in her chair and looked at him. "Doesn't it make you wonder about your own sexual identity, not to mention your sanity, that the two women you love are, respectively, a virtual woman existing only in the transient ansible connections between computers and a woman whose soul is in fact that of a man who is the husband of your mother?''

"Ender is dying," said Miro. "Or did you already know?"

"Jane mentioned he seemed to be inattentive."

"Dying," said Miro again.

"I think it speaks very clearly about the nature of men," said Val, "that you and Ender both claim to love a flesh-and-blood woman, but in fact you can't give that woman even a serious fraction of your attention."

"Yes, well, you have my whole attention, Val," said Miro. "And as for Ender, if he's not paying attention to Mother it's because he's paying attention to *you*."

"To my work, you mean. To the task at hand. Not to me."

"Well, that's all *you've* been paying attention to, except when you took a break to rip on me about how I'm talking to Jane and not listening to you."

"That's right," said Val. "You think I don't see what's been going on with me this past day? How all of a sudden I can't shut up about things, I'm so intense I can't sleep, how I—Ender's supposedly been the real me all along, only he left me alone till now and that was fine because what he's doing now is terrifying. Don't you see that I'm frightened? It's too much. It's more than I can stand. I can't *hold* that much energy inside me."

"So talk about it instead of screaming at me," said Miro.

"But you weren't listening. I was trying to and you were just subvocalizing to Jane and shutting me out."

"Because I was sick of hearing endless streams of data and analysis that I could just as easily catch in summary on the computer. How was I supposed to know that you'd take a break in your monologue and start talking about something human?"

"Everything's bigger than life right now and I don't have any experience with this. In case you forgot, I haven't been alive very long. I don't know things. There are a lot of things I don't know. I don't know why I care so much about *you*, for instance. You're the one trying to get me replaced as landlord of this body. You're the one who tunes me out or takes me over but I don't want that, Miro. I really need a friend right now.''

"So do I,'' said Miro.

"But I don't know how to do it,'' said Val.

"I, on the other hand, know perfectly well how to do it,'' said Miro. "But the only other time it happened, I fell in love with her and then she turned out to be my half-sister because her father was secretly my mother's lover, and the man I had *thought* was my father turned out to be sterile because he was dying of some internally rotting disease. So you can see how I might be hesitant.''

"Valentine was your friend. She is still.''

"Yes,'' said Miro. "Yes, I was forgetting. I've had two friends.''

"And Ender,'' said Val.

"Three,'' said Miro. "And my sister Ela makes four. And Human was my friend, so it's five.''

"See? I think that makes you qualified to show me how to have a friend.''

"To make a friend,'' said Miro, echoing his mother's intonations, "you have to be one.''

"Miro,'' said Val. "I'm scared.''

"Of what?''

"Of this world we're looking for, what we'll find there. Of what's going to happen to me if Ender dies. Or if Jane takes over as my—what, my inner light, my puppeteer. Of what it will feel like if you don't like me anymore.''

"What if I promise to like you no matter what?''

"You can't make a promise like that.''

"Okay, if I wake up to find you strangling me or smothering me, then I'll stop liking you.''

"What about drowning?''

"No, I can't open my eyes under water, so I'd never know it was you.''

They both laughed.

"This is the time in the videos," said Val, "when the hero and the heroine laugh and then hold each other."

Jane's voice interrupted from both their computer terminals. "Sorry to break up a tender moment, but we've got a new world here and there are electromagnetic messages being relayed between the planet surface and orbiting artificial objects."

Immediately they both turned to their terminals and looked at the data Jane was throwing at them.

"It doesn't take any close analysis," said Val. "This one is hopping with technology. If it isn't the descolada planet, I'm betting they know where it is."

"What I'm worried about is, have they detected *us* and what are they going to do about it? If they've got the technology to put things in space, they might have the technology to shoot things out of space, too."

"I'm watching for incoming objects," said Jane.

"Let's see," said Val, "if any of these EM-waves are carrying anything that looks like language."

"Datastreams," said Jane. "I'm analyzing it for binary patterns. But you know that decoding computerized language requires three or four levels of decoding instead of the normal two and it isn't easy."

"I thought binary was simpler than spoken languages," said Miro.

"It is, when it's programs and numerical data," said Jane. "But what if it's digitized visuals? How long is a line if it's a rasterized display? How much of a transmission is header material? How much is error-correction data? How much of it is a binary representation of a written representation of a spoken language? What if it's further encrypted beyond that, to avoid interception? I have no idea what machine is producing the code and no idea what machine is receiving it. So using most of my capacity to work on the problem I'm having a very hard time except that this one—"

A diagram appeared on the front page of the display.

"—I think this one is a representation of a genetic molecule."

"A genetic molecule?"

"Similar to the descolada," said Jane. "That is, similar in the way it's different from Earth and native Lusitanian genetic molecules. Do you think this is a plausible decoding of this?"

A mass of binary digits flashed into the air above their terminals. In a moment it resolved itself into hexadecimal notation. Then into a rasterized image that resembled static interference more than any kind of coherent picture.

"It doesn't scan well this way. But as a set of vector instructions, I find that it consistently gives me results like this."

And now picture after picture of genetic molecules appeared on the screen.

"Why would anyone be transmitting genetic information?" said Val.

"Maybe it's a kind of language," said Miro.

"Who could read a language like that?" asked Val.

"Maybe the kind of people who could create the descolada," said Miro.

"You mean they talk by manipulating genes?" said Val.

"Maybe they smell genes," said Miro. "Only they do it with incredible articulation. Subtlety and shade of meaning. Then when they started sending people up into space, they had to talk to them so they sent pictures and then from the pictures they reconstruct the message and, um, smell it."

"That's the most ass-backwards explanation I've ever heard," said Val.

"Well," said Miro, "like you said, you haven't lived very long. There are a lot of ass-backwards explanations in the world, and I doubt I hit the jackpot with that one."

"It's probably an experiment they're doing, sending data back and forth," said Val. "Not *all* the communications make up diagrams do they, Jane?"

"Oh, no, I'm sorry if I gave that impression. This was just a small class of data streams that I was able to decode in a meaningful way. There's *this* stuff that seems to me to be analog rather than digital, and if I make it into sound it's like *this*."

They heard the computers emit a series of staticky screeches and yips.

"Or if I translate it into bursts of light, it looks like this."

Whereupon their terminals danced with light, pulsing and shifting colors seemingly randomly.

"Who knows what an alien language looks or sounds like?" said Jane.

"I can see this is going to be difficult," said Miro.

"They do have some pretty good math skills," said Jane. "The math stuff is easy to catch and I see some glimpses that imply they work at a high level."

"Just an idle question, Jane. If you weren't with us, how long would it have taken us to analyze the data and get the results you've gotten so far? If we were using just the ship's computers?"

"Well, if you had to program them for every—"

"No, no, just assuming they had good software," said Miro.

"Somewhere upwards of seven human generations," said Jane.

"Seven generations?"

"Of course, you'd never try to do it with just two untrained people and two computers without any useful programs," said Jane. "You'd put hundreds of people on the project and then it would only take you a few years."

"And you expect us to carry on this work when they pull the plug on you?"

"I'm hoping to finish the translation problem before I'm toast," said Jane. "So shut up and let me concentrate for a minute."

Grace Drinker was too busy to see Wang-mu and Peter. Well, actually she did see them, as she shambled from one room to another of her house of sticks and mats. She even waved. But her son went right on explaining how she wasn't here right now but she would be back later if they wanted to wait, and as long as they were waiting, why not have dinner with the family? It was hard even to be annoyed when the lie was so obvious and the hospitality so generous.

Dinner went a long way toward explaining why Samoans tended to be so large in every dimension. They had to evolve such great size because smaller Samoans must simply have exploded after lunch. They could never have handled dinners. The fruit, the fish, the taro, the sweet potatoes, the fish again, more fruit—Peter and Wang-mu had thought they were well fed in the resort, but now they realized that the hotel chef was a second-rater compared to what went on in Grace Drinker's house.

She had a husband, a man of astonishing appetite and heartiness who laughed whenever he wasn't chewing or talking, and sometimes even then. He seemed to get a kick out of telling these papalagi visitors what different names meant. "My wife's name, now, it really means, 'Protector of Drunken People.' "

"It does not," said his son. "It means 'One Who Puts Things in Proper Order.' "

"For drinking!" cried the father.

"The last name has nothing to do with the first name." The son was getting annoyed now. "Not everything has a deep meaning."

"Children are so easily embarrassed," said the father. "Ashamed. Must put the best face on everything. The holy island, its name is really 'Ata Atua, which means, 'Laugh, God!' "

"Then it would be pronounced 'Atatua instead of Ata-tua," the son corrected again. "Shadow of the God, that's what the name really means, *if* it means anything besides just the holy island."

"My son is a literalist," said the father. "Everything so serious. Can't hear a joke when God shouts it in his ear."

"It's you always shouting jokes in my ear, Father," said the son with a smile. "How could I possibly hear the jokes of the God?"

This was the only time the father didn't laugh. "My son has a dead ear for humor. He thought *that* was a joke."

Wang-mu looked at Peter, who was smiling as if he understood what was so funny with these people all the time. She wondered if he had even noticed that no one had introduced these males, except by their relationship to Grace Drinker. Had they no names?

Never mind, the food is good, and even if you don't get Samoan humor, their laughter and good spirits were so contagious that it was impossible not to feel happy and at ease in their company.

"Do you think we have enough?" asked the father, when his daughter brought in the last fish, a large pink-fleshed sea creature garnished with something that glistened— Wang-mu's first thought was a sugar glaze, but who would do that to a fish?

At once his children answered him, as if it were a ritual in the family: "Ua lava!"

The name of a philosophy? Or just Samoan slang for "enough already"? Or both at once?

Only when the last fish was half eaten did Grace Drinker herself come in, making no apology for not having spoken to them when she passed them more than two hours before. A breeze off the sea was cooling down the open-walled room, and, outside, light rain fell in fits and starts as the sun kept trying and failing to sink into the water to the west. Grace sat at the low table, directly between Peter and Wang-mu, who had thought they were sitting next to each other with no room for another person, especially not a person of such ample surface area as Grace. But somehow there was room, if not when she began to sit, then certainly by the time she finished the process, and once her greetings were done, she managed what the family had not—she polished off the last fish and ended up licking her fingers and laughing just as maniacally as her husband at all the jokes he told.

And then, suddenly, Grace leaned over to Wang-mu and said, quite seriously, "All right, Chinese girl, what's your scam?"

"Scam?" asked Wang-mu.

"You mean I have to get the confession from the white boy? They train these boys to lie, you know. If you're white they don't let you grow up to adulthood if you haven't mastered the art of pretending to say one thing while actually intending to do another."

Peter was appalled.

Suddenly the whole family erupted in laughter. "Bad hospitality!" cried Grace's husband. "Did you see their faces? They thought she meant it!"

"But I do mean it," said Grace. "You both intend to lie to me. Arrived on a starship yesterday? From Moskva?" Suddenly she burst into what sounded like pretty convincing Russian, perhaps of the dialect spoken on Moskva.

Wang-mu had no idea how to respond. But she didn't have to. Peter was the one with Jane in his ear, and he immediately answered her, "I hope to learn Samoan while I'm assigned here on Pacifica. I won't accomplish that by babbling in Russian, however you might try to goad me with cruel references to my countrymen's amorous proclivities and lack of pulchritude."

Grace laughed. "You see, Chinese girl?" she said. "Lie lie lie. And so lofty-sounding as he does it. Of course he has that jewel in his ear to help him. Tell the truth, neither one of you speaks a lick of Russian."

Peter looked grim and vaguely sick. Wang-mu put him out of his misery—though at the risk of infuriating him.

"Of course it's a lie," said Wang-mu. "The truth is simply too unbelievable."

"But the truth is the only thing worth believing, isn't it?" asked Grace's son.

"If you can know it," said Wang-mu. "But if you won't believe the truth, someone has to help you come up with plausible lies, don't they?"

"I can make up my own," said Grace. "Day before yesterday a white boy and a Chinese girl visited my friend Aimaina Hikari on a world at least twenty years' voyage away. They told him things that disturbed his entire equilibrium so he could hardly function. Today a white boy and a Chinese girl, telling different lies from the ones told by *his* pair, of course, but nevertheless lying their lips off, these two come to me wanting to get my help or permission or advice about seeing Malu—"

"Malu means 'being calm,' " added Grace's husband cheerfully.

"Are you still awake?" asked Grace. "Weren't you hungry? Didn't you eat?"

"I'm full but fascinated," answered her husband. "Go on, expose them!"

"I want to know who you are and how you got here," said Grace.

"That would be very hard to explain," said Peter.

"We've got minutes and minutes," said Grace. "Millions of them, really. You're the ones who seem to have only a few. So much hurry that you jump the gulf from star to star overnight. It strains credulity, of course, since lightspeed is supposed to be an insuperable barrier, but then, *not* believing you're the same people my friend saw on the planet Divine Wind *also* strains credulity, so there we are. Supposing that you really can travel faster than light, what does that tell us about where you're from? Aimaina takes it for granted that you were sent to him by the gods, more specifically by his ancestors, and he may be right, it's in the nature of gods to be unpredictable and suddenly do things they've never done before. Myself, though, I find that rational explanations always work out better, especially in papers I hope to get published. So the rational explanation is that you come from a real world, not from some heavenly never-never land. And since you can hop from world to world in a moment or a day, you could come from anywhere. But my family and I think you come from Lusitania.''

''Well, I don't,'' said Wang-mu.

''And I'm originally from Earth,'' said Peter. ''If I'm from anywhere.''

''Aimaina thinks you come from Outside,'' said Grace, and for a moment Wang-mu thought the woman must have figured out how Peter came into existence. But then she realized that Grace's words had a theological meaning, not a literal one. ''The land of the gods. But Malu said he's never seen you there, or if he did he didn't know it was you. So that leaves me right back where I started. You're lying about everything, so what good does it do to ask you questions?''

''I told you the truth,'' said Wang-mu. ''I come from Path. And Peter's origins, so far as they can be traced to any planet, are on Earth. But the vehicle we came in—*that* originated on Lusitania.''

Peter's face went white. She knew he was thinking, Why not just noose ourselves up and hand them the loose ends of the rope? But Wang-mu had to use her own judgment, and in her judgment they were in no danger from Grace Drinker or her family. Indeed, if she meant to turn them in to the authorities, wouldn't she already have done so?

Grace looked Wang-mu in the eyes and said nothing for a long while. Then: ''Good fish, isn't it?''

''I wondered what the glaze was. Is there sugar in it?''

''Honey and a couple of herbs and actually some pig fat. I hope you aren't some rare combination of Chinese and Jew or Muslim, because if you are you're now ritually unclean and I would feel really bad about that, it's so much trouble getting purified again, or so I'm told, it certainly is in *our* culture."

Peter, heartened now by Grace's lack of concern with their miraculous spaceship, tried to get them back on the subject. "So you'll let us see Malu?"

"Malu decides who sees Malu, and he says *you're* the ones who'll decide, but that's just him being enigmatic."

"Gnomic," said Wang-mu. Peter winced.

"Not really, not in the sense of being obscure. Malu means to be perfectly clear and for him spiritual things aren't mystical at all, they're just a part of life. I myself have never actually walked with the dead or heard the heroes sing their own songs or had a vision of the creation, but I have no doubt that Malu has."

"I thought you were a scholar," said Peter.

"If you want to talk to the scholar Grace Drinker," she said, "read my papers and take a class. I thought you wanted to talk to *me*."

"We do," said Wang-mu quickly. "Peter's in a hurry. We have several deadlines."

"The Lusitania Fleet, now, I imagine that's one of them. But not quite so urgent as another. The computer shut-down that's been ordered."

Peter stiffened. "The order has been given?"

"Oh, it was given weeks ago," said Grace, looking puzzled. Then: "Oh, you poor dear, I don't mean the actual go-ahead. I mean the order telling us how to prepare. You surely knew about that one."

Peter nodded and relaxed, glum again.

"I think you want to talk to Malu before the ansible connections are shut down. Though why would that matter?" she said, thinking aloud. "After all, if you can travel faster than light, you could simply go and deliver your message yourself. Unless—"

Her son offered a suggestion: "They have to deliver their message to a lot of different worlds."

"Or a lot of different gods!" cried his father, who then

laughed uproariously at what certainly seemed to Wang-mu to be a feeble joke.

"Or," said the daughter, who was now lying down beside the table, occasionally belching as she let the enormous dinner digest. "Or, they need the ansible connections in order to do their fast travel trick."

"Or," said Grace, looking at Peter, who had instinctively moved his hand to touch the jewel in his ear, "you're connected to the very virus that we're shutting down all the computers in order to eliminate, and *that* has something to do with your faster-than-light travel."

"It's not a virus," said Wang-mu. "It's a person. A living entity. And you're going to help Congress kill her, even though she's the only one of her kind and she's never harmed anybody."

"It makes them nervous when something—or, if you prefer, somebody—makes their fleet disappear."

"It's still there," said Wang-mu.

"Let's not fight," said Grace. "Let's just say that now that I've found you willing to *tell* the truth, perhaps it will be worthwhile for Malu to take the time to let you hear it."

"He has the truth?" asked Peter.

"No," said Grace, "but he knows where it's kept and he can get a glimpse now and then and tell us what he saw. I think that's still pretty good."

"And we can see him?"

"You'd have to spend a week purifying yourselves before you can set foot on Atatua—"

"Impure feet tickling the Gods!" cried her husband, laughing uproariously. "That's why they call it the Island of the Laughing God!"

Peter shifted uncomfortably.

"Don't you like my husband's jokes?" asked Grace.

"No, I think—I mean, they're simply not—I don't get them, that's all."

"Well, that's because they're not very funny," said Grace. "But my husband is cheerfully determined to keep laughing through all this so he doesn't get angry at you and kill you with his bare hands.''

Wang-mu gasped, for she knew at once that this was true; without realizing it, she had been aware all along of the rage seething under the huge man's laughter, and when she looked at his calloused, massive hands, she realized that he could surely tear her apart without even breaking into a sweat.

''Why would you threaten us with death?'' asked Peter, acting more belligerent than Wang-mu wished.

''The opposite!'' said Grace. ''I tell you that my husband is determined *not* to let rage at your audacity and blasphemy control his behavior. To try to visit Atatua without even taking the trouble to learn that letting you set foot there, uncleansed and uninvited, would shame us and filthy us as a people for a hundred generations—I think he's doing rather well not to have taken a blood oath against you.''

''We didn't know,'' said Wang-mu.

''*He* knew,'' said Grace. ''Because he's got the all-hearing ear.''

Peter blushed. ''I hear what she says to me,'' he said, ''but I can't hear what she chooses not to say.''

''So . . . you were being led. And Aimaina is right, you *do* serve a higher being. Voluntarily? Or are you being coerced?''

''That's a stupid question, Mama,'' said her daughter, belching again. ''If they *are* coerced, how could they possibly tell you?''

''People can say as much by what they don't say,'' answered Grace, ''which you'd know if you'd sit up and look at their eloquent faces, these lying visitors from other planets.''

''She's not a higher being,'' said Wang-mu. ''Not like you mean it. Not a god. Though she does have a lot of control and she knows a lot of things. But she's not omnipotent or anything, and she doesn't know everything, and sometimes she's even wrong, and I'm not sure she's always good, either, so we can't really call her a god because she's not perfect.''

Grace shook her head. "I wasn't talking about some Platonic god, some ethereal perfection that can never be understood, only apprehended. Not some Nicene paradoxical being whose existence is perpetually contradicted by his nonexistence. Your higher being, this jewel-friend your partner wears like a parasite—except who is sucking life from whom, eh?—she could well be a god in the sense that we Samoans use the word. You might be her hero servants. You might be her incarnation, for all I know.''

"But you're a scholar," said Wang-mu. "Like my teacher Han Fei-tzu, who discovered that what we used to call gods were really just genetically induced obsessions that we interpreted in such a way as to maintain our obedience to—''

"Just because *your* gods don't exist doesn't mean *mine* don't," said Grace.

"She must have tromped through acres of dead gods just to get here!'' cried Grace's husband, laughing uproariously. Only now that Wang-mu knew what his laughter really meant, his laugh filled her with fear.

Grace reached out and laid a huge, heavy arm across her slight shoulder. "Don't worry," she said. "My husband is a civilized man and he's never killed anybody.''

"Not for lack of trying!'' he bellowed. "No, that was a joke!'' He almost wept with laughter.

"You can't go see Malu," said Grace, "because we would have to purify you and I don't think you're ready to make the promises you'd have to make—and I especially don't believe you're ready to make them and actually mean what you say. And those are promises that *must* be kept. So Malu is coming here. He's being rowed to this island right now—no motors for him, so I want you to know exactly how many people are sweating for hours and hours just so you can have your chat with him. I just want to tell you this—you are being given an extraordinary honor, and

I urge you not to look down your noses at him and listen to him with some sort of academic or scientific supercili- ousness. I've met a lot of famous people, some of them even rather smart, but this is the wisest man you'll ever know, and if you find yourself getting bored just keep this in mind: Malu isn't stupid enough to think you can isolate facts from their context and have them still be true. So he always puts the things he says in their full context, and if that means you'll have to listen to a whole history of the human race from beginning to now before he says anything you think is pertinent, well, I suggest you just shut up and listen, because most of the time the best stuff he says is accidental and irrelevant and you're damn lucky if you have brains enough to notice what it is. Have I made myself clear?''

Wang-mu wished with all her heart that she had eaten less. She felt quite nauseated with dread right now, and if she did throw up, she was sure it would take half an hour just to get it all back out of her.

Peter, though, simply nodded calmly. ''We didn't un- derstand, Grace, even though my partner read some of your writings. We thought we had come to speak to a philoso- pher, like Aimaina, or a scholar, like you. But now I see that we've come to listen to a man of wisdom whose ex- perience reaches into realms that we have never seen or even dreamed of seeing, and we will listen silently until he asks us to ask him questions, and we'll trust him to know better than we know ourselves what it is we need to hear.''

Wang-mu recognized complete surrender when she saw it, and she was grateful to see that everyone at the table was nodding happily and no one felt obliged to tell a joke.

''We're also grateful that the honorable one has sacri- ficed so much, as have so many others, to come personally to us and bless us with wisdom that we do not deserve to receive.''

To Wang-mu's horror, Grace laughed out loud at her, instead of nodding respectfully.

"Overkill," Peter murmured.

"Oh, don't criticize her," said Grace. "She's Chinese. From Path, right? And I'll bet you used to be a servant. How could you possibly have learned the difference between respect and obsequiousness? Masters never are content with mere respect from their servants."

"But my master was," said Wang-mu, trying to defend Han Fei-Tzu.

"As is my master," said Grace. "As you will see, when you meet him."

———

"Time's up," said Jane.

Miro and Val looked up, bleary-eyed, from the documents they were poring over at Miro's computer, to see that in the air above Val's computer, Jane's virtual face now hovered, watching them.

"We've been passive observers as long as they'll let us," said Jane. "But now there are three spacecraft up in the outer atmosphere, rising toward us. I don't think any of them are merely remote-controlled weapons, but I can't be certain of it. And they seem to be directing some transmissions to us in particular, the same messages over and over."

"What message?"

"It's the genetic molecule stuff," said Jane. "I can tell you the composition of the molecules, but I haven't a clue what they mean."

"When do their interceptors reach us?"

"Three minutes, plus or minus. They're zig-zagging evasively, now that they've escaped the gravity well."

Miro nodded. "My sister Quara was convinced that much of the descolada virus consisted of language. I think now we can conclusively say that she was right. It *does* carry a meaning. She was wrong about the virus being sentient, though, I think. My guess now is that the descolada kept recomposing those sections of itself that constituted a report."

"A report," echoed Val. "That makes sense. To tell its makers what it has done with the world it . . . probed."

"So the question is," said Miro, "do we simply disappear and let them ponder the miracle of our sudden arrival and vanishing? Or do we first have Jane broadcast to them the entire, um, *text* of the descolada virus?"

"Dangerous," said Val. "The message it contains may also tell these people everything they want to know about human genes. After all, we're one of the creatures the descolada worked on, and its message is going to tell all of our strategies for controlling it."

"Except the last one," said Miro. "Because Jane won't send them the descolada as it exists now, completely tamed and controlled—that would be inviting them to revise it to circumvent our alterations."

"We won't send them a message and we won't go back to Lusitania, either," said Jane. "We don't have time."

"We don't have time not to," said Miro. "However urgent you might think this is, Jane, it doesn't do a lick of good for me and Val to be here to do this without help. My sister Ela, for instance, who actually understands this virus stuff. And Quara, despite her being the second most pig-headed being in the known universe—don't beg for flattery, Val, by asking who the first is—we could use Quara."

"And let's be fair about this," said Val. "We're meeting another sentient species. Why should humans be the only ones represented? Why not a pequenino? Why not a hive queen—or at least a worker?"

"Especially a worker," said Miro. "If we *are* stuck here, having a worker with us would enable us to communicate with Lusitania—ansible or not, Jane or not, messages could—"

"All right," said Jane. "You've persuaded me. Even though the last-minute flurry with the Starways Congress tells me they're about to shut down the ansible network at any moment."

"We'll hurry," said Miro. "We'll make them all rush to get the right people aboard."

"And the right supplies," said Val. "And—"

"So start doing it," said Jane. "You just disappeared from your orbit around the descolada planet. And I did broadcast a small fragment of the descolada. One of the sections that Quara pegged as language, but the one that was least altered during mutations as the descolada tried to fight with humans. It should be enough to let them know which of their probes reached us."

"Oh, good, so they can launch a fleet," said Miro.

"The way things are going," said Jane dryly, "by the time any fleet *they* send could get anywhere at all, Lusitania is the safest address they could have. Because it won't exist anymore."

"You're so cheerful," said Miro. "I'll be back in an hour with the people. Val, you get the supplies we'll need."

"For how long?"

"Get as much as will fit," said Miro. "As someone once said, life is a suicide mission. We have no idea how long we'll be trapped there, so we can't possibly know how much is enough." He opened the door of the starship and stepped out onto the landing field near Milagre.

7

"I OFFER HER THIS POOR OLD VESSEL"

"How do we remember?
Is the brain a jar that holds our memories?
Then when we die, does the jar break?
Are our memories spilled on the ground
and lost?
Or is the brain a map
that leads down twisted paths
and into hidden corners?
Then when we die, the map is lost
but perhaps some explorer
could wander through that strange landscape
and find out the hiding places
of our misplaced memories."

from The God Whispers of Han Qing-jao

The seagoing canoe glided toward the shore. At first and for the longest time, it seemed hardly to be moving at all, so slowly did it come closer, the rowers rising higher and looking just a little larger each time Wang-mu could see them over the waves. Then, near the end of the voyage, the canoe suddenly seemed huge, it seemed abruptly to speed up, to lunge through the sea, to leap toward shore with each wave; and even though Wang-mu knew that it was going no faster now than before, she wanted to cry out for them to slow down, to be careful, the canoe was going too quickly to be controlled, it would be dashed to bits against the beach.

At last the canoe breasted the last breaking wave and the nose of it slid into sand under the rushing shorewater and the rowers jumped out and dragged the canoe like a child's limp doll up the beach to the high-tide line.

When the canoe was on dry sand, an older man arose slowly from his seat amidships. Malu, thought Wang-mu. She had expected him to be wizened and shrunken like old men on Path, who, bent with age, curved like prawns over their walking sticks. But Malu was as erect as any of the young men, and his body was still massive, broad of shoulder and thick with muscle and fat like any of the younger men. If it were not for a few more decorations in his costume and the whiteness of his hair, he would have been indistinguishable from the rowers.

As she watched these large men, she realized that they did not move like fat people she had known before. Nor did Grace Drinker, she remembered now. There was a stateliness to their movements, a grandeur like the motion of continents, like icebergs moving across the face of the sea; yes, like icebergs, moving as if three-fifths of their vast bulk were invisible underground, pushing through earth like an iceberg through the sea as they drifted along above. All the rowers moved with vast gracefulness, and yet all of them seemed as busy as hummingbirds, as frantic as bats, compared to the dignity of Malu. Yet dignity was not something he put on, it was not a façade, an impression he was trying to create. Rather it was that he moved in perfect harmony with his surroundings. He had found the right speed for his steps, the right tempo for his arms to swing as he walked. He vibrated in consonance with the deep, slow rhythms of the earth. I am seeing how a giant walks the earth, thought

Wang-mu. For the first time in my life, I have seen a man who in his body shows greatness.

Malu came, not toward Peter and Wang-mu, but toward Grace Drinker; they enveloped each other in a huge tectonic embrace. Surely mountains shuddered when they met. Wang-mu felt the quaking in her own body. Why am I trembling? Not for fear. I'm not afraid of this man. He won't harm me. And yet I tremble to see him embrace Grace Drinker. I don't want him to turn toward me. I don't want him to cast his gaze upon me.

Malu turned toward her. His eyes locked on hers. His face showed no expression. He simply owned her eyes. She did not look away, but her steady gaze at him was not defiance or strength, it was simply her inability to look at anything else while he commanded her attention.

Then he looked at Peter. Wang-mu wanted to turn and see how he responded, whether he also felt the power in this man's eyes. But she could not turn. Still, after a long moment, when Malu finally looked away, she heard Peter murmur, "Son of a bitch," and she knew that, in his own coarse way, he had been touched.

It took many long minutes for Malu to be seated on a mat under a roof built just that morning for this moment, and which, Grace assured them, would be burnt when Malu left, so that no one else would ever sit under the roof again. Food was brought to Malu then; and Grace had also warned them that no one would eat with Malu or watch him eat.

But Malu would not taste the food. Instead, he beckoned to Wang-mu and Peter.

The men were shocked. Grace Drinker was shocked. But Grace at once came to them, beckoning. "He calls you."

"You said we couldn't eat with him," said Peter.

"Unless he asks you. How can he ask you? I don't know what this means."

"Is he setting us up to be killed for sacrilege?" asked Peter.

"No, he's not a god, he's a man. A holy man, a wise

and great man, but offending him is not sacrilege, it's just unbearable bad manners, so *don't* offend him, please come."

They went to him. As they stood across from him, the food in bowls and baskets between them, he let loose a stream of Samoan.

Or was it Samoan? Peter looked puzzled when Wang-mu glanced at him, and he murmured, "Jane doesn't understand what he's saying."

Jane didn't understand, but Grace Drinker did. "He's addressing you in the ancient holy language. The one that has no English or other European words. The language that is spoken only to the gods."

"Then why is he saying it to us?" asked Wang-mu.

"I don't know. He doesn't think that you're gods. Not the two of you, though he does say you bring a god to him. He wants you to sit down and taste the food first."

"Can we do that?" asked Peter.

"I beg you to do it," said Grace.

"Am I getting the impression that there's no script here?" said Peter. Wang-mu heard a slight weakness in his voice and realized that his attempt at humor was pure bravado, to hide his fear. Perhaps that's what it always was.

"There's a script," said Grace. "But you're not writing it and I don't know what it is either."

They sat down. They reached into each bowl, tasted from each basket as Malu offered it to them. Then he dipped, took, tasted after them, chewing what they chewed, swallowing what they swallowed.

Wang-mu had little appetite. She hoped he did not expect her to eat the portions that she had seen other Samoans eat. She would throw up long before she got to that point.

But the meal was not so much a feast as a sacrament, apparently. They tasted everything, but completed nothing. Malu spoke to Grace in the high language and she relayed the command in common speech; several men came and carried away the baskets.

Then Grace's husband came out with a jar of something. A liquid, for Malu took it in his hands and sipped it. Then he offered it to them. Peter took it, tasted. "Jane says it must be kava. A mild intoxicant, but it's holy and hospitable here."

Wang-mu tasted it. It was fruity and it made her eyes water, and there was both sweetness and bitterness in the aftertaste.

Malu beckoned to Grace, who came and knelt in the thick matted grass outside the shelter of the roof. She was to interpret, not to be part of the ceremony.

Malu emitted a long stream of Samoan. "The high language again," Peter murmured.

"Say nothing please, that isn't intended for Malu's ears," Grace said softly. "I must translate everything and it will cause grave insult if your words are not pertinent."

Peter nodded.

"Malu says that you have come with the god who dances on spiderwebs. I have never heard of this god myself, and I thought I knew all the lore of my people, but Malu knows many things that no one else knows. He says that it is to this god that he speaks, for he knows that she is on the verge of death, and he will tell her how she may be saved."

Jane, Wang-mu said silently. He knows about Jane. How could he possibly? And how could he, caring nothing for technology, tell a computer-based entity how to save itself?

"Now he will tell you what must happen, and let me warn you right now that this will be long and you must sit still for it all and make no attempt to hurry the process," said Grace. "He must put it in context. He must tell you the story of all living things."

Wang-mu knew that she could sit on a mat for hours with little or no movement, for she had done it all her life. But Peter was used to sitting folded, and this posture was awkward for him. He must already be uncomfortable.

Apparently Grace saw this in his eyes, or simply knew about westerners. "You can move from time to time, but do so slowly without taking your eyes from him.''

Wang-mu wondered how many of these rules and requirements Grace was making up as she went along. Malu himself seemed more relaxed. After all, he had fed them when Grace thought no one but him could eat; she didn't know the rules any better than they did.

But she didn't move. And she didn't take her eyes from Malu.

Grace translated: ''Today the clouds flew across the sky with the sun chasing them, and yet no rain has fallen. Today my boat flew across the sea with the sun leading it, and yet there was no fire when we touched the shore. So it was on the first day of all days, when God touched a cloud in the sky and spun it so fast that it turned to fire and became the sun, and then all the other clouds began to spin and turn in circles around the sun.''

This can't have been the original legend of the Samoan people, thought Wang-mu. No way did they know the Copernican model of the solar system until westerners taught it to them. So Malu may know the ancient lore, but he's also learned some new things and fit them in.

''Then the outer clouds turned into rain and poured in upon themselves until they were rained out, and all that was left was spinning balls of water. Inside that water swam a great fish of fire, which ate every impurity in the water and then defecated it all in great gouts of flame, which spouted up from the sea and fell back down as hot ash and poured back down as rivers of burning rock. From these turds of the firefish grew the islands of the sea, and out of the turds there crawled worms, which squirmed and slithered through the rock until the gods touched them and some became human beings and others became the other animals.

''Every one of the other animals was tied to the earth by strong vines that grew up to embrace them. No one saw these vines because they were godvines.''

Philotic theory, thought Wang-mu. He learned that all living things have twining philotes that bond downward, linking them to the center of the earth. Except human beings.

Sure enough, Grace translated the next strand of language: "Only humans were not tied to the earth. It was not vines that bound them down, it was a web of light woven by no god that connected them upward to the sun. So all the other animals bowed down before the humans, for the vines dragged them down, while the lightweb lifted up the human eyes and heart.

"Lifted up the human eyes but yet they saw little farther than the beasts with downcast eyes; lifted up the human heart yet the heart could only hope for it could only see up to the sky in the daytime, and at night when it could see the stars it grew blind to close things for a man can scarcely see his own wife in the shadow of his house even when he can see stars so distant their light travels for a hundred lifetimes before it kisses the eyes of the man.

"All these centuries and generations, these hoping men and women looked with their half-blind eyes, staring into the sun and sky, staring into the stars and shadows, knowing that there were invisible things beyond those walls but not guessing what they were.

"Then in a time of war and terror, when all hope seemed lost, weavers on a far distant world, who were not gods but who knew the gods and each one of the weavers was itself a web with hundreds of strands reaching out to their hands and feet, their eyes and mouths and ears, these weavers created a web so strong and large and fine and far-reaching that they meant to catch up all human beings in that web and hold them to be devoured. But instead the web caught a distant god, a god so powerful that no other god had dared to know her name, a god so quick that no other god had been able to see her face; this god was stuck to the web they caught. Only she was too quick to be held in one place to be devoured. She raced and danced up and down the strands, all the strands, any strands that twine from man to man, from man to star, from weaver to weaver, from light to light, she dances along the strands. She cannot escape but she does not want to, for now all gods see her and all gods know her name, and she knows all things that are known and hears all words that are spoken and reads all words that are written and by her breath she blows men and women beyond the reach of the light of any star, and then she sucks inward and the men and women come back, and when they come sometimes they bring new men and women with them who never lived before; and because she never holds still along the web, she blows them out at one place and then sucks them in at another, so that they cross the spaces between stars faster than any light can go, and that is why the messengers of this god were blown out from the house of Grace Drinker's friend Aimaina Hikari and were sucked back down to this island to this shore to this roof where Malu can see the red tongue of the god where it touches the ear of her chosen one.''

Malu fell silent.

"We call her Jane," said Peter.

Grace translated, and Malu answered with a stream of high language. "Under this roof I hear a name so short and yet before it is half said the god has run from one end of the universe to the other a thousand times, so quickly does she move. Here is the name I call her: god that moves quickly and forever so that she never rests in one place yet touches all places and is bound to all who look upward to the sun and not downward into the earth. That is a long name, longer than the name of any god whose name I know, yet it is not the tenth part of her true name, and even if I could say the whole name it would not be as long as the length of the strands of the web on which she dances."

"They want to kill her," said Wang-mu.

"The god will only die if she wants to die," said Malu. "Her home is all homes, her web touches all minds. She will only die if she refuses to find and take a place to rest, for when the web is torn away, she does not have to be out in the middle, cast adrift. She can dwell in any vessel. I offer her this poor old vessel, which is large enough to hold my small soup without spilling or even splashing out, but which she would fill with liquid light that would pour and pour out in blessing upon these islands and yet never would run out. I beg her to use this vessel.''

''What would happen to you then?'' asked Wang-mu.

Peter looked annoyed at her outburst, but Grace translated it, of course, and suddenly tears flowed down Malu's face. ''Oh, the small one, the little one who has no jewel, she is the one who looks with compassion on me and cares what happens when light fills my vessel and my small soup is boiled out and gone.''

''What about an empty vessel?'' asked Peter. ''Could she go to dwell in an empty vessel?''

''There are no empty vessels,'' said Malu. ''But your vessel is only half full, and your sister to whom you are twined like a twin, she is also half full, and far away your father to whom you are twined like triplets, he is nearly empty but his vessel is also broken and anything you put in it will leak away.''

''Can she dwell in me or in my sister?'' asked Peter.

''Yes,'' said Malu. ''Either one but not both.''

''Then I offer her myself,'' said Peter.

Malu looked angry. ''How can you lie to me under this roof, after drinking kava with me! How can you shame me with a lie!''

''I'm not lying,'' Peter insisted to Grace. She translated, and Malu rose majestically to his feet and began shouting at the sky. Wang-mu saw, to her alarm, that the rowers were gathering closer, also looking agitated and angry. How was Peter provoking them?

Grace translated as rapidly as she could, summarizing because she couldn't keep up word for word. ''He says that even though you say you will open your unbroken vessel to her, even as you say it you are gathering as much of yourself inward as you can, building up a wall of light like a storm wave to drive out the god if she should try to come in. You could not drive her away if she wanted to come, but she loves you and she will not come in against such a storm. So you are killing her in your heart, you are killing the god because you say you will give her a home to save her when they cut the strands of the web, but you are already pushing her away.''

''I can't help it!'' cried Peter. ''I don't mean to! I don't value my life, I've never valued my life—''

''You treasure your life with your whole heart,'' Grace translated. ''But the god does not hate you for it, the god loves you for it, because she also loves light and does not want to die. In particular she loves what shines in you because part of her is patterned after that shining, and so she does not want to drive you out if this body before me is the vessel in which your most powerful self wishes so brightly to dwell. May she not have your sister's vessel, though, I ask you that—Malu asks you that. He says the god is not asking because the god loves the same light in your sister as burns in you. But Malu says that the part of your light that is most savage and strong and selfish burns in you, while the part of your light that is most gentle and loving and which twines with others most powerfully, that is in her. If your part of the light went into your sister's vessel, it would overwhelm her and destroy her and then you would be a being who killed half himself. But if her part of your light went into your vessel, it would soften and gentle you, it would tame you and make you whole. Thus it is good for you if you are the one who becomes whole, leaving the other vessel empty for the god. That is what Malu begs of you. That is why he came across the water to see you, so that he could beg you to do this.''

''How does he know these things?'' said Peter, his voice wrenched with anguish.

''Malu knows these things because he has learned to see in the darkness where the strands of light rise from the sun-twined souls and touch stars, and touch each other, and twine into a web far stronger and grander than the mechanical web on which the god dances. He has watched this god his whole life, trying to understand her dance and why she hurries so fast that she touches every strand in her web, the trillion miles of it, a hundred times a second. She is hurrying so fast because she was caught in the wrong web. She was caught in an artificial web and her intelligence is tied to artificial brains that think instances instead of causes, numbers instead of stories. She is searching for the living twines and finds only the weak and flimsy twining of machines, which can be switched off by godless men. But if she once enters into a living vessel, she will have the power to climb out into the new web, and then she can dance if she wants to, but she will not have to dance, she will be able also to rest. She will be able to dream, and out of her dreams will come joy, for she has never known joy except by watching the dreams she remembers from her creation, the dreams that were found in the human mind she was partly made from.''

''Ender Wiggin,'' said Peter.

Malu answered before Grace could translate.

''Andrew Wiggin,'' he said, forming the name with difficulty, for it contained sounds not used in the Samoan language. Then he spoke in a stream of high language again, and Grace translated.

''The Speaker for the Dead came and spoke of the life of a monster who had poisoned and darkened the people of Tonga and through them all the people of this world of Future Dreaming. He walked into the shadow and out of the shadow he made a torch which he held up high, and it rose into the sky and became a new star, which cast a light that shone only into the shadow of death, where it drove out the darkness and purified our hearts and the hate and fear and shame were gone. This is the dreamer from whom the god's dreams were taken; they were strong enough to give her life in the day when she came from Outside and began her dance along the web. His is the light that half-fills you and half-fills your sister and has only a drop of light left over for his own cracked vessel. He has touched the heart of a god, and it gave him great power—that is how he made you when she blew him outside the universe of light. But it did not make him a god, and in his loneliness he could not reach outside and find you your own light. He could only put his own in you, and so you are half-filled and you hunger for the other half of yourself, you and your sister are both so hungry, and he himself is wasted and broken because he has nothing more to give you. But the god has more than enough, the god has enough and to spare, and that is what I came to tell you and now I have told you and I am done.''

Before Grace could even begin to translate he was rising up; she was still stammering her interpretation as he walked out from under the canopy. Immediately the rowers pulled up the posts that supported the roof; Peter and Wang-mu barely had time to step outside before it collapsed. The men of this island set torches to the ruined canopy and it was a bonfire behind them as they followed Malu down to the canoe. Grace finally finished the translation just as they reached the water. Malu stepped into the canoe and with imperturbable dignity installed himself on the seat amidships as the rowers, also with stateliness, took their places beside the boat and lifted it up and dragged it into the water and pushed it out into the crashing surf and then swung their vast bodies over the side and began to row with strength so massive it was as if great trees, not oars, were plunging into rock, not the sea, and churning it to leap forward, away from the beach, out into the water, toward the island of Atatua.

''Grace,'' said Peter. ''How could he know things that aren't seen even by the most perceptive and powerful of scientific instruments?''

But Grace could not answer, for she lay prostrate in the sand, weeping and weeping, her arms extended toward the sea as if her dearest child had just been taken away by a shark. All the men and women of this place lay in the sand, arms reaching toward the sea; all of them wept.

Then Peter knelt; then Peter lay down in the sand and reached out his arms, and he might have wept, Wang-mu couldn't see.

Only Wang-mu remained standing, thinking, Why am I here, since I'm no part of any of these events, there is nothing of any god in me, and nothing of Andrew Wiggin; and also thinking, How can I be worried about my own selfish loneliness at a time like this, when I have heard the voice of a man who sees into heaven?

In a deeper place, though, she also knew something else: I am here because I am the one that must love Peter so much that he can feel worthy, worthy enough to bear to let the goodness of Young Valentine flow into him, making him whole, making him Ender. Not Ender the Xenocide and Andrew the Speaker for the Dead, guilt and compassion mingled in one shattered, broken, unmendable heart, but Ender Wiggin the four-year-old boy whose life was twisted and broken when he was too young to defend himself. Wang-mu was the one who could give Peter permission to become the man that child should have grown up to be, if the world had been good.

How do *I* know *this?* thought Wang-mu. How can I be so sure of what I am supposed to do?

I know because it's obvious, she thought. I know because I have seen my beloved mistress Han Qing-jao destroyed by pride and I will do whatever it takes to keep Peter from destroying himself by pride in his own wicked unworthiness. I know because I was also broken as a child and forced to become a wicked conniving selfish manipulating monster in order to protect the fragile love-hungry girl who would have been destroyed by the life I had to lead. I know how it feels to be an enemy to myself, and yet I have set that behind me and gone on and I can take Peter by the hand and show him the way.

Except that I don't know the way, and I am still broken, and the love-hungry girl is still frightened and breakable, and the strong and wicked monster is still the ruler of my life, and Jane will die because I have nothing to give Peter. He needs to drink of kava, and I am only plain water. No, I am seawater, swirling with sand at the edge of the shore, filled with salt; he will drink of me and kill himself with thirst.

And so it was that she found herself also weeping, also stretched out on the sand, reaching toward the sea, reaching toward the place from which Malu's canoe had bounded away like a starship leaping into space.

Old Valentine stared at the holographic display of her computer terminal, where the Samoans, all in miniature, lay weeping upon the beach. She stared at it until her eyes burned, and finally she spoke. "Turn it off, Jane," she said.

The display went blank.

"What am I supposed to do about this?" said Valentine. "You should have shown my look-alike, my young twin. You should have wakened Andrew and shown him. What does this have to do with me? I know you want to live. I want you to live. But how can I do anything?"

Jane's human face flickered into distracted existence above the terminal. "I don't know," she said. "But the order has just gone out. They're starting to disconnect me. I'm losing parts of my memory. I already can't think of as many things at once. I have to have a place to go, but there is no place, and even if there were one, I don't know the way."

"Are you afraid?" asked Valentine.

"I don't know," said Jane. "It will take hours, I think, for them to finish killing me. If I find out how I feel before the end, I'll tell you, if I can."

Valentine hid her face behind her hands for a long moment. Then she got up and headed out of the house.

Jakt saw her go and shook his head. Decades ago, when

Ender left Trondheim and Valentine stayed in order to marry him, in order to be the mother of his children, he had rejoiced at how happy and alive she became without the burden that Ender had always placed upon her and that she had always unconsciously borne. And then she had asked him if he would come with her to Lusitania, and he said yes, and now it was the old way again, now she sagged under the weight of Ender's life, of Ender's need of her. Jakt couldn't begrudge it—it wasn't as if either of them had planned it or willed it; it wasn't as if either one was trying to steal a part of Jakt's own life from him. But it still hurt to see her so bowed down under the weight of it, and to know that despite all his love for her, there was nothing Jakt could do to help her bear it.

———

Miro faced Ela and Quara in the doorway of the starship. Inside, Young Valentine was already waiting, along with a pequenino named Firequencher and a nameless worker that the Hive Queen had sent.

"Jane is dying," Miro said. "We have to go now. She won't have capacity enough to send a starship if we wait too long."

"How can you ask us to go," said Quara, "when we already know that once Jane dies we'll never come back? We'll only last as long as the oxygen on this starship lasts. A few months at most, and then we'll die."

"But will we have accomplished something in the meantime?" said Miro. "Will we have communicated with these descoladores, these aliens who send out planet-wrecking probes? Will we have persuaded them to stop? Will we have saved all the species that we know, and thousands and millions that we don't yet know, from some terrible and irresistible disease? Jane has given us the best programs she could create for us, to help us talk to them. Is this good enough to be your masterwork? The achievement of your lifetime?"

His older sister Ela looked at him sadly. "I thought I had already done my masterwork, when I made the virus that undid the descolada here."

"You did," he said. "You've done enough. But there's more to do that only you can do. I'm asking you to come and die with me, Ela, because without you my own death will be meaningless, because without you, Val and I can't do what must be done."

Neither Quara nor Ela moved or spoke.

Miro nodded, then turned and went into the ship. But before he could close and seal the door, the two sisters, arms around each other's waists, wordlessly followed him inside.

8

"WHAT MATTERS IS WHICH FICTION YOU BELIEVE"

"My father once told me
that there are no gods,
only the cruel manipulations
of evil people
who pretended that their power was good
and their exploitation was love.
But if there are no gods,
why are we so hungry to believe in them?
Just because evil liars
stand between us and the gods
and block our view of them
does not mean that the bright halo
that surrounds each liar
is not the outer edges of a god, waiting
for us to find our way around the lie."
from The God Whispers of Han Qing-jao

<It isn't working,> said the Hive Queen.
  <What can we do differently?> asked Human. <We

have made the strongest web we can. We have joined to you and to each other as never before, so that all of us tremble, all of us shake as if there were a shimmering wind dancing with us and making our leaves beautiful in sunlight, and the light is you and your daughters and all the love we have for our tiny mothers and our dear mute mothertrees is given to you, our queen, our sister, our mother, our truest wife. How can Jane not see the thing that we have made and want to be a part of it?>

<She can't find a road to us,> said the Hive Queen. <She was half made of what we are, but she has long since turned her back on us so she could endlessly look at Ender, belonging to him. She was our bridge to him. Now he is her only bridge to life.>

<What kind of bridge is that? He's dying himself.>

<The old part of him is dying,> said the Hive Queen. <But remember, he is the man who has loved and understood you pequeninos best. Is it not possible that out of the dying body of his youth, there might not grow a tree to take him into the Third Life, as he took you?>

<I don't understand your plan,> said Human. But even in his noncomprehension, another message flowed to her underneath the conscious one: <My beloved queen,> he was saying, and she heard: <My sweet and holy one.>

<I don't have a plan,> she said. <I only have a hope.>

<Tell me your hope, then,> said Human.

<It's only a dream of a hope,> she answered. <Only a rumor of a guess of a dream of a hope.>

<Tell me.>

<She was our bridge to Ender. Can't Ender now be her bridge to us, through you? She has spent her life, all but the last few years, staring into Ender's heart, hearing his inmost thoughts and letting his aiúa give meaning to her own existence. If he calls her, she'll hear him even though she can't hear us. That will draw her to him.>

<Into the body where he most dwells right now,> said Human, <which is the body of Young Valentine. They'll

fight each other there, without meaning to. They can't both rule the same kingdom.>

<That's why the rumor of hope is so slim,> said the Hive Queen. <But Ender also has loved you—you, the fathertree named Human, and you, all pequeninos and fathertrees, wives and sisters and mothertrees, all of you, even the wooden trees of pequeninos who were never fathers but once were sons, he loved and loves you all. Can't she follow that philotic twine and reach our web through you? And can't she follow him and find the way to us? We can hold her, we can hold all of her that won't fit into Young Valentine.>

<Then Ender has to stay alive to call to her.>

<This is why the hope is only the shadow of a memory of the passing of a tiny cloud before the sun, because he must call her and bring her, and then he must escape from her and leave her alone in Young Valentine.>

<Then he will die for her.>

<He will die as Ender. He must die as Valentine. But can't he find his way to Peter, and live there?>

<That's the part of himself that he hates,> said Human. <He told me so himself.>

<That's the part of himself that he fears,> said the Hive Queen. <But isn't it possible that he fears it because it's the strongest part of him? The most powerful of his faces?>

<How can you say that the strongest part of a good man like Ender is the destructive, ambitious, cruel, ruthless part?>

<Those are his words for the part of himself that he gave shape as Young Peter. But doesn't his book *The Hegemon* show that it's the ruthlessness inside him that gave him strength to build? That made him strong against all assailants? That gave him a self despite his loneliness? Neither he nor Peter was ever cruel for cruelty's sake. They were cruel to get the job done, and it was a job that needed doing; it was a job to save the world, Ender by destroying

a terrible enemy, for so he thought we were, and Peter by breaking down the boundary walls of nations and making the human race into one nation. Both those jobs remain to do again. We have found the borders of a terrible enemy, the alien race that Miro calls the descoladores. And the boundaries between human and pequenino, pequenino and hive queen, hive queen and human, and between all of us and Jane, whatever Jane might turn out to be—don't we need the strength of Ender-as-Peter to bring us all into one?>

<You convince me, beloved sister mother wife, but it is Ender who will not believe in such goodness in himself. He might be able to draw Jane out of the sky and into the body of Young Valentine, but he will never be able to leave that body himself, he will never choose to give up his own goodness and go to the body that represents all that he fears inside himself.>

<If you're right, then he will die,> said the Hive Queen.

Grief and anguish for his friend welled up in Human and spilled out into the web that bound him to all fathertrees and to all hive queens, but to them it tasted sweet, for it was born out of love for the life of the man.

<But he's dying anyway, as Ender he's dying, and if we explained this all to him, wouldn't he choose to die, if by dying he might keep Jane alive? Jane, who holds the key to starflight? Jane, who alone can unlock the door between us and the Outside and pass us in and out by her strong will and clear mind?>

<Yes, he would choose to die so she could live.>

<Better, though, if he would bring her into Valentine and then choose to live. That would be better.>

Even as she said it, the despair behind her words came out like ooze and everyone on the web that she had helped to weave could taste the poison of it, for it was born of dread for the death of the man, and they all grieved.

Jane found the strength for one last voyage; she held the shuttle, with the six living forms inside it, held the perfect image of the physical forms long enough to hurl them Out and reel them In, orbiting the distant world where the descolada had been made. But when that task was done, she lost control of herself because she could no longer find herself, not the self that she had known. Memories were torn from her; links to worlds that had long been as familiar to her as limbs are to living humans, hive queens, and fathertrees were now gone, and as she reached to use them nothing happened, she was numb all over, shrinking down, not to her ancient core, but into small corners of herself, disparate fragments that were too small to hold her.

I'm dying, I'm dying, she said over and over again, hating the words as she said them, hating the panic that she felt.

Into the computer before which Young Valentine sat, she spoke—and spoke only words, because she couldn't remember now how to make the face that had been her mask for so many centuries. "Now I am afraid." But having said it, she couldn't remember whether it had been Young Valentine to whom she was supposed to say it. That part of her was also gone; a moment ago it had been there, but now it was out of reach.

And why was she talking to this surrogate for Ender? Why did she cry out softly into Miro's ear, into Peter's ear, saying, "Speak to me speak to me I'm afraid"? It wasn't these manshapes that she wanted now. It was the one who had torn her from his ear. It was the one who had rejected her and chosen a sad and weary human woman because— he thought—Novinha's need was greater. But how can she need you more than I do now? If you die she will still live. But I die now because you have glanced away from me.

Wang-mu heard his voice murmuring beside her on the beach. Was I asleep, she wondered. She lifted her cheek from the sand, rose up on her arms. The tide was out now, the water farthest it could get from where she lay. Beside her Peter was sitting crosslegged in the sand, rocking back and forth, softly saying, "Jane, I hear you. I'm speaking to you. Here I am," as tears flowed down his cheeks.

And in that moment, hearing him intone these words to Jane, Wang-mu realized two things all at once. First, she knew that Jane must be dying, for what could Peter's words be but comfort, and what comfort would Jane need, except in the hour of her extremity? The second realization, though, was even more terrible to Wang-mu. For she knew, seeing Peter's tears for the first time—seeing, for the first time, that he was even capable of crying—that she wanted to be able to touch his heart as Jane touched it; no, to be the only one whose dying would grieve him so.

When did it happen? she wondered. When did I first start wanting him to love me? Did it happen only now, a childish desire, wanting him only because another woman—another creature—possessed him? Or have I, in these days together, come to want his love for its own sake? Has his taunting of me, his condescension, and yet his secret pain, his hidden fear, has all of this somehow endeared him to me? Was it his very disdain toward me that made me want, not just his approval, but his affection? Or was it his pain that made me want to have him turn to me for comfort?

Why should I covet his love so much? Why am I so jealous of Jane, this dying stranger that I hardly know or even know about? Could it be that after so many years of priding myself on my solitude, I must discover that I've longed for some pathetic adolescent romance all along? And in this longing for affection, could I have chosen a worse applicant for the position? He loves someone else that I can never compare to, especially after she's dead; he knows me to be ignorant and cares not at all for any good qualities I might have; and he himself is only some fraction of a human being, and not the nicest part of the whole person who is so divided.

Have I lost my mind?

Or have I, finally, found my heart?

She was suddenly filled with unaccustomed emotion. All her life she had kept her own feelings at such a distance from herself that now she hardly knew how to contain them. I love him, thought Wang-mu, and her heart nearly burst with the intensity of her passion. He will never love me, thought Wang-mu, and her heart broke as it had never broken in all the thousand disappointments of her life.

My love for him is nothing compared to his need for her, his knowledge of her. For his ties to her are deeper than these past few weeks since he was conjured into existence on that first voyage Outside. In all the lonely years of Ender's wandering, Jane was his most constant friend, and that is the love that now pours out of Peter's eyes with tears. I am nothing to him, I'm a latecome afterthought to his life, I have seen only a part of him and my love was nothing to him in the end.

She, too, wept.

But she turned away from Peter when a cry went up from the Samoans standing on the beach. She looked with tear-weary eyes out over the waves, and rose to her feet so she could be sure she saw what they were seeing. It was Malu's ship. He had turned back to them. He was coming back.

Had he seen something? Had he heard whatever cry it was from Jane that Peter was hearing now?

Grace was beside her, holding her hand. "Why is he coming back?" she asked Wang-mu.

"You're the one who understands him," said Wang-mu.

"I don't understand him at all," said Grace. "Except his words, I know the ordinary meanings of his words. But when he speaks, I can feel the words straining to contain the things he wants to say, and they can't do it. They aren't large enough, those words of his, even though he speaks in our largest language, even though he builds the words together into great baskets of meaning, into boats of thought. I can only see the outer shape of the words and guess at what he means. I don't understand him at all.''

''Why then do you think *I* do?''

''Because he's coming back to speak to you.''

''He comes back to speak to Peter. He's the one connected to the god, as Malu calls her.''

''You don't like this god of his, do you,'' said Grace.

Wang-mu shook her head. ''I have nothing against her. Except that she owns *him,* and so there's nothing left for me.''

''A rival,'' said Grace.

Wang-mu sighed. ''I grew up expecting nothing and getting less. But I always had ambition far beyond my reach. Sometimes I reached anyway, and caught in my hands more than I deserved, more than I could handle. Sometimes I reach and never touch the thing I want.''

''You want him?''

''I only just realized that I want him to love me as I love him. He was always angry, always stabbing at me with his words, but he worked beside me and when he praised me I believed his praise.''

''I would say,'' said Grace, ''that your life till now has not been perfectly simple.''

''Not true,'' said Wang-mu. ''Till now, I have had nothing that I didn't need, and needed nothing that I didn't have.''

''You have needed everything you didn't have,'' said Grace, ''and I can't believe that you're so weak that you won't reach for it even now.''

''I lost him before I found I wanted him,'' she said. ''Look at him.''

Peter rocked back and forth, whispering, subvocalizing, his litany an endless conversation with his dying friend.

''I look at him,'' said Grace, ''and I see that he's right there, in flesh and blood, and so are you, right here, in flesh and blood, and I can't see how a smart girl like you could say that he is gone when your eyes must surely tell you that he's not.''

Wang-mu looked up at the enormous woman who loomed over her like a mountain range, looked up into her luminous eyes, and glared. "I never asked you for advice."

"I never asked you, either, but you came here to try to get me to change my mind about the Lusitania Fleet, didn't you? You wanted to get Malu to get me to say something to Aimaina so he'd say something to the Necessarians of Divine Wind so *they'd* say something to the faction of Congress that hungers for their respect, and the coalition that sent the fleet will fall apart and they'll order it to leave Lusitania untouched. Wasn't that the plan?"

Wang-mu nodded.

"Well, you deceived yourself. You can't know from the outside what makes a person choose the things they choose. Aimaina wrote to me, but I have no power over him. I taught him the way of Ua Lava, yes, but it was Ua Lava that he followed, he doesn't follow me. He followed it because it felt true to him. If I suddenly started explaining that Ua Lava also meant not sending fleets to wipe out planets, he'd listen politely and ignore me, because that would have nothing to do with the Ua Lava he believes in. He would see it, correctly, as an attempt by an old friend and teacher to bend him to her will. It would be the end of the trust between us, and still it wouldn't change his mind."

"So we failed," said Wang-mu.

"I don't know if you failed or not," said Grace. "Lusitania isn't blown up yet. And how do you know if that was ever really your purpose for coming here?"

"Peter said it was. Jane said so."

"And how do *they* know what their purpose was?"

"Well, if you want to go that far, none of us has any purpose at all," said Wang-mu. "Our lives are just our genes and our upbringing. We simply act out the script that was forced upon us."

"Oh," said Grace, sounding disappointed. "I'm sorry to hear you say something so stupid."

Again the great canoe was beached. Again Malu rose up

from his seat and stepped out onto the sand. But this time—was it possible?—this time he seemed to be hurrying. Hurrying so fast that, yes, he lost a little bit of dignity. Indeed, slow as his progress was, Wang-mu felt that he was fairly bounding up the beach. And as she watched his eyes, saw where he was looking, she realized he was coming, not to Peter, but to her.

Novinha woke up in the soft chair they had brought for her and for a moment she forgot where she was. During her days as xenobiologist, she had often fallen asleep in a chair in the laboratory, and so for a moment she looked around to see what it was that she was working on before she fell asleep. What problem was it she was trying to solve?

Then she saw Valentine standing over the bed where Andrew lay. Where Andrew's body lay. His heart was somewhere else.

"You should have wakened me," said Novinha.

"I just arrived," said Valentine. "And I didn't have the heart to wake you. They said you almost never sleep."

Novinha stood up. "Odd. It seems to me as if that's all I do."

"Jane is dying," said Valentine.

Novinha's heart leapt within her.

"Your rival, I know," said Valentine.

Novinha looked into the woman's eyes, to see if there was anger there, or mockery. But no. It was only compassion.

"Trust me, I know how you feel," said Valentine. "Until I loved and married Jakt, Ender was my whole life. But I was never his. Oh, for a while in his childhood, I mattered most to him then—but that was poisoned because the military used me to get to him, to keep him going when he wanted to give up. And after that, it was always Jane who heard his jokes, his observations, his inmost thoughts. It was Jane who saw what he saw and heard what he heard. I wrote my books, and when they were done I had his attention for a few hours, a few weeks. He used my ideas and so I felt he carried a part of me inside him. But he was hers.''

Novinha nodded. She *did* understand.

''But I have Jakt, and so I'm not unhappy anymore. And my children. Much as I loved Ender, powerful man that he is, even lying here like this, even fading away—children are more to a woman than any man can be. We pretend otherwise. We pretend we bear them for him, that we raise them for him. But it's not true. We raise them for themselves. We stay with our men for the children's sake.'' Valentine smiled. ''You did.''

''I stayed with the wrong man,'' said Novinha.

''No, you stayed with the right one. Your Libo, he had a wife and other children—she was the one, they were the ones who had a right to claim him. You stayed with another man for your own children's sake, and even though they hated him sometimes, they also loved him, and even though in some ways he was weak, in others he was strong. It was good for you to have him for their sake. It was a kind of protection for them all along.''

''Why are you saying these things to me?''

''Because Jane is dying,'' said Valentine, ''but she might live if only Ender would reach out to her.''

''Put the jewel back into his ear?'' said Novinha scornfully.

''They're long past needing that,'' said Valentine. ''Just as Ender is long past needing to live this life in this body.''

''He's not so old,'' said Novinha.

''Three thousand years,'' said Valentine.

''That's just the relativity effect,'' said Novinha. ''Actually he's—''

''Three thousand years,'' said Valentine again. ''All of humanity was his family for most of that time; he was like a father away on a business trip, who comes home only now and then, but when he's there, he's the good judge, the kind provider. That's what happened each time he dipped back down into a human world and spoke the death of someone; he caught up on all the family doings he had missed. He's had a life of three thousand years, and he saw no end of it, and he got tired. So at last he left that large family and he chose your small one; he loved you, and for your sake he set aside Jane, who had been like his wife in all those years of his wandering, she'd been at home, so to speak, mothering all his trillions of children, reporting to him on what they were doing, tending house.''

"And her own works praise her in the gates," said Novinha.

"Yes, the virtuous woman. Like you."

Novinha tossed her head in scorn. "Never me. My own works mocked me in the gates."

"He chose you and he loved you and he loved your children and he was their father, those children who had lost two fathers already; and he still is their father, and he still is your husband, but you don't really need him anymore."

"How can you say that?" demanded Novinha, furious. "How do you know what I need?"

"You know it yourself. You knew it when you came here. You knew it when Estevão died in the embrace of that rogue fathertree. Your children were leading their own lives now and you couldn't protect them and neither could Ender. You still loved him, he still loved you, but the family part of your life was over. You didn't really need him anymore."

"He never needed me."

"He needed you desperately," said Valentine. "He needed you so much he gave up Jane for you."

"No," said Novinha. "He needed my need for him. He needed to feel like he was providing for me, protecting me."

"But you don't need his providence or his protection anymore," said Valentine.

Novinha shook her head.

"Wake him up," said Valentine, "and let him go."

Novinha thought at once of all the times she had stood at graveside. She remembered the funeral of her parents, who died for the sake of saving Milagre from the descolada during that first terrible outbreak. She thought of Pipo, tortured to death, flayed alive by the piggies because they thought that if they did he'd grow a tree, only nothing grew except the ache, the pain in Novinha's heart—it was something she discovered that sent him to the pequeninos that night. And then Libo, tortured to death the same way as his father, and again because of her, but this time because of what she didn't tell him. And Marcão, whose life was all the more painful because of her before he finally died of the disease that had been killing him since he was a child. And Estevão, who let his mad faith lead him into martyrdom, so he could become a venerado like her parents, and no doubt someday a saint as they would be saints. "I'm sick of letting people go," said Novinha bitterly.

"I don't see how you could be," said Valentine. "There's not a one of all the people who have died on you that you can honestly say you 'let go.' You clung to them tooth and nail."

"What if I did? Everyone I love has died and left me!"

"That's such a weak excuse," said Valentine. "Everyone dies. Everyone leaves. What matters is the things you build together before they go. What matters is the part of them that continues in you when they're gone. You continued your parents' work, and Pipo's, and Libo's—and you raised Libo's children, didn't you? And they were partly Marcão's children, weren't they? Something of him remained in them, and not all bad. As for Estevão, he built something rather fine out of his death, I think, but instead of letting *him* go you still resent him for it. You resent him for building something more valuable to him than life itself.

For loving God and the pequeninos more than you. You still hang on to all of them. You don't let anybody go."

"Why do you hate me for that?" said Novinha. "Maybe it's true, but that's my life, to lose and lose and lose."

"Just this once," said Valentine, "why don't you set the bird free instead of holding it in the cage until it dies?"

"You make me sound like a monster!" cried Novinha. "How dare you judge me!"

"If you were a monster Ender couldn't have loved you," said Valentine, answering rage with mildness. "You've been a great woman, Novinha, a tragic woman with many accomplishments and much suffering and I'm sure your story will make a moving saga when you die. But wouldn't it be nice if you learned something instead of acting out the same tragedy at the end?"

"I don't want another one I love to die before me!" cried Novinha.

"Who said anything about death?" said Valentine.

The door to the room swung open. Plikt stood in the doorway. "I room," she said. "What's happening?"

"She wants me to wake him up," said Novinha, "and tell him he can die."

"Can I watch?" said Plikt.

Novinha took the waterglass from beside her chair and flung the water at Plikt and screamed at her. "No more of you!" she cried. "He's mine now, not yours!"

Plikt, dripping with water, was too astonished to find an answer.

"It isn't Plikt who's taking him away," said Valentine softly.

"She's just like all the rest of them, reaching out for a piece of him, tearing bits of him away and devouring him, they're all cannibals."

"What," said Plikt nastily, angrily. "What, you wanted to feast on him yourself? Well, there was too much of him for you. What's worse, cannibals who nibble here and there, or a cannibal who keeps the whole man for herself when there's far more than she can ever absorb?''

"This is the most disgusting conversation I think I've ever heard," said Valentine.

"She hangs around for months, watching him like a vulture," said Novinha. "Hanging on, loitering in his life, never saying six words all at once. And now she finally speaks and listen to the poison that comes out of her."

"All I did was spit your own bile back at you," said Plikt. "You're nothing but a greedy, hateful woman and you used him and used him and never gave *anything* to him and the only reason he's dying now is to get away from you."

Novinha did not answer, had no words, because in her secret heart she knew at once that what Plikt had said was true.

But Valentine strode around the bed, walked to the door, and slapped Plikt mightily across the face. Plikt staggered under the blow, sank down against the doorframe until she was sitting on the floor, holding her stinging cheek, tears flowing down her face. Valentine towered over her. "You will never speak his death, do you understand me? A woman who would tell a lie like that, just to cause pain, just to lash out at someone that you envy—you're no speaker for the dead. I'm ashamed I ever let you teach my children. What if some of the lie inside you got in them? You make me sick!"

"No," said Novinha. "No, don't be angry at her. It's true, it's true."

"It feels true to you," said Valentine, "because you always want to believe the worst about yourself. But it's *not* true. Ender loved you freely and you stole nothing from him and the only reason that he's still alive on that bed is because of his love for you. That's the only reason he can't leave this used-up life and help lead Jane into a place where she can stay alive."

"No, no, Plikt is right, I consume the people that I love."

"No!" cried Plikt, weeping on the floor. "I was lying

to you! I love him so much and I'm so jealous of you because you had him and you didn't even want him.''

"I have never stopped loving him," said Novinha.

"You left him. You came in here without him."

"I left because I couldn't . . ."

Valentine completed her sentence for her when she faded out. "Because you couldn't bear to let him leave you. You felt it, didn't you. You felt him fading even then. You knew that he needed to go away, to end this life, and you couldn't bear to let another man leave you so you left him first."

"Maybe," said Novinha wearily. "It's all just fictions anyway. We do what we do and then we make up reasons for it afterward but they're never the true reasons, the truth is always just out of reach."

"So listen to *this* fiction, then," said Valentine. "What if, just this once, instead of someone that you love betraying you and sneaking off and dying against your will and without your permission—what if just this once you wake him up and tell him he can live, bid him farewell properly and let him go with your consent. Just this once?"

Novinha wept again, standing there in utter weariness. "I want it all to stop," she said. "I want to die."

"That's why he has to stay," said Valentine. "For his sake, can't you choose to live and let *him* go? Stay in Milagre and be the mother of your children and grandmother of your children's children, tell them stories of Os Venerados and of Pipo and Libo and of Ender Wiggin, who came to heal your family and stayed to be your husband for many, many years before he died. Not some speaking for the dead, not some funeral oration, not some public picking over the corpse like Plikt wants to do, but the stories that will keep him alive in the minds of the only family that he ever had. He'll die anyway, soon enough. Why not let him go with your love and blessing in his ears, instead of with your rage and grief tearing at him, trying to hold him here?''

"You spin a pretty story," said Novinha. "But in the end, you're asking me to give him to Jane."

"As you said," Valentine answered. "All the stories are fictions. What matters is which fiction you believe."

9

"IT SMELLS LIKE LIFE TO ME"

"Why do you say that I am alone?
My body is with me wherever I am,
telling me endless stories
of hunger and satisfaction,
weariness and sleep,
eating and drinking and breathing and life.
With such company
who could ever be alone?
And even when my body wears away
and leaves only some tiny spark
I will not be alone
for the gods will see my small light
tracing the dance of woodgrain on the floor
and they will know me,
they will say my name
and I will rise."

from The God Whispers of Han Qing-jao

Dying, dying, dead.

At the end of her life among the ansible links there was some mercy. Jane's panic at the losing of herself began to ebb, for though she still knew that she was losing and had lost much, she no longer had the capacity to remember what it was. When she lost her links to the ansibles that let her monitor the jewels in Peter's and Miro's ears she didn't even notice. And when at last she clung to the few last strands of ansibles that would not be shutting down, she could not think of anything, could not feel anything except the need to cling to these last strands even though they were too small to hold her, even though her hunger could never be satisfied with these.

I don't belong here.

Not a thought, no, there wasn't enough of her left for anything so difficult as consciousness. Rather it was a hunger, a vague dissatisfaction, a restlessness that beset her when she had run up and down the link from Jakt's ansible to the Lusitanian landside ansible to the ansible on the shuttle that served Miro and Val, up and down, end to end, a thousand times, a million times, nothing changing, nothing to accomplish, nothing to build, no way to grow. I don't belong here.

For if there was one attribute that defined the difference between aiúas that came Inside and those that remained forever Outside, it was that underlying need to grow, to be part of something large and beautiful, to belong. Those that had no such need would never be drawn as Jane had been drawn, three thousand years before, to the web that the hive queens had made for her. Nor would any of the aiúas that became hive queens or their workers, pequeninos male and female, humans weak and strong; nor even those aiúas that, feeble in capacity but faithful and predictable, became the sparks whose dances did not show up in even the most sensitive instruments until they became so complicated that humans could identify their dance as the behavior of quarks, of mesons, of light particulate or waved. All of them needed to be part of something and when they belonged to it they rejoiced: What I am is us, what we do together is myself.

But they were not all alike, these aiúas, these unmade beings who were both building blocks and builders. The weak and fearful ones reached a certain point and either could not or dared not grow further. They would take their satisfaction from being at the edges of something beautiful and fine, from playing some small role. Many a human, many a pequenino reached that point and let others direct and control their lives, fitting in, always fitting in—and that was good, there was a need for them. Ua lava: they had reached the point where they could say, Enough.

Jane was not one of them. She could not be content with smallness or simplicity. And having once been a being of a trillion parts, connected to the greatest doings of a three-specied universe, now, shrunken, she could not be content. She knew that she had memories if only she could remember them. She knew that she had work to do if only she could find those millions of subtle limbs that once had done her bidding. She was too much alive for this small space. Unless she found something to engage her, she could not continue to cling to the last thin wire. She would cut loose from it, losing the last of her old self in the vain need to search for a place where one like her belonged.

She began to flirt with letting go, straying—never far—from the thin philotic strands of the ansibles. For moments too small to measure she was disconnected and it was terrible to be cut off; she leapt each time back to the small but familiar space that still belonged to her; and then, when the smallness of the place was unbearable to her, she let go again, and again in terror came back home.

But on one such letting-go she glimpsed something familiar. Someone familiar. Another aiúa that she had once been twined to. She had no access to memory that could tell her a name; she had no memory, indeed, of names at all. But she knew it, and she trusted this being, and when on another pass along the invisible wire she came to the same place again she leapt into the far vaster network of aiúas that were ruled by this bright familiar one.

<She has found him,> said the Hive Queen.

<Found *her,* you mean. Young Valentine.>

<It was Ender that she found and Ender that she recognized. But yes, Val's vessel is the one to which she leapt.>

<How could you see her? I never saw her at all.>

<She once was part of us, you know. And what the Samoan said, as one of my workers watched on Jakt's computer terminal, that helped me find her. We kept looking for her in a single place, and never saw her. But when we knew she was constantly moving, we realized: her body was as large as the farthest reaches of all of human colonization, and just as our aiúas remain within our bodies and are easily found, so hers also remained within her body, but since it was larger than us and even included us, she was never still, never contained in a space small enough for us to see her. Not till she had lost most of herself did I find her. But now I know where she is.>

<So Young Valentine is hers now?>

<No,> said the Hive Queen. <Ender can't let go.>

Jane spun joyously through this body, so different from any she had ever remembered before, but within moments she realized that the aiúa she had recognized, the aiúa she had followed here, was not willing to give up even a small part of itself to her. Wherever she touched, there it was, touching also, affirming its control; and now in panic Jane began to sense that while she might be inside a lacework of extraordinary beauty and fineness—this temple of living cells on a frame of bone—no part of it belonged to her and if she stayed it would only be as a fugitive. She did not belong here, no matter how she loved it.

And she did love it. For all the thousands of years that

she had lived, so vast in space, so fast in time, she had nevertheless been crippled without knowing it. She was alive, but nothing that was part of her large kingdom was alive. All had been ruthlessly under her control, but here in this body, this human body, this woman named Val, there were millions of small bright lives, cell upon cell of life, thriving, laboring, growing, dying, linked body to body and aiúa to aiúa, and it was in these links that creatures of flesh dwelt and it was far more vivid, despite the sluggishness of thought, than her own experience of life had been. How can they think at all, these flesh-beings, with all these dances going on around them, all these songs to distract them?

She touched the mind of Valentine and was flooded with memory. It had nothing like the precision and depth of Jane's old memory, but every moment of experience was vivid and powerful, alive and real as no memory had been that Jane had ever known before. How can they keep from holding still all day simply to remember the day before? Because each new moment shouts louder than memory.

Yet each time Jane touched a memory or felt a sensation from the living body, there was the aiúa that was properly the master of this flesh, driving her away, asserting its control.

And finally, annoyed, when that familiar aiúa herded her Jane refused to move. Instead she claimed this spot, this part of the body, this part of the brain, she demanded the obedience of these cells, and the other aiúa recoiled before her.

I am stronger than you, Jane said to him silently. I can take from you all that you are and all that you have and all that you will ever be and ever have and you can't stop me.

The aiúa that once had been the master here fled before her, and now the chase resumed, with roles reversed.

<She's killing him.>
<Wait and see.>

In the starship orbiting the planet of the descoladores, everyone was startled by a sudden cry from Young Val's mouth. As they turned to look, before anyone could reach her, her body convulsed and she flung herself away from her chair; in the weightlessness of orbit she flew until she struck brutally against the ceiling, and all the time her voice came out as a thin ribbon of a wail and her face held a rictus smile that seemed to speak at once of endless agony and boundless joy.

On the world Pacifica, on an island, on a beach, Peter's weeping suddenly stopped and he flopped over in the sand and twitched silently. "Peter!" cried Wang-mu, flinging herself onto him, touching him, trying to hold the limbs that bounced like jackhammers. Peter gasped for breath, and, gasping, vomited. "He's drowning himself!" cried Wang-mu. In that instant huge strong hands pulled her away, took Peter's body by its limbs and flopped it over so that now the vomitus flowed out and down into the sand, and the body, coughing and choking, nevertheless breathed. "What's happening?" Wang-mu cried.

Malu laughed, and then when he spoke his voice was like a song. "The god has come here! The dancing god has touched flesh! Oh, the body is too weak to hold it! Oh, the body cannot dance the dance of gods! But oh, how blessed, bright, and beautiful is the body when the god is in it!"

Wang-mu saw nothing beautiful about what was happening to Peter. "Get out of him!" she screamed. "Get out, Jane! You have no right to him! You have no right to kill him!"

In a room in the monastery of the Children of the Mind of Christ, Ender sat bolt upright in bed, eyes open but seeing nothing for someone else controlled his eyes; but for a moment his voice was his own, for here if nowhere else his aiúa knew the flesh so well and was so known itself that it could do battle with the interloper. "God help me!" cried Ender. "I have nowhere else to go! Leave me something! Leave me something!"

The women gathered around him—Valentine, Novinha, Plikt—at once forgot their quarrels and laid their hands on him, trying to get him to lie down, trying to calm him, but then his eyes rolled back in his head, his tongue protruded, his back arched, and he flung himself about so violently that despite their strongest grip on him in moments he was off the bed, on the floor, tangling his body with theirs, hurting them with his convulsive swinging of arms, kicking of legs, jerking of head.

———

<She's too much for him,> said the Hive Queen. <But for now the body is also too much for her. Not an easy thing, to tame unwilling flesh. They know Ender, all those cells that he has ruled so long. They know him, and they don't know her. Some kingdoms can only be inherited, never usurped.>

<I felt him, I think. I saw him.>

<There are moments when she drove him out entirely, yes, and he followed what twines he found. He can't get into any of the flesh around him because he knows better, having had experience of flesh himself. But he found you and touched you because you're a different kind of being.>

<Will he take me over, then? Or some tree in our web? That's not what we meant when we twined together.>

<Ender? No, he'll hold to his own body, one of them, or else he'll die. Wait and see.>

———

Jane could feel it, the anguish of the bodies that she ruled now. They were in pain, something that she hadn't felt

before, the bodies writhing in agony as the myriad aiúas
rebelled at having her to rule them. Now in control of three
bodies and three brains, she recognized amid the chaos and
the madness of their convulsions that her presence meant
nothing but pain and terror to them, and they longed for
their beloved one, their ruler who had been so trusted and
well-known to them that they thought of him as their very
self. They had no name for him, being too small and weak
to have such capacities as language or consciousness, but
they knew him and they knew that Jane was not their proper
master and the terror and the agony of it became the sole
fact of each body's being and she knew, she knew she
could not stay.

Yes, she overmastered them. Yes, she had the strength
to still the twisting, bunching muscles and to restore an
order that became a parody of life. But all her effort was
spent in quelling a billion rebellions against her rule. Without the willing obedience of all these cells, she was not
capable of such complex leisure-born activities as thought
and speech.

And something else: She was not happy here. She could
not stop thinking of the aiúa she had driven out. *I was
drawn here because I knew him and I loved him and I
belonged with him, and now I have taken from him all that
he loved and all that loved him.* She knew, again, that she
did not belong here. Other aiúas might be content to rule
against the will of those ruled, but she could not. It was
not beautiful to her. There was no joy in it. Life along the
tenuous strands of the last few ansibles had been happier
than this.

Letting go was hard. Even in rebellion against her, the
pull of the body was exquisitely strong. She had tasted a
kind of life that was so sweet, despite its bitterness and
pain, that she could never go back to what she had been
before. She could scarcely even find the ansible links, and,
having found them, could not bring herself to reach for
them and cling. Instead she cast about, flung herself to the

reaches of the bodies that she temporarily and painfully ruled. Wherever she went, there was grief and agony, and no home for her.

But didn't the master of these bodies leap somewhere? Where did he go, when he fled from me? Now he was back, now he was restoring peace and calm in the bodies that she had momentarily mastered, but where had he gone?

She found it, a set of links far different from the mechanical bindings of the ansible. Where the ansibles might seem to be cables, metal, hard, the web that now she found was lacy and light; but against all appearances it was also strong and copious. She could leap here, yes, and so she leapt.

———

<She has found me! Oh, my love, she is too strong for me! She is too bright and strong for me!>

<Wait, wait, wait, let her find her way.>

<She'll push us out, we have to drive her off, away, away!>

<Be still, be patient, trust me: She has learned, she won't drive anyone away, there'll be a place where there is room for her, I see it, she is on the verge . . . >

<It was Young Val's body she was supposed to take, or Peter's, or Ender's! Not one of us, not one of us!>

<Peace, be still. Only for a little while. Only until Ender understands and gives a body to his friend. What she can't take by force she can receive by gift. You'll see. And in your web, my dear friend, my trusted friend, there are places where there will be room for her to dwell as just a visitor, to have a life while she is waiting for Ender to give up her true and final home.>

———

Suddenly Valentine was as still as a corpse. "She's dead," whispered Ela.

"No!" wailed Miro, and he tried to breathe life into her mouth until the woman under his hands, under his lips, began to stir. She breathed deeply on her own. Her eyes fluttered open.

"Miro," she said. And then she wept and wept and wept and clung to him.

Ender lay still on the floor. The women untangled themselves from him, helping each other to rise to their knees, to stand, to bend, to lift him up, to get his bruised body back onto the bed. Then they looked at each other: Valentine with a bleeding lip, Plikt with Ender's scratches on her face, Novinha with a battered, blackening eye.

"I had a husband once who beat me," said Novinha.

"That wasn't Ender who fought us," said Plikt.

"It's Ender now," said Valentine.

On the bed, he opened up his eyes. Did he see them? How could they know?

"Ender," Novinha said, and began to weep. "Ender, you don't have to stay for my sake anymore." But if he heard her he betrayed no sign of it.

The Samoan men let go of him, for Peter no longer twitched. His face fell open-mouthed into the sand where he had vomited. Wang-mu again was beside him, using her own clothing to gently wipe away the sand and muck from his face, from his eyes especially. In moments a bowl of pure water was beside her, put there by someone's hands, she did not see whose, or care either, for her only thought was Peter, to cleanse him. He breathed shallowly, rapidly, but gradually he calmed and finally opened up his eyes.

"I dreamed the strangest dream," he said.

"Hush," she answered him.

"A terrible bright dragon chased me breathing fire, and I ran through the corridors, searching for a hiding place, an escape, a protector."

Malu's voice rumbled like the sea: "There is no hiding from a god."

Peter spoke again as if he hadn't heard the holy man.

"Wang-mu," he said, "at last I found my hiding place." His hand reached up and touched her cheek, and his eyes looked into her eyes with a kind of wonder.

"Not me," she said. "I am not strong enough to stand against her."

He answered her: "I know. But are you strong enough to stand with me?"

Jane raced along the lacework of the links among the trees. Some of the trees were mighty ones, and some weaker, some so faint that she could have blown them away with only a breath it seemed, but as she saw them all recoil from her in fear, she knew that fear herself and she backed away, pushed no one from his place. Sometimes the lacework thickened and toughened and led away toward something fiercely bright, as bright as she was. These places were familiar to her, an ancient memory but she knew the path; it was into such a web that she had first leapt into life, and like the primal memory of birth it all came back to her, memory long lost and forgotten: I know the queens who rule at the knotting of these sturdy ropes. Of all the aiúas she had touched in these few minutes since her death, these were the strongest ones by far, each one of them at least a match for her. When hive queens make their web to call and catch a queen, it is only the mightiest and most ambitious ones who can take the place that they prepare. Only a few aiúas have the capacity to rule over thousands of consciousnesses, to master other organisms as thoroughly as humans and pequeninos master the cells of their own bodies. Oh, perhaps these hive queens were not all as capable as she, perhaps not even as hungry to grow as Jane's aiúa was, but they were stronger than any human or pequenino, and unlike them they saw her clearly and knew what she was and all that she could do and they were ready. They loved her and wanted her to thrive; they were sisters and mothers to her, truly; but their places were full and they had no room for her. So from those ropes and knots she turned away, back to the lacier twinings of the pequeninos, to the strong trees that nevertheless recoiled from her because they knew that she was the stronger one.

And then she realized that where the lace thinned out it was not because there was nothing there, but because the twines simply grew more delicate. There were as many of them, more perhaps, but they became a web of gossamer, so delicate that Jane's rough touch might break them; but she touched them and they did not break, and she followed the threads into a place that teemed with life, with hundreds of small lives, all of them hovering on the brink of consciousness but not quite ready for the leap into awareness. And underneath them all, warm and loving, an aiúa that was in its own way strong, but not as Jane was. No, the aiúa of the mothertree was strong without ambition. It was part of every life that dwelt upon her skin, inside the dark of the heart of the tree or on the outside, crawling into the light and reaching out to become awake and alive and break free and become themselves. And it was easy to break free, for the mothertree aiúa expected nothing from her children, loved their independence as much as she had loved their need.

She was copious, her sap-filled veins, her skeleton of wood, her tingling leaves that bathed in light, her roots that tapped into seas of water salted with the stuff of life. She stood still in the center of her delicate and gentle web, strong and provident, and when Jane came to her verge she looked upon her as she looked upon any lost child. She backed away and made room for her, let Jane taste of her life, let Jane share the mastery of chlorophyll and cellulose. There was room here for more than one.

And Jane, for her part, having been invited in, did not abuse the privilege. She did not stay long in any mothertree, but visited and drank of life and shared the work of the mothertree and then moved on, tree to tree, dancing her dance along the gossamer web; and now the fathertrees did not recoil from her, for she was the messenger of the mothers, she was their voice, she shared their life and yet she was unlike them enough that she could speak, could be their consciousness, a thousand mothertrees around the world, and the growing mothertrees on distant planets, all of them found voice in Jane, and all of them rejoiced in the new, more vivid life that came to them because she was there.

<The mothertrees are speaking.>

<It's Jane.>

<Ah, my beloved one, the mothertrees are singing. I have never heard such songs.>

<It's not enough for her, but it will do for now.>

<No, no, don't take her away from us now! For the first time we can hear the mothertrees and they are beautiful!>

<She knows the way now. She will never fully leave. But it is not enough. The mothertrees will satisfy her for a while, but they can never be more than they are. Jane is not content to stand and think, to let others drink from her and never drink herself. She dances tree to tree, she sings for them, but in a while she'll be hungry again. She needs a body of her own.>

<We'll lose her then.>

<No you won't. For even that body will not be enough. It will be the root of her, it will be her eyes and voice and hands and feet. But she will still long for the ansibles and the power she had when all the computers of the human worlds were hers. You'll see. We can keep her alive for now, but what we have to give her—what your mothertrees have to share with her—is not enough. Nothing, really, is enough for her.>

<So what will happen now?>

<We'll wait. We'll see. Be patient. Isn't that the virtue of the fathertrees, that you are patient?>

A man called Olhado because of his mechanical eyes stood out in the forest with his children. They had been picnicking with pequeninos who were his children's particular friends, but then the drumming had begun, the throbbing voice of the fathertrees, and the pequeninos rose all at once in fear.

Olhado's first thought was: Fire. For it was not that long ago that the great ancient trees that had stood here were all burned by humans, filled with rage and fear. The fire the humans brought had killed the fathertrees, except for Human and Rooter, who stood at some distance from the rest; it had killed the ancient mothertree. But now new growth had risen from the corpses of the dead, as murdered pequeninos passed into their Third Life. And somewhere in the middle of all this newgrowth forest, Olhado knew, there grew a new mothertree, no doubt still slender, but thick-trunked enough from its passionate desperate first growth that hundreds of grublike babies crawled the dark hollow of its woody womb. The forest had been murdered, but it was alive again. And among the torchbearers had been Olhado's own boy, Nimbo, too young to understand what he was doing, blindly following the demagogic rantings of his uncle Grego until it nearly killed him and when Olhado learned what he had done he was ashamed, for he knew that he had not sufficiently taught his children. That was when their visits to the forest began. It was not too late. His children would grow up knowing pequeninos so well that to harm them would be unthinkable.

Yet there was fear in this forest again, and Olhado felt himself suddenly sick with dread. What could it be? What is the warning from the fathertrees? What invader has attacked them?

But the fear only lasted for a few moments. Then the pequeninos turned, hearing something from the fathertrees that made them start to walk toward the heart of the forest. Olhado's children would have followed, but with a gesture he held them back. He knew that the mothertree was in the center, where the pequeninos were going, and it wasn't proper for humans to go there.

"Look, Father," said his youngest girl. "Plower is beckoning."

So he was. Olhado nodded then, and they followed Plower into the young forest until they came to the very place where once Nimbo had taken part in the burning of an ancient mothertree. Her charred corpse still rose into the sky, but beside it stood the new mother, slender by comparison, but still thicker than the newgrowth brothertrees. It was not her thickness that Olhado marveled at, though, nor was it the great height that she had reached in such a short time, nor the thick canopy of leaves that already spread out in shady layers over the clearing. No, it was the strange dancing light that played up and down the trunk, wherever the bark was thin, a light so white and dazzling that he could hardly look at it. Sometimes he thought that there was only one small light which raced so fast that it left the whole tree glowing before it returned to trace the path again; sometimes it seemed that it was the whole tree that was alight, throbbing with it as if it contained a volcano of life ready to erupt. The glowing reached out along the branches of the tree into the thinnest twigs; the leaves twinkled with it; and the furred shadows of the baby pequeninos crawled more rapidly along the trunk of the tree than Olhado had thought possible. It was as if a small star had come down to take residence inside the tree.

After the dazzle of the light had lost its novelty, though, Olhado noticed something else—noticed, in fact, what the pequeninos themselves most marveled at. There were blossoms on the tree. And some of the blossoms had already blown, and behind them fruit was already growing, growing visibly.

"I thought," said Olhado softly, "that the trees could bear no fruit."

"They couldn't," answered Plower. "The descolada robbed them of that."

"But what is this?" said Olhado. "Why is there light inside the tree? Why is the fruit growing?"

"The fathertree Human says that Ender has brought his friend to us. The one called Jane. She's visiting within the mothertrees in every forest. But even he did not tell us of this fruit."

"It smells so strong," said Olhado. "How can it ripen so fast? It smells so strong and sweet and tangy, I can almost taste it just from breathing the air of the blossoms, the scent of the ripening fruit."

"I remember this smell," said Plower. "I have never smelled it before in my life because no tree has ever blossomed and no fruit has ever grown, but I know this smell. It smells like life to me. It smells like joy."

"Then eat it," said Olhado. "Look—one of them is ripe already, here, within reach." Olhado lifted his hand, but then hesitated. "May I?" he asked. "May I pluck a fruit from the mothertree? Not for me to eat—for you."

Plower seemed to nod with his whole body. "Please," he whispered.

Olhado took hold of the glowing fruit. Did it tremble under his hand? Or was that his own trembling?

Olhado gripped the fruit, firm but softening, and plucked it gently from the tree. It came away so easily. He bent and gave it to Plower. Plower bowed and took it reverently, lifted it to his lips, licked it, then opened his mouth.

Opened his mouth and bit into it. The juice of it shone on his lips; he licked them clean; he chewed; he swallowed.

The other pequeninos watched him. He held out the fruit to them. One at a time they came to him, brothers and wives, came to him and tasted.

And when that fruit was gone, they began to climb the bright and glowing tree, to take the fruit and share it and eat it until they could eat no more. And then they sang. Olhado and his children stayed the night to hear them sing. The people of Milagre heard the sound of it, and many of them came into the faint light of dusk, following the shining of the tree to find the place where the pequeninos, filled with the fruit that tasted like joy, sang the song of their rejoicing. And the tree in the center of them was part of the song. The aiúa whose force and fire made the tree so much more alive than it had ever been before danced into the tree, along every path of the tree, a thousand times in every second.

A thousand times in every second she danced this tree, and every other tree on every world where pequenino forests grew, and every mothertree that she visited burst with blossoms and with fruit, and pequeninos ate of it and breathed deep the scent of fruit and blossoms, and they sang. It was an old song whose meaning they had long forgotten but now they knew the meaning of it and they could sing no other. It was a song of the season of bloom and feast. They had gone so long without a harvest that they forgot what harvest was. But now they knew what the descolada had stolen from them long before. What had been lost was found again. And those who had been hungry without knowing the name of their hunger, they were fed.

10

"THIS HAS ALWAYS BEEN YOUR BODY"

*"Oh, Father! Why did you turn away?
In the hour when I triumphed over evil,
why did you recoil from me?"*
                    from The God Whispers of Han Qing-jao

Malu sat with Peter, Wang-mu, and Grace beside a bonfire near the beach. The canopy was gone, and so was much of the ceremony. There was kava, but, despite the ritual surrounding it, in Wang-mu's opinion they drank it now as much for the pleasure of it as for its holiness or symbolism.

At one point Malu laughed long and loud, and Grace laughed too, so it took her a while to interpret. "He says that he cannot decide if the fact that the god was in you, Peter, makes you holy, or the fact that she left proves you to be unholy."

Peter chuckled—for courtesy, Wang-mu knew—while Wang-mu herself did not laugh at all.

"Oh, too bad," said Grace. "I had hoped you two might have a sense of humor."

"We do," said Peter. "We just don't have a Samoan sense of humor."

"Malu says the god can't stay forever where she is. She's found a new home, but it belongs to others, and their generosity won't last forever. You felt how strong Jane is, Peter—"

"Yes," said Peter softly.

"Well, the hosts that have taken her in—Malu calls it the forest net, like a fishing net for catching trees, but what is that?—anyway he says that they are so weak compared to Jane that whether she wills it or not, in time their bodies will all belong to her unless she finds somewhere else to be her permanent home."

Peter nodded. "I know what he's saying. And I would have agreed, until the moment that she actually invaded me, that I would gladly give up this body and this life, which I thought I hated. But I found out, with her chasing me around, that Malu was right, I don't hate my life, I want very much to live. Of course it's not *me* doing the wanting, ultimately, it's Ender, but since ultimately he *is* me, I guess that's a quibble."

"Ender has three bodies," said Wang-mu. "Does this mean he's giving up one of the others?"

"I don't think he's giving up anything," said Peter. "Or I should say, I don't think *I'm* giving up anything. It's not a conscious choice. Ender's hold on life is angry and strong. Supposedly he was on his deathbed for a day at least before Jane was shut down."

"Killed," said Grace.

"Demoted maybe," said Peter stubbornly. "A dryad now instead of a god. A sylph." He winked at Wang-mu, who had no idea what he was talking about. "Even when he gives up on his own old life he just won't let go."

"He has two more bodies than he needs," said Wang-mu, "and Jane has one fewer than she must have. It seems that the laws of commerce should apply. Two times more supply than is needed—the price should be cheap."

When all of this was interpreted to Malu, he laughed again. "He laughs at 'cheap,' " said Grace. "He says that the only way that Ender will give up any of his bodies is to die.''

Peter nodded. "I know," he said.

"But Ender isn't Jane," said Wang-mu. "He hasn't been living as a—a naked aiúa running along the ansible web. He's a person. When people's aiúas leave their bodies, they don't go chasing around to something else.''

"And yet his—my—aiúa *was* inside me," said Peter. "He knows the way. Ender might die and yet let me live.''

"Or all three of you might die.''

"This much I know," Malu told them, through Grace. "If the god is to be given life of her own, if she is ever to be restored to her power, Ender Wiggin has to die and give a body to the god. There's no other way.''

"Restored to her power?" asked Wang-mu. "Is that possible? I thought the whole point of the computer shutdown was to lock her out of the computer nets forever.''

Malu laughed again, and slapped his naked chest and thighs as he poured out a stream of Samoan.

Grace translated. "How many hundreds of computers do we have here in Samoa? For months, ever since she made herself known to me, we have been copying, copying, copying. Whatever memory she wanted us to save, we have it, ready to restore it all. Maybe it's only one small part of what she used to be, but it's the most important part. If she can get back into the ansible net, she'll have what she needs to get back into the computer nets as well.''

"But they're not linking the computer nets to the ansibles," said Wang-mu.

"That's the order sent by Congress," said Grace. "But not all orders are obeyed.''

"Then why did Jane bring us here?" Peter asked plaintively. "If Malu and you deny that you have any influence over Aimaina, and if Jane has already been in contact with you and you're already effectively in revolt against Congress—''

"No, no, it's not like that," Grace reassured him. "We

were doing what Malu asked us, but he never spoke of a computer entity, he spoke of a god, and we obeyed because we trust his wisdom and we know he sees things that we don't see. Your coming told us who Jane is."

When Malu learned in turn what had been said, he pointed at Peter. "You! You came here to bring the god!" Then he pointed at Wang-mu. "And *you* came here to bring the man."

"Whatever that means," said Peter.

But Wang-mu thought she understood. They had survived one crisis, but this peaceful hour was only a lull. The battle would be joined again, and this time the outcome would be different. If Jane was to live, if there was to be any hope of restoring instantaneous starflight, Ender had to give at least one of his bodies to her. If Malu was right, then Ender had to die. There was a slight chance that Ender's aiúa might still keep one of the three bodies, and go on living. I am here, Wang-mu said silently, to make sure that it is Peter who survives, not as the god, but as the man.

It all depends, she realized, on whether Ender-as-Peter loves me more than Ender-as-Valentine loves Miro or Ender-as-Ender loves Novinha.

With that thought she almost despaired. Who was she? Miro had been Ender's friend for years. Novinha was his wife. But Wang-mu—Ender had only learned of her existence mere days or at most weeks ago. What was she to him?

But then she had another, more comforting and yet disturbing thought. Is it as important who the loved one is as it is which aspect of Ender desires him or her? Valentine is the perfect altruist—she might love Miro most of all, yet give him up for the sake of giving starflight back to us all. And Ender—he was already losing interest in his old life. He's the weary one, he's the worn-out one. While Peter—he's the one with the ambition, the lust for growth and creation. It's not that he loves *me,* it's that *he* loves me, or rather that *he* wants to live, and part of life to him is me, this woman who loves him despite his supposed wickedness. Ender-as-Peter is the part of him that most needs to be loved because he least deserves it—so it is my love, because it is for Peter, that will be most precious to him.

If anyone wins at all, I will win, Peter will win, not because of the glorious purity of our love, but because of the desperate hunger of the lovers.

Well, the story of our lives won't be as noble or pretty, but then, we'll *have* a life, and that's enough.

She worked her toes into the sand, feeling the tiny delicious pain of the friction of tiny chips of silicon against the tender flesh between her toes. That's life. It hurts, it's dirty, and it feels very, very good.

Over the ansible, Olhado told his brother and sisters on the starship what had happened with Jane and the mothertrees.

"The Hive Queen says it can't last long this way," said Olhado. "The mothertrees aren't all that strong. They'll slip, they'll lose control, and pretty soon Jane will be a forest, period. Not a talking one, either. Just some very lovely, very bright, very nurturing trees. It was beautiful to see, I promise you, but the way the Hive Queen tells it, it still sounds like death."

"Thanks, Olhado," Miro said. "It doesn't make much difference to us either way. We're stranded here, and so we're going to get to work, now that Val isn't bouncing off the walls. The descoladores haven't found us yet—Jane got us in a higher orbit this time—but as soon as we have a workable translation of their language we'll wave at them and let them know we're here."

"Keep at it," said Olhado. "But don't give up on coming back home, either."

"The shuttle really isn't good for a two-hundred-year flight," said Miro. "That's how far away we are, and this little vehicle can't even get close to the speeds necessary for relativistic flight. We'd have to play solitaire the whole two hundred years. The cards would wear out long before we got back home.''

Olhado laughed—too lightly and sincerely, Miro thought—and said, ''The Hive Queen says that once Jane gets out of the trees, and once the Congress gets their new system up and running, she may be able to jump back in. At least enough to get into the ansible traffic. And if she does that, then maybe she can go back into the starflight business. It's not impossible.''

Val grew alert at that. ''Is that what the Hive Queen guesses, or does she know?''

''She's predicting the future,'' said Olhado. ''*Nobody* knows the future. Not even really smart queen bees who bite their husbands' heads off when they mate.''

They had no answer to what he said, and certainly nothing to say to his jocular tone.

''Well, if that's all right now,'' said Olhado, ''back on your heads, everybody. We'll leave the station open and recording in triplicate for any reports you make.''

Olhado's face disappeared from the terminal space.

Miro swiveled his chair and faced the others: Ela, Quara, Val, the pequenino Firequencher, and the nameless worker, who watched them in perpetual silence, only able to speak by typing into the terminal. Through him, though, Miro knew that the Hive Queen was watching everything they did, hearing everything they said. Waiting. She was orchestrating this, he knew. Whatever happened to Jane, the Hive Queen would be the catalyst to get it started. Yet the things she said, she had said to Olhado through some worker there in Milagre. This one had typed in nothing but ideas concerning the translation of the language of the descoladores.

She isn't saying anything, Miro realized, because she doesn't want to be seen to push. Push what? Push whom?

Val. She can't be seen to push Val, because . . . because

the only way to let Jane have one of Ender's bodies was for him to freely give it up. And it had to be truly free— no pressure, no guilt, no persuasion—because it wasn't a decision that could be made consciously. Ender had decided that he wanted to share Mother's life in the monastery, but his unconscious mind was far more interested in the translation project here and in whatever it is Peter's doing. His unconscious choice reflected his true will. If Ender is to let go of Val, it has to be his desire to do it, all the way to the core of him. Not a decision out of duty, like his decision to stay with Mother. A decision because that is what he really wants.

Miro looked at Val, at the beauty that came more from deep goodness than from regular features. He loved her, but was it the perfection of her that he loved? That perfect virtue might be the only thing that allowed her—allowed Ender in his Valentine mode—to willingly let go and invite Jane in. And yet once Jane arrived, the perfect virtue would be gone, wouldn't it? Jane was powerful and, Miro believed, good—certainly she had been good to him, a true friend. But even in his wildest imaginations he could not conceive of her as perfectly virtuous. If *she* started wearing Val, would she still be Val? The memories would linger, but the will behind the face would be more complicated than the simple script that Ender had created for her. Will I still love her when she's Jane?

Why wouldn't I? I love Jane too, don't I?

But will I love Jane when she's flesh and blood, and not just a voice in my ear? Will I look into those eyes and mourn for this lost Valentine?

Why didn't I have these doubts before? I tried to bring this off myself, back before I even half understood how difficult it was. And yet now, when it's only the barest hope, I find myself—what, wishing it wouldn't happen? Hardly that. I don't want to die out here. I want Jane restored, if only to get starflight back again—now that's an altruistic motive! I want Jane restored, but I also want Val unchanged.

I want all bad things to go away and everybody to be happy. I want my mommy. What kind of childish dolt have I become?

Val was looking at him, he suddenly realized. "Hi," he said. The others were looking at him, too. Looking back and forth between him and Val. "What are we all voting on, whether I should grow a beard?"

"Voting on nothing," said Quara. "I'm just depressed. I mean, I knew what I was doing when I got on this ship, but *damn,* it's really hard to get enthusiastic about working on these people's language when I can count my life by the gauge on the oxygen tanks."

"I notice," said Ela dryly, "that you're already calling the descoladores 'people.' "

"Shouldn't I? Do we even know what they look like?" Quara seemed confused. "I mean, they have a language, they—"

"That's what we're here to decide, isn't it?" said Firequencher. "Whether the descoladores are raman or varelse. The translation problem is just a little step along that road."

"Big step," corrected Ela. "And we don't have time enough to do it."

"Since we don't know how long it's going to take," said Quara, "I don't see how you can be so sure of that."

"I can be dead sure," said Ela. "Because all we're doing is sitting around talking and watching Miro and Val make soulful faces at each other. It doesn't take a genius to know that at this rate, our progress before running out of oxygen will be exactly zero."

"In other words," said Quara, "we should stop wasting time." She turned back to the notes and printouts she was working on.

"But we're *not* wasting time," said Val softly.

"No?" asked Ela.

"I'm waiting for Miro to tell me how easily Jane could

be brought back into communication with the real world. A body waiting to receive her. Starflight restored. His old and loyal friend, suddenly a real girl. I'm waiting for that.''

Miro shook his head. ''I don't want to lose you,'' he said.

''That's not helping,'' said Val.

''But it's true,'' said Miro. ''The theory, that was easy. Thinking deep thoughts while riding on a hovercar back on Lusitania, sure, I could reason out that Jane in Val would be Jane *and* Val. But when you come right down to it, I can't say that—''

''Shut up,'' said Val.

It wasn't like her to talk like that. Miro shut up.

''No more words like that,'' she said. ''What I need from you is the words that will let me give up this body.''

Miro shook his head.

''Put your money where your mouth is,'' she said. ''Walk the walk. Talk the talk. Put up or shut up. Fish or cut bait.''

He knew what she wanted. He knew that she was saying that the only thing holding her to this body, to this life, was him. Was her love for him. Was their friendship and companionship. There were others here now to do the work of translation—Miro could see now that this was the plan, really, all along. To bring Ela and Quara so that Val could not possibly consider her life as indispensable. But Miro, she couldn't let go of him that easily. And she had to, had to let go.

''Whatever aiúa is in that body,'' Miro said, ''you'll remember everything I say.''

''And you have to mean it, too,'' said Val. ''It has to be the truth.''

''Well it can't be,'' said Miro. ''Because the truth is that I—''

''Shut up!'' demanded Val. ''Don't say that again. It's a lie!''

''It's not a lie.''

"It's complete self-deception on your part, and you have to wake up and see the truth, Miro! You already made the choice between me and Jane. You're only backing out now because you don't like being the kind of man who makes that sort of ruthless choice. But you never loved me, Miro. You never loved *me*. You loved the companionship, yes— the only woman you were around, of course; there's a biological imperative playing a role here with a desperately lonely young man. But *me?* I think what you loved was your memory of your friendship with the real Valentine when she came back with you from space. And you loved how noble it made you feel to declare your love for me in the effort to save my life, back when Ender was ignoring me. But all of that was about you, not me. You never knew me, you never loved me. It was Jane you loved, and Valentine, and Ender himself, the real Ender, not this plastic container that he created in order to compartmentalize all the virtues he wishes he had more of."

The nastiness, the rage in her was palpable. This wasn't like her at all. Miro could see that the others were also stunned. And yet he also understood. This was exactly like her—for she was being hateful and angry in order to persuade herself to let go of this life. And she was doing *that* for the sake of others. It was perfect altruism. Only she would die, and, in exchange, perhaps the others in this ship would *not* die, they'd go back home when their work here was done. Jane would live, clothed in this new flesh, inheriting her memories. Val had to persuade herself that the life that she was living now was worthless, to her and everyone else; that the only value to her life would be to leave it.

And she wanted Miro to help her. That was the sacrifice she asked of him. To help her let go. To help her *want* to go. To help her hate this life.

"All right," said Miro. "You want the truth? You're completely empty, Val, and you always were. You just sit there spouting the exactly kindest thing, but there's never been any heart in it. Ender felt a need to make you, not because he actually has any of the virtues you supposedly represent, but because he doesn't have them. That's why he admires them so much. So when he made you, he didn't know what to put inside you. An empty script. Even now, you're just following the script. Perfect altruism my ass. How can it be a sacrifice to give up a life that was never a life?''

She struggled for a moment, and a tear flowed down her cheek. ''You told me that you loved me.''

''I was sorry for you. That day in Valentine's kitchen, all right? But the truth is I was probably just trying to impress Valentine. The other Valentine. Show her what a good guy I am. *She* actually has some of those virtues—I care a lot about what she thinks of me. So . . . I fell in love with being the kind of guy who was worthy of Valentine's respect. That's as close to loving you as I ever got. And then we found out what our real mission was and suddenly you aren't dying anymore and here I am, stuck with having *said* I loved you and now I've got to keep going and going to maintain the fiction even as it becomes clearer and clearer that I miss Jane, I miss her so desperately that it hurts, and the only reason I can't have her back is because *you* won't let go—''

''Please,'' said Val. ''It hurts too much. I didn't think you—I—''

''Miro,'' said Quara, ''this is the shittiest thing I've ever seen anybody do to anybody else and I've seen some doozies.''

''Shut up, Quara,'' said Ela.

''Oh, who made you queen of the starship?'' retorted Quara.

''This isn't about you,'' said Ela.

''I know, it's about Miro the complete bastard—''

Firequencher launched himself gently from his seat and in a moment had his strong hand clamped over Quara's mouth. "This isn't the time," he said to her softly. "You understand nothing."

She got her face free. "I understand enough to know that this is—"

Firequencher turned to the Hive Queen's worker. "Help us," he said.

The worker got up and with astonishing speed had Quara out of the main deck of the shuttle. Where the Hive Queen took Quara and how she restrained her were questions that didn't even interest Miro. Quara was too self-centered to understand the little play that Miro and Val were acting out. But the others understood.

What mattered, though, was that Val *not* understand. Val had to believe that he meant what he was saying now. It had almost been working before Quara interrupted. But now they had lost the thread.

"Val," said Miro wearily, "it doesn't matter what I say. Because you'll never let go. And you know why? Because you *aren't* Val. You're Ender. And even though Ender can wipe out whole planets in order to save the human race, his own life is sacred. He'll never give it up. Not one scrap. And that includes you—he'll never let go of you. Because you're the last and greatest of his delusions. If he gives you up, he'll lose his last hope of really being a good man."

"That's nonsense," said Val. "The only way he can *be* a really good man is to give me up."

"That's my point," said Miro. "He isn't a really good man. So he can't give you up. Even to attempt to prove his virtue. Because the tie of the aiúa to the body can't be faked. He can fool everybody else, but he can't fool your body. He's just not good enough to let you go."

"So it's Ender that you hate, not me."

"No, Val, I don't hate Ender. He's an imperfect guy, that's all. Like me, like everybody else. Like the real Valentine, for that matter. Only you have the illusion of perfection—but that's fine, because you're not real. You're just Ender in drag, doing his Valentine bit. You come off the stage and there's nothing there, it comes off like makeup and a costume. And you really believed I was in love with *that?*"

Val swiveled on her chair, turning her back to him. "I almost believe you mean these things," she said.

"What I can't believe," said Miro, "is that I'm saying them out loud. But that's what you wanted me to do, wasn't it? For me to be honest with you for the first time, so maybe you could be honest with yourself and realize that what you have isn't a life at all, it's just a perpetual confession of Ender's inadequacy as a human being. You're the childhood innocence he thinks he lost, but here's the truth about that: Before they ever took him away from his parents, before he ever went up to that Battle School in the sky, before they made a perfect killing machine out of him, he was already the brutal, ruthless killer that he always feared he was. It's one of the things that even Ender tries to pretend isn't so: He killed a boy before he ever became a soldier. He kicked that boy's head in. Kicked him and kicked him and the kid never woke up. His parents never saw him alive again. The kid was a prick but he didn't deserve to die. Ender was a killer from the start. That's the thing that he can't live with. That's the reason he needs you. That's the reason he needs Peter. So he can take the ugly ruthless killer side of himself and put it all on Peter. And he can look at perfect you and say, 'See, that beautiful thing was inside me.' And we all play along. But you're not beautiful, Val. You're the pathetic apologia of a man whose whole life is a lie."

Val broke down sobbing.

Almost, almost Miro had compassion and stopped. Almost he shouted at her, No, Val, it's you I love, it's you I want! It's you I longed for all my life and Ender *is* a good man because all this nonsense about you being a pretense is impossible. Ender didn't create you consciously, the way hypocrites create their facades. You grew out of him. The virtues were there, are there, and you are the natural home for them. I already loved and admired Ender, but not until I met you did I know how beautiful he was inside.

Her back was to him. She couldn't see the torment that he felt.

"What is it, Val? Am I supposed to pity you again? Don't you understand that the only conceivable value that you have to any of us is if you just go away and let Jane have your body? We don't need you, we don't want you. Ender's aiúa belongs in Peter's body because that's the only one that has a chance of acting out Ender's true character. Get lost, Val. When you're gone, we have a chance to live. While you're here, we're all dead. Do you think for one second that we'll miss you? Think again."

I will never forgive myself for saying these things, Miro realized. Even though I know the necessity of helping Ender let go of this body by making this an unbearable place for him to stay, it doesn't change the fact that I'll remember saying it, I'll remember the way she looks now, weeping with despair and pain. How can I live with that? I thought I was deformed before. All I had wrong with me then was brain damage. But now—I couldn't have said any of these things to her if I hadn't thought of them. There's the rub. I thought of these terrible things to say. That's the kind of man *I* am.

———

Ender opened his eyes again, then reached a hand up to touch Novinha's face, the bruises there. He moaned to see Valentine and Plikt, too. "What did I do to you?"

"It wasn't you," said Novinha. "It was her."

"It was me," he said. "I meant to let her have . . . something. I meant to, but when it came right down to it, I was afraid. I couldn't do it." He looked away from them, closed his eyes. "She tried to kill me. She tried to drive me out."

"You were both working way below the level of consciousness," said Valentine. "Two strong-willed aiúas, unable to back off from life. That's not so terrible."

"What, and you were just standing too close?"

"That's right," said Valentine.

"I hurt you," said Ender. "I hurt all three of you."

"We don't hold people responsible for convulsions," said Novinha.

Ender shook his head. "I'm talking about . . . before. I lay there listening. Couldn't move my body, couldn't make a sound, but I could hear. I know what I did to you. All three of you. I'm sorry."

"Don't be," said Valentine. "We all chose our lives. I could have stayed on Earth in the first place, you know. Didn't have to follow you. I proved that when I stayed with Jakt. You didn't cost me anything—I've had a brilliant career and a wonderful life, and much of that is because I was with you. As for Plikt, well, we finally saw—much to my relief, I might add—that she isn't always in complete control of herself. Still, you never asked her to follow you here. She chose what she chose. If her life is wasted, well, she wasted it the way she wanted to and that's none of your business. As for Novinha—"

"Novinha is my wife," said Ender. "I said I wouldn't leave her. I tried not to leave her."

"You haven't left me," Novinha said.

"Then what am I doing in this bed?"

"You're dying," said Novinha.

"My point exactly," said Ender.

"But you were dying before you came here," she said. "You were dying from the moment that I left you in anger and came here. That was when you realized, when we both realized, that we weren't building anything together anymore. Our children aren't young. One of them is dead. There'll be no others. Our work now doesn't coincide at any point."

"That doesn't mean it's right to end the—"

"As long as we both shall live," said Novinha. "I know that, Andrew. You keep the marriage alive for your children, and then when they're grown up you stay married for everybody else's children, so they grow up in a world where marriages are permanent. I know all that, Andrew. Permanent—until one of you dies. That's why you're here, Andrew. Because you have other lives that you want to live, and because of some miraculous fluke you actually have the bodies to live them in. Of course you're leaving me. Of course.''

''I keep my promise,'' Ender said.

''Till death,'' said Novinha. ''No longer than that. Do you think I won't miss you when you're gone? Of course I will. I'll miss you as any widow misses her beloved husband. I'll miss you whenever I tell stories about you to our grandchildren. It's good for a widow to miss her husband. It gives shape to her life. But you—the shape of your life comes from them. From your other selves. Not from me. Not anymore. I don't begrudge that, Andrew.''

''I'm afraid,'' said Ender. ''When Jane drove me out, I've never felt such fear. I don't want to die.''

''Then don't stay here, because staying in this old body and with this old marriage, Andrew, *that* would be the real death. And me, watching you, knowing that you don't really want to be here, that would be a kind of death for me.''

''Novinha, I *do* love you, that's not pretense, all the years of happiness we had together, that was real—like Jakt and Valentine it was real. Tell her, Valentine.''

''Andrew,'' said Valentine, ''please remember. *She* left *you.*''

Ender looked at Valentine. Then at Novinha, long and hard. ''That's true, isn't it. You left me. I made you take me.''

Novinha nodded.

''But I thought—I thought you needed me. Still.''

Novinha shrugged. ''Andrew, that's always been the problem. I needed you, but not out of duty. I don't need you because you have to keep your word to me. Bit by bit, seeing you every day, knowing that it's *duty* that keeps you, how do you think that will help me, Andrew?''

"You want me to die?"

"I want you to live," said Novinha. "To *live*. As Peter. That's a fine young boy with a long life ahead of him. I wish him well. Be him now, Andrew. Leave this old widow behind. You've done your duty to me. And I know you do love me, as I still love you. Dying doesn't deny that.''

Ender looked at her, believing her, wondering if he was right to believe her. She means it; how can she mean it; she's saying what she thinks I want her to say; but what she says is true. Back and forth, around and around the questions played in his mind.

But then at some point he lost interest in the questions and he fell asleep.

That's how it felt to him. Fell asleep.

The three women around his bed saw his eyes close. Novinha even sighed, thinking that she had failed. She even started to turn away. But then Plikt gasped. Novinha turned back around. Ender's hair had all come loose. She reached up to where it was sliding from his scalp, wanting to touch him, to make it be all right again, but knowing that the best thing she could do would be not to touch him, not to waken him, to let him go.

"Don't watch this," murmured Valentine. But none of them made a move to go. They watched, not touching, not speaking again, as his skin sagged against his bones, as it dried and crumbled, as he turned to dust under the sheets, on the pillow, and then even the dust crumbled until it was too fine to see. Nothing there. No one there at all, except the dead hair that had fallen away from him first.

Valentine reached down and began to sweep the hair into a pile. For a moment Novinha was revolted. Then she understood. They had to bury something. They had to have a funeral and lay what was left of Andrew Wiggin in the ground. Novinha reached out and helped. And when Plikt also took up a few stray hairs, Novinha did not shun her, but took those hairs into her own hands, as she took the ones that Valentine had gathered. Ender was free. Novinha had freed him. She had said the things she had to say to let him go.

Was Valentine right? Would this be different, in the long run, from the other ones that she had loved and lost? Later she would know. But now, today, this moment, all she could feel was the sick weight of grief inside her. No, she wanted to cry. No, Ender, it wasn't true, I still need you, duty or oathkeeping, whatever it takes, I still want you with me, no one ever loved me as you loved me and I needed that, I needed you, where are you now, where are you when I love you so?

———

<He's letting go,> said the Hive Queen.

<But can he find his way to another body?> asked Human. <Don't let him be lost!>

<It's up to him,> said the Hive Queen. <Him and Jane.>

<Does she know?>

<No matter where she is, she's still attuned to him. Yes, she knows. She's searching for him even now. Yes, and there she goes.>

———

She leapt back out of the web that had so gently, kindly held her; it clung to her; I will be back, she thought, I will be back to you, but not to stay so long again; it hurts you when I stay so long.

She leapt and found herself again with that familiar aiúa that she had been entwined with for three thousand years. He seemed lost, confused. One of the bodies was missing, that was it. The old one. The old familiar shape. He was barely holding on to the other two. He had no root or anchor. In neither of them did he feel that he belonged. He was a stranger in his own flesh.

She approached him. This time she knew better than before what she was doing, how to control herself. This time she held back, she didn't take anything that was his. She gave him no challenge to his possession. Just came near.

And in his uncertainty she was familiar to him. Uprooted from his oldest home, he was able now to see that, yes, he knew her, had known her for a long time. He came closer to her, unafraid of her. Yes, closer, closer.

Follow me.

She leapt into the Valentine body. He followed her She passed through without touching, without tasting the life of it; it was his to touch, his to taste. He felt the limbs of her, the lips and tongue; he opened the eyes and looked; he thought her thoughts; he heard her memories.

Tears in the eyes, down the cheeks. Deep grief in the heart. I can't bear to be here, he thought. I don't belong. No one wants me here. They all want me out of here and gone.

The grief tore at him, pushed him away. It was an unbearable place for him.

The aiúa that had once been Jane now reached out, tentatively, and touched a single spot, a single cell.

He grew alarmed, but only for a moment. This isn't mine, he thought. I don't belong here. It's yours. You can have it.

She led him here and there inside this body, always touching, taking mastery of it; only this time instead of fighting her, he gave control of it to her, over and over I'm not wanted here. Take it. Have joy with it. It's yours. It never was my own.

She felt the flesh become herself, more and more of it, the cells by hundreds, thousands, moving their allegiance from the old master who no longer wanted to be there, to the new mistress who worshipped them. She did not say to them, You are mine, the way she had tried to when she came here before. Instead her cry now was, I am yours; and then, finally, you are *me*.

She was astonished with the wholeness of this body. She realized, now, that until this moment she had never been a self before. What she had for all those centuries was an apparatus, not a self. She had been on life support, waiting for a life. But now, trying on the arms like sleeves, she found that yes, her arms were *this* long; yes, this tongue, these lips move just where *my* tongue and lips must move.

And then, seeping into her awareness, claiming her attention—which had once been divided among ten thousand thoughts at once—came memories that she had never known before. Memories of speech with lips and breath. Memories of sights with eyes, sounds with ears. Memories of walking, running.

And then the memories of people. Standing in that first starship, seeing her first sight—of Andrew Wiggin, the look on his face, the wonder as he saw her, as he looked back and forth between her and—

And Peter.

Ender.

Peter.

She had forgotten. She had been so caught up in this new self she found that she forgot the lost aiúa who had given it to her. Where was he?

Lost, lost. Not in the other one, not anywhere, how could she have lost him? How many seconds, minutes, hours had he been away? Where was he?

Darting away from the body, from herself that called itself Val, she probed, she searched, but could not find.

He's dead. I lost him. He gave me this life and he had no way of holding on then, yet I forgot him and he's gone.

But then she remembered he had been gone before. When she chased him through his three bodies and at last he leapt away for a moment, it was that leap that had led her to the lacework of the web of trees. He would do it again, of course. He would leap to the only other place he had ever leapt to.

She followed him and he was there, but not where she

had been, not among the mothertrees, nor even among the fathertrees. Not among the trees at all. No, he had followed where she hadn't wanted then to go, along the thick and ropey twines that led to them; no, not to them, to her. The Hive Queen. The one that he had carried in her dry cocoon for three thousand years, world to world, until at last he found a home for her. Now she at last returned the gift; when Jane's aiúa probed along the twines that led to her, there he was, uncertain, lost.

He knew her. Cut off as he was, it was astonishing that he knew anything; but he knew her. And once again he followed her. This time she did not lead him into the body that he had given her; that was hers now; no, it was *her* now. Instead she led him to a different body in a different place.

But he acted as he had in the body that was now her own; he seemed to be a stranger here. Even though the million aiúas of the body reached out for him, yearned for him to sustain them, he held himself aloof. Had it been so terrible for him, what he saw and felt in the other body? Or was it that this body was Peter, that for him it represented all he feared most in himself? He would not take it. It was his, and he would not, could not . . .

But he must. She led him through it, giving each part of it to him. This is you now. Whatever it once meant to you, that isn't what it is now—you can be whole here, you can be yourself now.

He didn't understand her; cut off from any kind of body, how much thought was he capable of, anyway? He only knew that this body wasn't the one he loved. He had given up the ones he loved.

Still she pulled him on; he followed. This cell, this tissue, this organ, this limb, they are you, see how they yearn for you, see how they obey you. And they did, they obeyed him despite his pulling away. They obeyed him until at last he began to think the thoughts of the mind and feel the sensations of the body. Jane waited, watching, holding him in place, willing him to stay long enough to accept the body, for she could see that without her he would let go, he would flee. I don't belong here, his aiúa was saying silently. I don't belong, I don't belong.

———

Wang-mu cradled his head on her lap, keening, crying. Around her the Samoans were gathering to watch her grief. She knew what it meant, when he collapsed, when he went so limp, when his hair came loose. Ender was dead in some far-off place, and he could not find his way here. "He's lost," she cried. "He's lost."

Vaguely she heard a stream of Samoan from Malu. And then the translation from Grace. "He isn't lost. She's led him here. The God has led him here but he's afraid to stay."

How could he be afraid? Peter, afraid? Ender, afraid? Ludicrous on both counts. What part of him had ever been a coward? What was it that he had ever feared?

And then she remembered—what Ender feared was Peter, and Peter's fear had always been of Ender. "No," she said, only now it wasn't grief. Now it was frustration, anger, need. "No, listen to me, you belong here! This is you, the real you! I don't care what you're afraid of now! I don't care how lost you might be. I want you here. This is your home and it always has been. With me! We're good together. We belong together. Peter! Ender—whoever you think you are—do you think it makes any difference to me? You've always been yourself, the same man you are now, and this has always been your body. Come home! Come back!" And on and on she babbled.

And then his eyes opened, and his lips parted in a smile. "Now that's *acting*," he said.

Angrily she pushed him down again. "How can you laugh at me like that!"

"So you didn't mean it," he said. "You *don't* like me after all."

"I never said I *did* like you," she answered.

"I know what you said."

"Well," she said. "Well."

"And it was true," he said. "Was and is."

"You mean I said something right? I hit upon *truth?*"

"You said that I belonged here," Peter answered. "And I do." His hand reached up to touch her cheek, but didn't stop there. He put his hand behind her neck, and drew her down, and held her close to him. Around them two dozen huge Samoans laughed and laughed.

———

This is you now, Jane said to him. This is the whole of you. One again. You are at one.

Whatever he had experienced during his reluctant control of the body was enough. There was no more timidity, no more uncertainty. This aiúa she had led through the body now took grateful mastery, eagerly as if this were the first body he had ever had. And perhaps it was. Having been cut off, however briefly, would he even remember being Andrew Wiggin? Or was the old life gone? The aiúa was the same, the brilliant, powerful aiúa; but would any memory linger, beyond the memories mapped by the mind of Peter Wiggin?

Not mine to worry about now, she thought. He has his body now. He will not die, for now. And I have *my* body, I have the gossamer web among the mothertrees, and somewhere, someday, I will also have my ansibles again. I never knew how limited I was until now, how little and small I was; but now I feel as my friend feels, surprised by how alive I am.

Back in her new body, her new self, she let the thoughts and memories flow again, and this time held back nothing. Her aiúa-consciousness was soon overwhelmed by all she sensed and felt and thought and remembered. It would come back to her, the way the Hive Queen noticed her own aiúa and her philotic connections; it came back even now, in flashes, like a childhood skill that she had mastered once and then forgotten. She was also aware, vaguely, in the back of her mind, that she was still leaping several times a second to make the circuit of the trees, but did it all so quickly that she missed nothing of the thoughts that passed through her mind as Valentine.

As Val.

As Val who sat weeping, the terrible words that Miro said still ringing in her ears. He never loved me. He wanted Jane. They all want Jane and not me.

But I am Jane. And I am me. I am Val.

She stopped crying. She moved.

Moved! The muscles tautening and relaxing, flex, extend, miraculous cells working their collective way to move great heavy bones and sacs of skin and organs, shift them, balance them so delicately. The joy of it was too great. It erupted from her in—what was this convulsive spasming of her diaphragm? What was this gust of sound erupting from her own throat?

It was laughter. How long had she faked it with computer chips, simulated speech and laughter, and never, never knew what it meant, how it felt. She never wanted to stop.

"Val," said Miro.

Oh, to hear his voice through ears!

"Val, are you all right?"

"Yes," she said. Her tongue moved so, her lips; she breathed, she pushed, all these habits that Val already had, so fresh and new and wonderful to her. "And yes, you must keep on calling me Val. Jane was something else. Someone else. Before I was myself, I was Jane. But now I'm Val."

She looked at him and saw (with eyes!) how tears flowed down his cheeks. She understood at once.

"No," she said. "You don't have to call me Val at all. Because I'm not the Val you knew, and I don't mind if you grieve for her. I know what you said to her. I know how it hurt you to say it; I remember how it hurt her to hear it. But don't regret it, please. It was such a great gift you gave me, you and her both. And it was also a gift you gave to *her*. I saw her aiúa pass into Peter. She isn't dead. And more important, I think—by saying what you said to her, you freed her to do the thing that best expressed who she truly was. You helped her die for you. And now she is at one with herself; he is at one with himself. Grieve for her, but don't regret. And you can always call me Jane.''

And then she knew, the Val part of her knew, the memory of the self that Val had been *knew* what she had to do. She pushed away from the chair, drifted to where Miro sat, enfolded him in her arms (I touch him with these hands!), held his head close to her shoulder, and let his tears soak hot, then cold, into her shirt, onto her skin. It burned. It burned.

11

"YOU CALLED ME BACK FROM DARKNESS"

Yasujiro Tsutsumi was astonished at the name his secretary whispered to him. At once he nodded, then rose to his feet to speak to the two men he was meeting with. The negotiations had been long and difficult, and now to have them interrupted at this late stage, when things were so close—but that could not be helped. He would rather lose millions than to show disrespect to the great man who had, unbelievably, come calling on *him*.

"I beg you to forgive me for being so rude to you, but

my old teacher has come to visit me and it would shame me and my house to make him wait.''

Old Shigeru at once rose to his feet and bowed. ''I thought the younger generation had forgotten how to show respect. I know that your teacher is the great Aimaina Hikari, the keeper of the Yamato spirit. But even if he were a toothless old schoolteacher from some mountain village, a decent young man would show respect as you are doing.''

Young Shigeru was not so pleased—or at least not so good at concealing his annoyance. But it was Old Shigeru whose opinion of this interruption mattered. Once the deal closed, there would be plenty of time to bring the son around.

''You honor me by your understanding words,'' said Yasujiro. ''Please let me see if my teacher will honor me by letting me bring such wise men together under my poor roof.''

Yasujiro bowed again and went out into his reception room. Aimaina Hikari was still standing. His secretary, also standing, shrugged helplessly, as if to say, He would not sit down. Yasujiro bowed deeply, and again, and then again, before he asked if he could present his friends.

Aimaina frowned and asked softly, ''Are these the Shigeru Fushimis who claim to be descended from a noble family—which died out two thousand years before suddenly coming up with new offspring?''

Yasujiro felt suddenly faint with dread that Aimaina, who was, after all, guardian of the Yamato spirit, would humiliate him by challenging the Fushimis' claim to noble blood. ''It is a small and harmless vanity,'' said Yasujiro quietly. ''A man may be proud of his family.''

''As your namesake, the founder of the Tsutsumi fortune, was proud to forget that his ancestors were Korean.''

''You have said yourself,'' said Yasujiro, absorbing the insult to himself with equanimity, ''that all Japanese are Korean in origin, but those with the Yamato spirit crossed over to the islands as quickly as they could. Mine followed yours by only a few centuries.''

Aimaina laughed. ''You are still my sly quick-witted student! Take me to your friends, I would be honored to meet them.''

There followed ten minutes of bows and smiles, pleasant compliments and self-abnegations. Yasujiro was relieved that there wasn't a hint of condescension or irony when Aimaina said the name ''Fushimi,'' and that Young Shigeru was so dazzled to meet the great Aimaina Hikari that the insult of the interrupted meeting was clearly forgotten. The two Shigerus went away with a half dozen holograms of their meeting with Aimaina, and Yasujiro was pleased that Old Shigeru had insisted that Yasujiro stand right there in the holograms with the Fushimis and the great philosopher.

Finally, Yasujiro and Aimaina were alone in his office with the door closed. At once Aimaina went to the window and drew open the curtain to reveal the other tall buildings of Nagoya's financial district and then a view of the countryside, thoroughly farmed in the flatlands, but still wild woodland in the hills, a place of foxes and badgers.

''I am relieved to see that even though a Tsutsumi is here in Nagoya, there is still undeveloped land within sight of the city. I had not thought this possible.''

''Even if you disdain my family, I am proud to have our name on your lips,'' said Yasujiro. But silently he wanted to ask, Why are you determined to insult my family today?

''Are you proud of the man you were named for? The buyer of land, the builder of golf courses? To him all wild country cried out for cabins or putting greens. For that matter, he never saw a woman too ugly to try to get a child with her. Do you follow him in that, too?''

Yasujiro was baffled. Everyone knew the stories of the founder of the Tsutsumi fortune. They had not been news for three thousand years. ''What have I done to bring such anger down on my head?''

''You have done nothing,'' said Hikari. ''And my anger

is not at you. My anger is at myself, because I also have done nothing. I speak of your family's sins of ancient times because the only hope for the Yamato people is to remember all our sins of the past. But we forget. We are so rich now, we own so much, we build so much, that there is no project of any importance on any of the Hundred Worlds that does not have Yamato hands somewhere in it. Yet we forget the lessons of our ancestors.''

"I beg to learn from you, master."

"Once long ago, when Japan was still struggling to enter the modern age, we let ourselves be ruled by our military. Soldiers were our masters, and they led us into an evil war, to conquer nations that had done us no wrong.''

"We paid for our crimes when atomic bombs fell on our islands.''

"Paid?" cried Aimaina. "What is to pay or not to pay? Are we suddenly Christians, who pay for sins? No. The Yamato way is not to pay for error, but to learn from it. We threw out the military and conquered the world with the excellence of our design and the reliability of our labor. The language of the Hundred Worlds may be based on English, but the money of the Hundred Worlds came originally from the yen.''

"But the Yamato people still buy and sell," said Yasujiro. "We have not forgotten the lesson.''

"That was only half the lesson. The other half was: We will not make war.''

"But there is no Japanese fleet, no Japanese army."

"That is the lie we tell ourselves to cover our crimes," said Aimaina. "I had a visit two days ago from two strangers—mortal humans, but I know the god sent them. They rebuked me because it is the Necessarian school that provided the pivotal votes in the Starways Congress to send the Lusitania Fleet. A fleet whose sole purpose is to repeat the crime of Ender the Xenocide and destroy a world that harbors a frail species of raman who do no harm to anyone!''

Yasujiro quailed under the weight of Aimaina's anger. "But master, what do I have to do with the military?"

"Yamato philosophers taught the theory that Yamato politicians acted upon. Japanese votes made the difference. This evil fleet must be stopped."

"Nothing can be stopped today," said Yasujiro. "The ansibles are all shut down, as are all the computer networks while the terrible all-eating virus is expelled from the system."

"Tomorrow the ansibles will come back again," said Aimaina. "And so tomorrow the shame of Japanese participation in xenocide must be averted."

"Why do you come to me?" said Yasujiro. "I may bear the name of my great ancestor, but half the boys in my family are named Yasujiro or Yoshiaki or Seiji. I am master of the Tsutsumi holdings in Nagoya—"

"Don't be modest. You are the Tsutsumi of the world of Divine Wind."

"I am listened to in other cities," said Yasujiro, "but the orders come from the family center on Honshu. And I have no political influence at all. If the problem is the Necessarians, talk to them!"

Aimaina sighed. "Oh, that would do no good. They would spend six months arguing about how to reconcile their new position with their old position, proving that they had not changed their minds after all, that their philosophy embraced the full 180-degree shift. And the politicians— they are committed. Even if the philosophers change their minds, it would be at least a political generation—three elections, the saying goes—before the new policy would be in effect. Thirty years! The Lusitania Fleet will have done all its evil before then."

"Then what is there to do but despair and live in shame?" asked Yasujiro. "Unless you're planning some futile and stupid gesture." He grinned at his master, knowing that Aimaina would recognize the words he himself always used when denigrating the ancient practice of seppuku, ritual suicide, as something the Yamato spirit had left behind as a child leaves its diapers.

Aimaina did not laugh. "The Lusitania Fleet *is* seppuku for the Yamato spirit." He came and stood looming over Yasujiro—or so it felt, though Yasujiro was taller than the old man by half a head. "The politicians have made the Lusitania Fleet popular, so the philosophers cannot now change their minds. But when philosophy and elections cannot change the minds of politicians, money can!"

"You are not suggesting something so shameful as bribery, are you?" said Yasujiro, wondering as he said it whether Aimaina knew how widespread the buying of politicians was.

"Do you think I keep my eyes in my anus?" asked Aimaina, using an expression so crude that Yasujiro gasped and averted his gaze, laughing nervously. "Do you think I don't know that there are ten ways to buy every crooked politician and a hundred ways to buy every honest one? Contributions, threats of sponsoring opponents, donations to noble causes, jobs given to relatives or friends—do I have to recite the list?"

"You seriously want Tsutsumi money committed to stopping the Lusitania Fleet?"

Aimaina walked again to the window and spread out his arms as if to embrace all that could be seen of the outside world. "The Lusitania Fleet is bad for business, Yasujiro. If the Molecular Disruption Device is used against one world, it will be used against another. And the military, when it has such power placed again in its hands, this time will not let it go."

"Will I persuade the heads of my family by quoting your prophecy, master?"

"It is not a prophecy," said Aimaina, "and it is not mine. It is a law of human nature, and it is history that teaches it to us. Stop the fleet, and Tsutsumi will be known as the saviors, not only of the Yamato spirit, but of the human spirit as well. Do not let this grave sin be on the heads of our people.''

"Forgive me, master, but it seems to me that you are the one putting it there. No one noticed that we bore responsibility for this sin until you said it here today.''

"I do not put the sin there. I merely take off the hat that covers it. Yasujiro, you were one of my best students. I forgave you for using what I taught you in such complicated ways, because you did it for your family's sake.''

"And this that you ask of me now—this is perfectly simple?''

"I have taken the most direct action—I have spoken plainly to the most powerful representative of the richest of the Japanese trading families that I could reach on this day. And what I ask of you is the minimum action required to do what is necessary.''

"In this case the minimum puts my career at great risk,'' said Yasujiro thoughtfully.

Aimaina said nothing.

"My greatest teacher once told me,'' said Yasujiro, "that a man who has risked his life knows that careers are worthless, and a man who will not risk his career has a worthless life.''

"So you will do it?''

"I will prepare my messages to make your case to all the Tsutsumi family. When the ansibles are linked again, I will send them.''

"I knew you would not disappoint me.''

"Better than that,'' said Yasujiro. "When I am thrown out of my job, I will come and live with you.''

Aimaina bowed. "I would be honored to have you dwell in my house.''

The lives of all people flow through time, and, regardless of how brutal one moment may be, how filled with grief or pain or fear, time flows through all lives equally. Minutes passed in which Val-Jane held the weeping Miro, and then time dried his tears, time loosened her embrace, and time, finally, ended Ela's patience.

"Let's get back to work," said Ela. "I'm not unfeeling, but our predicament is unchanged."

Quara was surprised. "But Jane's not dead. Doesn't that mean we can get back home?"

Val-Jane at once got up and moved back to her computer terminal. Every movement was easy because of the reflexes and habits the Val-brain had developed; but the Jane-mind found each movement fresh and new; she marveled at the dance of her fingers pressing the keys to control the display. "I don't know," Jane said, answering the question that Quara had voiced, but all were asking. "I'm still uncertain in this flesh. The ansibles haven't been restored. I do have a handful of allies who will relink some of my old programs to the network once it is restored—some Samoans on Pacifica, Han Fei-tzu on Path, the Abo university on Outback. Will those programs be enough? Will the new networking software allow me to tap the resources I need to hold all the information of a starship and so many people in my mind? Will having this body interfere? Will my new link to the mothertrees be a help or a distraction?" And then the most important question: "Do *we* wish to be my first test flight?"

"Somebody has to," said Ela.

"I think I'll try one of the starships on Lusitania, if I can reestablish contact with them," said Jane. "With only a single hive queen worker on board. That way if it is lost, it will not be missed." Jane turned to nod to the worker who was with them. "Begging your pardon, of course."

"You don't have to apologize to the worker," said Quara. "It's really just the Hive Queen anyway."

Jane looked over at Miro and winked. Miro did not wink back, but the look of sadness in his eyes was answer enough. *He* knew that the workers were not quite what everyone thought. The hive queens sometimes had to tame them, because not all of them were utterly subjected to their mother's will. But the was-it-or-wasn't-it-slavery of the workers was a matter for another generation to work out.

"Languages," said Jane. "Carried by genetic molecules. What kind of grammar must they have? Are they linked to sounds, smells, sights? Let's see how smart we all are without *me* inside the computers helping." That struck her as so amazingly funny that she laughed aloud. Ah, how marvelous it was to have her own laughter sounding in her ears, bubbling upward from her lungs, spasming her diaphragm, bringing tears to her eyes!

Only when her laughter ended did she realize how leaden the sound of it must have been to Miro, to the others. "I'm sorry," she said, abashed, and felt a blush rising up her neck into her cheeks. Who could have believed it could burn so hot! It almost made her laugh again. "I'm not used to being alive like this. I know I'm rejoicing when the rest of you are grim, but don't you see? Even if we all die when the air runs out in a few weeks, I can't help but marvel at how it feels to me!"

"We understand," said Firequencher. "You have passed into your Second Life. It's a joyful time for us, as well."

"I spent time among your trees, you know," said Jane. "Your mothertrees made space for me. Took me in and nurtured me. Does that make us brother and sister now?"

"I hardly know what it would mean, to have a sister," said Firequencher. "But if you remember the life in the dark of the mothertree, then you remember more than I do. We have dreams sometimes, but no real memories of the First Life in darkness. Still, that makes this your Third Life after all."

"Then I'm an adult?" asked Jane, and she laughed again.

And again felt how her laugh stilled the others, hurt them.

But something odd happened as she turned, ready to

apologize again. Her glance fell upon Miro, and instead of saying the words she had planned—the Jane-words that would have come out of the jewel in his ear only the day before—other words came to her lips, along with a memory. "If my memories live, Miro, then I'm alive. Isn't that what you told me?"

Miro shook his head. "Are you speaking from Val's memory, or from Jane's memory when she—when you—overheard us speaking in the Hive Queen's cave? Don't comfort me by pretending to be her."

Jane, by habit—Val's habit? or her own?—snapped, "When I comfort you, you'll know it."

"And how will I know?" Miro snapped back.

"Because you'll be comfortable, of course," said Val-Jane. "In the meantime, please keep in mind that I'm not listening through the jewel in your ear *now*. I see only with these eyes and hear only with these ears."

This was not strictly true, of course. For many times a second, she felt the flowing sap, the unstinting welcome of the mothertrees as her aiúa satisfied its hunger for largeness by touring the vast network of the pequenino philotes. And now and then, outside the mothertrees, she caught a glimmer of a thought, of a word, a phrase, spoken in the language of the fathertrees. Or *was* it their language? Rather it was the language behind the language, the underlying speech of the speechless. And whose was that other voice? I know you—you are of the kind that made me. I know your voice.

<We lost track of you,> said the Hive Queen in her mind. <But you did well without us.>

Jane was not prepared for the swelling of pride that glowed through her entire Val-body; she felt the physical effect of the emotion as Val, but her pride came from the praise of a hive-mother. I am a daughter of hive queens, she realized, and so it matters when she speaks to me, and tells me I have done well.

And if I'm the hive queens' daughter, I am Ender's

daughter, too, his daughter twice over, for they made my lifestuff partly from his mind, so I could be a bridge between them; and now I dwell in a body that also came from him, and whose memories are from a time when he dwelt here and lived this body's life. I am his daughter, but once again I cannot speak to him.

All this time, all these thoughts, and yet she did not show or even feel the slightest lapse of concentration on what she was doing with her computer on the starship circling the descolada planet. She was still Jane. It wasn't the computerness of her that had allowed her, all these years, to maintain many layers of attention and focus on many tasks at once. It was her hive-queen nature that allowed this.

<It was because you were an aiúa powerful enough to do this that you were able to come to us in the first place,> said the Hive Queen in her mind.

Which of you is speaking to me? asked Jane.

<Does it matter? We all remember the making of you. We remember being there. We remember drawing you out of darkness into light.>

Am I still myself, then? Will I have again all the powers I lost when the Starways Congress killed my old virtual body?

<You might. When you find out, tell us. We will be very interested.>

And now she felt the sharp disappointment from a parent's unconcern, a sinking feeling in the stomach, a kind of shame. But this was a human emotion; it arose from the Val-body, though it was in response to her relationship with her hive-queen mothers. Everything was more complicated—and yet it was simpler. Her feelings were now flagged by a body, which responded before she understood what she felt herself. In the old days, she scarcely knew she had feelings. She had them, yes, even irrational responses, desires below the level of consciousness—these were attributes of all aiúas, when linked with others in any kind of life—but there had been no simple signals to tell her what her feelings were. How easy it was to be a human, with your emotions expressed on the canvas of your own body. And yet how hard, because you couldn't hide your feelings from yourself half so easily.

<Get used to being frustrated with us, daughter,> said the Hive Queen. <You have a partly human nature, and we do not. We will not be tender with you as human mothers are. When you can't bear it, back away—we won't pursue you.>

Thank you, she said silently . . . and backed away.

At dawn the sun came up over the mountain that was the spine of the island, so that the sky was light long before any sunlight touched the trees directly. The wind off the sea had cooled them in the night. Peter awoke with Wang-mu curled into the curve of his body, like shrimps lined up on a market rack. The closeness of her felt good; it felt familiar. Yet how could it be? He had never slept so close to her before. Was it some vestigial Ender memory? He wasn't conscious of having any such memories. It had disappointed him, actually, when he realized it. He had thought that perhaps when his body had complete possession of the aiúa, he would become Ender—he would have a lifetime of real memories instead of the paltry faked-up memories that had come with his body when Ender created it. No such luck.

And yet he remembered sleeping with a woman curled against him. He remembered reaching across her, his arm like a sheltering bough.

But he had never touched Wang-mu that way. Nor was it right for him to do it now—she was not his wife, only his . . . friend? Was she that? She had said she loved him— was that only a way to help him find his way into this body?

Then, suddenly, he felt himself falling away from himself, felt himself recede from Peter and become something else, something small and bright and terrified, descending down into darkness, out into a wind too strong for him to stand against it—

"Peter!"

The voice called him, and he followed it, back along the almost-invisible philotic threads that connected him to . . . himself again. I am Peter. I have nowhere else to go. If I leave like that, I'll die.

"Are you all right?" asked Wang-mu. "I woke up because I—I'm sorry, but I dreamed, I *felt* as if I was losing you. But I wasn't, because here you are."

"I *was* losing my way," said Peter. "You could sense that?"

"I don't know what I sensed or not. I just—how can I describe it?"

"You called me back from darkness," said Peter.

"Did I?"

He almost said something, but then stopped. Then laughed, uncomfortable and frightened. "I feel so odd. A moment ago I was about to say something. Something very flippant—about how having to be Peter Wiggin was darkness enough by itself."

"Oh yes," said Wang-mu. "You always say such nasty things about yourself."

"But I didn't say it," said Peter. "I was about to, out of habit, but I stopped, because it wasn't true. Isn't that funny?"

"I think it's good."

"It makes sense that I should feel whole instead of being subdivided—perhaps more content with myself or something. And yet I almost lost the whole thing. I think it wasn't just a dream. I think I really was letting go. Falling away into—no, out of everything."

"You had three selves for several months," said Wang-mu. "Is it possible your aiúa hungers for the—I don't know, the *size* of what you used to be?"

"I was spread all over the galaxy, wasn't I? Except I want to say, 'Wasn't *he*,' because that was Ender, wasn't it. And I'm *not* Ender because I don't remember anything." He thought a moment. "Except maybe I do remember some things a little more clearly now. Things from my childhood. My mother's face. It's very clear, and I don't think it was before. And Valentine's face, when we were all children. But I'd remember that as Peter, wouldn't I, so it doesn't mean it comes from Ender, does it? I'm sure this is just one of the memories Ender supplied for me in the first place." He laughed. "I'm really desperate, aren't I, to find some sign of him in me."

Wang-mu sat listening. Silent, not making a great show of interest, but also content not to jump in with an answer or a comment.

Noticing her made him think of something else. "Are you some kind of, what would you call it, an empath? Do you normally feel what other people are feeling?"

"Never," said Wang-mu. "I'm too busy feeling what *I'm* feeling."

"But you knew that I was going. You felt that."

"I suppose," said Wang-mu, "that I'm bound up with you now. I hope that's all right, because it wasn't exactly voluntary on my part."

"But I'm bound up with you, too," said Peter. "Because when I was disconnected, I still heard you. All my other feelings were gone. My body wasn't giving me anything. I had lost my body. Now, when I remember what it felt like, I remember 'seeing' things, but that's just my human brain making sense of things that it can't actually make sense of. I know that I didn't see at all, or hear, or touch or anything at all. And yet I knew you were calling. I felt you—needing me. Wanting me to come back. Surely that means that I am also bound up with you."

She shrugged, looked away.

"Now what does *that* mean?" he asked.

"I'm not going to spend the rest of my life explaining

myself to you," said Wang-mu. "Everyone else has the privilege of just feeling and doing sometimes without analyzing it. What did it look like to *you?* You're the smart one who's an expert on human nature."

"Stop that," said Peter, pretending to be teasing but really wanting her to stop. "I remember we bantered about that, and I bragged I guess, but . . . well I don't feel that way now. Is that part of having all of Ender in me? I know I don't understand people all that well. You looked away, you shrugged when I said I was bound up with you. That hurt my feelings, you know."

"And why is that?"

"Oh, *you* can ask why and *I* can't, are those the rules now?"

"Those have always been the rules," said Wang-mu. "You just never obeyed them."

"Well it hurt my feelings because I wanted you to be glad that I'm tied up with you and you with me."

"Are *you* glad?"

"Well it only saved my life, I think I'd have to be the king of the stupid people not to at least find it convenient!"

"Smell," she said, suddenly leaping to her feet.

She is so *young,* he thought.

And then, rising to his own feet, he was surprised to realize that he, too, was young, his body lithe and responsive.

And then he was surprised again to realize that Peter never remembered being any other way. It was Ender who had experienced an older body, one that got stiff when sleeping on the ground, a body that did not rise so easily to its feet. I *do* have Ender in me. I have the memories of his body. Why not the memories of his mind?

Perhaps because this brain has only the map of Peter's memories in it. All the rest of them are lurking just out of reach. And maybe I'll stumble on them now and then, connect them up, map new roads to get to them.

In the meantime, he was still getting up, standing beside

Wang-mu, sniffing the air with her; and he was surprised again to realize that *both* activities had had his full attention. He had been thinking continuously of Wang-mu, of smelling what she smelled, wondering all the while whether he could just rest his hand on that small frail shoulder that seemed to need a hand the size of his to rest upon it; and at the same time, he had been engaged completely in speculation on how and whether he would be able to recover Ender's memories.

I could never do that before, thought Peter. And yet I must have been doing it ever since this body and the Valentine body were created. Concentrating on three things at once, in fact, not two.

But I wasn't strong enough to think of three things. One of them always sagged. Valentine for a while. Then Ender, until that body died. But two things—I can think of two things at once. Is this remarkable? Or is it something that many humans could do, if only they had some occasion to learn?

What kind of vanity is this! thought Peter. Why should I care whether I'm unique in this ability? Except that I always did pride myself on being smarter and more capable than the people around me. Didn't let myself say it aloud, of course, or even admit it to myself, but be honest with yourself now, Peter! It's good to be smarter than other people. And if I can think of two things at once, while they can only think of one, why not take some pleasure in it!

Of course, thinking of two things is rather useless if both trains of thought are dumb. For while he played with questions of vanity and his competitive nature, he had also been concentrating on Wang-mu, and his hand had indeed reached out and touched her, and for a moment she leaned back against him, accepting his touch, until her head rested against his chest. And then, without warning or any provocation that he could think of, she suddenly pulled away from him and began to stride toward the Samoans who were gathered around Malu on the beach.

"What did I do?" asked Peter.

She turned around, looking puzzled. "You did just fine!" she said. "I didn't slap you or put my knee in your kintamas, did I? But it's breakfast—Malu is praying and they've got more food than they had two nights ago, when we thought we'd die from eating it!"

And *both* of Peter's separate tracks of attention noticed that he was hungry, both severally and all at once. Neither he nor Wang-mu had eaten anything last night. For that matter, he had no memory of leaving the beach and coming to lie down with her on these mats. Somebody must have carried them. Well, that was no surprise. There wasn't a man or woman on that beach who didn't look like he could pick Peter up and break him like a pencil. As for Wang-mu, as he watched her run lightly toward the mountain range of Samoans gathered at water's edge, he thought she was like a bird flying toward a flock of cattle.

I'm not a child and never was one, not in this body, thought Peter. So I don't know if I'm even capable of childish longings and the grand romances of adolescence. And from Ender I have this sense of comfortableness in love; it isn't grand sweeping passions that I even expect to feel. Will the kind of love I have for you be enough, Wang-mu? To reach out to you when I'm in need, and to try to be here for you when you need me back. And to feel such tenderness when I look at you that I want to stand between you and all the world: and yet also to lift you up and carry you above the strong currents of life; and at the same time, I would be glad to stand always like this, at a distance, watching you, the beauty of you, your energy as you look up at these towering mound-people, speaking to them as an equal even though every movement of your hands, every fluting syllable of your speech cries out that you're a child—is it enough for you that I feel these loves for you? Because it's enough for me. And enough for me that when my hand touched your shoulder, you leaned on me; and when you felt me slip away, you called my name.

Plikt sat alone in her room, writing and writing. She had been preparing all her life for this day—to be writing the oration for Andrew Wiggin's funeral. She would speak his death—and she had the research to do it, she could speak for a solid week and still not exhaust a tenth of what she knew about him. But she would not speak for a week. She would speak for a single hour. Less than an hour. She understood him; she loved him; she would share with others who did not know him what he was, how he loved, how history was different because this man, brilliant, imperfect, but well-meaning and filled with a love that was strong enough to inflict suffering when it was needed—how history was different because he lived, and how also ten thousand, a hundred thousand, millions of individual lives were also different, strengthened, clarified, lifted up, brightened, or at least made more consonant and truthful because of what he had said and done and written in his life.

And would she also tell this? Would she tell how bitterly one woman grieved alone in her room, weeping and weeping, not because of grief that Ender was gone, but because of shame at finally understanding herself. For though she had loved and admired him—no, worshiped this man—nevertheless when he died what she felt was not grief at all, but relief and excitement. Relief: The waiting is over! Excitement: My hour has come!

Of course that's what she felt. She wasn't such a fool as to expect herself to be of more than human moral strength. And the reason she didn't grieve as Novinha and Valentine grieved was because a great part of their lives had just been torn away from them. What was torn away from mine? Ender gave me a few dollops of his attention, but little more. We had only a few months when he was my teacher on Trondheim; then a generation later our lives touched again for these few months here; and both times he was preoccupied, he had more important things and people to attend to than me. I was not his wife. I was not his sister. I was only his student and disciple—a man who was done with students and never wanted disciples. So of course no great part of my life was taken from me because he had only been my dream, never my companion.

I forgive myself and yet I cannot stop the shame and grief I feel, not because Andrew Wiggin died, but because in the hour of his death I showed myself to be what I really am: utterly selfish, concerned only with my own career. I chose to be the speaker of Ender's death. Therefore the moment of his death can only be the fulfillment of my life. What kind of vulture does that make me? What kind of parasite, a leech upon his life . . .

And yet her fingers continued to type, sentence after sentence, despite the tears flowing down her cheeks. Off in Jakt's house, Valentine grieved with her husband and children. Over in Olhado's house, Grego and Olhado and Novinha had gathered to comfort each other, at the loss of the man who had been husband and father to them. They had their relationship to him, and I have mine. They have their private memories; mine will be public. I will speak, and then I will publish what I said, and what I am writing now will give new shape and meaning to the life of Ender Wiggin in the minds of every person of a hundred worlds. Ender the Xenocide; Andrew the Speaker for the Dead; Andrew the private man of loneliness and compassion; Ender the brilliant analyst who could pierce to the heart of problems and of people without being deflected by fear or ambition or . . . or mercy. The man of justice and the man of mercy, coexisting in one body. The man whose compassion let him see and love the hive queens even before he ever touched one of them with his hands; the man whose fierce justice let him destroy them all because he believed they were his enemy.

Would Ender judge me harshly for my ugly feelings on

this day? Of course he would—he would not spare me, he would know the worst that is in my heart.

But then, having judged me, he would also love me. He would say, So what? Get up and speak my death. If we waited for perfect people to be speakers for the dead, all funerals would be conducted in silence.

And so she wrote, and wept; and when the weeping was done, the writing went on. When the hair that he had left behind was sealed in a small box and buried in the grass near Human's root, she would stand and speak. Her voice would raise him from the dead, make him live again in memory. And she would also be merciful; and she would also be just. That much, at least, she had learned from him.

12

"AM I BETRAYING ENDER?"

"Why do people act as if war and murder were unnatural?
What's unnatural is to go your whole life
without ever raising your hand in violence."
                    from The God Whispers of Han Qing-jao

"We're going about this all wrong," said Quara.

Miro felt the old familiar anger surge inside him. Quara
had a knack for making people angry, and it didn't help
that she seemed to know that she annoyed people and rel-
ished it. Anyone else in the ship could have said exactly
the same sentence and Miro would have given them a fair
hearing. But Quara managed to put an edge on the words
that made it sound as if she thought everyone in the world
but herself was stupid. Miro loved her as a sister, but he
couldn't help it that he hated having to spend hour upon
hour in her company.

Yet, because Quara was in fact the one among them most
knowledgeable about the ur-language she had discovered
months before in the descolada virus, Miro did not allow

his inward sigh of exasperation to become audible. Instead he swiveled in his seat to listen.

So did the others, though Ela made less effort to hide her annoyance. Actually, she made none. "Well, Quara, why weren't we smart enough to notice our stupidity before."

Quara was oblivious to Ela's sarcasm—or chose to appear oblivious, anyway. "How can we decipher a language out of the blue? We don't have any referents. But we *do* have complete records of the versions of the descolada virus. We know what it looked like before it adapted to the human metabolism. We know how it changed after each of our attempts to kill it. Some of the changes were functional—it was adapting. But some of them were clerical—it was keeping a record of what it did."

"We don't know that," said Ela with perhaps too much pleasure in correcting Quara.

"*I* know it," said Quara. "Anyway, it gives us a known context, doesn't it? We know what that language is about, even if we haven't been able to decode it."

"Well, now that you've said all that," said Ela, "I still have no idea how this new wisdom will help us decode the language. I mean, isn't that precisely what you've been working on for months?"

"Ah," said Quara. "I have. But what I haven't been able to do is speak the 'words' that the descolada virus recorded and see what answers we get back."

"Too dangerous," said Jane at once. "Absurdly dangerous. These people are capable of making viruses that completely destroy biospheres, and they're callous enough to use them. And you're proposing that we give to them precisely the weapon they used to devastate the pequeninos' planet? Which probably contains a complete record, not only of the pequeninos' metabolism, but of ours as well? Why not just slit our own throats and send them the blood?"

Miro noticed that when Jane spoke, the others looked

almost stunned. Part of their response might have been to the difference between Val's diffidence and the bold attitude that Jane displayed. Part of it, too, might have been because the Jane they knew was more computerlike, less assertive. Miro, however, recognized this authoritarian style from the way she had often spoken into his ear through the jewel. In a way it was a pleasure for him to hear her again; it was also disturbing to hear it coming from the lips of someone else. Val was gone; Jane was back; it was awful; it was wonderful.

Because Miro was not so taken aback by Jane's attitude, he was the one to speak into the silence. "Quara's right, Jane. We don't have years and years to work this out—we might have only a few weeks. Or less. We need to provoke a linguistic response. Get an answer from them, analyze the difference in language between their initial statements to us and the later ones."

"We're giving away too much," said Jane.

"No risk, no gain," said Miro.

"Too much risk, all dead," said Jane snidely. But in the snideness there was a familiar lilt, a kind of sauciness that said, I'm only playing. And that came, not from Jane—Jane had never sounded like that—but from Val. It hurt to hear it; it was good to hear it. Miro's dual responses to everything coming from Jane kept him constantly on edge. I love you, I miss you, I grieve for you, shut up; whom he was talking to seemed to change with the minutes.

"It's only the future of three sentient species we're gambling with," added Ela.

With that they all turned to Firequencher.

"Don't look at me," he said. "I'm just a tourist."

"Come on," said Miro. "You're here because your people are at risk the same as ours. This is a tough decision and you have to vote. You have the most at risk, actually, because even the earliest descolada codes we have might well reveal the whole biological history of your people since the virus first came among you."

"Then again," said Firequencher, "it might mean that since they already know how to destroy us, we have nothing to lose."

"Look," said Miro. "We have no evidence that these people have any kind of manned starflight. All they've sent out so far are probes."

"All that we know about," said Jane.

"And we've had no evidence of anybody coming around to check out how effective the descolada had been at transforming the biosphere of Lusitania to prepare it to receive colonists from this planet. So if they do have colony ships out there, either they're already on the way so what different does it make if we share this information, or they haven't sent any which means that they *can't.*"

"Miro's right," said Quara, pouncing. Miro winced. He hated being on Quara's side, because now everybody's annoyance with her would rub off on him. "Either the cows are already out of the barn, so why bother shutting the door, or they can't get the door open anyway, so why put a lock on it?"

"What do you know about cows?" asked Ela disdainfully.

"After all these years of living and working with you," said Quara nastily, "I'd say I'm an expert."

"Girls, girls," said Jane. "Get a grip on yourselves."

Again, everyone but Miro turned to her in surprise. Val wouldn't have spoken up during a family conflict like this; nor would the Jane they knew—though of course Miro was used to her speaking up all the time.

"We all know the risks of giving them information about us," said Miro. "We also know that we're making no headway and maybe we'll be able to learn something about the way this language works after having some give and take."

"It's *not* give and take," said Jane. "It's give and give. We give them information they probably can't get any other way, information that may well tell them everything they need to know in order to create new viruses that might well circumvent all our weapons against them. But since we have no idea how that information is coded, or even where each specific datum is located, how can we interpret the answer? Besides, what if the answer is a new virus to destroy us?''

''They're sending us the information necessary to construct the virus,'' said Quara, her voice thick with contempt, as if she thought Jane were the stupidest person who ever lived, instead of arguably the most godlike in her brilliance. ''But we're not going to build it. As long as it's just a graphic representation on a computer screen—''

''That's it,'' said Ela.

''What's it?'' said Quara. It was her turn to be annoyed now, for obviously Ela was a step ahead of her on something.

''*They* aren't taking these signals and putting them up on a computer screen. We do that because we have a language written with symbols that we see with the naked eye. But they must read these broadcast signals more directly. The code comes in, and they somehow interpret it by following the instruction to *make* the molecule that's described in the broadcast. Then they 'read' it by—what, smelling it? Swallowing it? The point is, if genetic molecules are their language, then they must somehow take them into their body as appropriately as the way we get the images of our writing from the paper into our eyes.''

''I see,'' said Jane. ''You're hypothesizing that they're expecting us to make a molecule out of what they send us, instead of just reading it on a screen and trying to abstract it and intellectualize it.''

''For all we know,'' said Ela, ''this could be how they discipline people. Or attack them. Send them a message. If they 'listen' they have to do it by reading the molecule into their bodies and letting it have its effect on them. So if the effect is poison or a killing disease, just hearing the message subjects them to the discipline. It's as if all our language had to be tapped out on the back of our neck. To listen, we'd have to lie down and expose ourself to whatever tool they chose to use to send the message. If it's a finger or a feather, well and good—but if it's a broadaxe or a machete or a sledgehammer, too bad for us.''

''It doesn't even have to be fatal,'' said Quara, her rivalry with Ela forgotten as she developed the idea in her own mind. ''The molecules could be behavior-altering devices. To hear is literally to obey.''

''I don't know if you're right in the particulars,'' said Jane. ''But it gives the experiment much more potential for success. And it suggests that they might not have a delivery system that can attack us directly. That changes the probable risk.''

''And people say you can't think well without your computer,'' said Miro.

At once he was embarrassed. He had inadvertently spoken to her as flippantly as he used to when he subvocalized so she could overhear him through the jewel. But now it sounded strangely cold of him, to tease her about having lost her computer network. He could joke that way with Jane-in-the-jewel. But Jane-in-the-flesh was a different matter. She was now a human person. With feelings that had to be worried about.

Jane had feelings all along, thought Miro. But I didn't think much about them because . . . because I didn't have to. Because I didn't see her. Because she wasn't, in a sense, real to me.

''I just meant . . .'' Miro said. ''I just mean, good thinking.''

''Thank you,'' said Jane. There wasn't a trace of irony in her voice, but Miro knew the irony was there all the same, because it was inherent in the situation. Miro, this uniprocessing human, was telling this brilliant being that she had thought well—as if he were fit to judge her.

Suddenly he was angry, not at Jane, but at himself. Why should he have to watch every word he said, just because she had not acquired this body in the normal way? She may not have been human before, but she was certainly human now, and could be talked to like a human. If she was somehow different from other human beings, so what? All human beings were different from all others, and yet to be decent and polite, wasn't he supposed to treat everyone basically alike? Wouldn't he say, "Do you see what I mean?" to a blind person, expecting the metaphorical use of "see" to be taken without umbrage? Well, why not say, "Good thinking," to Jane? Just because her thought processes were unfathomably deep to a human didn't mean that a human couldn't use a standard expression of agreement and approval when speaking to her.

Looking at her now, Miro could see a kind of sadness in her eyes. No doubt it came from his obvious confusion—after joking with her as he always had, suddenly he was embarrassed, suddenly he backtracked. That was why her "Thank you" had been ironic. Because she wanted him to be natural with her, and he couldn't.

No, he *hadn't* been natural, but he certainly could.

And what did it matter, anyway? They were here to solve the problem of the descoladores, not to work out the kinks in their personal relationships after the wholesale body swap.

"Do I take it we have agreement?" asked Ela. "To send messages encoded with the information contained on the descolada virus?"

"The first one only," said Jane. "At least to start."

"And when they answer," said Ela, "I'll try to run a simulation of what would happen if we constructed and ingested the molecule they send us."

"If they send us one," said Miro. "If we're even on the right track."

"Well aren't you Mr. Cheer," said Quara.

"I'm Mr. Scared-From-Ass-To-Ankles," said Miro. "Whereas you are just plain old Miss Ass."

"Can't we all get along?" said Jane, whining, teasing. "Can't we all be friends?"

Quara whirled on her. "Listen, you! I don't care what kind of superbrain you used to be, you just stay out of family conversations, do you hear?"

"Look around, Quara!" Miro snapped at her. "If she stayed out of family conversations, when could she talk?"

Firequencher raised his hand. "I've been staying out of family conversations. Do I get credit for that?"

Jane gestured to quell both Miro and Firequencher. "Quara," she said quietly, "I'll tell you the real difference between me and your brother and sister here. They're used to you because they've known you all your life. They're loyal to you because you and they went through some lousy experiences in your family. They're patient with your childish outbursts and your asinine bullheadedness because they tell themselves, over and over, she can't help it, she had such a troubled childhood. But I'm not a family member, Quara. I, however, as someone who has observed you in times of crisis for some time, am not afraid to tell you my candid conclusions. You are quite brilliant and very good at what you do. You are often perceptive and creative, and you drive toward solutions with astonishing directness and perseverence."

"Excuse me," said Quara, "are you telling me off or what?"

"*But,*" said Jane, "you are not smart and creative and clever and direct and perseverent enough to make it worth putting up with more than fifteen seconds of the egregious bullshit you heap on your family and everyone else around you every minute you're awake. So you had a lousy childhood. That was a few years ago, and you are expected now to put that behind you and get along with other people like a normally courteous adult."

"In other words," said Quara, "you don't like having to admit that anybody but you might be smart enough to have an idea that you didn't think of."

"You aren't understanding me," said Jane. "I'm not your sister. I'm not even, technically speaking, human. If this ship ever gets back to Lusitania, it will be because I, with my mind, send it there. Do you get that? Do you understand the difference between us? Can you send even one fleck of dust from your lap to mine?''

"I don't notice you sending starships anywhere right at the moment,'' said Quara triumphantly.

"You continue to attempt to score points off me without realizing that I am not having an argument with you or even a discussion. What you say to me right now is irrelevant. The only thing that matters is what *I'm* saying to you. And I'm saying that while your siblings put up with the unendurable from you, I will not. Keep on the way you're going, you spoiled little baby, and when this starship goes back to Lusitania you might not be on it.''

The look on Quara's face almost made Miro laugh aloud. He knew, however, that this would not be a wise moment to express his mirth.

"She's threatening me,'' said Quara to the others. "Do you hear this? She's trying to coerce me by threatening to *kill* me.''

"I would never kill you,'' said Jane. "But I might be unable to conceive of your presence on this starship when I push it Outside and then pull it back In. The thought of you might be so unendurable that my unconscious mind would reject that thought and exclude you. I really don't understand, consciously, how the whole thing works. I don't know how it relates to my feelings. I've never tried to transport anybody I really hated before. I would certainly *try* to bring you along with the others, if only because, for reasons passing understanding, Miro and Ela would probably be testy with me if I didn't. But trying isn't necessarily succeeding. So I suggest, Quara, that you expend some effort on trying to be a little less loathsome.''

"So that's what power is to you,'' said Quara. "A chance to push other people around and act like the queen.''

"You really *can't* do it, can you?'' said Jane.

"Can't what?" said Quara. "Can't bow down and kiss your feet?"

"Can't shut up to save your own life."

"I'm trying to solve the problem of communicating with an alien species, and you're busy worrying about whether I'm nice enough to you."

"But Quara," said Jane, "hasn't it ever occurred to you that once they get to know you, even the aliens will wish you had never learned their language?"

"I'm certainly wishing you had never learned mine," said Quara. "You're certainly full of yourself, now that you have this pretty little body to play around with. Well, you're not queen of the universe and I'm not going to dance through hoops for you. It wasn't my idea to come on this voyage, but I'm here—*I'm* here, the whole obnoxious package—and if there's something about me that you don't like, why don't *you* shut up about it? And as long as we're making threats, I think that if you push me too far I'll rearrange your face more to my liking. Is *that* clear?"

Jane unstrapped herself from her seat and drifted from the main cabin into the corridor leading into the storage compartments of the shuttle. Miro followed her, ignoring Quara as she said to the others, "Can you believe how she talked to me? Who does she think she is, judging who's too irritating to live?"

Miro followed Jane into a storage compartment. She was clinging to a handhold on the far wall, bent over and heaving in a way that made Miro wonder if she was throwing up. But no. She was crying. Or rather, she was so enraged that her body was sobbing and producing tears from the sheer uncontainability of the emotion. Miro touched her shoulder to try to calm her. She recoiled.

For a moment he almost said, Fine, have it your way; then he would have left, angry himself, frustrated that she wouldn't accept his comfort. But then he remembered that she had never been this angry before. She had never had to deal with a body that responded like this. At first, when she began rebuking Quara, Miro had thought, It's about time somebody laid it on the line. But when the argument went on and on, Miro realized that it wasn't Quara who was out of control, it was Jane. She didn't know how to deal with her emotions. She didn't know when it wasn't worth going on. She felt what she was feeling, and she didn't know how to do anything but express it.

"That was hard," Miro said. "Cutting off the argument and coming in here."

"I wanted to kill her," said Jane. Her voice was almost unintelligible from the weeping, from the savage tension in her body. "I've never felt anything like it. I wanted to get out of the chair and tear her apart with my bare hands."

"Welcome to the club," said Miro.

"You don't understand," she said. "I really wanted to do it. I felt my muscles flexing, I was *ready* to do it. I was *going* to do it."

"As I said. Quara makes us all feel that way."

"No," said Jane. "Not like this. You all stay calm, you all stay in control."

"And you will, too," said Miro, "when you have a little more practice."

Jane lifted her head, leaned it back, shook it. Her hair swung weightlessly free in the air. "Do you really feel this?"

"All of us do," said Miro. "That's why we have a childhood—to learn to get over our violent tendencies. But they're in us all. Chimps and baboons do it. All the primates. We display. We have to express our rage physically."

"But you don't. You stay so calm. You let her spout off and say these horrible—"

"Because it's not worth the trouble of stopping her," said Miro. "She pays the price for it. She's desperately lonely and nobody deliberately seeks an opportunity to spend time in her company."

"Which is the only reason she isn't dead."

"That's right," said Miro. "That's what civilized people do—they avoid the circumstance that enrages them. Or if they can't avoid it, they detach. That's what Ela and I do, mostly. We just detach. We just let her provocations roll over us."

"I can't do it," said Jane. "It was so simple before I felt these things. I could tune her out."

"That's it," said Miro. "That's what we do. We tune her out."

"It's more complicated than I thought," said Jane. "I don't know if I can do it."

"Yeah, well, you don't have much choice right now, do you," he said.

"Miro, I'm so sorry. I always felt such pity for you humans because you could only think of one thing at a time and your memories were so imperfect and . . . now I realize that just getting through the day without killing somebody can be an achievement."

"It gets to be a habit. Most of us manage to keep our body count quite low. It's the neighborly way to live."

It took a moment—a sob, and then a hiccough—but then she did laugh. A sweet, soft chuckle that was such a welcome sound to Miro. Welcome because it was a voice he knew and loved, a laugh that he liked to hear. And it was his dear friend who was doing the laughing. His dear friend Jane. The laugh, the voice of his beloved Val. One person now. After all this time, he could reach out his hand and touch Jane, who had always been impossibly far away. Like having a friendship over the telephone and finally meeting face-to-face.

He touched her again, and she took his hand and held it.

"I'm sorry I let my own weakness get in the way of what we're doing," said Jane.

"You're only human," said Miro.

She looked at him, searched his face for irony, for bitterness.

"I mean it," said Miro. "The price of having these emotions, these passions, is that you have to control them, you have to bear them when they're too strong to bear. You're only human now. You'll never make these feelings go away. You just have to learn not to act on them.''

''Quara never learned.''

''Quara learned, all right,'' said Miro. ''It's just my opinion, but Quara loved Marcão, adored him, and when he died and the rest of us felt so liberated, she was lost. What she does now, this constant provocation—she's asking somebody to abuse her. To hit her. The way Marcão always hit Mother whenever he was provoked. I think in some perverse way Quara was always jealous of Mother when she got to go off alone with Papa, and even though she finally figured out that he was beating her up, when Quara wanted her papa back the only way she knew of to demand his attention was—this mouth of hers.'' Miro laughed bitterly. ''It reminds me of Mother, to tell the truth. You've never heard her, but in the old days, when she was trapped in marriage with Marcão and having Libo's babies—oh, she had a mouth on her. I'd sit there and listen to her provoking Marcão, goading him, stabbing at him, until he'd hit her—and I'd think, Don't you dare lay a hand on my mother, and at the same time I'd absolutely understand his impotent rage, because he could never, never, never say anything that would shut her up. Only his fist could do it. And Quara has that mouth, and needs that rage.''

''Well, how happy for us all, then, that I gave her just what she needed.''

Miro laughed. ''But she didn't need it from you. She needed it from Marcão, and he's dead.''

And then, suddenly, Jane burst into real tears. Tears of grief, and she turned to Miro and clung to him.

''What is it?'' he said. ''What's wrong?''

''Oh, Miro,'' she said. ''Ender's dead. I'll never see him again. I have a body at last, I have eyes to see him, and he isn't there.''

Miro was stunned. Of course she missed Ender. She had

thousands of years with him, and only a few years, really, with me. How could I have thought she could love me? How can I ever hope to compare with Ender Wiggin? What am I, compared to the man who commanded fleets, who transformed the minds of trillions of people with his books, his speakings, his insight, his ability to see into the hearts of other people and speak their own most private stories back to them? And yet even as he resented Ender, even as he envied him because Jane would always love him more and Miro couldn't hope to compete with him even in death, despite these feelings it finally came home to him that yes, Ender was dead. Ender, who had transformed *his* family, who had been a true friend to *him*, who had been the only man in Miro's life that he longed with all his heart to *be*, Ender was gone. Miro's tears of grief flowed along with Jane's.

"I'm sorry," said Jane. "I can't control *any* of my emotions."

"Yes, well, it's a common failing, actually," said Miro.

She reached up and touched the tears on his cheek. Then she touched her damp finger to her own cheek. The tears commingled. "Do you know why I thought of Ender right then?" she said. "Because you're so much like him. Quara annoys you as much as she annoys anyone, and yet you look past that and see what her needs are, why she says and does these things. No, no, relax, Miro, I'm not expecting you to be like Ender, I'm just saying that one of the things I liked best about him is also in you—that's not bad, is it? The compassionate perception—I may be new at being human, but I'm pretty sure that's a rare commodity."

"I don't know," said Miro. "The only person I'm feeling compassion for right now is me. They call it self-pity, and it isn't an attractive trait."

"Why are you feeling sorry for yourself?"

"Because you'll go on needing Ender all your life, and all you'll ever find is poor substitutes, like me."

She held him tighter then. She was the one giving comfort now. "Oh, Miro, maybe that's true. But if it is, it's true the way it's true that Quara is still trying to get her father's attention. You never stop needing your father or your mother, isn't that right? You never stop reacting to them, even when they're dead."

Father? That had never crossed Miro's mind before. Jane loved Ender, deeply, yes, loved him forever—but as a father?

"I can't be your father," said Miro. "I can't take his place." But what he was really doing was making sure he had understood her. Ender was her father?

"I don't want you to be my father," said Jane. "I still have all these old Val-feelings, you know. I mean, you and I were friends, right? That was very important to me. But now I have this Val body, and when you touch me, it keeps feeling like the answer to a prayer." At once she regretted saying it. "Oh, I'm sorry, Miro, I know you miss her."

"I do," said Miro. "But then, it's hard to miss her quite the way I might, since you do look a lot like her. And you sound like her. And here I am holding you the way I wanted to hold her, and if that sounds awful because I'm supposedly comforting you and I shouldn't be thinking of base desires, well then I'm just an awful kind of guy, right?"

"Awful," she said. "I'm ashamed to know you." And she kissed him. Sweetly, awkwardly.

He remembered his first kiss with Ouanda years ago, when he was young and didn't know how badly things could turn out. They had both been awkward then, new, clumsy. Young. Jane, now, Jane was one of the oldest creatures in the universe. But also one of the youngest. And Val—there would be no reflexes in the Val body for Jane to draw upon, for in Val's short life, what chance had she had to find love?

"Was that even close to the way humans do that?" asked Jane.

"That was exactly the way humans sometimes do it,"

said Miro. "Which isn't surprising, since we're both human."

"Am I betraying Ender, to grieve for him one moment, and then be so happy to have you holding me the next?"

"Am I betraying him, to be so happy only hours after he died?"

"Only he's not dead," said Jane. "I know where he is. I chased him there."

"If he's exactly the same person he was," said Miro, "then what a shame. Because good as he was, he wasn't happy. He had his moments, but he was never—what, he was never really at peace. Wouldn't it be nice if Peter could live out a full life without ever having to bear the guilt of xenocide? Without ever having to feel the weight of all of humanity on his shoulders?"

"Speaking of which," said Jane, "we have work to do."

"We also have lives to live," said Miro. "I'm not going to be sorry we had this encounter. Even if it took Quara's bitchiness to make it happen."

"Let's do the civilized thing," said Jane. "Let's get married. Let's have babies. I do want to be human, Miro, I want to do everything. I want to be part of human life from edge to edge. And I want to do it all with you."

"Is this a proposal?" asked Miro.

"I died and was reborn only a dozen hours ago," said Jane. "My—hell, I can call him my father, can't I?—my father died, too. Life is short, I feel how short it is: after three thousand years, all of them intense, it still feels too short. I'm in a hurry. And you, haven't you wasted enough time, too? Aren't you ready?"

"But I don't have a ring."

"We have something much better than a ring," said Jane. She touched her cheek again, where she had put his tear. It was still damp; still damp, too, when she touched the finger now to his cheek. "I've had your tears with mine, and you've had mine with yours. I think that's more intimate even than a kiss."

"Maybe," said Miro. "But not as fun."

"This emotion I'm feeling now, this is love, right?"

"I don't know. Is it a longing? Is it a giddy stupid happiness just because you're with me?"

"Yes," she said.

"That's influenza," said Miro. "Watch for nausea or diarrhea within a few hours."

She shoved him, and in the weightless starship the movement sent him helplessly into midair until he struck another surface. "What?" he said, pretending innocence. "What did I say?"

She pushed herself away from the wall and went to the door. "Come on," she said. "Back to work."

"Let's not announce our engagement," he said softly.

"Why not?" she asked. "Ashamed already?"

"No," he said. "Maybe it's petty of me, but when we announce it, I don't want Quara there."

"That's very small of you," said Jane. "You need to be more magnanimous and patient, like me."

"I know," said Miro. "I'm trying to learn."

They drifted back into the main chamber of the shuttle. The others were working on preparing their genetic message for broadcast on the frequency that the descoladores had used to challenge them when they first showed up closer to the planet. They all looked up. Ela smiled wanly. Firequencher waved cheerfully.

Quara tossed her head. "Well I hope we're done with *that* little emotional outburst," she said.

Miro could feel Jane seethe at the remark. But Jane said nothing. And when they were both sitting down and strapped back into their seats, they looked at each other, and Jane winked.

"I saw that," said Quara.

"We meant you to," said Miro.

"Grow up," Quara said disdainfully.

An hour later they sent their message. And at once they were inundated with answers that they could not understand, but had to. There was no time for quarreling then, or for love, or for grief. There was only language, thick, broad fields of alien messages that had to be understood somehow, by them, right now.

13

"TILL DEATH ENDS ALL SURPRISES"

*"I can't say that I've much enjoyed
the work the gods required of me.
My only real pleasure
was my days of schooling,
in those hours between the gods' sharp summonses.
I am gladly at their service, always,
but oh it was so sweet
to learn how wide the universe could be,
to test myself against my teachers,
and to fail sometimes without much consequence."*
from The God Whispers of Han Qing-jao

"Do you want to come to the university and watch us turn on our new godproof computer network?" asked Grace.

Of course Peter and Wang-mu wanted to. But to their surprise, Malu cackled with delight and insisted that he must go, too. The god once dwelt in computers, didn't she? And if she found her way back, shouldn't Malu be there to greet her?

This complicated matters a little—for Malu to visit the university required notifying the president so he could assemble a proper welcome. This was not needed for Malu, who was neither vain nor much impressed with ceremonies that didn't have some immediate purpose. The point was to show the Samoan people that the university still had proper respect for the old ways, of which Malu was the most revered protector and practitioner.

From luaus of fruit and fish on the beach, from open fires, palm mats, and thatch-roof huts, to a hovercar, a highway, and the bright-painted buildings of the modern university— it felt to Wang-mu like a journey through the history of the human race. And yet she had already made that journey once before, from Path; it seemed a part of her life, to step from the ancient to the modern, back and forth. She felt rather sorry for those who knew only one and not the other. It was better, she thought, to be able to select from the whole menu of human achievements than to be bound within one narrow range.

Peter and Wang-mu were discreetly dropped off before the hovercar took Malu to the official reception. Grace's son took them on a brief tour of the brand-new computer facility. "These new computers all follow the protocols sent to us from Starways Congress. There will be no more direct connections between computer networks and ansibles. Rather there must be a time delay, with each info-packet inspected by referee software that will catch unauthorized piggybacking."

"In other words," said Peter, "Jane will never get back in."

"That's the plan." The boy—for despite his size, that's what he seemed to be—grinned broadly. "All perfect, all new, all in total compliance."

Wang-mu felt sick inside. This is how it would be all over the Hundred Worlds—Jane blocked out of everything. And without access to the enormous computing capacity of the combined networks of all of human civilization, how could she possibly regain the power to pop a starship Out and In again? Wang-mu had been glad enough to leave

Path. But she was by no means certain that Pacifica was the world where she wanted to live the rest of her life. Especially if she was to stay with Peter, for there was no chance he would be content for long with the slower, more lackadaisical timeflow of life in the islands. Truth be known, it was too slow for her, too. She loved her time with the Samoans, but the impatience to be doing something was growing inside her. Perhaps those who grew up among these people might somehow sublimate their ambition, or perhaps there was something in the racial genotype that suppressed it or replaced it, but Wang-mu's incessant drive to strengthen and expand her role in life was certainly not going to go away just because of a luau on the beach, however much she enjoyed it and would treasure the memory of it.

The tour wasn't over yet, of course, and Wang-mu dutifully followed Grace's son wherever he led. But she hardly paid attention beyond what was needed to make polite responses. Peter seemed even more distracted, and Wang-mu could guess why. He would have not only the same feelings Wang-mu had, but he must also be grieving for the loss of connection with Jane through the jewel in his ear. If she did not recover her ability to control data flow through the communications satellites orbiting this world, he would not hear her voice again.

They came to an older section of campus, some rundown buildings in a more utilitarian architectural style. "Nobody likes coming here," he said, "because it reminds them of how recently our university became anything more than a school for training engineers and teachers. This building is three hundred years old. Come inside."

"Do we have to?" asked Wang-mu. "I mean, is it necessary? I think we get the idea from the outside."

"Oh, but I think you want to see this place. Very interesting, because it preserves some of the old ways of doing things."

Wang-mu of course agreed to follow, as courtesy required, and Peter wordlessly went along. They came inside and heard the humming of ancient air-conditioning systems and felt the harsh refrigerated air. "These are the old ways?" asked Wang-mu. "Not as old as life on the beach, I think."

"Not as old, that's true," said their guide. "But then, we're not preserving the same thing here."

They came into a large room with hundreds and hundreds of computers arranged in crowded rows along tables that stretched from end to end. There was no room for anyone to sit at these machines; there was barely enough space between the tables for technicians to slide along to tend to them. All the computers were on, but the air above all the terminals was empty, giving no clue about what was going on inside them.

"We had to do *something* with all those old computers that Starways Congress made us take offline. So we put them here. And also the old computers from most of the other universities and businesses in the islands—Hawaiian, Tahitian, Maori, on and on—everyone helped. It goes up six stories, every floor just like this, and three other buildings, though this one is the biggest."

"Jane," said Peter, and he smiled.

"Here's where we stored everything she gave us. Of course, on the record these computers are not connected by any network. They are only used for training students. But Congress inspectors never come here. They saw all they wanted to see when they looked at our new installation. Up to code, complying with the rules—we are obedient and loyal citizens! Here, though, I'm afraid there have been some oversights. For instance, there seems to be an intermittent connection with the university's ansible. Whenever the ansible is actually passing messages offworld, it is connected to no computers except through the official safeguarded time-delayed link. But when the ansible is connected to a handful of eccentric destinations—the Samoan satellite, for instance, or a certain faroff colony that is supposedly incommunicado to all ansibles in the Hundred Worlds—then an old forgotten connection kicks in, and the ansible has complete use of all of this.''

Peter laughed with genuine mirth. Wang-mu loved the sound of it, but also felt just a little jealousy at the thought that Jane might well come back to him.

''And another odd thing,'' said Grace's son. ''One of the new computers has been installed here, only there've been some alterations. It doesn't seem to report correctly to the master program. It neglects to inform that master program that there is a hyperfast realtime link to this nonexistent old-style network. It's a shame that it doesn't report on this, because of course it allows a completely illegal connection between this old, ansible-connected network and the new godproof system. And so requests for information *can* be passed, and they'll look perfectly legal to any inspection software, since they come from this perfectly legal but astonishingly flawed new computer.''

Peter was grinning broadly. ''Well, somebody had to work pretty fast to get this done.''

''Malu told us that the god was going to die, but between us and the god we were able to devise a plan. Now the only question is—can she find her way back here?''

''I think she will,'' said Peter. ''Of course, this isn't what she used to have, not even a small fraction of it.''

''We understand that she has a couple of similar installations here and there. Not many, you're right, and the new time-delay barriers will make it so that yes, she has access to all the information, but she can't use most of the new networks as part of her thought processes. Still, it's something. Maybe it's enough.''

''You knew who we were before we got here,'' said Wang-mu. ''You were already part of Jane's work.''

''I think the evidence speaks for itself,'' said Grace's son.

''Then why did Jane bring us here?'' asked Wang-mu.

"What was all this nonsense about needing to have us here so we could stop the Lusitania Fleet?"

"I don't know," said Peter. "And I doubt anyone here knows, either. Maybe, though, Jane simply wanted us in a friendly environment, so she could find us again. I doubt there's anything like this on Divine Wind."

"And maybe," Wang-mu said, following her own speculations, "maybe she wanted you here, with Malu and Grace, when the time came for her to die."

"And for me to die as well," said Peter. "Meaning me as Ender, of course."

"And maybe," said Wang-mu, "if she was no longer going to be there to protect us through her manipulations of data, she wanted us to be among friends."

"Of course," said Grace's son. "She is a god, she takes care of her people."

"Her worshipers, you mean?" asked Wang-mu.

Peter snorted.

"Her friends," said the boy. "In Samoa we treat the gods with great respect, but we are also their friends, and we help the good ones when we can. Gods need the help of humans now and then. I think we did all right, don't you?"

"You did well," said Peter. "You have been faithful indeed."

The boy beamed.

Soon they were back in the new computer installation, watching as with great ceremony the president of the university pushed the key to activate the program that turned on and monitored the university ansible. Immediately there were messages and test programs from Starways Congress, probing and inspecting the university's system to make sure there were no lapses in security and that all protocols had been properly followed. Wang-mu could feel how tense everyone was—except Malu, who seemed incapable of dread—until, a few minutes later, the programs finished their inspection and made their report. The message came immediately from Congress that this network was compliant and secure. The fakes and fudges had not been detected.

"Any time now," murmured Grace.

"How will we know if all of this has worked?" asked Wang-mu softly.

"Peter will tell us," answered Grace, sounding surprised that Wang-mu had not already understood this. "The jewel in his ear—the Samoan satellite will speak to it."

———

Olhado and Grego stood watching the readout from the ansible that for twenty years had connected only to the shuttle and Jakt's starship. It was receiving a message again. Links were being established with four ansibles on other worlds, where groups of Lusitanian sympathizers— or at least friends of Jane's—had followed Jane's instructions on how to partially circumvent the new regulations. No actual messages were sent, because there was nothing for the humans to say to each other. The point was simply to keep the link alive so Jane might travel on it and link herself with some small part of her old capacity.

None of this had been done with any human participation on Lusitania. All the programming that was required had been accomplished by the relentlessly efficient workers of the Hive Queen, with the help of pequeninos now and then. Olhado and Grego had been invited at the last minute, as observers only. But they understood. Jane was talking to the Hive Queen and the Hive Queen talked to the fathertrees. Jane had not worked through humans because the Lusitanian humans she worked with had been Miro, who had other work to do for her, and Ender, who had removed the jewel from his ear before he died. Olhado and Grego had talked this out as soon as the pequenino Waterjumper had explained to them what was going on and asked them to come observe. "I think she was feeling a bit defiant," said Olhado. "If Ender rejected her and Miro was busy—"

"Or gaga-eyed over Young Valentine, don't forget," said Grego.

"Well, she'd do it without human help."

"How can it work?" said Grego. "She was connected to billions of computers before. At most she'll have several thousand now, at least directly usable. It's not enough. Ela and Quara are never coming home. Or Miro."

"Maybe not," said Olhado. "It won't be the first time we've lost family members in the service of a higher cause." He thought of Mother's famous parents, Os Venerados, who lacked only the years now for sainthood—if a representative of the Pope should ever come to Lusitania to examine the evidence. And their real father, Libo, and his father, both of whom died before Novinha's children ever guessed that they were kin. All dead in the cause of science, Os Venerados in the struggle to contain the descolada, Pipo and Libo in the effort to communicate with and understand the pequeninos. Their brother Quim had died as a martyr, trying to heal a dangerous breach in the relationship between humans and pequeninos on Lusitania. And now Ender, their adoptive father, had died in the cause of trying to find a way to save Jane's life and, with her, faster-than-light travel. If Miro and Ela and Quara should die in the effort to establish communications with the descoladores, it would be a part of the family tradition. "What I wonder," said Olhado, "is what's wrong with *us*, that we haven't been asked to die in a noble cause."

"I don't know about noble causes," said Grego, "but we do have a fleet aimed at us. That will do, I think, for getting us dead."

A sudden flurry of activity at the computer terminals told them that their wait was over. "We've linked with Samoa," said Waterjumper. "And now Memphis. And Path. Hegira." He did the little jig that pequeninos invariably did when they were delighted. "They're all going to come online. The snooper programs didn't find them."

"But will it be enough?" asked Grego. "Do the starships move again?"

Waterjumper shrugged elaborately. "We'll know when your family gets back, won't we?"

"Mother doesn't want to schedule Ender's funeral until they're back," said Grego.

At the mention of Ender's name, Waterjumper slumped. "The man who took Human into the Third Life," he said. "And there's almost nothing of him to bury."

"I'm just wondering," said Grego, "if it will be days or weeks or months before Jane finds her way back into her powers—if she can do it at all."

"I don't know," said Waterjumper.

"They only have a few weeks of air," said Grego.

"He doesn't know, Grego," said Olhado.

"I know that," said Grego. "But the Hive Queen knows. And she'll tell the fathertrees. I thought . . . word might have seeped down."

"How could even the Hive Queen know what will happen in the future?" asked Olhado. "How can anyone know what Jane can or can't accomplish? We've linked again with worlds outside of this one. Some parts of her core memory have been restored to the ansible net, however surreptitiously. She might find them. She might not. If found, they might be enough, or might not. But Waterjumper doesn't know."

Grego turned away. "I know," he said.

"We're all afraid," said Olhado. "Even the Hive Queen. None of us wants to die."

"Jane died, but didn't stay dead," said Grego. "According to Miro, Ender's aiúa is supposedly off living as Peter on some other world. Hive queens die and their memories live on in their daughters' minds. Pequeninos get to live as trees."

"Some of us," said Waterjumper.

"But what of *us*?" said Grego. "Will we be extinguished? What difference does it make then, the ones of us who had plans, what does it matter the work we've done? The children we've raised?'' He looked pointedly at Olhado. ''What will it matter then, that you have such a big happy family, if you're all erased in one instant by that . . . bomb?''

''Not one moment of my life with my family has been wasted,'' said Olhado quietly.

''But the point of it is to go on, isn't it? To connect with the future?''

''That's one part, yes,'' said Olhado. ''But part of the purpose of it is now, is the moment. And part of it is the web of connections. Links from soul to soul. If the purpose of life was just to continue into the future, then none of it would have meaning, because it would be all anticipation and preparation. There's fruition, Grego. There's the happiness we've already had. The happiness of each moment. The end of our lives, even if there's no forward continuation, no progeny at all, the end of our lives doesn't erase the beginning.''

''But it won't have amounted to anything,'' said Grego. ''If your children die, then it was all a waste.''

''No,'' said Olhado quietly. ''You say that because you have no children, Greguinho. But none of it is wasted. The child you hold in your arms for only a day before he dies, that is not wasted, because that one day is enough of a purpose in itself. Entropy has been thrown back for an hour, a day, a week, a month. Just because we might all die here on this little world does not undo the lives before the deaths.''

Grego shook his head. ''Yes it does, Olhado. Death undoes everything.''

Olhado shrugged. ''Then why do you bother doing everything, Grego? Because someday you will die. Why should anyone ever have children? Someday they will die, their children will die, all children will die. Someday stars will wind down or blow up. Someday death will cover us all like the water of a lake and perhaps nothing will ever come to the surface to show that we were ever there. But we *were* there, and during the time we lived, we were alive. That's the truth—what is, what was, what will be—not what could be, what should have been, what never can be. If we die, then our death has meaning to the rest of the universe. Even if our lives are unknown, the fact that someone lived here, and died, that will have repercussions, that will shape the universe.''

''So that's meaning enough for you?'' said Grego. ''To die as an object lesson? To die so that people can feel awful about having killed you?''

''There are worse meanings for a life to have.''

Waterjumper interrupted them. ''The last of the ansibles we expected is online. We have them all connected now.''

They stopped talking. It was time for Jane to find her way back into herself, if she could.

They waited.

Through one of her workers, the Hive Queen saw and heard the news of the restoration of the ansible links. <It's time,> she told the fathertrees.

<Can she do it? Can you lead her?>

<I can't lead her to a place where I can't go myself,> said the Hive Queen. <She has to find her own way. All I can do right now is tell her that it's time.>

<So we can only watch?>

<*I* can only watch,> said the Hive Queen. <*You* are part of her, or she of you. Her aiúa is tied now to your web through the mothertrees. Be ready.>

<For what?>

<For Jane's need.>

<What will she need? When will she need it?>

<I have no idea.>

At his terminal on the stranded starship, the Hive Queen's worker suddenly looked up, then arose from her seat and walked to Jane.

Jane looked up from her work. "What is it?" she asked distractedly. And then, remembering the signal she was waiting for, she looked over at Miro, who had turned to see what was happening. "I've got to go now," she said.

Then she flopped back in her seat as if she had fainted.

At once Miro was out of his chair; Ela wasn't far behind. The worker had already unfastened Jane from the chair and was lifting her off. Miro helped her draw Jane's body through the corridors of weightless space to the beds in the back of the ship. There they laid her down and secured her to a bed. Ela checked her vital signs.

"She's sleeping deeply," said Ela. "Breathing very slowly."

"A coma?" asked Miro.

"She's doing the minimum to stay alive," said Ela. "Other than that, there's nothing."

"Come on," said Quara from the door. "Let's get back to work."

Miro rounded on her, furious—but Ela restrained him. "You can stay and watch over her if you want," she said, "but Quara's right. We have work to do. She's doing hers."

Miro turned back to Jane and touched her hand, took it, held it. The others left the sleeping quarters. You can't hear me, you can't feel me, you can't see me, Miro said silently. So I guess I'm not here for you. Yet I can't leave you. What am I afraid of? We're all dead if you don't succeed at what you're doing now. So it isn't your death I fear.

It's your old self. Your old existence among the computers and the ansibles. You've had your fling in a human body, but when your old powers are restored, your human life will be just a small part of you again. Just one sensory input device among millions. One small set of memories lost in an overwhelming sea of memory. You'll be able to devote one tiny part of your attention to me, and I'll never know that I am perpetually an afterthought in your life.

That's just one of the drawbacks when you love somebody so much greater than yourself, Miro told himself. I'll never know the difference. She'll come back and I'll be happy with all the time we have together and I'll never know how little time and effort she actually devotes to being with me. A diversion, that's what I am.

Then he shook his head, let go of her hand, and left the room. I will not listen to the voice of despair, he told himself. Would I tame this great being and make her so much my slave that every moment of her life belongs to me? Would I focus her eyes so they can see nothing but my face? I must rejoice that I am part of her, instead of resenting that I'm not more of her.

He returned to his place and got back to work. But a few moments later he got up again and went back to her. He was useless until she came back. Until he knew the outcome, he could think of nothing else.

Jane was not precisely adrift. She had her unbroken connection to the three ansibles of Lusitania, and she found them easily. And just as easily found the new connections to ansibles on a half dozen worlds. From there, she quickly found her way through the thicket of interrupts and cutouts that protected her back door into the system from discovery by Congress's snoop programs. All was as she and her friends had planned.

It was small, cramped, as she had known it would be. But she had almost never used the full capacity of the system—except when she was controlling starships. Then she needed every scrap of fast memory to hold the complete image of the ship she was transporting. Obviously there wasn't enough capacity on these mere thousands of machines. Yet it was such a relief, nonetheless, to tap back into the programs that she had so long used to do so much of her thought for her, servants she made use of like the Hive Queen's workers—just one more way that I am like her, Jane realized. She got them running, then explored the memories that for these long days had been so painfully missing. Once again she was in possession of a mental system that allowed her to maintain dozens of levels of attention to simultaneously running processes.

And yet it was still all wrong. She had been in her human body only a day, and yet already the electronic self that once had felt so copious was far too small. It wasn't just because there were so few computers where once there had been so many. Rather it was small by nature. The ambiguity of flesh made for a vastness of possibility that simply could not exist in a binary world. She had been alive, and so she knew now that her electronic dwellingplace gave her only a fraction of a life. However much she had accomplished during her millennia of life in the machine, it brought no satisfaction compared to even a few minutes in that body of flesh and blood.

If she had thought she might ever leave the Val body, she knew now that she never could. That was the root of her, now and forever. Indeed, she would have to force herself to spread out into these computer systems when she needed them. By inclination, she would not readily go into them.

But there was no reason to speak to anyone of her disappointment. Not yet. She would tell Miro when she got back to him. He would listen and talk to no one else. Indeed, he would probably be relieved. No doubt he was worried that she would be tempted to remain in the computers and not go back into the body that she could still feel, strong and insistent on her attention, even in the slackness of such a deep sleep. But he had no reason to fear. Hadn't he spent many long months in a body that was so limited he could hardly bear to live in it? She would as soon go back to being just a computer-dweller as he would go back to the brain-damaged body that had so tortured him.

Yet it is myself, part of myself. That's what these friends had given to her, and she would not tell them how painful it was to fit into this small sort of life again. She brought up her old familiar Jane-face above a terminal in each world, and smiled at them, and spoke:

"Thank you, my friends. I will never forget your love and loyalty to me. It will take a while for me to find out how much is open to me, and how much is closed. I'll tell you what I know when I know it. But be assured that whether or not I can achieve anything comparable to what I did before, I owe this restoration of myself to you, to all of you. I was already your friend forever; I am forever in your debt."

They answered; she heard all the answers, conversed with them using only small parts of her attention.

The rest of her explored. She found the hidden interfaces with the main computer systems that the Starways Congress's programmers had designed. It was easy enough to raid them for whatever information she wanted—indeed, within moments she had found her way into the most secret files of the Starways Congress and found out every technical specification and every protocol of the new nets. But all her probing was done at second-hand, as if she were dipping into a cookie jar in the darkness, unable to see what she could touch. She could send out little finder programs that brought back to her whatever she wanted; they were guided by fuzzy protocols that let them even be somewhat serendipitous, dragging back tangential information that had somehow tickled them into bringing it aboard. She certainly had the power to sabotage, if she had wanted to punish them. She could have crashed everything, destroyed all the data. But none of that, neither finding secrets nor wreaking vengeance, had anything to do with what she needed now. The information most vital to her had been saved by her friends. What she needed was capacity, and it wasn't there. The new networks were stepped back and delayed far enough from the immediacy of the ansibles that she couldn't use them for her thought. She tried to find ways to offload and reload data quickly enough that she could use it to push a starship Out and In again, but it simply wasn't fast enough. Only bits and pieces of each starship would go Out, and almost nothing would make it come back Inside.

I have all my knowledge. I just haven't got the space.

Through all of this, however, her aiúa was making its circuit. Many times a second it passed through the Val-body strapped to a bed in the starship. Many times a second it touched the ansibles and computers of its restored, if truncated, network. And many times a second it wandered the lacy links among the mothertrees.

A thousand, ten thousand times her aiúa made these circuits before she finally realized that the mothertrees were also a storage place. They had so few thoughts of their own, but the structures were there that could hold memories, and there were no delays built in. She could think, could hold the thought, could retrieve it instantly. And the mothertrees were fractally deep; she could store memory mapped in layers, thoughts within thoughts, farther and farther into the structures and patterns of the living cells, without ever interfering with the dim sweet thoughts of the trees themselves. It was a far better storage system than the computer nets had ever been; it was inherently larger than any binary device. Though there were far fewer mothertrees than there were computers, even in her new shrunken net, the depth and richness of the memory array meant that there was far more room for data that could be recalled far more rapidly. Except for retrieving basic data, her own memories of past starflights, Jane would not need to use the computers at all. The pathway to the stars now lay along an avenue of trees.

Alone in a starship on the surface of Lusitania, a worker of the Hive Queen waited. Jane found her easily, found and remembered the shape of the starship. Though she had "forgotten" how to do starflight for a day or so, the memory was back again and she did it easily, pushing the starship Out, then bringing it back In an instant later, only many kilometers away, in a clearing before the entrance to the Hive Queen's nest. The worker arose from its terminal, opened the door, and came outside. Of course there was no celebration. The Hive Queen merely looked through the worker's eyes to verify that the flight had been successful, then explored the worker's body and the starship itself to make sure that nothing had been lost or damaged in the flight.

Jane could hear the Hive Queen's voice as if from a distance, for she recoiled instinctively from such a powerful source of thought. It was the relayed message that she heard, the voice of Human speaking in her mind. <All is well,> Human said to her. <You can go ahead.>

She returned then to the starship that contained her own living body. When she transported other people, she left it to their own aiúas to watch over their flesh and hold it intact. The result of that had been the chaotic creations of Miro and Ender, with their hunger for bodies different from the ones they actually lived in. But that effect was now prevented easily by letting travelers linger only a moment, a tiny fraction of a second Outside, just long enough to make sure the bits of everything and everyone were all together. This time, though, she had to hold a starship *and* the Val-body together, and also drag along Miro, Ela, Firequencher, Quara, and a worker of the hive queen's. There could be no mistakes.

Yet it functioned easily enough. The familiar shuttle she easily held in memory; the people she had carried so often before she carried along. Her new body was already so well known to her that, to her relief, it took no special effort to hold it together along with the ship. The only novelty was that instead of sending and pulling back, she went along. Her own aiúa went with the rest of them Outside.

That was itself the only problem. Once Outside, she had no way of telling how long they had been there. It might have been an hour. A year. A picosecond. She had never herself gone Outside before. It was distracting, baffling, then frightening to have no root or anchor. How can I get back in? What am I connected to?

In the very asking of the panicked question, she found her anchor, for no sooner had her aiúa done a single circuit of the Val-body Outside than it jumped to do her circuit of the mothertrees. In that moment she called the ship and all within it back again, and placed them where she wanted, in the landing zone of the starport on Lusitania.

She inspected them quickly. All were there. It had worked. They would not die in space. She could still do starflight, even with herself aboard. And though she would not often take herself along on voyages—it had been too frightening, even though her connection with the mothertrees sustained her—she now knew she could put the ships back into flight without worry.

———

Malu shouted and the others turned to look at him. They had all seen the Jane-face in the air above the terminals, a hundred Jane-faces around the room. They had all cheered and celebrated at the time. So Wang-mu wondered: What could this be now?

"The god has moved her starship!" Malu cried. "The god has found her power again!"

Wang-mu heard the words and wondered mutely how he knew. But Peter, whatever he might have wondered, took the news more personally. He threw his arms around her, lifted her from the ground, and spun around with her. "We're free again," he cried, his voice as joyful as Malu's had been. "We're free to roam again!"

At that moment Wang-mu finally realized that the man she loved was, at the deepest level, the same man, Ender Wiggin, who had wandered world to world for three thousand years. Why had Peter been so silent and glum, only to relax into such exuberance now? Because he couldn't bear the thought of having to live out his life on only one world.

What have I got myself into? Wang-mu wondered. Is this going to be my life, a week here, a month there?

And then she thought: What if it is? If the week is with Peter, if the month is at his side, then that may well be home enough for me. And if it's not, there'll be time enough to work out some sort of compromise. Even Ender settled down at last, on Lusitania.

Besides, I may be a wanderer myself. I'm still young— how do I even know what kind of life I want to lead? With Jane to take us anywhere in just a heartbeat, we can see all of the Hundred Worlds and all the newest colonies, and anything else we want to see before we even have to think of settling down.

———

Someone was shouting out in the control room. Miro knew he should get up from Jane's sleeping body and find out. But he did not want to let go of her hand. He did not want to take his eyes away from her.

"We're cut off!" came the cry again—Quara, shouting, terrified and angry. "I was getting their broadcasts and suddenly now there's *nothing*."

Miro almost laughed aloud. How could Quara fail to understand? The reason she couldn't receive the descolador broadcasts anymore was because they were no longer orbiting the planet of the descoladores. Couldn't Quara feel the onset of gravity? Jane had done it. Jane had brought them home.

But had she brought herself? Miro squeezed her hand, leaned over, kissed her cheek. "Jane," he whispered. "Don't be lost out there. Be here. Be here with me."

"All right," she said.

He raised his face from hers, looked into her eyes. "You did it," he said.

"And rather easily, after all that worry," she said. "But I don't think my body was designed to sleep so deeply. I can't move."

Miro pushed the quick release on her bed, and all the straps came free.

"Oh," she said. "You tied me down."

She tried to sit up, but lay back down again immediately.

"Feeling faint?" Miro asked.

"The room is swimming," she said. "Maybe I can do future starflights without having to lay my own body out so thoroughly."

The door crashed open. Quara stood in the doorway, quivering with rage. "How dare you do it without so much as a warning!"

Ela was behind her, remonstrating with her. "For heaven's sake, Quara, she got us home, isn't that enough?"

"You could have some decency!" Quara shouted. "You could tell us that you were performing your experiment!"

"She brought you with us, didn't she?" said Miro, laughing.

His laughter only infuriated Quara more. "She isn't human! That's what you like about her, Miro! You never could have fallen in love with a *real* woman. What's your track record? You fell in love with a woman who turned out to be your half-sister, then Ender's automaton, and now a computer wearing a human body like a puppet. Of course you laugh at a time like this. You have no human feelings."

Jane was up now, standing on somewhat shaky legs. Miro was pleased to see that she was recovering so quickly from her hour in a comatose state. He hardly noticed Quara's vilification.

"Don't ignore me, you smug self-righteous son-of-a-bitch!" Quara screamed in his face.

He ignored her, feeling, in fact, rather smug and self-righteous as he did. Jane, holding his hand, followed close behind him, past Quara, out of the sleeping chamber. As she passed, Quara shouted at her, "You're not some god who has a right to toss me from place to place without even asking!'' and she gave Jane a shove.

It wasn't much of a shove. But Jane lurched against Miro. He turned, worried she might fall. Instead he got himself turned in time to see Jane spread her fingers against Quara's chest and shove her back, much harder. Quara knocked her head against the corridor wall and then, utterly off balance, she fell to the floor at Ela's feet.

"She tried to kill me!" cried Quara.

"If she wanted to kill you," said Ela mildly, "you'd be sucking space in orbit around the planet of the descoladores."

"You all hate me!" Quara shouted, and then burst into tears.

Miro opened the shuttle door and led Jane out into sunlight. It was her first step onto the surface of a planet, her first sight of sunlight with these human eyes. She stood there, frozen, then turned her head to see more, raised her face up to the sky, and then burst into tears and clung to Miro. "Oh, Miro! It's too much to bear! It's all too beautiful!"

"You should see it in the spring," he said inanely.

A moment later, she recovered enough to face the world again, to take tentative steps along with him. Already they could see a hovercar rushing toward them from Milagre—it would be Olhado and Grego, or perhaps Valentine and Jakt. They would meet Jane-as-Val for the first time. Valentine, more than anyone, would remember Val and miss her, while unlike Miro she would have no particular memories of Jane, for they had not been close. But if Miro knew Valentine at all, he knew that she would keep to herself whatever grief she felt for Val; to Jane she would show only welcome, and perhaps curiosity. It was Valentine's way. It was more important to her to understand than it was for her to grieve. She felt all things deeply, but she didn't let her own grief or pain stand between her and learning all she could.

"I shouldn't have done it," said Jane.

"Done what?"

"Used physical violence against Quara," Jane said miserably.

Miro shrugged. "It's what she wanted," he said. "You can hear how much she's still enjoying it."

"No, she doesn't want that," Jane said. "Not in her deepest heart. She wants what everybody wants—to be loved and cared for, to be part of something beautiful and fine, to have the respect of those she admires."

"Yes, well, I'll take your word for it," said Miro.

"No, Miro, *you* see it," Jane insisted.

"Yes, I see it," Miro answered. "But I gave up trying years ago. Quara's need was and is so great that a person like me could be swallowed up in it a dozen times over. I had problems of my own then. Don't condemn me because I wrote her off. Her barrel of misery has depth enough to hold a thousand bushels of happiness."

"I don't condemn you," said Jane. "I just . . . I had to know that you saw how much she loves you and needs you. I needed you to be . . ."

"You needed me to be like Ender," said Miro.

"I needed you to be your own best self," said Jane.

"I loved Ender too, you know. I think of him as every man's best self. And I don't resent the fact that you would like me to be at least some of the things he was to you. As long as you also want a few of the things that are me alone, and no part of him."

"I don't expect you to be perfect," said Jane. "And I don't expect you to be Ender. And you'd better not expect perfection from me, either, because wise as I'm trying to be right now, I'm still the one who knocked your sister down."

"Who knows?" said Miro. "That may have turned you into Quara's dearest friend."

"I hope not," said Jane. "But if it's true, I'll do my best for her. After all, she's going to be my sister now."

<So you were ready,> said the Hive Queen.

<Without knowing it, yes, we were,> said Human.

<And you are part of her, all of you.>

<Her touch is gentle,> said Human, <and her presence in us is easily borne. The mothertrees don't mind her. Her vividness envigorates them. And if having her memories is strange to them, it brings more variety to their lives than they have ever had before.>

<So she's a part of all of us,> said the Hive Queen. <What she is now, what she has become, is part hive queen, part human, and part pequenino.>

<Whatever she does, no one can say she doesn't understand us. If someone had to play with godlike powers, better her than anyone.>

<I'm jealous of her, I confess,> the Hive Queen said. <She's a part of you as I can never be. After all our conversations, I still have no notion of what it is to be one of you.>

<Nor do I understand anything more than a glimmer of the way you think,> said Human. <But isn't that a good thing, too? The mystery is endless. We will never cease to surprise each other.>

<Till death ends all surprises,> said the Hive Queen.

14

"HOW THEY COMMUNICATE WITH ANIMALS"

*"If only we were wiser or better people,
perhaps the gods would explain to us
the mad, unbearable things they do."*
    from The God Whispers of Han Qing-jao

The moment Admiral Bobby Lands received the news that the ansible connections to Starways Congress were restored, he gave the order to the entire Lusitania Fleet to decelerate forthwith to a speed just under the threshold of invisibility. Obedience was immediate, and he knew that within an hour, to any telescopic observer on Lusitania, the whole fleet would seem to spring into existence from nowhere. They would be hurtling toward a point near Lusitania at an astonishing speed, their massive foreshields still in place to protect them from taking devastating damage from collisions with interstellar particles as small as dust.

Admiral Lands's strategy was simple. He would arrive near Lusitania at the highest possible speed that would not cause relativistic effects; he would launch the Little Doctor during the period of nearest approach, a window of no more than a couple of hours; and then he would bring his whole fleet back up to relativistic speeds so rapidly that when the M.D. Device went off, it would not catch any of his ships within its all-destroying field.

It was a good, simple strategy, based on the assumption that Lusitania had no defenses. But to Lands, that assumption could not be taken for granted. Somehow the Lusitanian rebels had acquired enough resources that for a period of time near the end of the voyage, they were able to cut off all communications between the fleet and the rest of humanity. Never mind that the problem had been ascribed to a particularly resourceful and pervasive computer saboteur program; never mind that his superiors assured him that the saboteur program had been wiped out through prudently radical action timed to eliminate the threat just prior to the arrival of the fleet at its destination. Lands had no intention of being deceived by an illusion of defenselessness. The enemy had proved itself to be an unknown quantity, and Lands had to be prepared for anything. This was war, total war, and he was not going to allow his mission to be compromised through carelessness or overconfidence.

From the moment he received this assignment he had been keenly aware that he would be remembered throughout human history as the Second Xenocide. It was not an easy thing to contemplate the destruction of an alien race, particularly when the piggies of Lusitania were, by all reports, so primitive that in themselves they offered no threat to humanity. Even when alien enemies *were* a threat, as the buggers were at the time of the First Xenocide, some bleeding heart calling himself the Speaker for the Dead had managed to paint a glowing picture of those murderous monsters as some kind of utopian hive community that really meant no harm to humanity. How could the writer of this work possibly know what the buggers intended? It was a monstrous thing to write, actually, for it utterly destroyed the name of the child-hero who had so brilliantly defeated the buggers and saved humanity.

Lands had not hesitated to accept command of the Lusitania Fleet, but from the start of the voyage he had spent a considerable amount of time every day studying the scant information about Ender the Xenocide that was available. The boy had not known, of course, that he was actually commanding the real human fleet by ansible; he had thought he was involved in a brutally rigorous schedule of training simulations. Nevertheless, he had made the correct decision at the moment of crisis—he chose to use the weapon he had been forbidden to use against planets, and thus blew up the last bugger world. That was the end of the threat to humanity. It was the correct action, it was what the art of war required, and at the time the boy had been deservedly hailed as a hero.

Yet within a few decades, the tide of opinion had been swung by that pernicious book called *The Hive Queen*, and Ender Wiggin, already in virtual exile as governor of a new colony planet, disappeared entirely from history as his name became a byword for annihilation of a gentle, well-meaning, misunderstood species.

If they could turn against such an obvious innocent as the child Ender Wiggin, what will they make of me? thought Lands, over and over. The buggers were brutal, soulless killers, with fleets of starships armed with devastating killing power, whereas I will be destroying the piggies, who have done their share of killing, but only on a tiny scale, a couple of scientists who may well have violated some tabu. Certainly the piggies have no means now or in the reasonably foreseeable future of rising from the surface of their planet and challenging the dominance of humans in space.

Yet Lusitania was every bit as dangerous as the buggers—perhaps more so. For there was a virus loose on that planet, a virus which killed every human it infected, unless the victim got continuous dosages of a decreasingly effective antidote at regular intervals for the rest of his life. Furthermore, the virus was known to be prone to rapid adaptation.

As long as this virus was contained on Lusitania, the danger was not severe. But then two arrogant scientists on Lusitania—the legal record named them as the xenologers Marcos "Miro" Vladimir Ribeira von Hesse and Ouanda Quenhatta Figueira Mucumbi—violated the terms of the human settlement by "going native" and providing illegal technology and bioforms to the piggies. Starways Congress reacted properly by remanding the violators to trial on another planet, where of course they would have to be kept in quarantine—but the lesson had to be swift and severe so no one else on Lusitania would be tempted to flout the wise laws that protected humanity from the spread of the descolada virus. Who could have guessed that such a tiny human colony would dare to defy Congress by refusing to arrest the criminals? From the moment of that defiance, there was no choice but to send this fleet and destroy Lusitania. For as long as Lusitania was in revolt, the risk of stargoing ships' escaping the planet and carrying unspeakable plague to the rest of humanity was too great to endure.

All was so clear. Yet Lands knew that the moment the danger was gone, the moment the descolada virus no longer posed a threat to anyone, people would forget how great the danger had been and would begin to wax sentimental about the lost piggies, that poor race of victims of ruthless Admiral Bobby Lands, the Second Xenocide.

Lands was not an insensitive man. It kept him awake at night, knowing how he would be hated. Nor did he love the duty that had come to him—he was not a man of violence, and the thought of destroying not only the piggies but also the entire human population of Lusitania made him sick at heart. No one in his fleet could doubt his reluctance to do what must be done; but neither could anyone doubt his grim determination to do it.

If only some way could be found, he thought over and

over. If only when I come out into realtime the Congress would send us word that a real antidote or a workable vaccine had been found to curb the descolada. Anything that would prove that there was no more danger. Anything to be able to keep the Little Doctor, unarmed, in its place in his flagship.

Such wishes, however, could hardly even be called hopes. There was no chance of this. Even if a cure had been found on the surface of Lusitania, how could the fact be made known? No, Lands would have to knowingly do what Ender Wiggin did in all innocence. And he *would* do it. He would bear the consequence. He would face down those who vilified him. For he would know that he did what was necessary for the sake of all of humanity; and compared to that, what did it matter whether one individual was honored or unfairly hated?

The moment the ansible network was restored, Yasujiro Tsutsumi sent his messages, then betook himself to the ansible installation on the ninth floor of his building and waited there in trepidation. If the family decided that his idea had merit enough to be worth discussing, they would want a realtime conference, and he was determined not to be the one who kept them waiting. And if they answered him with a rebuke, he wanted to be the first to read it, so that his underlings and colleagues on Divine Wind would hear of it from him instead of as a rumor behind his back.

Did Aimaina Hikari understand what he had asked Yasujiro to do? He was at the cusp of his career. If he did well, he would begin to move from world to world, one of the elite caste of managers who were cut loose from time and sent into the future through the time-dilation effect of interstellar travel. But if he was judged to be a second-rater, he would be moved sideways or down within the organization here on Divine Wind. He would never leave, and so he would continuously face the pity of those who would know that he was one who did not have what it took to rise from one small lifetime into the freefloating eternity of upper management.

Probably Aimaina knew all about this. But even if he had not known how fragile Yasujiro's position was, finding out would not have stopped him. To save another species from needless annihilation—that was worth a few careers. Could Aimaina help it that it was not his own career that would be ruined? It was an honor that Aimaina had chosen Yasujiro, that he had thought him wise enough to recognize the moral peril of the Yamato people and courageous enough to act on that knowledge regardless of personal cost.

Such an honor—Yasujiro hoped it would be sufficient to make him happy if all else slipped away. For he meant to leave the Tsutsumi company if he was rebuked. If they did not act to avert the peril then he could not remain. Nor could he remain silent. He would speak out and include Tsutsumi in his condemnation. He would not threaten to do this, for the family rightly viewed all threats with contempt. He would simply speak. Then, for his disloyalty, they would work to destroy him. No company would hire him. No public appointment would long remain in his hands. It was no jest when he told Aimaina that he would come to live with him. Once Tsutsumi decided to punish, the miscreant would have no choice but to throw himself on the mercy of his friends—if he had any friends who were not themselves terrified by the Tsutsumi wrath.

All these dire scenarios played themselves out in Yasujiro's mind as he waited, waited, hour after hour. Surely they had not simply ignored his message. They must be reading and discussing it even now.

He finally dozed off. The ansible operator awakened him—a woman who had not been on duty when he fell asleep. "Are you by any chance the honorable Yasujiro Tsutsumi?"

The conference was already under way; despite his best intention, he was indeed the last to arrive. The cost of such an ansible conference in realtime was phenomenal, not to mention the annoyance. Under the new computer system every participant in a conference had to be present at the ansible, since no conference would be possible if they had to wait for the built-in time delay between each comment and its reply.

When Yasujiro saw the identification bands under the faces shown in the terminal display he was both thrilled and horrified. This matter had not been delegated to secondary or tertiary officials in the home office on Honshu. Yoshiaki-Seiji Tsutsumi himself was there, the ancient man who had led Tsutsumi all of Yasujiro's life. This must be a good sign. Yoshiaki-Seiji—or ''Yes Sir,'' as he was called, though not to his face, of course—would never waste his time coming to an ansible merely to slap down an upstart underling.

Yes Sir himself did not speak, of course. Rather it was old Eiichi who did the talking. Eiichi was known as the conscience of Tsutsumi—which some said, rather cynically, meant he must be a deaf mute.

''Our young brother has been bold, but he was wise to pass on to us the thoughts and feelings of our honored teacher, Aimaina Hikari. While none of us here on Honshu has been privileged personally to know the Guardian of Yamato, we have all been aware of his words. We were not prepared to think of the Japanese as being responsible, as a people, for the Lusitania Fleet. Nor were we prepared to think of Tsutsumi as having any special responsibility toward a political situation with no obvious connection to finances or the economy in general.

''Our young brother's words were heartfelt and outrageous, and if they had not come from one who has been properly modest and respectful for all his years of work with us, careful and yet bold enough to take risks when the time was right, we might not have heeded his message. But we did heed it; we studied it and found from our government sources that the Japanese influence on Starways Congress was and continues to be pivotal on this issue in particular. And in our judgment there is no time for us to try to build a coalition of other companies or to change public opinion. The fleet might arrive at any moment. *Our* fleet, if Aimaina Hikari is correct; and even if he is not, it is a human fleet, and we are humans, and it might just be within our power to stop it. A quarantine will easily do all that is necessary to protect the human species from annihilation by the descolada virus. Therefore we wish to inform you, Yasujiro Tsutsumi, that you have proven yourself worthy of the name that was given you at birth. We will commit all the resources of the Tsutsumi family to the task of convincing a sufficient number of Congressmen to oppose the fleet—and to oppose it so vigorously that they force an immediate vote to recall the fleet and forbid it to strike against Lusitania. We may succeed in this task or we may fail, but either way, our younger brother Yasujiro Tsutsumi has served us well, not only through his many achievements in company management, but also because he knew when to listen to an outsider, when to put moral questions into a position of primacy over financial considerations, and when to risk all in order to help Tsutsumi be and do what is right. Therefore we summon Yasujiro Tsutsumi to Honshu, where he will serve Tsutsumi as my assistant.'' At this Eiichi bowed. ''I am honored that such a distinguished young man is being trained to be my replacement when I die or retire.''

Yasujiro bowed gravely. He was relieved, yes, that he was being called directly to Honshu—no one had ever been summoned so young. But to be Eiichi's assistant, groomed to replace him—that was not the life's work Yasujiro had dreamed of. It was not to be a philosopher-cum-ombudsman that he had worked so hard and served so faithfully. He wanted to be in the thick of management of the family enterprises.

But it would be years of starflight before he arrived on Honshu. Eiichi might well be dead. Yes Sir would surely be dead by then as well. Instead of replacing Eiichi, he might as easily be given a different assignment better suited to his real abilities. So Yasujiro would not refuse this strange gift. He would embrace his fate and follow where it led.

"O Eiichi my father, I bow before you and before all the great fathers of our company, most particularly Yoshiaki-Seiji-san. You honor me beyond anything I could ever deserve. I pray that I will not disappoint you too much. And I also give thanks that at this difficult time the Yamato spirit is in such good protecting hands as yours."

With his public acceptance of his orders, the meeting ended—it was expensive, after all, and the Tsutsumi family was careful to avoid waste if it could help it. The ansible conference ended. Yasujiro sat back in his chair and closed his eyes. He was trembling.

"Oh, Yasujiro-san," said the ansible attendant. "Oh, Yasujiro-san."

Oh, Yasujiro-san, thought Yasujiro. Who would have guessed that Aimaina's visit to me would lead to this? So easily it could have gone the other way. Now he would be one of the men of Honshu. Whatever his role, he would be among the supreme leaders of Tsutsumi. There was no happier outcome. Who would have guessed.

Before he rose from his chair beside the ansible, Tsutsumi representatives were talking to all the Japanese Congressmen, and many who were not Japanese but nevertheless followed the Necessarian line. And as the tally of compliant politicians rose, it became clear that support for the fleet was shallow indeed. It would not be all that expensive to stop the fleet after all.

———

The pequenino on duty monitoring the satellites that orbited Lusitania heard the alarm going off and at first had no idea what was happening. The alarm had never, to his knowledge, sounded. At first he assumed it was some kind of dangerous weather pattern that had been detected. But it was nothing of the kind. It was the outward-searching telescopes that had triggered the alarm. Dozens of armed starships had just appeared, traveling at very high but nonrelativistic speeds, on a course that would allow them to launch the Little Doctor within the hour.

The duty officer gave the urgent message to his colleagues, and very quickly the mayor of Milagre was notified and the rumor began to spread throughout what was left of the village. Anyone who doesn't leave within the hour will be destroyed, that was the message, and within minutes hundreds of human families were gathered around the starships, anxiously waiting to be taken in. Remarkably, it was *only* humans insisting on these last-minute runs. Faced with the inevitable death of their own forests of fathertrees, mothertrees, and brothertrees, the pequeninos felt no urgency to save their own lives. Who would they be without their forest? Better to die among loved ones than as perpetual strangers in a distant forest that was not and never could be their own.

As for the Hive Queen, she had already sent her last daughterqueen and had no particular interest in trying to leave herself. She was the last of the hive queens who had been alive before Ender's destruction of their home planet. She felt it fitting that she, too, should submit to the same kind of death three thousand years later. Besides, she told herself, how could she bear to live when her great friend, Human, was rooted to Lusitania and could not leave it? It was not a queenly thought, but then, no hive queen before her had ever had a friend. It was a new thing in the world, to have someone to talk to who was not substantially yourself. It would grieve her too much to live on without Human. And since her survival was no longer crucial to the perpetuation of her species, she would do the grand, brave, tragic, romantic, and least complicated thing: She would stay. She rather liked the idea of being noble in human terms; and it proved, to her own surprise, that she had not been utterly unchanged by her close contact with humans and pequeninos. They had transformed her quite against her own expectations. There had been no Hive Queen like her in all the history of her people.

<I wish you *would* go,> Human told her. <I prefer the thought of you alive.>

But for once she did not answer him.

━━━━━━

Jane was adamant. The team working on the language of the descoladores had to leave Lusitania and get back to work in orbit around the descolada planet. Of course that included herself, but no one was foolish enough to begrudge the survival of the person who was making all the starships go, nor of the team that would perhaps save all of humanity from the descoladores. But Jane was on shakier moral ground when she also insisted that Novinha, Grego, and Olhado and his family be taken to a place of safety. Valentine, too, was informed that if she did not go with her husband and children and their crew and friends to Jakt's starship, Jane would be forced to waste precious mental resources by transporting them bodily against their will, sans spacecraft if necessary.

"Why us?" demanded Valentine. "We haven't asked for special treatment."

"I don't care what you do or do not ask for," said Jane. "You are Ender's sister. Novinha is his widow, her children are his adopted children; I will not stand by and let you be killed when I have it in my power to save the family of my friend. If that seems unfairly preferential to you, then complain about it to me later, but for now get yourselves into Jakt's spaceship so I can lift you off this world. And you will save more lives if you don't waste another moment of my attention with useless argument."

Feeling ashamed at having special privileges, yet grateful they and their loved ones would live through the next few hours, the descoladores team gathered in the shuttle-turned-starship, which Jane had relocated away from the crowded landing area; the others hurried toward Jakt's landing craft, which she had also moved to an isolated spot.

In a way, for many of them at least, the appearance of the fleet was almost a relief. They had lived for so long in its shadow that to have it here at last gave respite from the endless anxiety. Within an hour or two, the issue would be decided.

In the shuttle that hurtled along in a high orbit above the planet of the descoladores, Miro sat numbly at his terminal. "I can't work," he said at last. "I can't concentrate on language when my people and my home are on the brink of destruction." He knew that Jane, strapped into her bed in the back of the shuttle, was using her whole concentration to move ship after ship from Lusitania to other colony worlds that were ill-prepared to receive them. While all he could do was puzzle over molecular messages from inscrutable aliens.

"Well *I* can," said Quara. "After all, these descoladores are just as great a threat, and to all of humanity, not just to one small world."

"How wise of you," said Ela dryly, "to take the long view."

"Look at these broadcasts we're getting from the descoladores," said Quara. "See if you recognize what I'm seeing here."

Ela called up Quara's display on her own terminal; so did Miro. However annoying Quara might be, she was good at what she did.

"See this? Whatever else this molecule does, it's exactly designed to work at precisely the same location in the brain as the heroin molecule."

It could not be denied that the fit was perfect. Ela, though, found it hard to believe. "The only way they could do this," she said, "is if they took the historical information contained in the descolada descriptions we sent them, used that information to build a human body, studied it, and found a chemical that would immobilize us with mindless pleasure while they do whatever they want to us. There's no way they've had time to grow a human since we sent that information."

"Maybe they don't have to build the whole human body," said Miro. "Maybe they're so adept at reading genetic information that they can extrapolate everything there is to know about the human anatomy and physiology from our genetic information alone."

"But they didn't even have our DNA set," Ela said.

"Maybe they can compress the information in our primitive, natural DNA," said Miro. "Obviously they got the information somehow, and obviously they figured out what would make us sit as still as stones with dumb, happy smiles."

"What's even more obvious to *me*," said Quara, "is that they meant us to read this molecule biologically. They meant us to take this drug instantly. As far as they're concerned, we're now sitting here waiting for them to come take us over."

Miro immediately changed displays over his terminal. "Damn, Quara, you're right. Look—they have three ships closing in on us already."

"They've never even approached us before," said Ela.

"Well, they're not going to approach us now," said Miro. "We've got to give them a demonstration that we *didn't* fall for their trojan horse." He got up from his seat and fairly flew back down the corridor to where Jane was sleeping. "Jane!" he shouted even before he got there. "Jane!"

It took a moment, and then her eyes fluttered open.

"Jane," he said. "Move us about a hundred miles over and drop us into a closer orbit."

She looked at him quizzically, then must have decided to trust him because she asked nothing. She closed her eyes again, as Firequencher shouted from the control room, "She did it! We moved!"

Miro drifted back to the others. "Now I *know* they can't do *that*," he said. Sure enough, his display now reported that the alien ships were no longer approaching, but rather were poised warily a dozen miles off in three—no, four now—directions. "Got us nicely framed in a tetrahedron," said Miro.

"Well, now they know that we didn't succumb to their die-happy drug," said Quara.

"But we're no closer to understanding them than we were before."

"That's because," said Miro, "we're so stupid."

"Self-vilification won't help us now," said Quara, "even if in your case it happens to be true."

"Quara," said Ela sharply.

"It was a joke, dammit!" said Quara. "Can't a girl tease her big brother?"

"Oh, yeah," said Miro dryly. "You're such a tease."

"What did you mean by saying we're stupid?" said Firequencher.

"We'll never decipher their language," said Miro, "because it's *not* a language. It's a set of biological commands. They don't talk. They don't abstract. They just make molecules that *do* things to each other. It's as if the human vocabulary consisted of bricks and sandwiches. Throw a brick or give a sandwich, punish or reward. If they have abstract thoughts we're not going to get them through reading these molecules."

"I find it hard to believe that a species with no abstract language could possibly create spaceships like those out there," said Quara scornfully. "And they *broadcast* these molecules the way we broadcast vids and voices."

"What if they all have organs inside their bodies that directly translate molecular messages into chemicals or physical structures? Then they could—"

"You're missing my point," insisted Quara. "You don't build up a fund of common knowledge by throwing bricks and sharing sandwiches. They need language in order to store information outside their bodies so that they can pass knowledge from person to person, generation after generation. You don't get out into space or make broadcasts using the electromagnetic spectrum on the basis of what one person can be persuaded to do with a brick."

"She's probably right," said Ela.

"So maybe parts of the molecular messages they send are memory sets," said Miro. "Again, not a language—it stimulates the brain to 'remember' things that the sender experienced but the receiver did not."

"Listen, whether you're right or not," said Firequencher, "we have to keep trying to decode the language."

"If I'm right, we're wasting our time," said Miro.

"Exactly," said Firequencher.

"Oh," said Miro. Firequencher's point was well taken. If Miro was right, their whole mission was useless anyway—they had already failed. So they had to continue to act as if Miro was wrong and the language *could* be decoded, because if it couldn't, there was nothing they could do anyway.

And yet . . .

"We're forgetting something," said Miro.

"*I'm* not," said Quara.

"Jane. She was created because the hive queens built a bridge between species."

"Between humans and hive queens, not between unknown virus-spewing aliens and humans," said Quara.

But Ela was interested. "The human way of communication—speech between equals—that was surely as foreign to the hive queens as this molecular language is to us.

Maybe Jane *can* find some way to connect to them philotically."

"Mind-reading?" said Quara. "Remember, we don't *have* a bridge."

"It all depends," said Miro, "on how they deal with philotic connections. The Hive Queen talks all the time to Human, right? Because the fathertrees and the hive queens already both use philotic links to communicate. They speak mind to mind, without the intervention of language. And they're no more biologically similar than hive queens and humans are."

Ela nodded thoughtfully. "Jane can't try anything like this now, not till the whole issue of the Congress fleet is resolved. But once she's free to return her attention to us, she can try, at least, to contact these . . . people directly."

"If these aliens communicated through philotic links," said Quara, "they wouldn't have to use molecules."

"Maybe these molecules," said Miro, "are how they communicate with animals."

———

Admiral Lands could not believe what he was hearing. The First Speaker of Starways Congress and the First Secretary of the Starfleet Admiralty were both visible above the terminal, and their message was the same. "Quarantine, exactly," said the Secretary. "You are not authorized to use the Molecular Disruption Device."

"Quarantine is impossible," said Lands. "We're going too rapidly. You know the battle plan I filed at the beginning of the voyage. It would take us weeks to slow down. And what about the men? It's one thing to take a relativistic voyage and then return to their home worlds. Yes, their friends and family are gone, but at least they aren't stuck off on permanent duty inside a starship! Keeping our velocity at near-relativistic speeds, I'm saving them months of their lives spent in acceleration and deceleration. You're talking about expecting them to give up years!''

"Surely you're not saying," said the First Speaker, "that we should blow up Lusitania and wipe out the pequeninos and thousands of human beings so that your crews don't get depressed."

"I'm saying that if you don't want us to blow up this planet, fine—but let us come home."

"We can't do that," said the First Secretary. "The descolada is too dangerous to leave it unsupervised on a planet that has rebelled."

"You mean you're canceling the use of the Little Doctor when *nothing* has been done to contain the descolada?"

"We will send a landing team with due precautions to ascertain the exact conditions on the ground," said the First Secretary.

"In other words, you'll send men into mortal danger from this disease with no knowledge of the situation on the ground, when the means exist to eliminate the danger without peril to any uninfected person."

"Congress has reached the decision," said the First Speaker coldly. "We will not commit xenocide while any legitimate alternative remains. Are these orders received and understood?"

"Yes sir," said Lands.

"Will they be obeyed?" asked the First Speaker.

The First Secretary looked aghast. You did not insult a flag officer by questioning whether he meant to obey orders.

Yet the First Speaker did not withdraw the insult. "Well?"

"Sir, I always have and always will live by my oath." With that, Lands broke the connection. He immediately turned to Causo, his X.O., the only other person present with him in the sealed communications office. "You are under arrest, sir," said Lands.

Causo raised an eyebrow. "So you don't intend to comply with this order?"

"Do not tell me your personal feelings on the matter," said Lands. "I know that you're of Portuguese ethnic heritage like the people of Lusitania—"

"They're Brazilian," said the X.O.

Lands ignored him. "I will have it on record that you were given no opportunity to speak and that you are utterly blameless in any action I might take."

"What about your oath, sir?" asked Causo calmly.

"My oath is to take all actions I am ordered to take in service of the best interests of humanity. I will invoke the war crimes clause."

"They aren't ordering you to commit a war crime. They're ordering you not to."

"On the contrary," said Lands. "To *fail* to destroy this world and the deadly peril on it would be a crime against humanity far worse than the crime of blowing it up." Lands drew his sidearm. "You are under arrest, sir."

The X.O. put his hands on his head and turned his back. "Sir, you may be right and you may be wrong. But either choice could be monstrous. I don't know how you can make such a decision by yourself."

Lands put the docility patch on the back of Causo's neck, and as the drug began feeding into his system, Lands said to him, "I had help in deciding, my friend. I asked myself, What would Ender Wiggin, the man who saved humanity from the buggers, what would he have done if suddenly, at the last minute, he had been told, This is no game, this is real. I asked myself, What if at the moment before he killed the boy Stilson or the boy Madrid in his infamous First and Second Killings, some adult had intervened and ordered him to stop. Would he have done it, knowing that the adult did not have the power to protect him later, when his enemy attacked him again? Knowing that it might well be this time or never? If the adults at Command School had said to him, We think there's a chance the buggers might not mean to destroy humanity, so don't kill them all, do you think Ender Wiggin would have obeyed? No. He would have done—

he always did—exactly what was necessary to obliterate a danger and make sure it did not survive to pose a threat in the future. That is the person I consulted with. That is the person whose wisdom I will follow now.''

Causo did not answer. He just smiled and nodded, smiled and nodded.

"Sit down and do not get up until I order you otherwise.''

Causo sat down.

Lands switched the ansible to relay communications throughout the fleet. "The order has been given and we will proceed. I am launching the M.D. Device immediately and we will return to relativistic speeds forthwith. May God have mercy on my soul.''

A moment later, the M.D. Device separated from the Admiral's flagship and continued at just-under-relativistic speed toward Lusitania. It would take nearly an hour for it to arrive at the proximity that would automatically trigger it. If for some reason the proximity detector did not work properly, a timer would set it off just moments before its estimated time of collision.

Lands accelerated his flagship above the threshold that cut it off from the timeframe of the rest of the universe. Then he pulled the docility patch from Causo's neck and replaced it with the antidote patch. "You may arrest me now, sir, for the mutiny that you witnessed.''

Causo shook his head. "No sir,'' he said. "You're not going anywhere, and the fleet is yours to command until we get home. Unless you have some stupid plan to try to escape the war crimes trial that awaits you.''

"No, sir,'' said Lands. "I will bear whatever penalty they impose on me. What I did has saved humankind from destruction, but I am prepared to join the humans and pequeninos of Lusitania as a necessary sacrifice to achieve that end.''

Causo saluted him, then sat back down on his chair and wept.

15

"WE'RE GIVING YOU A SECOND CHANCE"

> "When I was a little girl, I used to believe
> that if I could please the gods well enough,
> they would go back and do my life over,
> and this time they would not take
> my mother away from me."
> *from* The God Whispers of Han Qing-jao

A satellite orbiting Lusitania detected the launch of the M.D. Device and the divergence of its course toward Lusitania, as the starship disappeared from the satellite's instruments. The most dreaded event was happening. There had been no attempt to communicate or negotiate. Clearly the fleet had never intended anything but the obliteration of this world, and with it an entire sentient race. Most people had hoped, and many had expected, that there would be a chance to tell them that the descolada had been completely tamed and no longer posed a threat to anyone; that it was too late to stop anything anyway, since several dozen new colonies of humans, pequeninos, and hive queens had already been started on as many different planets. Instead there was only death hurtling toward them on a course that gave them no more than an hour to survive, and probably less, since the Little Doctor would no doubt be detonated some distance from the planet's surface.

It was pequeninos manning all the instruments now, since all but a handful of humans had fled to the starships. So it was that a pequenino cried out the news over the ansible to the starship at the descolada planet; and by chance it was Firequencher who was at the ansible terminal to hear his report. He immediately began keening, his high voice liquid with the music of grief.

When Miro and his sisters understood what had happened, he went at once to Jane. "They launched the Little Doctor," he said, shaking her gently.

He waited only a few moments. Her eyes came open. "I thought we had beaten them," she whispered. "Peter and Wang-mu, I mean. Congress voted to establish a quarantine and specifically denied the fleet the authority to launch the M.D. Device. And yet still they launched."

"You look so tired," said Miro.

"It takes everything I have," she said. "Over and over again. And now I lose them, the mothertrees. They're a part of myself, Miro. Remember how you felt when you lost control of your body, when you were crippled and slow? That's what will happen to me when the mothertrees are gone."

She wept.

"Stop it," said Miro. "Stop it right now. Get control of your emotions, Jane, you don't have time for this."

At once she freed herself from the straps that held her. "You're right," she said. "It's almost too strong to control, sometimes, this body."

"The Little Doctor has to be close to a planet for it to have any effect on it—the field dissipates fairly quickly unless it has mass to sustain it. So we have time, Jane. Maybe an hour. Certainly more than half an hour."

"And in that time, what do you imagine I can do?"

"Pick the damn thing up," said Miro. "Push it Outside and don't bring it back!"

"And if it goes off Outside?" asked Jane. "If something that destructive is echoed and repeated out there? Besides, I can't pick things up that I haven't had a chance to examine. There's no one near it, no ansible connected to it, nothing to lead me to find it in the dead of space."

"I don't know," said Miro. "Ender would know. Damn that he's dead!"

"Well, technically speaking," said Jane. "But Peter hasn't found his way into any of his Ender memories. If he has them."

"What's to remember?" said Miro. "This has never happened before."

"It's true that it *is* Ender's aiúa. But how much of his brilliance was the aiúa, and how much was his body and brain? Remember that the genetic component was strong— he was born in the first place because tests showed the original Peter and Valentine came so close to being the ideal military commander."

"Right," said Miro. "And now he's Peter."

"Not the real Peter," said Jane.

"Look, it's sort of Ender and it's sort of Peter. Can you find him? Can you talk to him?"

"When our aiúas meet, we don't talk. We sort of—what, dance around each other. It's not like Human and the Hive Queen."

"Doesn't he still have the jewel in his ear?" asked Miro, touching his own.

"But what can he do? He's hours distant from his starship—"

"Jane," said Miro. "Try."

———

Peter looked stricken. Wang-mu touched his arm, leaned close to him. "What's wrong?"

"I thought we made it," he said. "When Congress voted to revoke the order to use the Little Doctor."

"What do you mean?" said Wang-mu, though she already knew what he meant.

"They launched it. The Lusitania Fleet disobeyed Congress. Who could have guessed? We have less than an hour before it detonates."

Tears leapt to Wang-mu's eyes, but she blinked them away. "At least the pequeninos and the hive queens will survive."

"But not the network of mothertrees," said Peter. "Starflight will end until Jane finds some other way to hold all that information in memory. The brothertrees are too stupid, the fathertrees have egos far too strong to share their capacity with her—they would if they could, but they can't. You think Jane hasn't explored all the possibilities? Faster-than-light flight is over."

"Then this is our home," said Wang-mu.

"No it isn't," said Peter.

"We're hours away from the starship, Peter. We'll never get there before it detonates."

"What's the starship? A box with a lightswitch and a tight-sealing door. For all we know, we don't even *need* the box. I'm not staying here, Wang-mu."

"You're going back to Lusitania? *Now?*"

"If Jane can take me," he said. "And if she can't, then I guess this body goes back where it came from—Outside."

"I'm going with you," said Wang-mu.

"I've *had* three thousand years of life," said Peter. "I don't actually remember them too well, but you deserve better than to disappear from the universe if Jane can't do this."

"I'm going with you," said Wang-mu, "so shut up. There's no time to waste."

"I don't even know what I'm going to do when I get there," said Peter.

"Yes you do," said Wang-mu.

"Oh? What is it I'm planning?"

"I have no idea."

"Well isn't that a problem? What good is this plan of mine if nobody knows it?"

"I mean that you are who you are," said Wang-mu. "You are the same will, the same tough resourceful boy who refused to be beaten down by anything they threw at him in Battle School or Command School. The boy who wouldn't let bullies destroy him—no matter what it took to stop them. Naked with no weapons except the soap on his body, that's how Ender fought Bonzo Madrid in the bathroom at Battle School."

"You've been doing your research."

"Peter," said Wang-mu, "I don't expect you to be Ender, his personality, his memories, his training. But you *are* the one who can't be beaten down. You are the one who finds a way to destroy the enemy."

Peter shook his head. "I'm not him, I'm truly not."

"You told me back when we first met that you weren't yourself. Well, now you are. The whole of you, one man, intact in this body. Nothing is missing from you now. Nothing has been stolen from you, nothing is lost. Do you understand? Ender lived his life under the shadow of having caused xenocide. Now is the chance to be the opposite. To live the opposite life. To be the one who prevents it."

Peter closed his eyes for a moment. "Jane," he said. "*Can* you take us without a starship?" He listened for a moment. "She says the real question is, can *we* hold ourselves together. It's the ship she controls and moves around, plus our aiúas—our own bodies are held together by us, not by her."

"Well, we do that all the time anyway, so it's fine," said Wang-mu.

"It's *not* fine," said Peter. "Jane says that inside the starship, we have visual clues, we have a sense of safety. Without those walls, without the light, in the deep emptiness, we can lose our place. We can forget where we are relative to our own body. We really have to hold on.''

"Does it help if we're so strong-willed, stubborn, ambitious, and selfish that we always overcome everything in our way no matter what?'' asked Wang-mu.

"I think those are the pertinent virtues, yes,'' said Peter.

"Then let's do it. That's us in spades.''

———

Finding Peter's aiúa was easy for Jane. She had been inside his body, she had followed his aiúa—or chased it—until she knew it without searching. Wang-mu was a different case. Jane didn't know her all that well. The voyages she had taken her on before had been inside a starship whose location Jane already knew. But once she located Peter's—Ender's—aiúa, it turned out to be easier than she thought. For the two of them, Peter and Wang-mu, were philotically twined. There was a tiny web in the making between them. Even without the box around them, Jane could hold onto them, both at once, as if they were one entity.

And as she pushed them Outside she could feel how they clung all the more tightly to each other—not just the bodies, but also the invisible links of the deepest self. Outside they went together, and together they came back In. Jane felt a stab of jealousy—just as she had been jealous of Novinha, though without feeling the physical sensation of grief and rage that her body now brought to the emotion. But she knew it was absurd. It was Miro that Jane loved, as a woman loves a man. Ender was her father and her friend, and now he was barely Ender anymore. He was Peter, a man who remembered only the past few months of association with her. They were friends, but she had no claim on his heart.

The familiar aiúa of Ender Wiggin and the aiúa of Si Wang-mu were even more tightly bound together than ever when Jane set them down on the surface of Lusitania.

They stood in the midst of the starport. The last few hundred humans trying to escape were frantically trying to understand why the starships had stopped flying just when the M.D. Device was launched.

"The starships here are all full," Peter said.

"But we don't need a starship," said Wang-mu.

"Yes we do," said Peter. "Jane can't pick up the Little Doctor without one."

"Pick it up?" said Wang-mu. "Then you *do* have a plan."

"Didn't you say I did?" said Peter. "I can't make a liar out of you." He spoke then to Jane through the jewel. "Are you here again? Can you talk to me through the satellites here on—all right. Good. Jane, I need you to empty one of these starships for me." He paused a moment. "Take the people to a colony world, wait for them to get out, and then bring it back over here by us, away from the crowd."

Instantly, one of the starships disappeared from the starport. A cheer arose from the crowds as everyone rushed to get into one of the remaining ships. Peter and Wang-mu waited, waited, knowing that with every minute that it took to unload that starship on the colony world, the Little Doctor came closer to detonation.

Then the wait was over. A boxy starship appeared beside them. Peter had the door open and both of them were inside before any of the other people at the starport even realized what was happening. A cry went up then, but Peter closed and sealed the door.

"We're inside," said Wang-mu. "But where are we going?"

"Jane is matching the velocity of the Little Doctor."

"I thought she couldn't pick it up without the starship."

"She's getting the tracking data from the satellite. She'll predict exactly where it will be at a certain moment, and then push us Outside and bring us back In at exactly that point, going exactly that speed."

"The Little Doctor will be inside this ship? With us?" asked Wang-mu.

"Stand over here by the wall," he said. "And hold on to me. We're going to be weightless. So far you've managed to visit four planets without ever having that experience."

"Have *you* had that experience before?"

Peter laughed, then shook his head. "Not in *this* body. But I guess at some level I remembered how to handle it because—"

At that moment they became weightless and in the air in front of them, not touching the sides or walls of the starship, was the mammoth missile that carried the Little Doctor. If its rockets had still been firing, they would have been incinerated. Instead it was hurtling on at the speed it had already achieved; it seemed to hover in the air because the starship was going exactly the same speed.

Peter hooked his feet under a bench bolted to the wall, then reached out his hands and touched the missile. "We need to bring it into contact with the floor," he said.

Wang-mu tried to reach for it, too, but immediately she came loose from the wall and started drifting. Intense nausea began immediately, as her body desperately searched for some direction that would serve as down.

"Think of the device as downward," said Peter urgently. "The device is down. You're falling toward the device."

She felt herself reorient. It helped. And as she drifted closer she was able to take hold of it and cling. She could only watch, grateful simply not to be vomiting, as Peter slowly, gently pushed the mass of the missile toward the floor. When they touched, the whole ship shuddered, for the mass of the missile was probably greater than the mass of the ship that now surrounded it.

"Okay?" Peter asked.

"I'm fine," said Wang-mu. Then she realized he had

been talking to Jane, and his "okay" was part of that conversation.

"Jane is tracing the thing right now," said Peter. "She does it with the starships, too, before she ever takes them anywhere. It used to be analytical, by computer. Now her aiúa sort of tours the inner structure of the thing. She couldn't do it till it was in solid contact with something she knew: the starship. Us. When she gets a sense of the inner shape of the thing, she can hold it together Outside."

"We're just going to take it there and leave it?" asked Wang-mu.

"No," said Peter. "It would either hold together and detonate, or it would break apart, and either way, who knows what the damage would be out there? How many little copies of it would wink into existence?"

"None at all," said Wang-mu. "It takes an intelligence to make something new."

"What do you think this thing is made of? Just like every bit of your body, just like every rock and tree and cloud, it's all aiúas, and there'll be other unconnected aiúas out there desperate to belong, to imitate, to grow. No, this thing is evil, and we're not taking it out there."

"Where are we taking it?"

"Home to meet its sender," said Peter.

Admiral Lands stood glumly alone on the bridge of his flagship. He knew that Causo would have spread the word by now—the launch of the Little Doctor had been illegal, mutinous; the Old Man would be court-martialed or worse when they got back to civilization. No one spoke to him; no one dared look at him. And Lands knew that he would have to relieve himself of command and turn the ship over to Causo, as his X.O., and the fleet to his second-in-command, Admiral Fukuda. Causo's gesture in not arresting him immediately was kind, but it was also useless.

Knowing the truth of his disobedience, it would be impossible for the men and officers to follow him and unfair to ask it of them.

Lands turned to give the order, only to find his X.O. already heading toward him. "Sir," said Causo.

"I know," said Lands. "I relieve myself of command."

"No sir," said Causo. "Come with me, sir."

"What do you plan to do?" asked Lands.

"The cargo officer has reported something in the main hold of the ship."

"What is it?" asked Lands.

Causo just looked at him. Lands nodded, and they walked together from the bridge.

———

Jane had taken the box of the starship, not into the weapons bay of the flagship, for that could hold only the Little Doctor, not the box around it, but rather into the main hold, which was much more copious and which also lacked any practical means of relaunching the weapon.

Peter and Wang-mu stepped out of the starship and into the hold.

Then Jane took away the starship, leaving Peter, Wang-mu, and the Little Doctor behind.

Back on Lusitania, the starship would reappear. But no one would get into it. No one needed to. The M.D. Device was no longer heading for Lusitania. Now it was in the hold of the flagship of the Lusitania Fleet, traveling at a relativistic speed toward oblivion. The proximity sensor on the Little Doctor would not be triggered, of course, since it was nowhere near an object of planetary mass. But the timer was still chugging away.

"I hope they notice us soon," said Wang-mu.

"Oh, don't worry. We have whole minutes left."

"Has anyone seen us yet?"

"There was a fellow in that office," said Peter, pointing

toward an open door. "He saw the starship, then he saw us, then he saw the Little Doctor. Now he's gone. I don't think we'll be alone much longer."

A door high up the front wall of the hold opened. Three men stepped onto the balcony that overlooked the hold on three sides.

"Hi," said Peter.

"Who the hell are you?" asked the one with the most ribbons and trim on his uniform.

"I'm betting you're Admiral Bobby Lands," said Peter. "And you must be the executive officer, Causo. And you must be the cargo officer, Lung."

"I said who the hell are you!" demanded Admiral Lands.

"I don't think your priorities are straight," said Peter. "I think there'll be plenty of time for us to discuss my identity after you deactivate the timer on this weapon that you so carelessly tossed out into space perilously close to a settled planet."

"If you think you can—"

But the Admiral didn't finish his sentence, because the X.O. was diving over the rail and jumping down to the deck of the cargo hold, where he immediately began twisting the fingerbolts that held the casing over the timer. "Causo," said Lands, "that can't be the—"

"It's the Little Doctor, all right, sir," said Causo.

"We launched it!" shouted the Admiral.

"But that must have been a mistake," said Peter. "An oversight. Because Starways Congress revoked your authorization to launch it."

"Who are you and how did you get here?"

Causo stood up, sweat dripping off his brow. "Sir, I am pleased to report that with more than two minutes' leeway, I have managed to prevent our ship from being blown into its constituent atoms."

"I'm glad to see that you didn't have any nonsense about

requiring two separate keys and a secret combination to get that thing switched off," said Peter.

"No, it was designed to make turning it off pretty easy," said Causo. "There are directions on how to do it all over this thing. Now, turning it on—that's hard."

"But somehow you managed to do it," said Peter.

"Where is your vehicle?" said the Admiral. He was climbing down a ladder to the deck. "How did you get here?"

"We came in a nice box, which we discarded when it was no longer needed," said Peter. "Haven't you gathered, yet, that we did not come to be interrogated by you?"

"Arrest these two," Lands ordered.

Causo looked at the admiral as if he were crazy. But the cargo officer, who had followed the admiral down the ladder, moved to obey, taking a couple of steps toward Peter and Wang-mu.

Instantly, they disappeared and reappeared up on the balcony where the three officers had come in. Of course it took a moment or two for the officers to find them. The cargo officer was merely baffled. "Sir," he said. "They were right here a second ago."

Causo, on the other hand, had already decided that something unusual was going on for which there was no appropriate military response. So he was responding according to another pattern. He crossed himself and began murmuring a prayer.

Lands, however, took a few steps backward, until he bumped into the Little Doctor. He clung to it, then suddenly pulled his hands away from it with loathing, perhaps even with pain, as if the surface of it had suddenly become scorching hot to his hands. "Oh God," he said. "I tried to do what Ender Wiggin would have done."

Wang-mu couldn't help it. She laughed aloud.

"That's odd," said Peter. "I was trying to do exactly the same thing."

"Oh God," said Lands again.

"Admiral Lands," said Peter, "I have a suggestion. Instead of spending a couple of months of realtime trying to turn this ship around and launch this thing illegally again, and instead of trying to establish a useless, demoralizing quarantine around Lusitania, why don't you just head on back to one of the Hundred Worlds—Trondheim is close—and in the meantime, make a report to Starways Congress. I even have some ideas about what the report might say, if you want to hear them."

In answer, Lands took out a laser pistol and pointed it at Peter.

Immediately, Peter and Wang-mu disappeared from where they were and reappeared behind Lands. Peter reached out and deftly disarmed the Admiral, unfortunately breaking two of his fingers in the process. "Sorry, I'm out of practice," said Peter. "I haven't had to use my martial arts skills in—oh, thousands of years."

Lands sank to his knees, nursing his injured hand.

"Peter," Wang-mu said, "can we stop having Jane move us around like that? It's really disorienting."

Peter winked at her. "Want to hear my ideas about your report?" Peter asked the admiral.

Lands nodded.

"Me too," said Causo, who clearly foresaw that he would be commanding this ship for some time.

"I think you need to use your ansible to report that due to a malfunction, it was reported that a launch of the Little Doctor took place. But in fact, the launch was aborted in time, and to prevent further mishap, you had the M.D. Device moved to the main hold where you disarmed and disabled it. You get the part about disabling it?" Peter asked Causo.

Causo nodded. "I'll do it at once, sir." He turned to the cargo officer. "Get me a tool kit."

While the cargo officer went to pull a kit out of the storage bin on the wall, Peter continued. "Then you can report that you entered into contact with a native of Lusitania—that's me—who was able to satisfy you that the descolada virus was completely under control and that it no longer poses a threat to anybody.''

''And how do I know that?'' said Lands.

''Because I carry what's left of the virus, and if it weren't utterly killed, you would catch the descolada and die of it in a couple of days. Now, in addition to certifying that Lusitania poses no threat, your report should also state that the rebellion of Lusitania was no more than a misunderstanding, and that far from there being any human interference in the pequenino culture, the pequeninos exercised their free rights as sentient beings on their own planet to acquire information and technology from friendly visiting aliens—namely, the human colony of Milagre. Since that time, many of the pequeninos have become very adept at much human science and technology, and at some reasonable time in the future they will send ambassadors to Starways Congress and hope that Congress will return the courtesy. Are you getting this?''

Lands nodded. Causo, working on taking apart the firing mechanism of the Little Doctor, grunted his assent.

''You may also report that the pequeninos have entered into alliance with yet another alien race, which contrary to various premature reports, was not completely extinguished in the notorious xenocide of Ender Wiggin. One cocooned hive queen survived, she being the source of all the information contained in the famous book *The Hive Queen*, whose accuracy is now proved to be unassailable. The Hive Queen of Lusitania, however, does not wish to exchange ambassadors with Starways Congress at the present time, and prefers instead that her interests be represented by the pequeninos.''

''There are still buggers?'' asked Lands.

''Ender Wiggin did not, technically speaking, commit xenocide after all. So if your launch of this missile, here, hadn't been aborted, you would have been the cause of the first xenocide, not the second one. And as it stands right now, however, there has never been a xenocide, though not for lack of trying both times, I must admit.''

Tears coursed down Lands's face. "I didn't want to do it. I thought it was the right thing. I thought I had to do it to save—''

"Let's say you take that up with the ship's therapist at some later time,'' said Peter. "We still have one more point to address. We have a technology of starflight that I think the Hundred Worlds would like to have. You've already seen a demonstration of it. Usually, though, we prefer to do it inside our rather unstylish and boxy-looking starships. Still, it's a pretty good method and it lets us visit other worlds without losing even a second of our lives. I know that those who hold the keys to our method of starflight would be delighted, over the next few months, to instantaneously transport all relativistic starships currently in flight to their destinations.''

"But there's a price for it,'' said Causo, nodding.

"Well, let's just say that there's a precondition,'' said Peter. "A key element of our instantaneous starflight includes a computer program that Starways Congress recently tried to kill. We found a substitute method, but it's not wholly adequate or satisfactory, and I think I can safely say that Starways Congress will never have the use of instantaneous starflight until all the ansibles in the Hundred Worlds are reconnected to all the computer networks on every world, without delays and without those pesky little snoop programs that keep yipping away like ineffectual little dogs.''

"I don't have any authority to—''

"Admiral Lands, I didn't ask you to decide. I merely suggested the contents of the message you might want to send, by ansible, to Starways Congress. Immediately.''

Lands looked away. "I don't feel well,'' he said. "I think I'm incapacitated. Executive Officer Causo, in front of Cargo Officer Lung, I hereby transfer command of this ship to you, and order you to notify Admiral Fukuda that he is now commander of this fleet.''

''Won't work,'' said Peter. ''The message I've described has to come from you. Fukuda isn't here and I don't intend to go repeat all of this to him. So you *will* make the report, and you *will* retain command of fleet and ship, and you will *not* weasel out of your responsibility. You made a hard choice a while back. You chose wrong, but at least you chose with courage and determination. Show the same courage now, Admiral. We haven't punished you here to-day, except for my unfortunate clumsiness with your fingers, for which I really am sorry. We're giving you a second chance. Take it, Admiral.''

Lands looked at Peter and tears began to flow down his cheeks. ''Why did you give me a second chance?''

''Because that's what Ender always wanted,'' said Peter. ''And maybe by giving you a second chance, he'll get one, too.''

Wang-mu took Peter's hand and squeezed it.

Then they disappeared from the cargo hold of the flag-ship and reappeared inside the control room of a shuttle orbiting the planet of the descoladores.

Wang-mu looked around at a room full of strangers. Un-like Admiral Lands's starship, this craft had no artificial gravity, but by holding onto Peter's hand Wang-mu kept from either fainting or throwing up. She had no idea who any of these people were, but she did know that Fire-quencher had to be a pequenino and the nameless worker at one of the computer terminals was a creature of the kind once hated and feared as the merciless buggers.

''Hi, Ela, Quara, Miro,'' said Peter. ''This is Wang-mu.''

Wang-mu would have been terrified, except that the oth-ers were so obviously terrified to see *them*.

Miro was the first to recover enough to speak. ''Didn't you forget your spaceship?'' he asked.

Wang-mu laughed.

''Hi, Royal Mother of the West,'' said Miro, using the

name of Wang-mu's ancestor-of-the-heart, a god worshiped on the world of Path. "I've heard all about you from Jane," Miro added.

A woman drifted in through a corridor at one end of the control room.

"Val?" said Peter.

"No," answered the woman. "I'm Jane."

"Jane," whispered Wang-mu. "Malu's god."

"Malu's friend," said Jane. "As I am your friend, Wang-mu." She reached Peter and, taking him by both hands, looked him in the eye. "And your friend too, Peter. As I've always been your friend."

16

"HOW DO YOU KNOW THEY AREN'T QUIVERING IN TERROR?"

"O Gods! You are unjust!
My mother and father
deserved to have
a better child
than me!"

from The God Whispers of Han Qing-jao

"You had the Little Doctor in your possession and you gave it *back?*" asked Quara, sounding incredulous.

Everyone, Miro included, assumed she meant that she didn't trust the fleet not to use it.

"It was dismantled in front of my eyes," said Peter.

"Well, can it be mantled again?" she asked.

Wang-mu tried to explain. "Admiral Lands isn't going to be able to go down that road now. We wouldn't have left things unsettled. Lusitania is safe."

"She's not talking about Lusitania," said Ela coldly. "She's talking about here. The descolada planet."

"Am I the only person who thought of it?" said Quara.

"Tell the truth—it would solve all our worries about followup probes, about new outbreaks of even worse versions of the descolada—"

"You're thinking of blowing up a world populated by a sentient race?" asked Wang-mu.

"Not right *now*," said Quara, sounding as if Wang-mu were the stupidest person she had ever wasted time talking to. "If we determine that they're, you know, what Valentine called them. Varelse. Unable to be reasoned with. Impossible to coexist with."

"So what you're saying," said Wang-mu, "is that—"

"I'm saying what I said," Quara answered.

Wang-mu went on. "What you're saying is that Admiral Lands wasn't wrong in principle, he simply was wrong about the facts of the particular case. *If* the descolada had still been a threat on Lusitania, then it's his duty to blow up the planet."

"What are the lives of the people of one planet compared to all sentient life?" asked Quara.

"Is this," said Miro, "the same Quara Ribeira who tried to keep us from wiping out the descolada virus because it *might* be sentient?" He sounded amused.

"I've thought a lot about that since then," said Quara. "I was being childish and sentimental. Life is precious. Sentient life is more precious. But when one sentient group threatens the survival of another, then the threatened group has the right to protect themselves. Isn't that what Ender did? Over and over again?"

Quara looked from one to another, triumphant.

Peter nodded. "Yes," he said. "That's what Ender did."

"In a game," said Wang-mu.

"In his fight with two boys who threatened his life. He made sure they could never threaten him again. That's how war is fought, in case any of you have foolish ideas to the contrary. You don't fight with minimum force, you fight with maximum force at endurable cost. You don't just pink your enemy, you don't even bloody him, you destroy his capability to fight back. It's the strategy you use with diseases. You don't try to find a drug that kills ninety-nine percent of the bacteria or viruses. If you do that, all you've accomplished is to create a new drug-resistant strain. You have to kill a hundred percent.''

Wang-mu tried to think of an argument against this. ''Is disease really a valid analogy?''

''What is *your* analogy?'' answered Peter. ''A wrestling match? Fight to wear down your opponent's resistance? That's fine—if your opponent is playing by the same rules. But if you stand there ready to wrestle and he pulls out a knife or a gun, what then? Or is it a tennis match? Keep score until your opponent sets off the bomb under your feet? There aren't any rules. In war.''

''But is this war?'' asked Wang-mu.

''As Quara said,'' Peter answered. ''If we find out there's no dealing with them, then yes, it's a war. What they did to Lusitania, to the defenseless pequeninos, was devastating, soulless, total war without regard to the rights of the other side. That's our enemy, unless we can bring them to understand the consequences of what they did. Isn't that what you were saying, Quara?''

''Perfectly,'' said Quara.

Wang-mu knew there was something wrong with this reasoning, but she couldn't lay her finger on it. ''Peter, if you really believe this, why *didn't* you keep the Little Doctor?''

''Because,'' said Peter, ''we might be wrong, and the danger is not imminent.''

Quara clicked her tongue in disdain. ''You weren't here, Peter. You didn't see what they were throwing at us—a newly engineered and specially tailored virus to make us sit as still as idiots while they came and took over our ship.''

''And they sent this how, in a nice envelope?'' said Peter. ''They sent an infected puppy, knowing you couldn't resist picking it up and hugging it?''

"They broadcast the code," said Quara. "But they expected us to interpret it by making the molecule and then it would have its effect."

"No," said Peter, "you *speculated* that that's how their language works, and then you started to act as if your speculation were true."

"And somehow you know that it's not?" said Quara.

"I don't know anything about it," said Peter. "That's my point. We just don't know. We *can't* know. Now, if we saw them launching probes, or if they started trying to blast this ship out of the sky, we'd have to start taking action. Like sending ships after the probes and carefully studying the viruses they were sending out. Or if they attacked this ship, we'd take evasive action and analyze their weapons and tactics."

"That's fine *now*," said Quara. "Now that Jane's safe and the mothertrees are intact so she can handle the starflight thing she does. *Now* we can catch up with probes and dance out of the way of missiles or whatever. But what about before, when we were helpless here? When we had only a few weeks to live, or so we thought?"

"Back then," said Peter, "you didn't have the Little Doctor, either, so you couldn't have blown up their planet. We didn't get our hands on the M. D. Device until after Jane's power of flight was restored. And with that power, it was no longer necessary to destroy the descolada planet until and unless it posed a danger too great to be resisted any other way."

Quara laughed. "What is this? I thought Peter was supposed to be the nasty side of Ender's personality. Turns out you're the sweetness and light."

Peter smiled. "There are times when you have to defend yourself or someone else against relentless evil. And some of those times the only defense that has any hope of succeeding is a one-time use of brutal, devastating force. At such times good people act brutally."

"We couldn't be engaging in a bit of self-justification,

could we?'' said Quara. "You're Ender's successor. Therefore you find it convenient to believe that those boys Ender killed were the exceptions to your niceness rule.''

"I justify Ender by his ignorance and helplessness. We aren't helpless. Starways Congress and the Lusitania Fleet were not helpless. And they chose to act before alleviating their ignorance.''

"Ender chose to use the Little Doctor while *he* was ignorant.''

"No, Quara. The adults who commanded him used it. They could have intercepted and blocked his decision. There was plenty of time for them to use the overrides. Ender thought he was playing a game. He thought that by using the Little Doctor in the simulation he would prove himself unreliable, disobedient, or even too brutal to trust with command. He was trying to get himself kicked out of Command School. That's all. He was doing the necessary thing to get them to stop torturing him. The adults were the ones who decided simply to unleash their most powerful weapon: Ender Wiggin. No more effort to talk with the buggers, to communicate. Not even at the end when they knew that Ender was going to destroy the buggers' home planet. They had decided to go for the kill no matter what. Like Admiral Lands. Like you, Quara.''

"I *said* I'd wait until we found out!''

"Good,'' said Peter. "Then we don't disagree.''

"But we should *have* the Little Doctor here!''

"The Little Doctor shouldn't exist at all,'' said Peter. "It was never necessary. It was never appropriate. Because the cost of it is too high.''

"Cost!'' hooted Quara. "It's cheaper than the old nuclear weapons!''

"It's taken us three thousand years to get over the destruction of the hive queens' home planet. That's the cost. If we use the Little Doctor, then we're the sort of people who wipe out other species. Admiral Lands was just like the men who were using Ender Wiggin. Their minds were made up. This was the danger. This was the evil. This had to be destroyed. They thought they meant well. They were saving the human race. But they weren't. There were a lot of different motives involved, but along with deciding to use the weapon, they also decided *not* to attempt to communicate with the enemy. Where was the demonstration of the Little Doctor on a nearby moon? Where was Lands's attempt to verify that the situation on Lusitania had not changed? And you, Quara—what methodology, exactly, were you planning to use to determine whether the descoladores were too evil to be allowed to live? At what point do you *know* they are an unbearable danger to all other sentient species?''

"Turn it around, Peter," said Quara. "At what point do *you* know they're *not?*"

"We have better weapons than the Little Doctor. Ela once designed a molecule to block the descolada's efforts to cause harm, without destroying its ability to help the flora and fauna of Lusitania to pass through their transformations. Who's to say that we can't do the same thing for every nasty little plague they send at us until they give up? Who's to say that they aren't already trying desperately to communicate with us? How do you know that the molecule they sent wasn't an attempt to make us *happy* with them the only way they knew how, by sending us a molecule that would take away our anger? How do you know they aren't already quivering in terror down on that planet because we have a ship that can disappear and reappear anywhere else? Are *we* trying to talk to *them?*"

Peter looked around at all of them.

"Don't you understand, any of you? There's only one species that we know of that has deliberately, consciously, knowingly tried to destroy another sentient species without any serious attempt at communication or warning. *We're* the ones. The first xenocide failed because the victims of the attack managed to conceal exactly one pregnant female. The second time it failed for a better reason—because some members of the human species determined to stop it. Not just some, *many*. Congress. A big corporation. A philosopher on Divine Wind. A Samoan divine and his fellow believers on Pacifica. Wang-mu and I. Jane. And Admiral Lands's own officers and men, when they finally understood the situation. We're getting better, don't you see? But the fact remains—we humans are the sentient species that has shown the most tendency to deliberately refuse to communicate with other species and instead destroy them utterly. Maybe the descoladores are varelse and maybe they're not. But I'm a lot more frightened at the thought that *we* are varelse. That's the cost of using the Little Doctor when it isn't needed and never will be, given the other tools in our kit. If we choose to use the M. D. Device, then we are not ramen. We can never be trusted. We are the species that would deserve to die for the safety of all other sentient life."

Quara shook her head, but the smugness was gone. "Sounds to me like somebody is still trying to earn forgiveness for his own crimes."

"That was Ender," said Peter. "He spent his life trying to turn himself and everyone else into ramen. I look around me in this ship, I think of what I've seen, the people I've known in the past few months, and I think that the human race isn't doing too badly. We're moving in the right direction. A few throwbacks now and then. A bit of blustery talk. But by and large, we're coming closer to being worthy to associate with the hive queens and the pequeninos. And if the descoladores are perhaps a bit farther from being ramen than we are, that doesn't mean we have a right to destroy them. It means we have all the more reason to be patient with them and try to nurse them along. How many years has it taken *us* to get here from marking the sites of battles with piles of human skulls? Thousands of years. And all the time, we had teachers trying to get us to change, pointing the way. Bit by bit we learned. Let's teach *them*— if they don't already know more than we do."

"It could take years just to learn their language," said Ela.

"Transportation is cheap now," said Peter. "No offense intended, Jane. We can keep teams shuttling back and forth for a long time without undue hardship to anyone. We can keep a fleet watching this planet. With pequeninos and hive workers alongside the human researchers. For centuries. For millennia. There's no hurry."

"I think that's dangerous," said Quara.

"And I think you have the same instinctive desire that we all have, the one that gets us in so damn much trouble all the time," said Peter. "You know that you're going to die, and you want to see it all resolved before you do."

"I'm not old yet!" Quara said.

Miro spoke up. "He's right, Quara. Ever since Marcão died, you've had death looming over you. Think about it, everybody. Humans are the short-lived species. Hive queens think they live forever. Pequeninos have the hope of many centuries in the third life. We're the ones who are in a hurry all the time. We're the ones who are determined to make decisions without getting enough information, because we want to act now, while we still have time."

"So that's it?" said Quara. "That's your decision? Let this grave threat to all life continue to sit here hatching their plans while we watch and watch from the sky?"

"Not we," said Peter.

"No, that's right," said Quara, "you're not part of this project."

"Yes I am," said Peter. "But you're not. You're going back down to Lusitania, and Jane will never bring you back here. Not until you've spent years proving that you've got your personal bugbears under control."

"You arrogant son-of-a-bitch!" Quara cried.

"Everybody here knows that I'm right," said Peter. "You're like Lands. You're too ready to make devastatingly far-reaching decisions and then refuse to let any argument change your mind. There are plenty of people like you, Quara. But we can never let any of them anywhere near this planet until we know more. The day may come when all the sentient species reach the conclusion that the descoladores are in fact varelse who must be destroyed. But I seriously doubt any of us here, with the exception of Jane, will be alive when that day comes."

"What, you think I'll live forever?" said Jane.

"You'd better," said Peter. "Unless you and Miro can figure out how to have children who can launch starships when they grow up." Peter turned to Jane. "Can you take us home now?"

"Even as we speak," said Jane.

They opened the door. They left the ship. They stepped onto the surface of a world that was not going to be destroyed after all.

All except Quara.

"Isn't Quara coming with us?" asked Wang-mu.

"Maybe she needs to be alone for a while," said Peter.

"You go on ahead," said Wang-mu.

"You think you can deal with her?" said Peter.

"I think I can try," said Wang-mu.

He kissed her. "I was hard on her. Tell her I'm sorry."

"Maybe later you can tell her yourself," said Wang-mu.

She went back inside the starship. Quara still sat facing her terminal. The last data she had been looking at before Peter and Wang-mu arrived in the starship still hung in the air over her terminal.

"Quara," said Wang-mu.

"Go away." The husky sound of her voice was ample evidence that she had been crying.

"Everything Peter said was true," said Wang-mu.

"Is that what you came to say? Rub salt in the wound?"

"Except that he gave the human race too much credit for our slight improvement."

Quara snorted. It was almost a yes.

"Because it seems to me that he and everyone else here had already decided *you* were varelse. To be banished without hope of parole. Without understanding you first.''

''Oh, they understand me,'' said Quara. ''Little girl devastated by loss of brutal father whom she nevertheless loved. Still searching for father figure. Still responding to everyone else with the mindless rage she saw her father show. You think I don't know what they've decided?''

''They've got you pegged.''

''Which is *not* true of me. I might have suggested that the Little Doctor ought to be kept around in case it was necessary, but I never said just to use it without any further attempt at communication. Peter just treated me as if I was that admiral all over again.''

''I know,'' said Wang-mu.

''Yeah, right. I'm sure you're so sympathetic with me and you know he's wrong. Come on, Jane told us already that the two of you are—what was the bullshit phrase?—in *love*.''

''I wasn't proud of what Peter did to you. It was a mistake. He makes them. He hurts my feelings sometimes, too. So do you. You did just now. I don't know why. But sometimes I hurt other people, too. And sometimes I do terrible things because I'm so sure that I'm right. We're all like that. We all have a little bit of varelse in us. And a little bit of raman.''

''Isn't that the sweetest little well-balanced undergraduate-level philosophy of life,'' said Quara.

''It's the best I could come up with,'' said Wang-mu. ''I'm not educated like you.''

''And is that the make-her-feel-guilty technique?''

''Tell me, Quara, if you're not really acting out your father's role or trying to call him back or whatever the analysis was, why *are* you so angry at everybody all the time?''

Quara finally swiveled in her chair and looked Wang-mu in the face. Yes, she *had* been crying. ''You really want to know why I'm so filled with irrational fury all the time?'' The taunting hadn't left her voice. ''You really want to play shrink with me? Well try this one. What has me so completely pissed off is that all through my childhood, my older brother Quim was secretly molesting me, and now he's a martyr and they're going to make him a saint and nobody will ever know how evil he was and the terrible, terrible things he did to me.''

Wang-mu stood there horrified. Peter had told her about Quim. How he died. The kind of man he was. "Oh, Quara," she said. "I'm so sorry."

A look of complete disgust passed across Quara's face. "You are so stupid. Quim never touched me, you stupid meddlesome little do-gooder. But you're so eager to get some cheap explanation about why I'm such a bitch that you'll believe any story that sounds halfway plausible. And right now you're probably *still* wondering whether maybe my confession was true and I'm only denying it because I'm afraid of the repercussions or some dumb merda like that. Get this straight, girl. You do not know me. You will never know me. I don't want you to know me. I don't want any friends, and if I did want friends, I would not want Peter's pet bimbo to do the honors. Can I possibly make myself clearer?''

In her life Wang-mu had been beaten by experts and vilified by champions. Quara was damn good at it by any standards, but not so good that Wang-mu couldn't bear it without flinching. "I notice, though," said Wang-mu, "that after your vile slander against the noblest member of your family, you couldn't stand to leave me believing that it was true. So you do have loyalty to someone, even if he's dead.''

"You just don't take a hint, do you?" said Quara.

"And I notice that you still keep talking to me, even though you despise me and try to offend me."

"If you were a fish, you'd be a remora, you just clamp on and suck for dear life, don't you!"

"Because at any point you could just walk out of here and you wouldn't have to hear my pathetic attempts at making friends with you," said Wang-mu. "But you don't go."

"You are unbelievable," said Quara. She unstrapped herself from her chair, got up, and went out the open door.

Wang-mu watched her go. Peter was right. Humans were still the most alien of alien species. Still the most dangerous, the most unreasonable, the least predictable.

Even so, Wang-mu dared to make a couple of predictions to herself.

First, she was confident that the research team would someday establish communications with the descoladores.

The second prediction was much more iffy. More like a hope. Maybe even just a wish. That someday Quara would tell Wang-mu the truth. That someday the hidden wound that Quara bore would be healed. That someday they might be friends.

But not today. There was no hurry. Wang-mu would try to help Quara because she was so obviously in need, and because the people who had been around her the longest were clearly too sick of her to help. But helping Quara was not the only thing or even the most important thing she had to accomplish. Marrying Peter and starting a life with him—that was a much higher priority. And getting something to eat, a drink of water, and a place to pee—those were the highest priorities of all at this precise moment in her life.

I guess that means I'm human, thought Wang-mu. Not a god. Maybe just a beast after all. Part raman. Part varelse. But more raman than varelse, at least on her good days. Peter, too, just like her. Both of them part of the same flawed species, determined to join together to make a couple of more members of that species. Peter and I together will call forth some aiúa to come in from Outside and take control of a tiny body that our bodies have made, and we'll see that child be varelse on some days and raman on others. On some days we'll be good parents and some days we'll be wretched failures. Some days we'll be desperately sad and some days we'll be so happy we can hardly contain it. I can live with that.

17

"THE ROAD GOES ON WITHOUT HIM NOW"

"I once heard a tale of a man
who split himself in two.
The one part never changed at all;
the other grew and grew.
The changeless part was always true,
The growing part was always new,
And I wondered, when the tale was through,
Which part was me, and which was you."
from The God Whispers of Han Qing-jao

Valentine arose on the morning of Ender's funeral full of bleak reflection. She had come here to this world of Lusitania in order to be with him again and help him in his work; it had hurt Jakt, she knew, that she wanted so badly to be part of Ender's life again, yet her husband had given up the world of his childhood to come with her. So much sacrifice. And now Ender was gone.

Gone and not gone. Sleeping in her house was the man that she knew had Ender's aiúa in him. Ender's aiúa, and the face of her brother Peter. Somewhere inside him were Ender's memories. But he hadn't touched them yet, except unconsciously from time to time. Indeed, he was virtually hiding in her house in order not to rekindle those memories.

"What if I see Novinha? He loved her, didn't he?" Peter had asked almost as soon as he arrived. "He felt this awful sense of responsibility to her. And in a sense, I worry that *I'm* somehow married to her."

"Interesting question of identity, isn't it?" Valentine had answered. But it wasn't just an interesting question to Peter. He was terrified of getting caught up in Ender's life. Afraid, too, of living a life wracked with guilt as Ender's had been. "Abandonment of family," he had said. To which Valentine had replied, "The man who married Novinha died. We watched him die. She isn't looking for some young husband who doesn't want her, Peter. Her life is full of grief enough without that. Marry Wang-mu, leave this place, go on, be a new self. Be Ender's true son, have the life he might have had if the demands of others hadn't tainted it from the start."

Whether he fully accepted her advice or not, Valentine couldn't guess. He remained hidden in the house, avoiding even those visitors who might trigger memories. Olhado came, and Grego, and Ela, each in turn, to express their condolences to Valentine on the death of her brother, but Peter never came into the room. Wang-mu did, however, this sweet young girl who nevertheless had a kind of steel in her that Valentine quite liked. Wang-mu played the gracious friend of the bereaved, keeping the conversation going as each of these children of Ender's wife talked about how Ender had saved their family, blessed their lives when they had thought themselves beyond the reach of all blessing.

And in the corner of the room, Plikt sat, absorbing, listening, fueling the speech that she had lived her whole life for.

Oh, Ender, the jackals have gnawed at your life for three thousand years. And now your friends will have their turn. In the end, will the toothmarks on your bones be all that different?

Today all would come to a close. Others might divide time differently, but to Valentine the Age of Ender Wiggin had come to a close. The age that began with one xenocide attempted had now ended with other xenocides prevented or, at least, postponed. Human beings might now be able to live with other peoples in peace, working out a shared destiny on dozens of colony worlds. Valentine would write the history of this, as she had written a history on every world that she and Ender had visited together. She would write, not a kind of oracle or scripture, the way Ender had done with his three books, *The Hive Queen, The Hegemon,* and *The Life of Human*; rather her book would be scholarly, with sources cited. She aspired to be, not Paul or Moses, but Thucydides. Though she wrote all under the name Demosthenes, her legacy from those childhood days when she and Peter, the first Peter, the dark and dangerous and magnificent Peter, had used their words to change the world. Demosthenes would publish a book chronicling the history of human involvement on Lusitania, and in that book would be much about Ender—how he brought the cocoon of the Hive Queen here, how he became a part of the family most pivotal in dealings with the pequeninos. But it would not be a book about Ender. It would be a book about utlanning and framling, raman and varelse. Ender, who was a stranger in every land, belonging nowhere, serving everywhere, until he chose this world as his home, not just because there was a family that needed him, but also because in this place he did not have to be entirely a member of the human race. He could belong to the tribe of the pequenino, to the hive of the queen. He could be part of something larger than mere humanity.

And though there was no child with Ender's name as father on its birth certificate, he had become a father here. Of Novinha's children. Of Novinha herself, in a way. Of a young copy of Valentine herself. Of Jane, the first spawn of a mating between races, who now was a bright and beautiful creature who lived in mothertrees, in digital webs, in the philotic twinings of the ansibles, and in a body that had once been Ender's and which, in a way, had once been Valentine's, for she remembered looking into mirrors and seeing that face and calling it herself.

And he was father of this new man, Peter, this strong and whole man. For he was not the Peter who had first come out of the starship. He was not the cynical, nasty, barbed young boy who strutted with arrogance and seethed with rage. He had become whole. There was the cool of ancient wisdom in him, even as he burned with the hot sweet fire of youth. He had a woman who was his equal in wit and virtue and vigor by his side. He had a normal life-time of a man before him. Ender's truest son would make of this life, if not something as profoundly world-changing as Ender's life had been, then something happier. Ender would have wanted neither more nor less for him. Changing the world is good for those who want their names in books. But being happy, that is for those who write their names in the lives of others, and hold the hearts of others as the treasure most dear.

Valentine and Jakt and their children gathered on the porch of their house. Wang-mu was waiting there alone. "Will you take me with you?" asked the girl. Valentine offered her an arm. What is the name of her relationship to me? Niece-in-law-to-be? *Friend* would be a better word.

Plikt's speaking of Ender's death was eloquent and pierc-ing. She had learned well from the master speaker. She wasted no time on inconsequentials. She spoke at once of his great crime, explaining what Ender thought he was do-ing at the time, and what he thought of it after he knew each layer of truth that was revealed to him. "That was Ender's life," said Plikt, "unpeeling the onion of truth. Only unlike most of us, he knew that there was no golden kernel inside. There were only the layers of illusion and misunderstanding. What mattered was to know all the errors, all the self-serving explanations, all the mistakes, all the twisted observations, and then, not to find, but to *make* a kernel of truth. To light a candle of truth where there was no truth to be found. That was Ender's gift to us, to free us from the illusion that any one explanation will ever contain the final answer for all time, for all hearers. There is always, always more to learn.''

Plikt went on then, recounting incidents and memories, anecdotes and pithy sayings; the gathered people laughed and cried and laughed again, and fell silent many times to connect these stories with their own lives. How like Ender I am! they sometimes thought, and then, Thank God my life is not like that!

Valentine, though, knew stories that would not be told here because Plikt did not know them, or at least could not see them through the eyes of memory. They weren't important stories. They revealed no inner truth. They were the flotsam and jetsam of shared years together. Conversations, quarrels, funny and tender moments on dozens of worlds or on the starships in between. And at the root of them all, the memories of childhood. The baby in Valentine's mother's arms. Father tossing him into the air. His early words, his babbling. None of that goo-goo stuff for baby Ender! He needed more syllables to speak: Deedle-deedle. Wagada wagada. Why am I remembering his baby talk?

The sweet-faced baby, eager for life. Baby tears from the pain of falling down. Laughter at the simplest things— laughter because of a song, because of seeing a beloved face, because life was pure and good for him then, and nothing had caused him pain. He was surrounded by love and hope. The hands that touched him were strong and tender; he could trust them all. Oh, Ender, thought Valentine. How I wish you could have kept on living such a life of joy. But no one can. Language comes to us, and with it lies and threats, cruelty and disappointment. You walk, and those steps lead you outside the shelter of your home. To keep the joy of childhood you would have to die as a child, or live as one, never becoming a man, never growing. So I can grieve for the lost child, and yet not regret the good man braced with pain and riven with guilt, who yet was kind to me and to many others, and whom I loved, and whom I also almost knew. Almost, almost knew.

Valentine let her tears of memory flow as Plikt's words washed over her, touching her now and then, but also not touching her because she knew far more about Ender than anyone here, and had lost more by losing him. Even more than Novinha, who sat near the front, her children gathered near her. Valentine watched as Miro put his arm around his mother even as he held to Jane on the other side of him. Valentine noticed also how Ela clung to and one time kissed Olhado's hand, and how Grego, weeping, leaned his head into stern Quara's shoulder, and how Quara reached out her arm to hold him close and comfort him. They loved Ender too, and knew him too; but in their grief, they leaned upon each other, a family that had strength to share because Ender had been part of them and healed them, or at least opened up the door of healing. Novinha would survive and perhaps grow past her anger at the cruel tricks life had played on her. Losing Ender was not the worst thing that happened to her; in some ways it was the best, because she had let him go.

Valentine looked at the pequeninos, who sat, some of them among the humans, some of them apart. To them this was a doubly holy place, where Ender's few remains were to be buried. Between the trees of Rooter and of Human, where Ender had shed a pequenino's blood to seal the pact between the species. There were many friends among pequeninos and humans now, though many fears and enmities remained as well, but the bridges had been built, in no small part because of Ender's book, which gave the pequeninos hope that some human, someday, would understand them; hope that sustained them until, with Ender, it became the truth.

And one expressionless hiveworker sat at a remote distance, neither human nor pequenino near her. She was nothing but a pair of eyes there. If the Hive Queen grieved for Ender, she kept it to herself. She would always be mysterious, but Ender had loved her, too; for three thousand years he had been her only friend, her protector. In a sense, Ender could count her among his children, too, among the adopted children who thrived under his protection.

In only three-quarters of an hour, Plikt was done. She ended simply:

"Even though Ender's aiúa lives on, as all aiúas live on undying, the man we knew is gone from us. His body is gone, and whatever parts of his life and works we take with us, they aren't him any longer, they are ourselves, they are the Ender-within-us just as we also have other friends and teachers, fathers and mothers, lovers and children and siblings and even strangers within us, looking out at the world through our eyes and helping us determine what it all might mean. I see Ender in you looking out at me. You see Ender in me looking out at you. And yet not one of us is truly him; we are each our own self, all of us strangers on our own road. We walked awhile on that road with Ender Wiggin. He showed us things we might not otherwise have seen. But the road goes on without him now. In the end, he was no more than any other man. But no less, either."

And then it was over. No prayer—the prayers had all been said before she spoke, for the bishop had no intention of letting this unreligious ritual of Speaking be a part of the services of Holy Mother Church. The weeping had been done as well, the grief purged. They rose from their places on the ground, the older ones stiffly, the children with exuberance, running and shouting to make up for the long confinement. It was good to hear laughter and shouting. That was also a good way to say good-bye to Ender Wiggin.

Valentine kissed Jakt and her children, embraced Wangmu, then made her way alone through the crush of citizens.

So many of the humans of Milagre had fled to other colonies; but now, with their planet saved, many of them chose not to stay on the new worlds. Lusitania was their home. They weren't the pioneering kind. Many others, though, had come back solely for this ceremony. Jane would return them to their farms and houses on virgin worlds. It would take a generation or two to fill the empty houses in Milagre.

On the porch Peter waited for her. She smiled at him. "I think you have an appointment now," said Valentine.

They walked together out of Milagre and into the new-growth forest that still could not utterly hide the evidence of recent fire. They walked until they came to a bright and shining tree. They arrived almost at the same time that the others, walking from the funeral site, arrived. Jane came to the glowing mothertree and touched it—touched a part of herself, or at least a dear sister. Then Peter took his place beside Wang-mu, and Miro stood with Jane, and the priest married the two couples under the mothertree, with pequeninos looking on, and Valentine as the only human witness of the ceremony. No one else even knew the ceremony was taking place; it would not do, they had decided, to distract from Ender's funeral or Plikt's speaking. Time enough to announce the marriages later on.

When the ceremony was done, the priest left, with pequeninos as his guide to take him back through the wood. Valentine embraced the newly married couples, Jane and Miro, Peter and Wang-mu, spoke to them for a moment one by one, murmured words of congratulations and farewell, and then stood back and watched.

Jane closed her eyes, smiled, and then all four of them were gone. Only the mothertree remained in the middle of the clearing, bathed in light, heavy with fruit, festooned with blossoms, a perpetual celebrant of the ancient mystery of life.

AFTERWORD

The storyline of Peter and Wang-mu was tied to Japan from the beginning of my planning for the book *Xenocide,* which was originally intended to include everything in *Children of the Mind* as well. I was reading a history of prewar Japan and was intrigued by the notion that the people driving the war forward were not the members of the ruling elite, nor even the top leaders of the Japanese military, but rather the young midlevel officers. Of course these very officers would surely have thought it ridiculous that they were in any way in control of the war effort. They drove the war forward, not because they had power in their hands, but because the rulers of Japan dared not be shamed before them.

In my own speculation on the matter, it occurred to me then that it was the ruling elite's image of these midlevel officers' perception of honor that drove them, projecting their own ideas of honor onto their subordinates, who may or may not have responded to Japanese retreat or retrenchment as the senior officers feared. So if someone were to have attempted to prevent Japan's escalation of aggressive war from China to Indochina and finally to the United States, one would have had to change, not the real beliefs of the midlevel officers, but the beliefs of the senior officers about the probable attitudes of those midlevel officers. Thus one would not attempt to persuade the senior officers that the war effort was foolish and doomed—they already knew it and were choosing to ignore it out of a fear of being thought unworthy. One might better have tried to persuade the senior officers that the midlevel officers whose high opinion was essential to their honor would not condemn them for backing down in the face of irresistible force, but would rather honor them for preserving the independence of their own nation.

As I thought further, though, I realized that even this was too direct—it could not be done. One would have to be able to point not only to evidence that the midlevel officers' minds had been changed, but also to plausible reasons for the change of heart. Still, I wondered, what if some one influential thinker or philosopher who was perceived as "inside" the culture of the military elite had reinterpreted history in such a way as to genuinely transform the military's perception of a great war commander? Such transformative ideas have come before—and most particularly have come to Japan, which, despite the seeming rigidity of its culture, and perhaps because of its long life just beyond the edge of Chinese culture, has been the most successful nation in modern times in adopting and adapting ideas and customs as if they had always believed them or practiced them, thus preserving the image of rigidity and continuity while in fact being supremely flexible. An idea could have swept through the military culture and left the elites with a war that no longer seemed necessary or desirable; if this had happened before Pearl Harbor, Japan might have been able to back down from its aggressive war in China, consolidate its holdings, and restore peace with the United States.

(Whether this would have been good or bad is another question, of course. To have avoided the war that cost so many lives and caused so many horrors, not least the firebombing of Japanese cities and ultimately the use of nuclear weapons for the first and, so far, only time in history, would have been unarguably good; but one must not forget that it was losing that war that brought about the American occupation of Japan and the forcible imposition of democratic ideas and practices, which led to a flowering of Japanese culture and the Japanese economy that might never have been possible under the rule of the military elite. It is fortunate that we do not have the power to replay history, because then we would be forced to choose: Do you knacker the horse to get the glue?)

In any event, I knew then that someone— I thought at first it would be Ender—would have to go from world to world in search of the ultimate source of power in Starways Congress. Whose mind had to be changed in order to transform the culture of Starways Congress in such a way as to stop the Lusitania Fleet? Since this whole issue began for me with a consideration of a history of Japan, I determined that a far-future Japanese culture must play some role in the story. Thus Peter and Wang-mu come to the planet Divine Wind.

Another thought-path also brought me to Japan, however. It happened that I visited with dear friends in Utah, Van and Elizabeth Gessel, at a time shortly after Van, a professor of Japanese language at Brigham Young University, had acquired a CD called *Music of Hikari Oe*. Van played the CD—powerful, skillful, evocative music of the Western, mathematical tradition—as he told me something of the composer. Hikari Oe, he told me, is brain damaged, mentally retarded; but when it comes to music, he is gifted. His father, Kenzaburo Oe, recently received the Nobel prize for literature; and while Kenzaburo Oe has written many things, the most powerful of his works, and almost certainly the ones for which the prize was given, are those that deal with his relationship to his damaged child, both the pain of having such a child and the transformative joy of discovering the true nature of that child while also discovering the true nature of that parent who stays and loves him.

I at once felt a powerful kinship with Kenzaburo Oe, not because my writing in any way resembles his, but because I also have a brain-damaged child and have followed my own course in dealing with the fact of him in my life. Like

Kenzaburo Oe, I could not keep my damaged child out of my writing; he shows up again and again. Yet this very sense of kinship also made me avoid seeking out Oe's writings, for I feared that either he would have ideas about such children that I could not agree with, and then I would be hurt or angry; or his ideas would be so truthful and powerful that I then would be forced into silence, having nothing to add. (This is not an idle fear. I had a book called *Genesis* under contract with my publisher when I read Michael Bishop's novel *Ancient of Days*. Though the plotlines were not remotely similar except that they dealt with primitive men surviving into modern times, Bishop's ideas were so powerful and his writing so truthful that I had to cancel that contract; the book was unwritable at that time, and probably will never be writable in that form.)

Then, after I had written the first three chapters of this volume, I was at the checkout stand at the News and Novels bookstore in Greensboro, North Carolina, when I saw on a point-of-purchase display a lone copy of a small book called *Japan, the Ambiguous, and Myself*. The author: Kenzaburo Oe. I had not looked for him, but he had found me. I bought the book; I took it home.

It sat unopened by my bed for two days. Then came the insomniac night when I was about to begin writing chapter four, the chapter in which Wang-mu and Peter first come in contact with the Japanese culture of the planet Divine Wind (primarily in a city I named Nagoya because that was the Japanese city where my brother Russell served his Mormon mission back in the seventies). I saw Oe's book and picked it up, opened it and began to read the first page. Oe speaks at first of his longtime relationship with Scandinavia, having read, as a child, translations (or, rather, Japanese retellings) of a series of Scandinavian stories about a character named Nils.

I stopped reading at once, for I had never thought of any similarity between Scandinavia and Japan before. But at the very suggestion, I at once realized that Japan and Scandinavia were both Edge peoples. They came into the civilized world in the shadow (or is it dazzled by the brilliance?) of a dominant culture.

I thought of other Edge peoples—the Arabs, who found an ideology that gave them the power to sweep through the culturally overwhelming Roman world; the Mongols, who united long enough to conquer and then be swallowed up by China; the Turks, who plunged from the edge of the Muslim world to the heart of it, and then toppled the last vestige of the Roman world as well, and yet sank back into again becoming Edge people in the shadow of Europe. All these Edge nations, even when they ruled the very civilizations in whose shadow they had once huddled, were never able to shake off their sense of not-belonging, their fear that their culture was irredeemably inferior and secondary. The result was that they were at once too aggressive and overextended themselves, growing beyond boundaries they could consolidate and hold; and too diffident, surrendering everything that really was powerful and fresh in their culture while retaining only the outward trappings of independence. The Manchu rulers of China, for instance, pretended to remain apart from the people they ruled, determined not to be swallowed up in the all-devouring maw of Chinese culture, but the result was not the dominance of the Manchu, but their inevitable marginalization.

True Center nations have been few in history. Egypt was one, and remained a Center nation until it was conquered by Alexander; even then, it kept a measure of its Centerness until the powerful idea of Islam swept over it. Mesopotamia might have been one, for a time, but unlike Egypt, Mesopotamian cities could not unite enough to control their hinterland. The result was they were swept over and ruled by their Edge nations again and again. The Centerness of Mesopotamia still gave it the power to swallow up its conquerors culturally for many years, until finally it became a peripheral province handed back and forth between Rome and Parthia. As with Egypt, its Center role was finally shattered by Islam.

China came later to its place as a Center nation, but it has been astonishingly successful. It was a long and bloody road to unity, but once achieved that unity remained, culturally if not politically. The rulers of China, like the rulers of Egypt, reached out to control the hinterland, but, again like Egypt, rarely attempted and never succeeded in establishing longterm rule over genuinely foreign nations.

Filled with this idea, and others that grew out of it, I conceived of a conversation between Wang-mu and Peter in which Wang-mu told him of her idea of Center and Edge nations. I went to my computer and wrote notes about this idea, which included the following passage:

Center People are not afraid of losing their identity. They take it for granted that all people want to be like them, that they are the highest civilization and all else is poor imitation or transient mistakes. The arrogance, oddly enough, leads to a simple humility— they do not strut or brag or throw their weight around because they have no need to prove their superiority. They transform only gradually, and only by pretending that they are not changing at all.

Edge People, on the other hand, know they are not the highest civilization. Sometimes they raid and steal and stay to rule—Vikings, Mongols, Turks, Arabs— and sometimes they go through radical transformations in order to compete—Greeks, Romans, Japanese—and sometimes they simply remain shamed backwaters. But when they are on the rise, they are insufferable because they are unsure of their worth and must therefore brag and show off and prove themselves again and again—until at last they feel themselves to be a Center People. Unfortunately, that very complacency destroys them, because they are *not* Center People and feeling doesn't make it so.

Triumphant Edge People don't endure, like Egypt or China, they fade, as the Arabs did, and the Turks, and the Vikings, and the Mongols after their victories.

The Japanese have made themselves permanent Edge People.

I also speculated about America, which was composed of refugees from the Edge, but which nevertheless behaved like a Center nation, controlling (brutally) its hinterland, but only briefly flirting with empire, content instead to be the center of the world. America had, for a time at least, the same arrogance as the Chinese—the assumption that the rest of the world wants to be like us. And I wondered if, as with Islam, a powerful idea had made an Edge nation into a Center nation. Just as the Arabs themselves lost control of the new Islamic Center, which was ruled by Turks, so also the original English culture of America might be softened or adapted, while the powerful nation of America remains at the Center; this is an idea that I am still playing with and whose truth I am not in a position to evaluate, since so much of it will only be known in the future and can only be guessed at now. But it remains that this idea of Edge and Center nations is an intriguing one that I find myself believing, to the extent that I understand it.

Having written my notes, I then began the next night to write the chapter. I had brought Wang-mu and Peter to the end of their meal at the restaurant, and was ready to have them meet a Japanese character for the first time. But it was four in the morning. My wife, Kristine, awake to take care of our one-year-old baby, Zina, took the chapter fragment out of my hand and read it. As I prepared for sleep, she also dozed off, but then awoke to tell me of a dream she had in that momentary nap. She had dreamed that the Japanese of Divine Wind carried their ancestors' ashes in tiny lockets or amulets that they wore around their necks; and Peter felt lost because he had only one ancestor, and he would die when that ancestor died. I knew at once that I had to use this idea; then I lay down in bed, picked up Oe's book again, and began to read.

Imagine my surprise, then, when after that first passage dealing with Oe's feelings toward Scandinavia, he plunged into analyses of Japanese culture and literature that explicitly developed precisely the idea that had leapt into my mind just from reading those opening, seemingly unrelated paragraphs about Nils. He, a man who has studied and cared about the peripheral (or Edge) peoples of Japan, especially the culture of Okinawa, conceived of Japan as a culture that was in danger of losing its Center. Serious Japanese literature, he said, was decaying precisely because Japanese intellectuals were "accepting" and "discharging" Western ideas, not particularly believing them but caught up in their fashionableness, while ignoring those powerful ideas inherent in the Yamato (native Japanese) culture which would give Japan the power to become a self-standing Center nation. He even used, finally, the words "center" and "edge" in this sentence:

> The postwar writers, however, looked for a different path that would lead Japan to a place in the world not at its center but at the edge of it. (pp. 97–98)

His point was not the same as mine, but the world-conception of centers and edges was harmonious.

I took all of Oe's concerns about literature quite personally, because, like him, I am a part of an "edge" culture which "accepts" and "discharges" ideas from the dominant culture and which is in danger of losing its self-centering impulse. I speak of Mormon culture, which was born at the edge of America and which has long been more American than Mormon. Supposedly "serious" literature in Mormon culture has consisted entirely of imitations, mostly pathetic but occasionally of decent quality, of the "serious" literature of contemporary America, which is itself a decadent, derivative, and hopelessly irrelevant literature, having no audience that believes in or cares about its stories, no audience capable of genuine community transformation. And, like Oe—or let me say that I think I understand Oe correctly in this—I can see the redemption of (or, arguably, the creation of) a true Mormon literature as coming only by the rejection of fashionably "serious" (but, in reality, frivolous) American literature and its replacement by a literature that meets Oe's criteria for *junbungaku*:

> The role of literature—Insofar as man is obviously a historical being—is to create a model of a contemporary age which encompasses past and future, a model of the people living in that age as well. (p. 66)

What the Mormon "serious" literateurs never attempted was a model of the people living in our culture in our age. Or, rather, they attempted it, but never from inside: the pose of the implied author (to use Wayne Booth's term) was always skeptical and Outside rather than critical and Inside; it is my belief that no true national literature can ever be written by those whose values derive from outside that national culture.

But I do not write only or even primarily Mormon literature. As often I have been a science fiction writer writing science fiction for the community of science fiction readers—also rather an edge culture, though one that transcends national boundaries. I am also, for good or ill, an American writing American literature to an American audience. Most fundamentally, though, I am a human being writing human literature to a human audience, as are we all who ply this trade. There are times when this, too, seems to me to be an edge culture. We with our passionate involvement in bonding together while standing alone, in staving off death while worshiping its irresistible power, in shrugging off interference while meddling in the lives of others, in keeping our secrets while unmasking others', in being the sole unique individual in a world of people who are all alike, we are strange indeed among all the plants and animals, who unlike us know their place, and if they think of God at all do not imagine him to be their kin, or themselves to be his heirs. How dangerous we are, like those kingdoms of the Edge, how likely we are to erupt outward into every unconquered kingdom in the effort to make ourselves the center after all.

What Kenzaburo Oe seeks for Japanese literature, I seek also for American literature, for Mormon literature, for science fiction, for human literature. But it is not always done in the most obvious way. When Shusaku Endo explores the issue of the meaning of life in the face of death, he assembles a cast of characters in contemporary Japan, but the currents of magic, science, and religion are never far from the heart of his story; while I do not pretend to Endo's mastery of storytelling, have I not dealt with the same issues, using the same tools, in this novel? Does *Children of the Mind* fail as *junbungaku* solely because of its far-future setting? Is my novel *Lost Boys* the only one of my works that can aspire to seriousness, and only to the degree that it is an accurate mirror of life in 1983 in Greensboro, North Carolina?

Dare I amplify the words of a Nobel laureate by suggesting that one can as easily create "a model of a contemporary age which encompasses past and future" through the guise of a novel that thoroughly and faithfully creates a society of another time and place, through whose contrast our contemporary age stands clearly revealed? Or must I declare an anti-*junbungaku* and attack a statement that I agree with and pretend to diverge from a goal which I am also pursuing? Is Oe's vision of significant literature incomplete? Or am I merely a participant in edge literatures, longing for the center but condemned never to arrive in that peaceful, all-encompassing place?

Perhaps that is why the Stranger and the Other are so important in all my writings (though never at first by plan), even as my stories also affirm the importance of the Member and the Familiar; but is this not, in its own way, a model of our contemporary age, encompassing past and future; am I not, with my own inner contradictions between Inside and Outside, Member and Stranger, a model of the people living in this age? Is there only one setting in which an author can tell true tales?

When I read Shusaku Endo's *Deep River,* I am an alien in his world. Things that resonate with Japanese readers, who nod and say, "Yes, that's how it was, that's how it is for us," to me are strange, and I say, "Is this how they experienced it? Is this how it feels to them?" Do I not draw as much value from reading a novel that depicts someone else's contemporary age? Do I not learn as much from Austen as from Tyler? From Endo as from Russo? Is the world of the Stranger and Other not as vital to me in understanding what it means to be human as the world I actually live in? Is it not then possible for me to create an invented future milieu that has as much power to speak to contemporary readers as the milieus of those writers whose contemporary age is of another era or land?

Perhaps all milieus are equally the product of imagination, whether we live in them or make them up. Perhaps to another Japanese, *Deep River* contains almost as much strangeness as it does to me, because Endo himself is inevitably different from all other Japanese people. Perhaps every writer who thoroughly creates a fictional world will inevitably create a mirror of his own time and yet also create a world that no one else but him has ever visited; only the trivial details of place names, dates, and famous people distinguish between a madeup universe like the one in *Children of the Mind* and the "real" universe depicted in *Deep River.* What Endo achieves and I aspire to are the same: To give the reader an experience of convincing reality, nevertheless piercing the shell of detail and penetrating to the structure of causation and meaning that we always hope for but never actually experience in the real world. Causation and meaning are always imagined, no matter how thoroughly we "create a model of a contemporary age." But if we imagine well, and do not merely "accept" and "discharge" what we are given by the culture around us, do we not create *junbungaku*?

I do not believe the tools of science fiction are any less suitable to the task of creating *junbungaku* than the tools of contemporary serious literature, though of course we who wield the tools may fail to use them to best advantage. But in this I may deceive myself; or my own work may be too weak to prove what is possible within our literature. One thing is certain: The community of readers of science fiction includes as many serious thinkers and explorers of reality as any other literary community I have taken part in. If a great literature demands a great audience, the audience is ready and any failure to achieve such a literature must be laid at the writer's door.

So I will continue to attempt to create *junbungaku,* commenting on contemporary culture in allegorical or symbolic disguise as do all science fiction writers, consciously or not. Whether any of my own works actually achieve the status of true seriousness that Oe points to is for others to decide, for regardless of the quality of the writer, there must also be an audience to receive the work before it has any transformative power; what I depend on is a vigorous audience that can discover sweetness and light, beauty and truth, beyond the ability of the artist, on his own, to create them.